BOXED

Stephen Johnson

Clan Destine
PRESS

First published by Clan Destine Press in 2021

Clan Destine Press
PO Box 121, Bittern
Victoria, 3918 Australia

National Library of Australia Cataloguing-In-Publication data:

Johnson, Stephen

BOXED

ISBN: 978-0-6450021-7-1 (paperback)
ISBN: 978-0-6450426-8-9 (eBook)

Cover Design by © Willsin Rowe
Design & Typesetting by Clan Destine Press

Dedicated to my parents, Marie and Len Johnson

Day 133

The limestone crumbled easily beneath the makeshift stylus, as it did every night. A breath blew away fine grains as the screw recorded another day in captivity. Her finger traced the new log that couldn't quell dreams it might be the last. *I'll be free again soon.* Each line on the wall beside the single bed was about three centimetres long. They were mostly straight, as much as an amateur engraver could make them. They were grouped in blocks of 30 and 31, just the one section of 28. That was 49 notches ago.

The prisoner hadn't seen sunlight since incarceration, but the calendar was accurate. She was semi-conscious when dragged by the hair and bloodied clothing to her prison on a Monday morning. Three blows to the head and face knocked her down; the first came from behind, giving her no chance to fight back. There were a dozen stone steps to the cellar. For a fortnight, her legs and hips bore the bruises of that descent into terror. She could see them darken by the day until nature worked its healing powers. The facial wounds were never seen. The prison held no mirrors to examine that damage. Or the broken nose.

The injuries slowly repaired. She had seen worse during her previous life with the British Army and International Red Cross. A nurse had to be physically and mentally tough to survive the daily traumas in war zones like Chechnya, Iraq, the former Yugoslav republic, Iraq and Afghanistan. Nurses were trained for situations like this. Security was always taken seriously, although towns and villages at her last posting provided more danger from IEDs than capture by the enemy. There was greater fear of limbs being severed by Semtex than becoming a toy for the Taliban.

The survival in captivity lessons were learned more than two decades ago. Refresher courses ensured the prisoner retained the key points. She recited the same mantra every night before sleep. *Stay strong. I will survive.*

Chapter 1

Fear clawed at Kim Prescott's stomach. Did something slither past her foot?

'Do snakes come out at night?'

It was a reasonable question from the current affairs reporter, crouching in long grass on a farm near Steiglitz, 90 kilometres west of Melbourne. Less than two metres in front of Kim's face was an infrared camera. Four metres to her left was another. Both were framed and rolling to record her intro to their story, yet Kim could barely see them or the operators. She missed the shrug from the point man, senior TV op Dugal Cameron. It was his second-in-command, Ken Withers, who stoked her jitters.

'Shit yeah,' he whispered. 'This is snake heaven, Kim. They spend their days in rocks or under bark and corrugated iron. But they've gotta eat. They love it when the lizards and frogs go walkabout.'

Kim leapt to her feet as an amphibian croak from an unseen pond fuelled her paranoia.

'Ugh! Then why am I snake bait?'

Dugal paused his recording. 'Um, I think this moonlight escapade was your idea, wasn't it?'

The 24-year-old *Melbourne Spotlight* reporter shivered. It wasn't from the cool Saturday night air: she wore jeans, thick leather hiking boots and a black mountain fleece hoody. It was the thought of a venom-laden reptile wanting to snuggle that gave her the willies.

'What snakes are likely to be out here? Any poisonous ones?'

Withers was the crew's self-appointed snake expert.

'Jeezus Kim, every kind. Tiger snakes, copperheads, brown snakes, red-bellied black snakes. They're among the deadliest in the world and they love long grass. We're probably on the snake super-highway to that frog banquet. You can forget about collecting the next journalism award if one of them gives you a love bite. We'd have enough time to record your final sign-off – maybe.'

Kim retreated a few steps towards the safety of the crew car a dozen metres away on the gravel road.

Dugal laughed softly. 'Ignore him, Kim. It's mid-autumn; there's not likely to be any serpents to spoil your story. By now they're shacked up with a sexy mate for the winter. Anyway, Kenny's farts from the dim sims at Werribee would gas anything below waist level. How much soy sauce did you put on – a bottle?'

'Only half.' Withers was indignant. 'And what would a Scottish git know about fine cuisine and the wildlife dangers of Terra Australis?'

'I think my ancestors arrived here about the same time as your Sassenach relatives. And mine paid their way as free settlers – they weren't shackled below decks.'

Withers wore his family's convict heritage like a badge of honour.

'At least we got a free ocean voyage. And someone had to clean the dunnies for you bloody toffs.'

Both camera ops laughed, the banter a practiced routine that never wounded any dignity. Withers was almost two-metres tall and stocky, but that didn't stop Kim swatting a broad shoulder.

'Shhhh, you dimwits. They'll hear your chuckling in Geelong.'

Dugal was a few centimetres shorter than his mate and 10 kilos leaner, but Kim normally didn't need to playfully slap him into line. She looked at the ground, then at the property they would investigate after recording her introduction. *If* she was brave enough to lie down in the snake-filled grass. The frogs revived their chorus. Kim hoped they were more attractive to creepy reptiles.

There was a dull glare from an old security light behind a timber building 120-metres away. Nobody was home. It was a safe assumption, Kim believed; research revealed the occupant and his workers were normally in Broadmeadows on Saturday nights.

'Okay, let's get this done. My intro …' Kim paused as she knelt. 'Hang on. I think I saw movement near that large shed.' She eagerly stood. 'Ken, give me your night vision thingy.'

Withers was miffed but handed over his 'thingy.'

'That's a Spartan Night Vision Monocular, $500 of precision technology, I'll have you know. Anyway, I thought this place was supposed to be empty.'

Kim jammed the monocle against her right eye. 'It is.'

The scope didn't turn darkness into daylight, but it showed enough to confirm there wasn't anyone lurking around the buildings. The black and white image outlined the 30-metre-long structure, two smaller sheds – one of which was burnt timbers and roofing iron – the main house and the rails of the track. No human movement. 'I guess my eyes are playing tricks.'

Kim handed back the monocle. 'Nifty device that. It's not often we get to do night surveillance work. What do you use it for?'

Withers tucked it into the side of a backpack filled with electronic goodies for their nocturnal mission. 'Shooting. It's not top of the range, but it's good enough to spot roos, rabbits and rogue politicians.'

'State or Federal?' Dugal asked.

'They're all fair game to me, mate.'

Two palms slapped. Somehow the camera operators connected for a high five.

Kim shook her head, not that anyone could see. 'Right.' She lowered herself to the ground and was grateful to find nothing crawling past. 'Now, a reminder that I'll talk to Dugal's camera. When I'm finished, I'll stand and both of us walk towards the fence. Ken, you track us until we go past that thick gum tree 10-metres to your left.'

'Got it.'

Kim lowered her head to compose herself and recall her script.

Dugal adjusted his headphones. 'Give me another sound check Kim. I want to make sure the radio mic hasn't shifted.'

'Testing, one, two, three. Testing. This is Kim Prescott of *Melbourne Spotlight*, reporting from the Brisbane Ranges for our next scintillating scoop of the year. Good enough for you?'

'Yep.' Dugal laughed quietly. 'But I can't imagine anything beating our Tugga's Mob extravaganza.'

'Well, I hope it wasn't a once-in-a-career story, Dugal. This one deserves a lot of attention. Remember the outcry after the ABC's Four Corners exposé? Everyone thought the industry learned from its mistakes. But maybe they haven't. It's time to find out.'

Kim ensured her hair was tucked inside the hoody and reclaimed the backpack from Withers. She crouched beside it on the grass, hoping it might side-track fanged predators. She looked towards Dugal and nodded; the investigative reporter was ready for work. Five seconds later the cameramen whispered in unison. 'Recording.'

'A few metres in front of me is the property under investigation. It's about 40-kilometres north of Geelong and is a mixed bag of sheep grazing and canola crops. However, it is the owner's passion for training greyhounds that has brought us here tonight. We've been told that this is the venue for something more sinister.

'It's alleged the track is used to blood greyhounds – live rabbits, piglets and possums are strapped to a mechanical lure to give racers a taste for the chase. It could be the winning edge in a gambling industry worth billions of dollars.

'It's hard to believe the practice continues following the media exposé on cruelty in the industry. Yet, we have credible information that live-baiting happens here every third Sunday morning.

'Tonight, my camera crew and I will infiltrate the property to set up mini cameras to gather evidence.'

Kim stood and shouldered the backpack containing the mini cams. Dugal picked up his kit and they walked beyond the designated tree; the movements recorded on the second infrared camera.

'Right, got that guys,' Withers said. 'It looked fine to me; how did you feel Kim?'

'I'm happy – but I know you're going to tell me to do another recording.'

'Yep, always best to do a safety. There might have been a red belly slithering past in the dark and nobody noticed.'

Kim squirmed again. 'Thanks for reminding me. Okay, let's get this done. It will take time to scout locations and set up those mini cams.'

There were verbal stumbles during the second, third and fourth takes, which annoyed Kim. She prided herself on clean deliveries for most pieces to camera after six months as a reporter. With two clean introductions they recorded their entrance to the property. Dugal provided the walking point of view footage, Withers the wider shots of his colleagues trudging through grass to the three-metre-high fence.

The pictures created drama and were necessary for Kim's script. She slipped through the convenient gap in the fence first, the cameras followed. It was *convenient* because the hole was exactly where the anonymous tip-off declared it would be. Withers squinted at the wires as he squeezed through. They had been cut. How recent was hard to tell, but it was obvious their informant wanted the TV current affairs crew to easily gain access.

'Where's the welcome mat?'

Kim's brow wrinkled in the darkness. 'What do you mean?'

'We get a tip about live-baiting, the hole's where the message indicated, the wire's been tampered with – are we being set up?'

It was Kim's turn to be nettled. She had established her bona fides as a solid researcher for *Melbourne Spotlight* before promotion to the on-air role. It rankled that a colleague might consider her naïve, or gullible. It wasn't the time to be pissy with Withers. She swallowed her pride.

'Our job is to investigate. Live-baiting is barbaric. If this trainer is dumb enough to try it after that furore created by activists and the ABC, we have a duty to disclose it so the courts and parliament can stop them.'

'I understand that, Kim. I'm worried that we are being led by the nose.'

Dugal kept a diplomatic silence as they weighed that possibility. Cruelty in the greyhound racing industry became an emotional topic after the exposé by Four Corners in 2015.

Australians were shocked by surveillance footage of live animals tied to mechanical lures on private tracks in Queensland, New South Wales and Victoria. They were chased, caught and savaged by dogs in horrific scenes that appalled viewers. The practice was known as blooding; the theory was that greyhounds chased harder if they caught a live animal during training. They developed a taste for winning. Administrators and trainers denied the practice existed. Some of those deniers were caught in the scandal when their crimes – recorded by activists – appeared on Four Corners.

The fall out was immense. Widespread condemnation was the first reaction. Suspensions, court cases and inquiries followed. In New South Wales, evidence of systemic animal cruelty – the euthanising of dogs too slow to race – saw the State Government ban the sport. Then it made an embarrassing back flip before the ban was even enforced. The public was upset about the treatment of greyhounds, but the mood was against ruining the livelihoods of thousands because of a guilty few. The sport survived, but all participants knew major reforms were needed.

'Okay,' Withers sighed. 'Where do we go from here Kim?'

They had manoeuvred through three rows of gum trees which obscured much of the track from the road.

'I want to check the mechanical lure for blood – it might be our first indicator. Then we'll look in that small shed nearby in case tomorrow's bait is caged there.'

Kim pulled the monocle from Wither's pack and raised it to her eye. The operators did the same with their cameras. 'We should look at that burnt shed as well. Can you see it near the starting traps?'

'Yep.' Dugal responded. 'You go ahead of us Kim. I'll do the close ups and the snake charmer can get the wide shots. Are we going near the kennels?'

'Safer not to. I'm not sure how many dogs they took to the track tonight, but there might be one or two left behind. We don't want to get them agitated. Do a few wide shots of the building when you get a chance. Once we check the layout, you guys can select the best positions to hide the mini cams.'

The trio used the electronics to navigate the final 60 metres. They reached the training track first; it wasn't impressive. The metal railing was rickety; no timber support post stood vertical. The mechanical lure was mounted another 30 metres away, closer to the traps. Wither's scepticism hadn't waned.

'It would be a miracle if anything mechanical could move around this track.'

Kim ignored the sarcasm and pressed on towards the lure with the scope held to her right eye. Something unusually bulky had caught her attention.

'Guys. Look at the lure. I'm sure there's something on it.'

They moved closer, both cameras recording, Kim in the lead. Within a few steps it became obvious the mechanical arm that extended over the track contained more than a fluffy fake lure.

'Oh my – that's…that's a possum tied to it.'

The two cameras recorded Kim as she edged around the evidence. If it really was evidence. The possum was face down on the arm, its torso and limbs held in place by bungy cords. Ready for the morning feast?

It was barely breathing. Kim looked closer and found a bloody gash behind the left ear. The injury didn't appear life-threatening, but serious enough to stun the poor animal. Kim stepped back and spotted a palm-sized rock a metre inside the decrepit railing.

Withers lowered his camera. 'This stinks.'

Dugal buttoned off as well; his mate wasn't referring to the half-dead possum. He drifted away from the looming confrontation between enthusiastic reporter and grumpy cameraman.

'This is wrong.' Withers didn't bother whispering. 'Who would tie a possum like that a night before the blooding session? I bet an animal activist stunned it to make sure we found *evidence*. You probably did see something earlier Kim. Some Greenie was tying this poor bugger with the bungy cords. Honestly – what trainer would do this?'

Kim knew they were legitimate questions. The tip-off about the *alleged* dodgy trainer was anonymous, arriving at the *Spotlight* office in a plain brown envelope. It was the detail about the property, the trainer and the days when live baiting allegedly happened that convinced senior producers it was worth an investigation. Kim eagerly agreed to tackle the story; she had a personal interest.

Her Richmond flat-mate was Sexy Rexy – a former racer who took up residence via the Greyhound Adoption Program. Kim believed greyhounds were pawns in the original scandal; they merely followed natural instincts. It was the trainers, breeders and owners who were at fault and she wanted to snuff out any attempts to revive the abhorrent practice. But faking evidence against trainers wasn't right.

'It doesn't look good, I agree.' Kim shook her head, bewildered. Why would anyone try to mislead them?

'This stinks.' Dugal chipped in.

'Doh,' Withers said. 'I think we've already established that Sherlock.'

'No, not that possum, which we should release soon if it's going to survive. There's a stench coming from these.' Dugal gestured towards two rusty starting boxes.

Withers joined his colleague three metres from the practice traps; there was enough flaky paint left to display their race heritage as boxes four and five.

'Smells like it's coming from the squeeze box – the five' Withers said. 'If a slow dog draws that in a race, they often get squeezed out of the field by the first turn. Say goodbye to your money.' Withers sniffed twice, then a third time. 'I hope the trainer hasn't forgotten some mutt. Or punished it.'

Kim put a hand over her nose and mouth as she approached. 'How do we raise the doors?

Withers walked behind the boxes and found a manual release. He pulled the lever – the doors sprang open. Kim and Dugal raised their night vision equipment and gasped.

Chapter 2

The traps clanged for the start of Race 7 at The Meadows track on Saturday night. Eight greyhounds burst into the lights in manic pursuit of the cheeky critter trying to escape. It was instinctive; they were sight hounds – they chase. Nothing else mattered until they caught it. The track was a blur of dogs and coloured rugs – red, white, blue, yellow, green, black, stripes and pink – over hyper extended muscles and paws.

The lure was nothing like the live hares and rabbits their ancestors hounded to death. This speedster was like a court jester's hat – blue with dangling threads of yellow and white. It taunted them, always a few strides beyond their reach as they sprinted. It breezed through the turns which compressed the chasers; bodies ricocheted as they sought a clear run to the prize.

The dog from box one edged ahead by half a length down the back straight. At the home turn it was the bearers of the red, blue and green rugs in contention. They were oblivious to the shouts from the five punters lining the fence. The race commentary was mere background noise to the four-legged flyers. They swept past the finish line in 30.15 seconds, a good time, but their pace didn't slacken.

In the blink of an eye the lure accelerated like a Formula One car and was swiftly beyond their reach. Staff swung a barrier across the track to create the catching pen; a new distraction on rope was cast before the panting chasers. The dogs couldn't fight the impulse to follow the diversion and catchers swooped to claim their charges. Race

7 at Broadmeadows was over – in 20 minutes another eight hopefuls would repeat that exercise in futility.

Inside the lounges of The Meadows patrons shrugged or raised a glass of beer according to the TAB ticket in their hands. The track was home to nine Group 1 races every year; the big money events which drew the fastest dogs from around the country. None was on the program for that evening; few of the 223 patrons in the facility saw any need to step beyond the warmth of the bar and tote. It meant they avoided the boring chorus from the group behind The Terrace.

'Stop animal cruelty. Stop animal cruelty. Stop animal cruelty.'

The race for line honours was over; off track the skirmish for audio supremacy continued between the commentator and a dozen animal rights protestors. The skittering of paws, the whirring of the electronic lure and the race call had faded. That allowed the Hound Liberation Party a few precious seconds to shout their message from beyond the fence.

'Stop animal cruelty. Stop animal cruelty. Stop animal cruelty.'

The announcer dutifully read the finishing order, race times, margins and the dividends. By the time he finished there was no competition – the protestors were silent. The studio director had moved television coverage to the harness meeting at Menangle, New South Wales. The vocal outrage was wasted on the dogs, their catchers and the punters behind the floor-to-ceiling glass windows at The Meadows.

The protesters made no impression on 23-three-year old Dwayne Milligan as he led Flyin' Frisco through the kennels. Strands of saliva dripped from her mouth and muzzle. Eighth in the black rug; the seven-box was always unlucky for them. In fact, the evening was grim for the whole kennel; seven races and only one dog in the money with a third placing. That wouldn't pay the wages. Not that Milligan had to worry about providing the payroll; he was an employee. But if the boss, Conor O'Leary, didn't have any prize money then it could become a problem for Milligan. He lived week-by-week in a Geelong flat on a modest salary and the fluctuations of his TAB account.

Home wasn't far from the track in Corio. It was, however, roughly 30-minutes to Tara – O'Leary's training kennels, near Steiglitz. The commute back and forth seven days a week was expensive in his Commodore SV6 ute. The green beast guzzled fuel faster than a Cats supporter at Kardinia Park on match day. Milligan's lead foot didn't help; long, straight roads and a six-speed manual gear box were temptations to imitate Bathurst legend, Peter Brock. Milligan and co-worker Rene Harding often coasted home to the flat on fumes at the end of the pay week when their punting form was poor.

O'Leary nagged Milligan to ditch the ute for a Toyota. 'They run on the smell of an oily rag and they last forever.'

That was blasphemous to Milligan. The SV6 was a hand-me-down from his father. 'Ted would roll over in his grave if I ever drove a Jap car.'

Ted Milligan bought the ute in 2012 when Green Moon won the Melbourne Cup and paid $22.50. No numerical system – or horse sense – made the 52-year-old Ford factory worker rich until he tried a new system: a trifecta of saddle cloth numbers that added up to his birthday on November 28. His combination of 14, 11 and 3 worked, big time – a $45,941.60 pay out.

The celebrations were boisterous, Ted was barely sober when he marched into the Geelong Holden dealer the next morning and bought the first green vehicle he saw – the SV6 ute. He felt no loyalty to his employer; Ford was about to close the Geelong operation. A bright new Holden in the car park would make a nice poke in the eye for his bosses.

Ford executives didn't have to suffer the Holden indignity for long – just a week. Ted's pub carousing continued until his luck ran out on the Saturday night after the cup. He was caught driving under the influence of alcohol by a police patrol. A 12-month licence suspension saw the green machine parked in the family garage in North Geelong. It was too powerful for his wife Cheryl to drive and young Dwayne didn't have a licence. Ted consoled himself with more pub visits until the week before Christmas. He didn't check for passing traffic after exiting the late bus; Ted was killed instantly when crossing the road.

Dwayne Milligan lost a father but inherited a beautiful V6. It took him three attempts to get a driving licence after his 18th birthday; the examiners didn't understand it was impossible to keep the beast under the speed limit. Every spare bit of cash went into maintaining the ute in pristine condition. Not that there was much left in the pay packet.

Milligan had been fixated on greyhounds since he was 12; the wheels allowed him to pursue a racing dream when a vacancy opened at O'Leary's kennels. The 54-year-old expat Irishman took a chance on the kid who had been a regular at the track with his father for years. Milligan was a natural with the dogs; within 12 months O'Leary assured him he had a future as a trainer. Greyhounds and the green ute were Dwayne's passions, although girls ran a close third. He liked a regular punt but never drank more than two beers when driving. Ted's death was a reminder to stay under the breath alcohol limit.

Milligan removed the muzzle from Flyin' Frisco as they reached the van. He retrieved a water bowl from the trailer, filled it from a plastic container and watched the dog lap it up. There was no need for a post-race swab, there hadn't been for seven weeks. He liked the four-year-old bitch; she was an easy dog to handle on the track and at home. A year ago, O'Leary would have considered the lack of form justification to retire her to a friendly family, or an adoption program. But a run of bad luck over the past six months meant Flyin' Frisco was still part of the racing pack; there weren't many other chasers left in the kennels.

Milligan left Flyin' Frisco to finish the bowl as he tidied the van. The race night was almost over for the team from Steiglitz; Milligan was worried there might not be many more appearances at The Meadows, or other tracks. Their problems started with a mysterious shed fire in November.

It was a Wednesday, a racing afternoon; O'Leary, Harding and Milligan were at Broadmeadows as usual. Ironically, it was a successful trip: two wins, a second, two thirds. It was always exciting to get dais time at the metropolitan meetings – bigger crowds, more prize money – and the trio celebrated with a McDonalds feast on the way home. The stars weren't left out: slushies and ice creams were their treats.

The burgers soured when the trio arrived home to find the smoking ruin. It didn't make sense. It was a tin shed around a timber frame with nothing of value inside: broken farm equipment, out-of-date feed bags. It wasn't even locked. The kennels were saved by a neighbour who saw the smoke; he used a hose to stop the resultant grass fire from spreading. An investigation found an accelerant was used, but the police never caught the culprits.

The fire puzzled the O'Leary team. If it was arson, who was the target and why? Conor O'Leary was a moderately successful trainer, popular with colleagues, fans and the media for his witty personality.

He came from Cork and claimed to have kissed the Blarney Stone while still in nappies. He was always ready for boisterous discussions on greyhounds, racing and any topic that took his fancy over a pint of Guinness. Milligan knew most people loved O'Leary. The exception was his former wife.

Siobhan O'Leary returned to Ireland before Milligan joined the kennel. Along with being loquacious, her husband was renowned for being flirtatious, and that didn't sit well with Mrs O'Leary's rules on fidelity. Rene Harding, who at 25 had been with the trainer for almost a decade, gleefully shared the story of the final dust up.

'Conor offered to drive Emma Crowe home from the Geelong track. You know Emma – the busty blonde from the kennels on the Bellarine Peninsula? Thirty Ks in the opposite direction from Steiglitz!

'They stopped in Eastern Park for a more *intimate* discussion – and that's when Siobhan pounced. She was hiding under a blanket in the back of the van.

'Apparently she was screaming like a banshee. Emma scarpered – but Conor wasn't so lucky. He got tangled in the seat belt as Siobhan smacked him about the head. The black eye took a fortnight to fade. Boy, did he cop some stick after that escapade!'

That was six years ago; Milligan knew his boss didn't miss his ex-wife, judging by the variety of ladies who joined him for drinks after the races.

The O'Leary's domestic problems were ancient history for Milligan. There was more recent trouble at Cnoc na Teamhrach. The attendant could never pronounce the Irish name plate that hung beside the homestead's front door. He knew it meant Hill of Tara, the traditional base for the high-kings of Ireland near the River Boyne. Conor explained that the opportunity to own land in Australia made him feel like a king. For most people, the Steiglitz property was known as Tara.

O'Leary started with sheep 30 years ago, then introduced canola crops when neighbours showed they were profitable. Two greyhounds were bought as a hobby after a decade. The racers became an obsession and the kennels expanded, although most of the 100-hectare farm was still dedicated to the oil-rich seed and grazing. All income streams were needed as droughts were prevalent in farming and racing. O'Leary had fenced the dog areas well, which allowed them to roam when the ground wasn't baking. Most greyhounds are notoriously lazy: a sprint, some play, a feed and they're happy to sleep the rest of the time. O'Leary loved to boast that his charges were free-range chasers.

Over summer that freedom to wander turned deadly. Three dogs died from snake bites: one before Christmas, the second at New Year, the third on Australia day. It's traditionally the most active time for snakes, but three deaths defied the odds. There hadn't been an attack in the previous three decades.

Milligan and Harding regularly saw brown snakes. A few red bellies as well, even the occasional tiger and copperhead. But they usually kept a distance from humans and the animals. Their prey were lizards, frogs, or mice; Milligan could never recall chasing reptiles away from the dogs. There was lots of junk metal and wood piles around the property, but it was instinctive to avoid them in the summer. Even in the colder months Milligan and Harding belted the piles with sticks – and waited – before moving anything.

To lose three dogs to snakes was bad. To lose Paddy, Bubs and Missy – their kennel names – was catastrophic. They were O'Leary's best chasers, all with Group victories to their credit. They were the kennel stars, the breadwinners for their block mates and two-legged minders. Missy had good genes and was expected to produce one or two Group 1 champions after her track career.

Word of the snake problems at Steiglitz spread quickly. The 15 best dogs, and a handful of average performers, were relocated to other trainers by mid-February. The spooked owners were apologetic, but the kennel was jinxed. Milligan knew the boss was desperate to secure a big-name chaser. If the dogs didn't make the dais – and O'Leary's cheery mug wasn't on television for interviews – owners ignored you. And that could mean everyone – Milligan, Harding and the remaining dogs – being out of work.

Flyin Frisco was their last chaser for The Meadows on Saturday night. There were two more races, but O'Leary didn't have any entries. Rene Harding was content with the early finish as he returned to the 10-dog trailer.

'You get Frisco settled and I'll go order the drinks.'

It would take five minutes for Milligan to reach the bar, but he knew

Harding would down two pots in that time. *He* didn't have to drive. They didn't have the green ute, but Milligan was on duty to pilot the van and trailer back to Steiglitz.

'No problems, mate. Make sure mine's a light beer. That new barmaid gave me a full-strength pot last week.'

'She was probably trying to get you legless, Dwayne. Wanted to jump you in the back of the ute.'

Milligan laughed. 'Tell her that space is reserved for hot bitches.'

Harding snorted. Greyhound racing is the only profession where casual references to bitches weren't treated as sexist. Most of the time.

'I wonder if the boss is upstairs.'

'Probably got a harem of ladies in a corner hanging on every silver-tongued word.'

'Yeah, he could charm the panties off a nun.' They laughed as Harding turned for the lounge.

Milligan counted the leads and muzzles; he was thorough with their track night routine. Normally it was the two attendants left to the pack up as O'Leary shouted the first beers. Not that Saturday night. It was weird – O'Leary didn't make it to the track.

That hadn't happened before. The boss always went to the races, summer and winter, good weather and bad. He could be dripping rivers of snot from the worst case of man-flu, but O'Leary fulfilled his duty to his greyhounds and their owners.

Everyone noticed his absence; Milligan and Harding were peppered with questions.

'What have you done with Conor? Lost him at the pub?'

'Has the Missus come back from Ireland and clobbered the randy bugger?'

The attendants laughed away the banter. They had a ready reply.

'He had a late meeting with a new owner. Someone who didn't want to be seen at the track. He could be stealing your best brindles.'

Most attendants and catchers accepted that explanation. A few trainers suddenly grew nervous the wily Irishman might lure away their star performers. They dashed off to count the owners, more concerned about who was missing.

By race four there was no sign of the boss. Milligan and Harding weren't worried, they only had seven chasers and could handle the duties between them. Even by their final run, and still no O'Leary, the attendants weren't fussed. Perhaps he signed a rich client? Were they toasting the new partnership with a Jameson Irish Whiskey?

Another thought struck Milligan as he locked the van and pocketed the keys. Did Conor have a run in with the protestors? There was already bad blood between Conor and the activists. They were noisy before and after every race – when they knew the track was on live television – but that was standard. The Hound Liberation Party had targeted the Broadmeadows track every month since the end of winter. The numbers varied from six protestors on wet nights to about 30 in summer. Milligan looked across the car park and counted 10 protestors. They hadn't been as loud or aggressive as previous demonstrations.

The first encounters between supporters and opponents of greyhound racing were ugly. There was pushing and shoving, lots of swearing. Conor had been in the front-line for the trainers. He cleverly put one loud protestor on his butt at The Meadows in October without being spotted by the TV cameras. There were no arrests, but greyhound industry officials acted quickly to head off a PR disaster. Attendants, catchers, trainers and owners were urged to stay calm, button their lips and focus on the welfare of their greyhounds whenever confronted by the Hound Liberation Party.

The protestors liked The Meadows because the bespoke facility enabled them to get close to the track. They weren't permitted inside the venue, but their monotonous chants could reach the sound effects microphones from the road behind The Terrace. The impact of their message was often thwarted by tight television schedules.

Producers constantly struggled to squeeze in every horse and dog race broadcast in Australia and New Zealand. Inevitably races ran late because horses refused to enter barriers; or cunning club managers delayed starts to maximise betting revenues. The dish lickers were at the bottom of the television food chain because of the tote turnovers. At a minimum, they were given enough coverage for the markets, the race and the dividends, maybe. Animal rights protestors learned their antics were ignored by cameras that never veered away from the dogs. They persisted because their chanting could be heard over the race commentary at some venues.

Milligan saw the HLP protestors huddle for the next race: it looked like business as usual. Surely O'Leary hadn't belted a greenie and been arrested? Everyone would have heard that commotion. The Irishman was 185 centimetres tall and strong from a lifetime farming. Guinness had expanded his midriff, but not enough to slow him in a donnybrook against people trying to ruin his sport. O'Leary wouldn't hit the women, but weedy men were fair game.

O'Leary had a second and more violent run-in with the HLP in early December after the shed fire. The protestor who landed on his backside in the first stoush – normally the loudest – blocked their van and trailer at The Meadows. When O'Leary emerged from the passenger seat, ready for a *debate*, the protestor accused him of 'burning evidence of animal cruelty.'

O'Leary grabbed the angry man by the throat and smashed him against the van. Fortunately, there was no serious damage to limb or pride as wiser heads prevailed. Milligan and Harding wrestled the boss away and the protestors hauled the loudmouth to safety. The Irish trainer wasn't harangued again, even after media reports about snakes killing his top three chasers.

The twice-humbled protestor kept a wary distance from O'Leary after that encounter. Milligan couldn't see him amongst the small band of protestors. Eight dogs and their attendants approached The Terrace and the HLP launched into the familiar refrain.

'Stop animal cruelty. Stop animal cruelty. Stop animal cruelty.'

The chorus annoyed Milligan: the activists would never convert anyone at the track, the repetition drove everyone barmy. Perhaps that's why few punters stood trackside during the races? In the lounge they could focus on their dogs and TAB tickets, and not listen to zealots.

'Stop animal cruelty. Stop animal cruelty. Stop animal cruelty.'

Milligan finally reached the sanctuary of the bar and blocked the chanting.

Chapter 3

Dugal Cameron's hamburger from the Werribee shop threatened to stain his boots. Fortunately, the reflux stopped with a belch, the takeaway stayed in place.

'Jeezus Kenny. You and Kim are better than cadaver dogs.'

Withers hoisted his camera, pressed record and returned to the front. He pointed his lens at the traps and recoiled.

'Oh fuck!'

Inside the box was a body: a man, most likely. It was difficult to confirm without a head attached. The legs and arms had also been removed; they were stacked on the bloodied torso which was wedged in sideways. The victim's bulk indicated he was probably a male. Race boxes are constructed to hold greyhounds that weigh between 25 to 30 kilograms, not a human that probably tipped the scales at more than 90 kilos – when fully assembled.

It was gruesome, the trio stood silently for almost a minute. They were reluctant to look at the dismembered body but couldn't tear their eyes away from the night vision gear. The black and white imagery sanitised some of the horrific scene. Eventually Kim forced herself to move closer; she had a job to do. She turned to Withers.

'Can you believe it? Another body?'

It wasn't the second body related to her investigation, but a murder victim at their feet wasn't an unfamiliar sight for the reporter and cameraman. Barely six months previously – during the Tugga's Mob story – Kim and Withers discovered their interviewee stabbed to death on the doorstep of his Geelong flat. The killer had fled moments before their arrival. The victim held vital information about a 30-year-old crime which sparked a Trans-Tasman trail of revenge. The investigation led the *Spotlight* crew back to their own television station in Melbourne where the chief financial officer, not so affectionately known as The Hatchet, was trapped in the crosshairs of the killer in January. The story was headline news in Australia and New Zealand for weeks. It elevated the current affairs show to one of the highest rating programs and launched Kim's reporting career.

Dugal stepped wider on the track to film his colleagues and the murder scene. 'Okay, you guys know that you're part of the new story. The live-baiting angle is secondary to the death of this poor bastard. It doesn't add up – the bait and the body – but we'll let the cops sort that out. Kim, stay close to Kenny and I'll pick up his reactions on your radio mic. Kenny, I know it's tough, but you need to look inside the box. Can you see a head?'

Kim wiped her mouth with a sleeve, it settled the queasiness. They were the crew that found Eddie Malone – it made sense to focus on them with this body, whoever he was.

Withers pushed his camera to the front of the trap.

'Gah! It's like a butcher's fridge in there. But I can't see a head – there's no room for much else.' He backed away after 10 seconds and swallowed deeply. The extreme close-up pictures would never be used on *Spotlight,* they were too ghastly. Dugal's wider shots of the traps and current affairs duo would be enough for sensitive news audiences.

Kim quickly composed a report and turned to Dugal. 'I'm ready to record a short piece. Are you still rolling?'

'Yep, go for it.'

Kim placed both hands in the pockets of her hoody and stood in profile to the boxes behind.

'We were led to this property by an anonymous tip-off about live-baiting in the greyhound industry.

'Instead, we've found something more sinister – a body. Two bodies, in fact. First, we found a stunned possum tied to a mechanical lure on the track. It appeared to be verification that animals are used to blood greyhounds at this site.

'However, a disgusting smell brought us to these starting traps and the body of what we believe to be a man. He's been butchered – torn apart limb by limb and stacked inside. We are about to call the police as this media investigation is now a homicide inquiry.'

Kim turned to the trap and Dugal buttoned off five seconds later. They stared at the crime scene for another 10 seconds before Withers spoke.

'I can imagine the news producers and Mac scrapping over who gets to use that piece to camera.'

'Yeah, I guess we'll have to do a news treatment, then think about something different for us on Monday,' said Kim. 'They might even find the killer by then – that makes Channel 5 News the priority.'

'We'll have time for both before the cops get here,' Withers said. 'Let's do the same as November – film everything possible and hide the discs in the crew car in case the cops confiscate it.'

'Good idea. You and Dugal be careful; I might have seen the killer lurking earlier.'

'I'm sure this guy was killed a few hours ago, judging by the smell of the body. The killer should be miles away.'

Dugal swept his camera around the boxes again. 'Have you noticed there isn't much blood outside?'

Withers copied the move. 'I see what you mean. He was probably killed near the sheds, or house, then carried here – piece by piece. I'll see if I can find that death spot. I reckon the killer chopped him up with a chainsaw. It's messy – but effective.'

'That's too gross to think about,' Kim said. 'Dugal leave me your phone. I'll call the cops on my mobile and use yours to text the newsroom and wake up Mac. The police kept me on the phone for ages last time, ordering me not to disturb anything.'

Dugal was impressed. 'You two are crime scene experts.' He looked at the body. 'By the way, any clues as to who *he* might be?'

Chapter 4

Milligan nursed his glass of low-alcohol beer. Harding had already consumed three full-strength pots and was ready for a fourth.

'Are you sure you won't have another Dwayne? Two thimbles of cat's piss won't put you over the limit.'

'I'm good mate.' He watched the wiry Harding weave through the crowd to the bar, pausing occasionally to greet another attendant or trainer. Race night is all business with little time to chat until the last race. Often trainers want to get dogs home to the kennels as soon their racing is finished. O'Leary was more relaxed; he liked to socialise with owners and punters.

'The dogs can sleep anywhere. It never hurts them to wait for us to have a couple of beers.'

Milligan looked around the lounge, surprised there were still 30 people as the last race had been run. Some nights people were in the mood to linger if they had been successful at the TAB. He saw the Dapper Pom on the fringe of the tables. Benedict Beacham's eyes were also scanning the crowd. Milligan presumed he was looking for his girlfriend; a cute, perky late-30s blonde who loved to chat. Abigail hated a conversation vacuum, which meant Milligan tried to avoid her. She was attractive, but he needed time to think.

Beacham's sweep reached Milligan. The 53-year-old was dressed in a stylish suit, as always. It was grey with a light blue shirt and dark blue tie. Not many punters dressed that elegantly for the dogs, even for the Group races. Hence, Beacham earned the classy moniker.

He was of average height, trim, tanned and most of his hair was still brown, just a few grey tufts over his ears and sideboards. The only flaw was a gammy left leg. Track gossip suggested it was from a car accident, although he never spoke about it.

Beacham smiled at Milligan, raised a glass, returned to his search. He wasn't a toff but insisted on being called by his full first name, not the Australian abbreviation of Benny. The fools who tried to greet him as *Benny Beach* were given short shrift.

The Dapper Pom appeared on the local racing scene five years previously. The flash suits and late model Commodore indicated he knew his greyhounds and their form. The inside word was that Beacham sold an electrical business to get away from the northern hemisphere winters. He was married when he arrived, but not anymore.

Milligan always believed the wife was nice enough: friendly, slim, attractive. She was like Abigail in many ways: pretty, chatty, popular. But Carolyn dropped out of the racing scene before Christmas. Beacham said she couldn't tolerate the searing summer heat. Plus, she missed England's social life. The husband was apparently given an ultimatum – return to cooler climes or stay. The Dapper Pom said Melbourne's snow-free winters made it an easy choice.

Milligan watched as the only other suit-wearing patron joined the Dapper Pom. Chauncey Quayle was never seen without a jacket and tie – even when the mercury edged past 40 degrees. Everyone joked that Chauncey was born in a Fletcher Jones suit, the same woollen garment he'd worn for 70 years. It was always rumpled, yet he wore it like a uniform, complete with cufflinks.

A bookie had to look the part. He didn't want to appear too prosperous, otherwise punters would take their cash elsewhere. Around the Victorian gallops, harness and dog tracks Chauncey looked like he was one race away from the breadline. He couldn't afford fancier suits because his odds were too generous; wise punters were coining it from his bag. Outdoors, a battered fedora, a bulbous nose, eyebrows that needed a hedge trimmer to control and a lanky frame completed the ensemble of the battling bookie.

Milligan learned from track gossip it was a deliberate image. It worked for almost half a century – until the growth in online betting services convinced Chauncey it was time to hang up his bag. Retirement didn't produce a better wardrobe. The bookie still loved the excitement of racing and visited a track, or two, every day. But he wasn't silly enough to let his former punters know he played them for mugs for 50 years.

Chauncey held a large Bundy and coke – his favourite bracer – as he chatted to Beacham. Milligan watched them draw Harding into their huddle when he returned from the bar with one and half pots, both for him. They talked for a few moments before the trio walked to Milligan's table.

'G'day Dwayne,' Chauncey said. 'Benedict and I have been asking young Rene here about your missing boss. Did he get too hammered on his cheap Irish plonk and you've had to cover his arse for the night?'

Milligan and Harding knew there was no love lost between O'Leary and the former bookie. They never learned the source of the antagonism – probably an old debt – but they knew the bitterness was mutual. The pair usually restricted the dislike to baiting and teasing; neither wanted to be banned from the track. There were rumours, however, that they came to blows 20 years ago when away from the stewards' view.

Milligan noticed that Beacham winced at the belligerent tone of the bookie. The Dapper Pom had no beef with anyone, from what Milligan ever saw. He presumed Beacham was curious, like the rest of the room. Milligan was loyal to his boss.

'No Mr Quayle, he told us a new owner wanted to visit. On the quiet, you know? He wanted to check out the kennels, the long run, the feed and whatever else Conor could offer. Maybe they're still talking business – or celebrating?'

'Have you tried calling him?'

Milligan shrugged. 'A couple of times. But it went to voice mail. He's not the greatest with answering the mobile anyway.'

Chauncey snorted. 'It's a wonder he's got enough brains to charge it.' The bookie took a deep swig of rum. 'You collected one third tonight. I can't imagine he'll convince any owners to send their best chasers to that ghost town at Steiglitz. O'Leary's best training days are behind him – there's too many snakes out there. My advice to you young lads is to talk to other kennels. I can't see the Irish rogue staying in the greyhound business much longer.'

Milligan bristled, but held his tongue. The Dapper Pom squirmed, that left Harding to fill the void.

'We appreciate the advice Mr Quayle, we really do. But Conor has been a good boss to us. He's positive things will improve. The canola crop was good last season. We'll get by.' Harding swallowed the rest of his pot and took a gulp from the second.

Beacham chose that moment to make his escape. 'There's Abigail! We must get to Albert Park so time to round up the chatterbox. I'm sure things will get better at Tara. I wish you good luck lads, and your boss.'

He turned to Quayle. 'Are you coming back on Wednesday Chauncey?'

'Most likely. I've got a dog running.' Chauncey took another swallow as he eyed the Dapper Pom. 'When are you going to get your hands dirty Benedict? Invest some of the cash you hauled out of my bag. You've never bought a dog – or a horse. You've got a few hectares at Mount Macedon. You ever going to give something back to the industry?'

Beacham shrugged and smiled. 'Then I would be as poor as the rest of you chaps. I'll stick to punting thanks Chauncey. Perhaps I'll see you all mid-week? Cheers.'

The group watched Beacham limp through the remaining punters and exit the lounge. Milligan couldn't see Abigail, perhaps she went to the ladies before the drive back into the city.

'Lucky bastard.' Chauncey muttered. 'Money and the pretty women.'

'He's okay Mr Quayle,' Harding said. 'The Dapper Pom always shouts a few beers when he backs a winner.'

'He's too fortunate for my liking Rene. We avoided the charmed ones. They'd empty your bags quicker than a Collingwood goal sneak.' Chauncey drained his glass. 'Time for me to hit the road as well. Remember my advice. You should look for new kennels as Conor O'Leary's future looks bloody bleak.'

Chapter 5

Freddie Mercury and Queen belted out the chorus of *We Are The Champions* on the radio of Alan Deveraux's Mazda 6 wagon early Sunday morning. Deveraux joined them for the first time since starting his Christmas holiday; at the top of his voice and badly out of tune. He didn't care, his three sons had been delivered to their soccer fields.

He wasn't ecstatic about unloading the boys; he really wanted to watch their matches. His job as a weekend television news producer made his kid's sport an occasional treat. A need to feed the future sporting heroes and a fat mortgage tipped the scales in favour of turning up for duty. Deveraux often completed the journey from the Burwood venue to the South Melbourne studios with a heavy dose of guilt. But not that morning. Even the traffic was unusually co-operative. The weekday kamikazes were still slumbering, he rarely had to stop for red lights. It was a smooth trip all the way – apart from the horrendous singing.

Deveraux knew it was going to be a magical day as he entered the Channel 5 newsroom a few minutes before nine o'clock. The only person present was his chief of staff, Ciaran O'Malley. That was a good sign as the weekend roster included four reporters and a matching number of camera operators. Empty desks indicated they were already allocated jobs, another boost for the producer's good mood. A phone call from his colleague at 5.17am alerted Deveraux they already had the best story of the day in the can, thanks to the *Spotlight* crew.

'Maybe we should pay Kim and Withers to freelance for us every Friday and Saturday night. They seem to have the luck of the Irish – finding bodies at least.'

O'Malley pursed his lips. 'That was a little too close to home.'

Deveraux was puzzled. O'Malley was bubbling with excitement on the dawn call, declaring his love for Kim and the two camera operators. An inside scoop on a grisly murder delivered before breakfast was a dream start to a news gatherer's day. But O'Malley listlessly twirled a half-empty coffee mug on his untidy desk.

'I got confirmation from the crew about the victim's identity. He was Irish: Conor O'Leary from County Cork.'

'Oh Christ Ciaran. I'm sorry – you knew him?'

'No, but he's an Irish expat like me – I'm bound to know half a dozen people that know him. Well, *knew* him.'

'Okay, my bad. Blood's thicker than Guinness for you folks. Anyway, who was Conor O'Leary – and why did he deserve to be sliced, diced and boxed? And you'd better bring me up to speed on what everyone else is doing.'

O'Malley snapped out of his maudlin mood; he would drink a toast to O'Leary after work. 'I've got Stephanie Grant working on a bio piece: his greyhound racing, farming life, family, friends. He was an above average trainer. Loved his dogs, had a few big wins but was never a threat for the premiership. *Spotlight* were working on a tip off that he was dirty – supposedly used live baits to blood the dogs. Kim says they found a possum strapped to the lure on his track, but they reckon it was a set up. I don't think those allegations will stand up now, but it's obvious someone really hated O'Leary.'

Deveraux nodded. 'It's tough for his family, but we have to spell out the facts. What about Kim – will she be free to do the lead story and a live cross at six?'

'Yep, they're tired and shocked, naturally, but we've got plenty of time to prepare. Mac McKenzie rang; he or Curly Rogers will drop in later.'

'What? They want to make sure we blow *Spotlight's* trumpet for breaking the story?'

'Probably. I think they also want a heads-up on what the vision is like, so they can prepare for Monday.'

'Speaking of that footage – how gruesome is it? A chain-saw dissection is going to be too much for a news audience.'

'Dugal and Withers were using infrared cameras. It's already grainy and some pixilation in editing shouldn't make viewers barf. The boys are pros – they shot the scene knowing what can be used and what can't.'

'Great. What about some live talent to join Kim? Is there a distraught wife?'

'Not in Steiglitz. She went back to County Cork a few years ago. O'Leary lived alone at the property and was helped by two young guys. One helped with the farm and they were all passionate about the dogs. I'm sure Kim can talk one of them into face time on TV.'

Deveraux turned for the kitchenette and the first of many coffees. 'Are they suspects for the cops? Did they chop up the boss before going to the track? With no wife around, they might inherit the farm and the dogs.'

O'Malley shook his head. 'Nah. I suppose anything's possible, but Kim and the guys were filming when they arrived home with the dogs. They were genuinely shocked to see what happened to O'Leary. The cops asked them to identify the clothing and his boots – that was enough to make one of the lads spew. The crime scene officers found the victim's head inside the box. The killer must have expected it to be opened from the rear – his noggin was posed to greet whoever raised the panel. Not pleasant I imagine.' O'Malley swallowed the final dregs of his coffee and grimaced.

'What about the protestors at the track? The Hound Liberation Party – I think they're called. Are the cops talking to them?'

'Not yet – but we are. I've got Mike Berry at their Fitzroy headquarters right now. According to O'Leary's attendants, their boss had a couple of run-ins with them a few months ago. It got physical.'

Chapter 6

The LED video lights provided enough illumination for a television interview in the 19th century Victorian terrace in North Fitzroy. They didn't brighten the mood of Mike Berry's interviewee. Kristin Webb was ready for battle.

'What do you mean physical?' demanded the HLP communications manager. 'Are you implying that Mr O'Leary and one of our members fought at the racetrack?'

Berry wasn't ruffled by her belligerence. 'We've been told – by eye-witnesses – that there was a confrontation between the deceased, Conor O'Leary, and an *aggressive* member of the Hound Liberation Party.'

Kristin didn't flinch. The reporter was using word association – *aggressive* and the HLP in the same sentence – to provoke her. At 37, Webb was a 15-year veteran of skirmishes with the media. Young reporters were easy to handle: a bit of charm, flattery and the reporter would soon relay her message *du jour*. Berry was 34, equally experienced. This story would be different. A greyhound trainer was dead and already the media was floating the theory an animal rights activist might be involved. The inference was that passive resistance had escalated to murder. Webb didn't know about the chainsaw aspect of the case, yet, but the reporter made it clear the trainer's death was brutal.

To suggest any member of the Hound Liberation Party could be angry enough to kill was ludicrous. They were pacifists: passionate about animal welfare, but never inclined to cause harm to people or property. The party was formed in the wake of the New South Wales government's capitulation to public pressure in 2016. That was gutless and shameful, according to Kristin and her 572 party members. How could Premier Mike Baird ban the sport for cruelty to greyhounds, then change his mind a few months later? Webb understood the threat of losing parliamentary seats outweighed sympathy for dogs, but it couldn't quell her indignation.

Kristin had fronted for dozens of television, radio and press interviews since the party formation. It was easy after the Four Corners exposé to push their message about greyhound racing. What loving owners subjected their dogs to danger on the track for the sake of entertainment? Why would they kill them when they were too slow to race? Kristin had all the statistics at her fingertips, but they wouldn't be required for this chat. The focus wasn't about greyhounds – the reporter wanted to link the Hound Liberation Party to O'Leary's death.

Kristin couldn't show any weakness, but there was a niggle at the back of her mind. A small one that couldn't be examined properly before the interview. She had been at the track in December when one of their group blocked O'Leary's van, accused him of burning evidence and was body-slammed. It shocked everyone; the protests had been noisy but relatively calm for several months.

The spring confrontations were mostly verbal, apart from one occasion. Three placards were smashed and a male protestor was deliberately tripped. It was cunningly done as the TV cameras missed the instigator, but not the result – their activist on his backside. That was the extent of the physical contact. The boundaries were marked out, the cold war continued until the pre-Christmas fracas. Both incidents involved Julian Oliver, the most vocal member of the HLP. He was the irritant that Kristin didn't want to reveal to the news reporter.

'Please don't equate chanting to aggression Mr Berry. We are proud of our opposition to the cruel treatment of greyhounds. They're exploited for money, ill-treated, dumped or killed when they're …'

The reporter sighed. 'This isn't a political platform for your party Ms Webb. A man has been butchered. The facts are that one of your members recently abused Mr O'Leary. Your man came off second best in that confrontation. He was thumped against the trainer's van and had to be rescued. The protestor was then heard to threaten the trainer. What can you tell us about that?'

Kristin paused and that was fatal in a TV interview – was she withholding information?

'Nothing.' Kristin hoped a short answer would get the question and her slow reaction edited from the story. This was news; anything longer than a seven second grab was normally a luxury.

'You don't know about the confrontation – or the threat? Our sources tell us you were at the protest Ms Webb. And you helped drag the *aggressor* away. You don't deny that your man blocked the trainer's vehicle and accused him of – and I quote – 'burning evidence of animal cruelty.'

'I believe it was something like that.'

'This was shortly after the trainer's valuable equipment shed was burned to the ground by an arsonist? A crime that hasn't been solved.'

'Yes, but you can't blame that on us. It wasn't anything important anyway, just some old farm rubbish. We had nothing to do with the fire.'

The reporter smiled; Kristin gritted her teeth. She drifted off track and Berry won that round.

'But your protestor decided to poke at a raw wound for the trainer – and was humiliated.'

Kristin wanted to repudiate that sentence but knew it was futile; that's essentially what happened. Julian Oliver saw a chance to score a cheap shot and took it.

The reporter smirked. 'So, after trying to annoy the trainer – then getting thrown around by a man twice his age – he tried to have the parting jab. As he was hauled away, he was heard to say he would *get even.* What can you say about that threat Ms Webb?'

'I never heard anything like that. And really Mr Berry this is a waste of time. We are non-violent people dedicated to ending the greyhound racing industry in Australia. To try to involve the party in this case is ridiculous.'

Kristin reached for the lapel microphone to end the interview. It was time to cut her losses before the reporter asked the crucial question: the name of the angry protestor. Unfortunately, Mike Berry was smart enough to make his final question count.

'Can you tell us where that party member was last night, Ms Webb? Was he at the track with you?'

Chapter 7

Ciaran O'Malley's chair was at full tilt, his feet on the news desk. He raised a chilled bottle of Crown Lager. 'May God grant you a generous share of eternity, Conor O'Leary.'

David 'Mac' McKenzie drank the toast with the news chief of staff without taking his eyes from the three television news services on the monitors above. Mac, senior program producer for *Melbourne Spotlight,* was similarly inclined. 'I thought you didn't know the guy?'

'No, I didn't. But we Irish are a sentimental lot. Especially away from home.'

Mac snorted at the lilt that suddenly infiltrated O'Malley's voice. His colleague left the Emerald Isle as a babe in arms, that was more than 40 years ago. He forgave the expat a touch of melancholy; O'Malley's workday had exceeded 13 hours and the clock was still ticking.

That wasn't all bad. A rise in news ratings since the Tugga's Mob saga – they were still behind Channels 7 and 9 but well ahead of 10, the ABC and SBS – had improved the station's finances. Overtime, if it couldn't be taken in lieu, was now paid. The extended leave-of-absence for The Hatchet – aka chief financial officer Andrew Hackett – had loosened the purse strings for the hospitality budget. Hence the beers the journos sipped: leftovers from *Spotlight's* Friday night gathering.

The pair lapsed into silence again as they watched the news program. They smashed the opposition channels with their content, all remotely packaged by Kim with a little help from Mac in the edit suite. It wasn't even a fair contest. The other stations were left with daytime pictures of police driving in and out of the property, stills of the victim and file shots of greyhound races. How could anyone compete with a television crew with a knack for finding murder victims? Mind you, it was one thing to locate the bodies – it took journalistic skill to turn the footage into a ratings-winning program.

Mac watched Kim anchor the O'Leary stories from the crime scene near Steiglitz. He hadn't been required to work his police contacts to ensure Kim was available for the news report and live crosses. The crew didn't leave the property all day, finding convenient ways to help detectives. They were suitably rewarded when the senior officer allowed Kim to host the news segment from the property. A live shot showing where Conor O'Leary had been boxed beat a Melbourne studio set. Mac would have paid a fortune to watch the faces of the 7, 9, 10, ABC and SBS journos as Channel 5's live broadcast truck rolled past them at the front gate.

Kim's main story about finding the trainer's body ran two and a half minutes – a lifetime in a half hour commercial news program. She then introduced a background feature from Stephanie Grant which, while shorter, could put O'Leary on the path to sainthood. That was until reporters tracked down the former Mrs O'Leary in Ireland. Canonisation plans could be shelved before the wake. For the moment, O'Leary's brutal death was a blessing for a greyhound racing industry under intense scrutiny and pressure to reform. The greyhounds weren't the only victims.

The biography finished, Kim turned to a live interview with one of the kennel's two attendants, Dwayne Milligan. He was lean, a fraction taller than Kim's height of 176 cm but scruffier in work jeans and a tattered sweatshirt, a far cry from the race night uniform of black waterproof-jacket and trousers.

Milligan was nervous, his eyes red-rimmed. Mac could see the young man was upset; was he grieving – or angry? Kim didn't have time to dwell on O'Leary as a boss or trainer; she wanted to get to a potential cause for the horrific slaying.

'Now Dwayne, I understand the kennels have had a run of terrible luck over the past six months.'

Milligan looked at the ground and shuffled his feet. Kim gently clasped his right elbow to keep him in camera frame.

'Yeah, we've had tough times since before Christmas. Someone burnt down a shed, then three of our best chasers died from snake bites. And now the boss gets chopped up with a chainsaw. Yeah, things have been pretty shitty.'

Kim almost fainted earlier in the day when detectives revealed the snake deaths. But further discussions raised doubts about the unusual cluster.

'Let's focus on the snakes for a moment, Dwayne. Have they been prolific on the property?'

'They've always been around. We all know that. But I've been here six years and we've never had a problem. No bites, no deaths until recently. Mr O'Leary said he'd never lost a dog before that in 20 years. They're smart animals – dogs and snakes – they know when to avoid each other. From what I've read, dogs only get bit when they try to save their owners. Snakes getting three dogs in a few weeks was weird.'

Kim allowed a moment for her television audience to absorb that anomaly.

'We've heard from Stephanie Grant's story how popular Mr O'Leary was in the greyhound racing community. Is there anyone who would have a grudge against your boss?'

'He never really had an enemy in the world. Everyone loved him at the track. The only problem I ever saw was last December when a protestor bailed us up at The Meadows, just after the fire.'

'What happened then?'

'This guy jumped in front of the van as we arrived. I had to slam on the brakes and it really shook up the dogs. Then he started abusing Mr O'Leary, saying he burnt his own shed to hide evidence of cruelty to the dogs. The boss was pissed off and smashed the guy into the van. We'd just lost Paddy that day as well – the first of the dogs to the snakes. I don't blame the boss for being riled. But Rene and I grabbed him, the protestors dragged their guy away, so we settled things pretty quickly.'

'But it didn't end there, did it Dwayne?'

'No, the idiot threatened Mr O'Leary. He yelled that he would get even.'

It was the perfect ending and Mac watched in admiration as Kim thanked the attendant and segued to Mike Berry's interview with the Hound Liberation Party. They ran the full combative clip – questions and answers. The only positive for the HLP was that it ended before the angry protestor was named. The communications manager had discarded the microphone and walked off camera by that point. Kim wrapped the segment and handed back to the studio anchor for the day's other news.

It was an impressive performance and Mac was proud of his youngest reporter. 'Well done Kim.' He turned to O'Malley. 'But that is where the spirit of inter-departmental co-operation ends.'

'Oh, come on Mac! She owns this story: she finds the body, reveals the motive and now she's pointed the cops in the direction of the killer. She must stay on the story – you know, be there for the arrest. She's so sweet with the country cops they'll probably let her put the handcuffs on the guy.'

'I don't think the police will move that quickly and I'm sure you'll be back with the brat pack by tomorrow. The news directors at 7, 9 and 10 are probably screaming at the police media lackeys right now. That was a coup to be inside the cordon tonight, but it won't happen again. Your reporters can handle it from here.'

O'Malley shrugged. He would be yelling at the cops too if his crew was outside the fence at Steiglitz. But he wouldn't give up the fight for Kim easily. 'How about we ask her? I bet she wants to stay on the story.'

'She will – but for us. We need a new angle for *Spotlight* and I've already told Curly to put on his thinking cap.'

Mac stood; at almost two metres, 110 kilos and a ginger mane, he could discourage dissent in a maximum-security prison. His news colleague wasn't going to stress about the issue; the afternoon promos ensured the TV audience was the biggest for the year. It was job well done for O'Malley and Deveraux, time to hand the baton to the weekday crew and enjoy their days off.

Mac drained his lager and dumped the bottle in the kitchenette bin. It was almost full after the news department's Friday drinks; the extra cash didn't cover weekend cleaners. The current affairs producer didn't need to see the rest of the bulletin; his mind was focussed on what *Spotlight* could do with the exclusive footage. He waved goodbye to O'Malley and navigated the rabbit warren of the South Melbourne complex to the news studio. He stuck his head through the doorway of the control room and gave Deveraux a thumbs up. The accolade was similarly acknowledged.

Mac detoured via the current affairs office to collect his car keys. Out of habit, he checked the fridge: empty, he'd shared the last two beers with O'Malley. Mac picked up the coffee kitty and gave it a shake: a few coins. *Bugger!*

Mac's kitty pilfering days were over, mostly. The new beer and wine largesse from management had eased that financial pressure. It occasionally provided short-term loans to cover hot tips for a fast nag at Flemington, Caulfield, or Moonee Valley. Fortunately, the tipster's horse sense had improved: Mac was able to make repayments without being sprung by the guardian, Josephine Trescowthick. But the rattling tin heralded bad times ahead.

The coffee-addicted Jo would badger producers, reporters, editors and camera ops for a $5 top-up at the Monday production meeting. It could be ugly if Jo's home espresso machine had one of its regular hissy fits. Eighteenth century Royal Navy press gangs looked like choir boys compared to Jo on collection day. Mac would need to sneak a few coins from his wife's purse in the morning.

Mac looked around the office before switching off the lights. It wasn't an inspiring room at that moment; it was a box without windows. The dungeon, as the crew called it, held everything a current affairs program required: an internal glass-partitioned office for executive producer and *Spotlight* presenter, Richard Templeton, a conference room with formica table and 10 chairs, the central producer command post, eight desks with mandatory computers, three edit suites, two 60-inch televisions, a kitchenette and the all-important booze fridge.

The walls and ceiling had been painted in earthy tones in the past three months, another small reward for improved ratings. There were new *Spotlight* posters to add a dash of colour, yet it still looked bland. Put a dozen resourceful people in that space Monday to Friday and everything changed for Mac. It became a creative hub and that's what motivated the 55-year-old veteran to get out of bed every day.

Despite news expectations of a swift resolution, Mac believed the story was more complicated. The facts pointed to a person with a grievance against the murder victim. The obvious suspect was the protestor from the HLP. There had been a physical confrontation at the track, a threat was made, the trainer was dead. Case over once the accused could be found. It looked obvious, but Mac knew it wasn't. For him, the facts didn't stack up.

Spotlight's involvement started with the anonymous letter about live baiting. It arrived the previous Monday. Jo had retrieved it from the station mail room, along with two dozen other PR handouts seeking publicity. Mac had given it a cursory examination with his second in command, Curly Rogers. The allegations seemed implausible. After the furore generated by the Four Corners exposé, who would be stupid enough to try live baiting again? The greyhound racing fraternity was on notice: another scandal could close the industry forever, regardless of job losses.

Curly insisted there was enough detail in the letter to warrant further investigation. Their resident greyhound expert – Kim – was the obvious choice to dig deeper. Pete Benson was initially miffed to be overlooked. The senior reporter was a racing connoisseur: horses, dogs, cars, bikes, trucks, humans – anything that went fast. He even did a story once about racing penny farthings. The bruised ego was mollified when Mac reminded Benson he was booked to fly to England on Thursday. If his international media contacts came through, Benson's dream holiday would include the Monaco Formula 1 Grand Prix and Royal Ascot. Perhaps he might see the Queen? The dish lickers didn't compare to that experience.

The story potential excited Kim. Her discreet inquiries into Conor O'Leary didn't raise any red flags. He was well respected by owners, trainers, attendants and punters. Even the administrators. However, Kim argued he might be too clever for animal welfare investigators.

O'Leary wasn't implicated in the first scandal; did that encourage him to keep blooding dogs below the radar? If surveillance mini cams recorded evidence of animal cruelty, they had a story that would captivate all Australia. If they found nothing, so be it. It would only cost them a couple of nights in the bush – one to set up the cameras, the second to retrieve them. Kim's youthful enthusiasm swayed the senior producers to take a gamble.

Mac squeezed his large frame into the driver's seat of his wife's Suzuki Swift and decided to be honest: that original punt failed. Yes, Kim and the cameras found so-called evidence of live baiting at O'Leary's property. But it was fake, most likely planted by animal rights campaigners. Or was it one activist; the man who threatened to *get even* with the trainer who humiliated him?

And that's where Mac's problems with the HLP man as a suspect started. Did getting even extend to chopping the trainer into small pieces and shoving him inside a starting box? Even if it did, why would the avenger invite the media to the event? He virtually laid a trail of crumbs for them to follow. They were tempted with details of a heinous practice, who the perpetrator was, where it was going to happen and when. The instructions for the crew to enter the property were exact. Ken Withers told Mac in a private call that he was certain the wire was cut. Why would the activist set up a story about live baiting and then kill the man committing that crime? It would only draw attention to his own more serious crime.

If that was the case. There could be another scenario. Was he discovered while faking the evidence? Did he kill O'Leary in a panic? If so, why the brutality? That was over the top for a bit of a push and shove at a greyhound track.

Mac pointed the Swift towards home in Beaumaris as those questions did laps around his brain. The more he thought about it, the less sense it made. That wasn't his problem though; the police had to solve the case. The longer detectives took to arrest a suspect, the more time it gave *Spotlight* to poke around the story. What could they produce by Monday?

Chapter 8

Kristin Webb was angry, mobile phone-smashing angry; the screen finally cracked as it was slammed onto the wooden table at her terrace for the tenth time. She couldn't reach Julian Oliver. The first attempt was at 9.55am – soon after she had shown that arrogant Mike Berry the door. It was 6.11 and her mood was volcanic after the stitch-up job by Channel 5 News.

Kristin was appalled the reporter used the *whole* interview, including her clumsy exit. It wasn't easy to gracefully remove a microphone and step over power cables while fighting the urge to throttle the reporter. The interview was bad in every respect for the HLP. She didn't deal well with Berry's probing about the track confrontation. And the walkout to avoid naming the activist made her look guilty. That would have an impact on party donations and membership.

Her effort was futile anyway as the television station would soon discover Julian's name. It would probably be leaked by one of their former party colleagues, the incident in December spooked a dozen members. Three resigned from the party, declaring it was no longer aligned with their non-violent beliefs. The other nine wanted Julian removed. It took two meetings to pacify the dissenters. They finally accepted a compromise: Julian would be suspended for a month.

It was such a storm in a teacup. Julian hadn't been violent – *he* was subjected to violence by the trainer. He was more surprised by the experience than any of the protestors. Webb knew that because she drove a chastened Julian home.

'It was a cheap shot,' Julian admitted. 'I knew about the fire, then I heard about the snake death. I wanted to be provocative Kristin, but I never meant to provoke that sort of response. I'm sorry.'

Kristin recalled her subdued compatriot as he slouched in the passenger seat of her Corolla; he looked more like a naughty schoolboy than a barrier-storming agitator. The suspension was an easy fix; Kristin knew Julian had booked a holiday away from Melbourne for Christmas.

The frustrating part was the four hours it took to appease grumpy party members. Everyone had to speak, several times. What would those members do if the murder investigation focussed on Julian? It was a crisis for the HLP. Kristin had two goals when the party was formed: to end greyhound racing and to gain a seat in the Victorian parliament. Both were in jeopardy if Julian Oliver was connected to the death of the trainer. It could destroy the party – unless Webb used her communications skills to spin the story their way.

She believed Julian was innocent, despite missing the protest in Broadmeadows. Julian wasn't at the usual pick-up point in Carlton. It was a rare non-show as Julian was passionate about animal cruelty and humanitarian causes. The drives to various protests had given her a chance to learn about Julian's involvement.

He'd left Auckland University in his native New Zealand 10 years before to join the Red Cross. Julian told her he needed to physically get involved with helping communities, rather than talk about it. The Red Cross job had taken him to crises throughout the Pacific and southern Asia: cyclones, floods, a tsunami and other natural disasters. Fatigue had overwhelmed him after eight years and he moved to Australia for a change of scene. The greyhound scandal had re-ignited his social conscience, and eventually led him to the door of the Hound Liberation Party headquarters.

Julian's commitment and fervour had inspired a handful of younger protestors. Older HLP members described him as *intense*, and for most the December incident was water under the bridge.

Until last night. Julian's absence from the regular protest team was hard to explain. Kristin picked up the battered mobile phone. The screen lit up; she pressed Julian's number again.

Please answer Julian!

Chapter 9

Kim Prescott was dog-tired as she walked Sexy Rexy beside the Yarra River late on Sunday. Professionally it had been an exhilarating day-and-a-half; physically it was brutal on the body once the adrenalin dissipated – even for a 24-year-old. She hadn't slept since Friday night. She could claim a day in lieu to recover. Not that she would dream of doing that; it would allow another reporter to steal *her* story. It was going to remain her yarn – after a run for Rex and a solid sleep.

The fawn brindle missed his morning trot and Kim knew a night walk meant a fox hunt. Foxes in central Melbourne were an urban myth until residents with cameras revealed they had adapted to life in the burbs. Their own close encounter came on Domain Road behind the Shrine of Remembrance. Rex almost ripped Kim's arm off on a midnight ramble when he spotted a fox padding across the grass towards the botanical gardens. The chaser instinct was still strong; by the time Kim controlled Rex the fox had wisely disappeared; too late to retrieve the mobile from her bomber jacket. That was a pity because few colleagues were inclined to believe her. Wildlife expert Ken Withers was the most sceptical. 'Did you have a late night at the pub Kim?'

Rex's latest fox expedition was delayed until after Kim watched the news update on the murder. Detectives wouldn't name a suspect, so Channel 5 did it for them. Two former HLP party members were keen to distance themselves from police inquiries and eagerly threw Julian Oliver under the bus for the journalists.

The snitches wouldn't appear on camera, but provided pictures of the 30-year-old expat Kiwi at earlier HLP protests. Someone also tracked down a photo of Julian working for the Red Cross in the aftermath of the catastrophic Christchurch earthquake in 2011. He looked more like a carer than a killer to Kim. Not that she was a good judge. The Tugga's Mob terminator worked at Channel 5 for several weeks while plotting the final murder. No one suspected anything until it was too late.

Julian Oliver was dressed the same in the protest photos: a green anorak, black jeans, shoulder length dark hair. The lens usually caught him wearing a beret and mid chant with a raised fist. He wasn't a modern-day Che Geuvara, but Kim admitted the pictures portrayed charisma. He was about five years older than the conservative Red Cross snap and thinner. Was O'Leary's murder a heat-of-the-moment reaction? Julian was humiliated twice by the trainer; did he get the upper hand the third time they met?

The evening dog walks were always valuable time for analysis. The Stieglitz trip didn't go as expected, but it still produced a story of national interest. Kim had spoken to Mac and Curly about her *Spotlight* feature. They also had fresh ideas; everything would be thrashed out at the Monday morning production meeting. They could be feisty encounters, much like family dinners with everyone wanting to be heard at the same time. She knew Mac relished the brainstorming sessions; he sieved the advice before deciding *Spotlight's* focus for the day.

Kim and Rex faced a walk sign on the traffic lights at Punt Road but instinctively waited a few more seconds to avoid a colour-blind motorist. A police van also flashed through the intersection with lights on. It reminded Kim of the friendly cop who made their life at the crime scene much easier.

Detective Sergeant Nathan Potter had worked on the Eddie Malone homicide inquiry in November. Kim remembered him well: he was the same height as Ken Withers, more athletic and much cuter. The detective's first words at Steiglitz made Kim laugh.

'Wouldn't you rather meet over a coffee instead of a body?'

It was meant to settle nerves as the forensic examiners were grumpy with the television crew. Kim, Dugal and Withers trampled all around the starting traps – mangling footprints the killer might have left – before they even knew it was a crime scene. Kim earned kudos with the detective by pointing the CSOs towards the kennels. Her phantom might have been real.

The Norlane inquisition in November was tense. Kim wanted to help the police, but she desperately needed time to work on the biggest story of her career. There wasn't the same deadline pressure as in November. Kim and Withers were familiar with homicide procedures and patiently answered questions when required. She was content to repeat their story half a dozen times to more senior officers. The longer the police needed them, the longer they stayed inside the cordon.

Dugal had ducked through the trees before the first patrol car arrived to hide the initial recordings. He returned with their regular XDCAMS and spare batteries. Daylight revealed the property was in better shape than they expected.

The ramshackle greyhound circuit was no longer in use. It must have been abandoned years ago. Instead, there was a 400-metre dirt run which was well-maintained. The plywood kennel block was sturdy, spacious and recently painted. The house was a 1980s brown brick ranch style with wide verandas. It had been painted and repaired diligently through the decades, reflecting the work of proud owners.

Kim spent the time between talking to detectives and story preparations with Dwayne Milligan and Rene Harding. Their boss was dead, but they still had dogs to look after. Many of the animals were stressed, prowling their enclosures and not settling for long snoozes like normal. Police wouldn't allow the attendants to release the dogs for a romp, which was another change in routine. Kim tagged along and petted greyhounds who sought attention. It helped chill Milligan; Kim was able to glean more information. She learned that O'Leary was a good boss and was well-liked in the racing community, mostly. Former bookie Chauncey Quayle wasn't a member of the O'Leary fan club.

'You think he hated your boss?'

'Hate's a bit strong,' said Milligan.

'Do you know what caused the animosity?'

'Nah. It was way before Rene and I joined him. They probably forget what started it themselves. Much of the time I think they enjoyed winding each other up. You know, just to get a reaction. They both had the gift of the gab and people often laughed at their insults.'

'You don't think police would be looking at him then as a possible killer?'

'Nah. They've been sparring for so many years – why would Mr

Quayle suddenly take a chainsaw to Conor? He's too old anyway. Must be over 70 and the boss was pretty fit for a 60-year-old.'

The bookie as a possible murderer didn't excite Kim either, but she would do more research to be sure. Kim directed the two camera operators to set up camp near the trees, away from the police forensic operations. Her goal was to be on site at six o'clock and to learn more from the kennel workers. Milligan relaxed as Kim tagged along, displaying a natural affinity with the greyhounds. He explained the kennels shift from circuit training to a drag lure.

'The circuit was dumped years ago, well before I arrived. Conor said it was impractical but didn't bother pulling the posts out. He occasionally gave younger dogs a run around it, to give them experience on an oval track.'

Kim looked at the winch on the long run. Milligan said it was set to a speed to allow dogs to catch the lure; a reward for the chase and an incentive to keep running on race day.

'So, whoever tried to frame him for live-baiting had never been to the property during daylight? They didn't know the mechanical lure on the circuit wasn't operational.'

'It must be those animal activists,' said Harding. 'Everyone knows we only do the long run and drag. Greyhound people wouldn't have tied an animal to the old lure. No way. They know we're clean.'

Kim felt guilty about her intended story. She *was* being led by somebody with an agenda to hurt greyhound racing and its participants. The murder of O'Leary changed her focus. Were the two connected? Most probably, but she couldn't see how. The police had the responsibility of solving the homicide case; perhaps Kim could solve the mystery that connected the sabotage to the death? She could have a new ally in that cause.

DS Potter was taking more than an official interest. He convinced his superior it would help publicise the case if Channel 5 reported the news from inside the property. He emphasised they were an integral part of the story as they found the victim. The *Spotlight* trio was ecstatic when their broadcast truck was given access to the property. Kim suspected either DS Potter or the police would require a *quid pro quo* for that favour.

Kim and Rex returned to the apartment a few minutes past eleven. There weren't any distractions on their latest jaunt as Kim's lifeline was left at home. It was an accidental disconnect, missed in Rex's eagerness to get out the door. The phone hadn't been idle in her absence. It listed two calls and a text. They were all from *Spotlight's* PA, Jo Trescowthick. Kim checked the text first.

Call me! I know suspect!!!

Day 134

The Sunday dinner was better than usual: beef stir fry with broccoli, cauliflower, onions, carrots and cashew nuts swimming in sauce. It had to be a takeaway as the jailer didn't possess those culinary skills. She didn't need the sodium overdose, but the vegetables were welcome. The standard fare was stodgy: casseroles, tinned soups, baked beans, cottage pies, sandwiches – meals that could be consumed without a knife and fork. The only utensils allowed in the cell were plastic.

The prisoner was surprised her daily record was permitted. He knew about the screw from the first time it scraped the wall. He merely shrugged; it was too small to be a threat. She found it poking from a wine-rack after waking with the first concussion. There had been half a dozen more unprovoked assaults in the following months. She learned the warning signs of that madness and minimised the damage with whatever bedding could be clawed over her body. A separate record of that brutality was hidden.

Many prisoners would rate the cell as comfortable. It was a five-metre by three-metre rectangle with a two-metre high stud. She had almost worn a groove in the floor to stop her leg muscles from atrophying. There was a bed with two blankets and a separate en-suite with toilet, vanity and shower. The roof, walls and floor were stone, the only access was via the locked steel door. It was built as a storeroom in the 19th century, modernised before the millennium and turned into a wine cellar. The expensive bottles departed with the previous owner and the empty shelves taunted the occupant; she loved a regular tipple: red, white, bubbles.

The alcohol-free diet had done wonders for her waistline. There were no scales to chart the kilos shed, but the prison uniform of track suit pants and tee shirts were much looser. Sweatshirts or jumpers were never required in her dungeon. The temperature was meticulously controlled. It wasn't for her benefit. It was for the other inhabitants. Out there.

Chapter 10

Curly Rogers removed his ear plugs as he approached the *Spotlight* office Monday morning. Jimmy Barnes and Cold Chisel were singing *Khe Sanh*, but experience taught him it was wiser to switch off the iPod before entering. It was silent ahead: no cursing or yelling. That was usually a good sign; Jo hadn't clipped Mac's ankles or shins with her death chariot – yet!

Jo considered it was a waste of energy to walk in the office. Not when she could propel herself back and forth in the nifty, black mesh chair on five casters. The optional adjustable arms were jettisoned the first day; they slowed Jo's access to the kitchenette. Only the foolish entered that alley when Jo needed a coffee fix. Unfortunately, Mac's command post was in the middle of the track. Crushed toes, gashes and bruises still hadn't taught Mac to improve his evasion techniques.

Curly entered the room to find Mac was the only occupant. He was slouched in his chair, arms folded and legs at full stretch. He didn't acknowledge Curly, just stared at the dark windows of the edit suites.

'Morning Mac. Are you thinking – or sulking about your losses at Flemington?'

Mac grunted but didn't shift his gaze. 'Did you know Ms Ben Hur has legs?'

Curly smiled at one of Jo's many office nicknames. 'Really? I thought she was a torso on wheels.' There was no sign of Jo. 'Did you record it? The crew won't believe you.' Curly dumped the shoulder bag on his desk.

'Bizarre things have been happening my loyal scribe.' Mac swivelled to face Curly, his trusted producer and friend. 'She was here when I arrived. Not much unusual about that I admit. But she didn't have a coffee on the desk – she was drinking *peppermint tea!*'

Curly was shocked. 'That is strange – for Jo. Is she sick?'

'I asked her that, after picking my jaw off the floor. She didn't answer because Kim walked through the door. That's when it got truly weird – Jo *leapt* to her feet, *ran* to Kim and dragged her in there.' The chair turned again as Mac pointed at Edit 2. 'And that's where they've been for the last 10 minutes.'

Curly peered at the tinted glass; he could barely see the outline of the reporter or production assistant. 'It must be serious. When did Jo last leave that chair?'

'Must have been the Christmas party. Ken Withers was twirling Jo around the dance floor and smashed her into the bandstand. Jo had to walk away from the wreckage. I thought it was the end of the death chariot, but she forged my signature to get a more lethal machine. I'm sure she has blades attached to the sides. That meeting must involve a life-or-death crisis – but is it personal, or work?'

Curly shrugged and was saved from guessing when the edit suite door opened. Kim emerged first, followed by a downcast Jo. Curly broke the ice.

'Morning Kim, Jo. Anything we can help you with?'

Jo's eyes were red. Curly couldn't tell whether it was from caffeine withdrawal or lack of sleep. She wore a blue blouse and jeans, standard attire for the 29-year-old – a dress or skirt impeded the chariot speed. Jo was never short of attitude, but she currently lacked her normal spark. She looked at the reporter who nodded assurance.

'I have a confession – about that greyhound trainer. The one Kim found dead on Saturday.'

Curly was relieved. Jo didn't reach one and a half metres in her tallest boots. Primary school kids towered over her; no way did Jo have the strength to dissect a greyhound trainer. Nor would she have a reason to. The crisis wasn't going to be too dramatic. He was about to encourage Jo to continue, but Mac beat him to it.

'We know you couldn't lift a chainsaw, Jo. What do you know about it?'

Jo was horrified that Mac even considered she was the mysterious chopper. 'I didn't bloody kill him!' She paused and lowered her head again. 'But I might know who did.'

It was Mac and Curly's turn to be shocked. Four eyebrows were at full elevation as they turned to Kim. She nodded. 'Don't worry. Jo's not connected to the act, as such – but she…she knows the main suspect. Julian Oliver. Tell them Jo.'

Jo shuffled her feet and looked longingly at her chair. 'I met Julian 10 days ago. At a pub in Brunswick.'

'Was it a date? A Tinder hook up – or something more casual?' asked Mac.

Jo blushed, another first for the producers. The office Jo was feisty and took no prisoners. She wasn't scared to call a spade a fucking shovel when she needed to be assertive. Mostly her private life was kept under the radar. Curly and Mac heard occasional rumours of flings – sometimes with station staff – but never saw the evidence at work. It wasn't their business anyway, apart from wanting to enjoy office gossip about colleagues. But her latest dalliance couldn't be kept under wraps, not if Julian Oliver was a killer. Curly tried to settle his colleague's frayed nerves.

'Come on Jo. It's us – we're almost family. We're not going to judge you about after-hours liaisons. We need to know more about Julian and whether he's dangerous.'

'That's the thing Curly – I don't believe he's evil. I know the evidence points his way – he clashed with the dead trainer, he threatened to get even, he was missing in action on Saturday night and someone planted the possum.'

Mac shrugged. 'That's not hard evidence Jo. A good defence lawyer could make that look circumstantial for a jury if Julian can provide an alibi. Were you with him?'

'No. It was just a random hook up for a night. He was sweet, charming, we both had lots to drink. It just happened.'

'You can say five Hail Marys and save yourself a trip to the confessional next Saturday morning,' said Mac. Everyone laughed, the tension eased. 'But what can you tell us about him? Do you know where he lives?'

'Not exactly. It was Carlton – I think.' A small smile appeared. 'We caught an Uber to his place…but we weren't exactly paying attention to the scenery.' Jo turned to Kim. 'He was very cute.'

'Okay, what about later – or the next morning? Did you notice where you were when you left? How did you get home to South Melbourne?'

'It was another Uber. And no, I won't have the pick-up details. He was a proper gentleman and used his account. It was about seven o'clock and all those terraces look the same.'

'Phone number?' Curly asked.

'No.'

'Email?'

'Nup.'

'It was random?'

'Yup. Right time and place for both of us to have some fun.'

'What about his home, apartment or whatever it was? Did he have any flatmates?'

'I think so, but they weren't around after midnight.' Jo brightened. 'Maybe one of them will come forward? Or even the Hound Liberation Party?'

Mac shook his head. 'I wouldn't count on any help from the HLP after Mike Berry's job on the news. Did you talk to Julian about the greyhounds Jo?'

'At the start. He's passionate about animal rights and humanitarian causes in general. He told me how cruel the sport was and that he was positive trainers were still blooding their dogs – yada yada. I listened, mostly. He had such lovely dark eyes and long lashes.' Jo sighed. 'He got more excited when I told him I worked at Melbourne *Spotlight*. He insisted we should do an exposé and–'

'Hang on,' Mac interrupted. 'This was, what – Friday week ago?'

'Yes.'

'And on Monday we received the *anonymous* tip about live-baiting at O'Leary's property.'

Kim intervened. 'It arrived in the post on Monday morning.'

Jo blushed again. 'Not exactly.'

'Eh?' Mac said. 'You didn't do a personal delivery for Julian Oliver I hope.'

'No!' Embarrassment transitioned to indignation. 'I was on my way back from the mail room when reception handed me the envelope. They said a security guard found it under the door on Sunday evening. He forgot to put it in the mail room and left it on the reception desk.'

'Did you guess it was from your Romeo?'

'I…considered it. But it was you guys who made the decision to investigate the story. You thought it was possible. My sleeping with the potential writer was irrelevant – at that time.'

Curly grimaced. 'It would have helped to know about your date Jo. We would have been more cautious. I guess we got too excited about cracking a big story. We didn't do enough preliminary investigations. My fault really. I should have thought about groups with a vested interest. The HLP would have been one of the first to consider.'

'No need to fall on your sword Curly,' said Mac. 'I sent Kim and the boys to set up the cameras. There was always potential. We didn't get the story we wanted – but still ended up with something explosive.'

'It grates that we were being led. But the result doesn't stack up for me – anyone disagree? Why send us to the property to do a live-baiting story and then kill the trainer before we get there?'

Jo was the first to answer. 'That's what kept me awake all night.' She shook her head. 'I couldn't believe that Julian was involved, but everything points towards him. Did he go to plant the live bait and was confronted by O'Leary? Julian isn't a big guy; but did he kill the trainer in self-defence?'

Kim was quiet throughout Jo's revelations. 'Maybe there *was* an unexpected showdown between Julian and O'Leary. The death might be accidental. We'll know more about that from the autopsy report today. But it doesn't explain why the body was chopped up and stuffed in the starting trap. That, to me, was a brutal and vindictive act. Was that Julian?'

Chapter 11

'We should have kicked him out last December. Not let him off with a slap on the wrist. That mad Kiwi was always a loose cannon. Now he's going to destroy the party – the dogs will suffer.'

Ryan Mathison stroked the head of the dark brindle greyhound that patiently stood beside him in the HLP office. Molly was a former racer who saw more of Victoria in retirement as Mathison's loyal companion. They were back from a weekend fund-raising trip to Horsham in the north-west. The 38-year-old's tirade was directed towards Kristin Webb who was slumped over a desk, head in her hands. 'What did you tell the cops? Are they pointing the finger at anyone else in our group?'

Mathison was the co-founder of the HLP. He was a veteran activist: much of the previous two decades were spent with Greenpeace, People for the Ethical Treatment of Animals, Animals Australia and other welfare causes. Mathison wanted to try a new approach with the dogs. Instead of ranting against the establishment, he wanted to work from the inside. The Hound Liberation Party was his pathway to a political career.

Kristin knew her party co-founder genuinely cared for animals. But she wondered if Mathison was more concerned about his political ambitions for parliament. Could they be derailed by the murder investigation? She had watched him morph into a *candidate* over the past 12 months. Gone were the dreadlocks that were proudly cultivated for 17 years. His dark hair was styled in a fashion more acceptable amongst Collins Street stockbrokers. The Op Shop wardrobe was binned for chinos, dress shirts and sports coats. Mathison had even worn ties for television interviews. Smart casual was Mathison's ticket to the classically designed power base on Spring Street. The image change wasn't a sell-out, but Kristin knew the grooming could be wasted if the HLP was collateral damage in a homicide inquiry. Was that the source of Mathison's real ire?

'Was it Julian alone, or do you know if he had any help?'

Kristin pulled her fingers from her tangled mop of auburn curls. 'Don't be stupid. Julian didn't kill the trainer, and nobody else from the party would have done it either.' She stood, stomped to the sideboard and turned on the kettle.

'How can you say that?' asked Mathison in a milder tone. 'You haven't heard from Julian, have you?'

'No.'

'And he was supposed to be at the track on Saturday night?'

'Yes.'

'And we all heard Julian threaten O'Leary?'

'We knew that was bravado. He's a talker – not a killer.'

'We know bugger all about him.' Mathison walked to a cupboard above the kettle and retrieved two cups and a packet of jasmine green tea. 'He appeared at the door – what? Eight months ago. Supposedly from New Zealand via Sydney. A burnout from too much tragedy with the Red Cross. Then he gets all hot and bothered about Baird's back flip on the ban. He doesn't have any history with animal rights groups, yet he's the loudest mouth at our protests. He was lucky a few race goers didn't take a swing at his snide comments. He provoked a showdown with an old trainer – and now that guy is dead. Tell me why the cops shouldn't be crawling all over him?'

The kettle boiled; hot water was poured over the tea bags. Kristin didn't respond.

'Okay, I'll tell you why the cops are *very* interested in our expat loudmouth – because they can't find him! He's done a runner. Probably trying to swim back to the Shaky Isles. Which leaves the HLP behind to wipe the shit off the fan.'

Mathison reached over to the biscuit bin and pulled out two Arnott's milk coffees. He broke one in half and flicked it to Molly. She caught it cleanly and waited obediently for the other half. 'How many party members are threatening to quit?'

'Fifty-one have cancelled their memberships. Another 15 are *thinking* about it.' Kristin helped herself to a biscuit and dunked it in her tea. 'That's too close to the party threshold.'

'Christ. We'll only have Molly, you and I left as members by the end of the month at this rate. They're bloody pathetic – a whiff of scandal and they run faster than the dogs.' Mathison slumped into a battered leather armchair and sipped his tea. Molly nuzzled his arm and was rewarded with the second treat.

'Don't be such a gloom merchant. I'm sure the cops will find the real killer. I know Julian – he's not a brutal man.'

Mathison looked at his party co-founder, house mate and former lover, but didn't say anything.

Kristin bristled. 'What's that look about?'

'Nothing.'

'Go on say it – you think because I slept with Julian it's tainted my judgement?'

Mathison shook his head and stared at his tea.

'You can't see that he cares about people, dogs, animals, the planet. Julian has a heart of gold. He doesn't have a mean bone in his body. He's one of our members – he's family. We have a duty to help and protect him as much as the greyhounds. You need to get over your own jealousy.'

Mathison snorted but avoided that distraction. 'Are the cops coming back today?'

'I don't think so. I had to give them Julian's address and phone number. I spoke to a flatmate – they haven't seen him since Friday night. The cops asked me to call a Detective Sergeant Potter if Julian turned up here.'

'I'll drive him to police headquarters myself if he shows his face through that door.'

Kristin shook her head and sat in front of her computer. 'Are you going to be here for the rest of the day? I need help keeping our party intact.'

Mathison picked up his travel bag. 'Yeah. I'll drop this in my room and hit the phones to calm the nervous nellies. We have to keep our numbers above 500 or we're stuffed as a party.'

'What did you do with the money from the Horsham fund-raiser?'

'I'll put it in the bank tomorrow.' Mathison left the room.

'How much did you collect?' There was no reply, only the creaking of timber stairs as Mathison climbed to the bedrooms on the first floor. Home and the HLP headquarters were conveniently in the same building in Brunswick Street, close to the Edinburgh Gardens. Kristin inherited the 19th century terrace three years previously when her maternal grandmother, Bessy, died at the age of 97. It was spacious, with four bedrooms and two reception rooms – the downstairs formal lounge was converted into the HLP Headquarters – and desperately needed modernising. Renovations were a low priority for the granddaughter. Their prime concern was ending greyhound racing. A seat – or two – in the Victorian Parliament was next on the list. Mathison wasn't the only activist with ambition.

Kristin stared at her laptop screen which displayed an incomplete email to party members. The page had the date and a headline: *HLP Not involved in Trainer Death*. It was a bid to rally the party faithful, yet she struggled with inspiration to sway the weak-minded. Kristin ran a hand through tangled curls once more and sipped tea.

The past 24 hours had been brutal. There was the shock of the murder and the immediate suspicion that fell upon Julian, even from within their own ranks. Her stress levels spiked when Julian dropped off the grid. They went to the red zone during the unpleasant interview with the Channel 5 reporter. Julian's silence continued to agitate Kristin and then the cops came calling in the afternoon.

The police interview was more difficult than the journalist's probing. And she couldn't stand up in a huff and walk out on the detectives. Kristin wanted to – several times – especially when their questions focussed on her relationship to the suspect. Julian wasn't her boyfriend; couldn't even be called her lover. He was good looking with soulful eyes and an easy charm. They had tumbled into her bed on a handful of occasions, usually after drinks which followed a protest at one of the tracks. It was casual and fun, although Kristin wouldn't have objected if Julian wanted to get more serious. That wasn't likely to happen now, even if Julian could be found – and was innocent.

Kristin felt like a traitor when she revealed Julian's Carlton address and mobile number to the police. Not that it would help with their investigation: Julian was gone. Kristin wasn't totally honest with the cops when they asked if she had spoken to Julian – or had any contact. Strictly speaking that was true – she hadn't.

They didn't ask if she had *seen* Julian Oliver. That would have been a problem because she did – late on Sunday morning. Frustrated by his silence and worried about his safety – perhaps Julian was targeted by the same deranged nutter – Kristin had walked to his home.

She didn't need to knock on the door. Julian was striding away from the rented terrace he shared with two nurses and about to turn the corner into Lygon Street. Kristin was 250 metres away. She shouted Julian's name, but he didn't respond. By the time Kristin ran to the main road there was no sign of him. There was just a tram trundling to the north.

Kristin's tears had dried long before the detectives sat down at her table. The interview focussed on the December confrontation. The cops wanted every detail: prodding her to reveal the protagonists' positions, language, temperaments, reactions. They also wanted names of other party members who witnessed the encounter.

It was clear that Julian was their main – and possibly only – suspect. The more she sought to portray him as a caring activist, the more sceptical the cops became. They had also been told about the October altercation. Their implication was that an innocent person didn't hide from the police.

Kristin trusted her instincts and didn't feel guilty about skirting the truth on contact with Julian. She had seen him, not spoken to him. The fact that he was carrying a daypack indicated he might be leaving Melbourne. But it wasn't her job to tell the police that. Her responsibility now was the HLP. The party couldn't be allowed to fragment under the glare of police and media scrutiny. Kristin plucked a hair band from beside the laptop, tamed her curls, and summoned the creativity required to stem the membership bleeding.

Chapter 12

Mac's body bore the scars of Jo's anxiety about the impending police interview. Three toes on his left foot were smashed by Jo's chariot before the production meeting. He hobbled into the conference room but was poorly positioned again. His right ankle lost a chunk of flesh as Jo did a handbrake stop and slammed the coffee kitty onto the table.

'Ker-rist Jo!' Mac clutched his new battle wound and fell into his seat. 'I'm going to dump that death machine in the bay.'

Jo kept her hand on the tin and moved her files to the left. 'Are you a haemophiliac?'

'No.'

'Well stop whining. You'll live. Unlike me. The coffee kitty's empty again.' Jo raised the tin and rattled the lone coin. Two had mysteriously disappeared since Sunday night: the price of a vending machine chocolate treat. The 10 members of the production crew assembled around the table hurriedly reached for wallets and purses, a flurry of violet soon rained on the table. Five dollars was the minimum Jo would accept. Executive producer and program presenter Richard Templeton slid a red note across to Jo. Twenty dollars was the price for being at the top of the pyramid.

Technically the kitty was no longer required as station management supplied coffee for each department. The seal on the container in *Spotlight* had never been pierced. Journalists, producers, editors and camera ops had standards. Nothing less than heart-jolting, quality caffeine could enter their veins before the end of the program. After seven the life blood was alcohol. The evening could finish with an Irish coffee which satisfied all requirements.

A lone moth circled the lights as the last $5 fell on the table. All eyes turned to Dugal Cameron. He was often accused by colleagues of having deep pockets and short arms. Dugal played the game and theatrically blew the *dust* from an empty wallet. Jo switched her glare to the final hold-out, Ken Withers. His chair was at full backward tilt, arms folded across his chest, eyes focussed on the moth. Jo knew he was defiant and mightily pissed off after hearing about her tryst with the murder suspect. She didn't press him for a contribution which was a lose-lose situation.

For half the production crew it confirmed rumours about Jo's summer fling with Withers. For the other half, who already knew, it established the affair was dead. At least for Jo it was long over. A fortnight at least. Days before she slept with Julian Oliver – the Conor O'Leary murder suspect.

Jo turned her attention to *Spotlight* duties as Mac laid out their agenda.

'Right, in case some of you don't know, we have a greater involvement in this case than the cadaver crew finding the body.' Mac paused as several people hooted and poked fun at their colleagues.

'It's not safe to invite you lot for dinner,' said Stephanie Grant. She was on secondment to the program from News during Pete Benson's holiday.

Senior editor Ralph James tried to top that. 'Imagine their Halloween party? Real bodies hanging from the rafters!'

'All right, leave them be. At least they're digging up stories,' said Mac to a chorus of groans. Jo's chariot suddenly reversed and sped off to the command post to answer an insistent phone. Normally she would have ignored it until after the meeting. It was prudent to be absent as Mac told the rest of the team about her shagging the killer. Suspect. Or whatever Julian was. Jo was only two-metres from the door and could still hear.

'We know the police suspect is Julian Oliver from the HLP. He had a confrontation with the victim and threatened him. He's now Missing in Action. We have also learned he knows our Jo. They met at a pub in Fitzroy – or Carlton or somewhere grungy – about 10 days ago.'

Several colleagues cast glances at Withers whose eyes stayed glued to the ceiling. It was the newcomer from News who pushed the boundaries of etiquette.

'Did they share more than a few drinks – and conversation?' asked Stephanie Grant.

Jo blushed; she was grateful to focus on the communications console in front of the desk. It wasn't an important call; a PR company chasing television coverage for an '80s pop star down on his luck. Normally Jo would have dispensed with the beggar inside 30 seconds. Today she was happy to listen to the full pitch while Mac publicly dealt with her sex life.

'Jo spent one evening with Mr Oliver. They talked about his passionate campaign to end greyhound racing and other matters. We've told the police, and detectives have arranged to chat to Jo later to flesh out more details on his personality, state of mind etcetera. The concern for us is the *anonymous* tip about live-baiting at the Steiglitz property that arrived the Monday after Jo's meeting. Mr Oliver was aware that Jo worked for *Spotlight*. It seems he is the most likely candidate for providing that information. Given what happened on Friday night, we were apparently set up.'

Jo breathed a silent prayer for her boss. He hadn't thrown her reputation to the wolves. Instead, he focussed his crew on the story and *Spotlight*'s role. She vowed to be more careful when her chariot flew down the Valley of Death. For a week at least. Jo understood that her colleagues automatically assumed that she slept with Julian. Wither's sulky mood made it obvious. But Mac's handling of the matter had set the moral compass for the office – Jo's sex life was off limits in this story. She dumped the PR woman 10 seconds later and returned to the fray in the conference room. The chariot glided gracefully to a halt a good 10 cm from Mac's shins.

'That gives us another advantage over the competition with tonight's story. They don't know the suspect contacted us. Jo will record an interview after she's chatted to the detectives. That will be a stand-alone item as it will give us a chance to personalise Julian Oliver. Is he mad, bad or an innocent person in this drama? No one else will have that inside knowledge as the HLP people are sticking their heads in the sand. Stephanie?'

The reporter lifted her eyes from the doodles in her notebook. The dark-haired 28-year-old was eager to get involved.

'Are you happy to pull that story together? More elements will emerge throughout the day and it could be a rush job at the end – if the police find him.'

A broad smile stretched from ear to ear. Stephanie was being offered a big bone on her first day in current affairs. 'I'll be ready Mac. You can count on me.'

Mac nodded and turned to Curly. 'I'll need you to help Kim pull together the main package at the top of the program. Kim. Tell us what extra footage you shot that wasn't used by news.'

Kim sat up and adjusted her notes, not that she needed them. 'O'Leary's body in the starting trap is the most compelling clip, especially when Ken flicked the lever to open the gate. We didn't use that on the news, even with heavy pixilation, because it would have freaked out half of Melbourne. I think – with a suitable warning from Richard – we can get away with it tonight.'

Kim then cast a guilty look at Stephanie. 'We also shot pictures close to the murder site before the cops arrived. It was obvious where the killer chopped up O'Leary. The chainsaw was gone, but there was a massive pool of blood and flesh on the gravel near the kennels. Sorry for not sharing with you guys, Steph, but we needed something extra for us. News had plenty of exclusive material already.'

Jo watched the news reporter shrug. No big deal. Stephanie Grant was part of the *Spotlight* crew until the end of June; Jo knew she wanted to make the secondment to current affairs permanent. Ambition determined loyalties for the next few weeks.

'I recorded several pieces to camera to link it together. I also did a first draft of a script that won't take me long to bash into shape. I'll knock that off after the meeting so Curly can do some tweaks. I want to see if the cops will allow me to sit with Jo during her interview. I might be able to glean more information.'

'Good idea Kim,' said Mac. 'I'm sure they'll have follow-up questions for you, they might be happy to talk to both of you. Make sure we get pictures of you and the cops going into and out of the interview.' Mac looked at the sulking Withers and turned to his senior camera op. 'Can you look after that Dugal?'

Mac guided the meeting through more discussion about the stories they would produce and their exclusive angles. Jo scooted in and out to organise cameras and interviews as assignments were allocated. On one mission past the command post her personal mobile chirped. She snatched it immediately as the call was from Sue in reception. The front office was sometimes the first line of defence from disgruntled viewers, debt collectors and other assorted pests. Occasionally they were the first alert for a story. That was the case when a guest left a studio interview and was stabbed at the front door. The victim survived as the ambulance was called immediately after the newsroom was notified. In this case Sue had the news Jo was dreading – the cops wanted to book a station car park for 12.30.

Chapter 13

Chauncey Quayle fanned his face with a battered fedora as he scanned the dry paddocks of Conor O'Leary's property in the midday sun. They were empty: the canola crops hadn't been planted, the sheep were grazing in paddocks down the road. No dogs were running, playing or lazing in the shade. One small rabbit hopped into view 100 metres south of the kennels and long run. The bunny wouldn't have had the audacity to show itself a week ago.

Chauncey replaced the hat over thinning grey hair and strode back down the long run, raising small clouds of dust that coated his Clark's shoes. His stride was long and steady for a 70-year-old with a gut that indicated a fondness for starchy foods. Grey eyes matched the Fletcher Jones suit, the only real colour coming from a sky-blue tie with a Windsor knot. Gold cufflinks were Chauncey's one exception to the modest public persona, although easily explained away as family heirlooms from his grandfather.

Dwayne Milligan and Rene Harding watched the bookie from the front of the house. It didn't seem polite to stand under the veranda despite Chauncey turning up unannounced. It was the first time the attendants had seen him at Tara, yet he ambled around as if he owned the place, or soon would.

Milligan and Harding shuffled their feet in the driveway gravel, hands in pockets. There wasn't much else to do as the kennels held only two greyhounds. The rest were collected by their owners and transported to new racing homes in the past six hours. The kennel was out of business without a licenced trainer. The remaining pair were only in residence because their owner was on holiday in Bali. He was due back on Thursday; Milligan suspected the dogs would be gone by the end of the week.

'You fancy a cup of tea?' asked Harding.

'Yeah. Earl Grey thanks. Check the milk – I think it's getting chunky. Better get a cup out for Chauncey too.'

Harding nodded and went inside the house. They had been using O'Leary's kettle and fridge since Saturday night. The crime scene officers had commandeered their tearoom for a forensic base. The last cop departed at breakfast, but neither attendant saw any need to change the new routine. The ex-boss wasn't going to complain. Mrs O'Leary would, but they assumed she was at least another two days away from arriving. Milligan and Harding were grateful to be spared the onerous duty of informing Siobhan about the murder. Social media must have broken the news in Ireland as she called Victorian police.

The lads were surprised to learn from the cops that Mrs O'Leary wasn't the ex-wife after all – the couple hadn't divorced. Conor was content to keep his wife half a world away; the price was maintaining the façade of a marriage in name only. Her husband's death made Siobhan the new proprietor. Harding returned while the water boiled to offer his thoughts on what the future might involve.

'Siobhan never shared Conor's passion for greyhounds. Normally she was the practical one, keeping an eye on the wool business and pushing Conor into growing canola crops. But she did have a secret obsession – gold!'

'Didn't they scrape every ounce of gold out of Steiglitz last century?'

'No, no. They reckon there's tonnes still under the town – if you know where to dig. There's a legend the first graziers found a massive gold reef, right here on Tara, while digging a well in the 1850s. Charles von Stieglitz must have been filthy rich – or bloody mad – because he filled the hole in again. He didn't want prospectors all over his property. Chuck retired to Ireland a few years later without telling anyone about the gold. I reckon Siobhan heard those stories before she came to Australia. She spent hours roaming the gullies and old mines with a steel-tipped walking stick, prodding here and there. Maybe she'll want to search for the lost mine again?'

Milligan had heard about a gold reef at the pub but disregarded it as a furphy. However, he was always puzzled by the name of the township. Steiglitz, was never spelled the same as the original settlers – von Stieglitz. The township was now part of a historic park covering 469 hectares, although the number of permanent residents couldn't muster a cricket team at the last census.

Milligan eyed Chauncey as he approached the house from the long run. His inspection was bad form, rude in fact. Not that Milligan would dare to tick off the bookie. Seniority and decades in the racing industry brought some respect. And besides, Chauncey might become his new boss if Siobhan wanted to sell Tara and not dig for gold.

It was a tidy property, not flashy, but attractive to either a sheep farmer, a cropper or another greyhound trainer. That was the part that confused Milligan; Chauncey was neither a grazier nor a trainer. What would he do with the land? Harding learned farming skills from Conor O'Leary, but he wasn't experienced enough to take over the main duties by himself. Chauncey could hire someone to run the sheep and plant the crops; or lease the kennels to a trainer. But how much was that worth in the long-term? Milligan knew the bookie had three retired racehorses on a life-style block near Gisborne, but nothing else that stamped him as a working man of the land. His four greyhounds were spread between two trainers at Bacchus Marsh. Was Chauncey bored with retirement and this was a new venture to supplement his superannuation?

Those thoughts were pushed aside as Milligan's mobile phone vibrated with a message. It was Kim Prescott.

Hi Dwayne. Can you help with pictures of Conor? I need him in kennels, at track etc. Anything appreciated. Kim

Milligan was happy to help. The TV reporter was pretty and polite; not pushy or overbearing like the other journalists who covered the murder. Kim was genuinely interested in greyhounds and she handled Conor's death sensitively in her first story. By Sunday afternoon Kim had charmed Milligan into appearing on Channel 5 News to talk about Conor and the protestor.

Milligan laughed about that experience. He was used to the media and cameras at the track. They were an integral part of every race meeting; Milligan had been on the telly hundreds of times parading dogs to the boxes and catching them after the race. Conor took over at the dais for interviews. If Milligan wanted to be a licenced trainer, he needed to be as smooth as his former mentor. Harding called Milligan a poser after the live Chanel 5 segment. That prompted another laugh: Milligan knew his mate was envious because he performed well. That's what Kim said.

Milligan swiped to his photo gallery on the shattered screen of the mobile. It had been like that for three months, ever since he dropped it in the car park at The Meadows. O'Leary's death dashed hopes of replacing it with a new model on his birthday. Forget about the dream of an iPhone. There wouldn't be any annual pay rise either.

At least the picture gallery worked: it was full of hundreds of images from the kennels, paddocks, tracks. Milligan selected six photos of Conor to send. He was smiling in each one and that's how Milligan wanted *Spotlight* viewers to remember the Irish trainer.

He found a final group photo of Conor with Paddy after a win at Broadmeadows. He was surrounded by the Beachams – Benedict and his then-wife Carolyn – and another trainer, Henry Wright. Milligan studied the photo for a moment as it seemed an odd group; neither the Beachams nor Wright owned Paddy.

Milligan couldn't remember taking that snap. Perhaps Harding did it while he was packing the trailer. His mate was hopeless with mobiles, breaking or losing one every few months. That record meant Harding never wasted money on quality phones. If he couldn't buy a replacement in a Kmart special, Harding helped himself to Milligan's.

Milligan sent the photos to Kim. He wondered for a moment whether to add the names of the people with O'Leary. He decided against it as they weren't relevant to the story; it was meant to be a tribute to Conor. Milligan didn't know the word for it, but the last image – the group shot – made him feel…*unsettled?* Conor and Paddy were both dead. And Carolyn was no longer on the racing scene, or even in the country. She went home to England because of the scorching Australian heat. Funny, thought Milligan, she was in a sleeveless yellow dress in the photo and her arms and face were bronzed. Maybe it was the nights where the mercury refused to dip below 35 degrees that drove her away? Those nights made everyone go barmy.

Harding returned to the veranda with three mugs, a pot of tea, sugar and a packet of Tim Tams on a silver tray. It was a trophy for one of the victories. He placed it on a wooden table as Chauncey Quayle walked up the stairs fanning himself with the hat.

'Aren't your cooking skills up to scones, jam and cream, Rene?'

'They don't extend beyond bacon, eggs and a tin of baked beans Mr Quayle.' Harding smiled. 'You should be grateful I can boil a billy.'

Chauncey snagged a chocolate biscuit as the tea was poured. 'Milk and two sugars thanks lad.' He took the mug and assessed its rainbow stripes. 'Probably a wise move not to use Siobhan's best crockery. Any word on when she's arriving?'

'Wednesday at the earliest, although we haven't heard anything,' said Harding.

Chauncey sipped his Earl Grey. 'How did you get on with Siobhan? She was a strong-willed lady.'

Harding snared a Tim Tam and took a bite before answering. 'Things were good the first few years I was here. She was a straight-up lady. Didn't take any nonsense. But if you did the work, she was generous with lunches, afternoon teas and other treats. She loved her baking – lots of sourdough bread and cakes. Conor lost a heap of weight after she left.'

Harding tugged his own baggy denims and belt. 'I think we all did.'

'She turned bitter when she found out about Conor and his lady friends?'

'Yeah.' Harding reached for another biscuit. 'She obviously suspected for a while because it got really tense. Dwayne hadn't arrived, so I copped as much shit as Conor. She couldn't prove anything – until that night she jumped on them at Eastern Park.'

Milligan joined in the laughter at the thought of a wild Siobhan O'Leary scaring the crap out of her husband and the female attendant. It was a legend that was embellished with every repetition. He watched Chauncey finish his tea and prepare to depart. Should he broach the subject about the reason for the bookie's visit? He played safe.

'Are you likely to drop in to pay your respects to Mrs O'Leary ahead of the funeral?'

Chauncey fitted his hat. 'I may do lad. Thanks for the tea and bikkies. Time for me to get home again. Sorry to learn the kennels are almost empty. If I hear any trainers need help, I'll let you know.' He touched the brim and walked down the stairs to his green Jaguar X-Type and drove away. It was 10-years-old, still natty and projected the right image.

Harding broke the silence. 'Is that our new boss?'

Milligan shook his head. 'I can't see it, Rene. He's not really a dog man and he's not a farmer. I don't know why he's checking out the property. Maybe he was being ghoulish, wanted to see the murder site?'

'I noticed he spent a lot of time near the boxes and the kennels, you know – where the killer butchered Conor.'

Milligan placed his empty mug on the tray and grabbed the last Tim Tam a fraction of a second before Harding.

'It was a bit creepy. Maybe he thinks that gold story is true – there really is a reef waiting to be discovered? Or the land could be turned into a housing estate or life-style sub-division?'

Harding picked up the tray. 'Nah. Too much work for him.' He paused as he reached the front door. 'Hey! Was he trying to walk the crime scene? You know, prove he's been to the property in case the cops find his DNA on the chainsaw. Whenever they find that.'

Milligan laughed. 'You've been watching too many crime shows on TV. He needed to be here *before* Conor was killed.' But the possibility Chauncey Quayle could be a suspect made Milligan think about Saturday night.

'I wonder what time Chauncey arrived at the track? When did you see him?'

Harding replaced the tray on the table. 'Not until the bar. But we were in the kennels or on the track, parading and catching. He could have been there from race one and we wouldn't know.'

'I guess not. And he's never out of that Fletcher Jones suit. I didn't see any blood on it. You couldn't chop up a man and avoid the splatter. He didn't look flustered either, did he?'

'Nah. But Chauncey has been around racing all his life. You get to meet a few shady characters after 50 years in the business. He must know some muscle men from back in the day when he carried a lot of cash. Would Chauncey get one of them to do it?'

Chapter 14

Jo struggled not to stare at the opulence of Channel 5's 10th floor. The executive suite featured floor-to-ceiling windows, plush dark carpet, two white leather sofas and four abstract prints – or were they original water colours? The botanical garden was framed through the northern view, Port Phillip Bay on the southern side. She didn't want to leave the safety of the lift; few news and current affairs staff survived ascents to the top floor.

Five metres across the foyer an attractive blonde woman sat behind a silver laptop on a glass-topped desk. It was the legendary Zara Hennessy, executive assistant to the financial controller, Andrew Hackett. Zara had survived his extended absence, a sure indicator she was a skilled corporate tactician. Jo turned to Kim who wasn't so awe-struck. 'Why do we have to do the interview up here – so close to the bosses?'

'Don't panic Jo. I've been up here heaps of times.'

'Yeah – but your Dad's on the bloody board!'

The lift pinged for closure. Kim held her arm over the doors and nudged Jo forward. Behind them was Withers with his camera and tripod. 'Thank you, ladies. I was wondering if you wanted me to set up in the lift. That would have been cosy.'

'Fuck you, Kenny!' hissed Jo. 'You don't have to talk to the cops under the station manager's nose.'

'No, I don't.' Withers dumped his kit on the carpet. 'I haven't been shagging any killers.' His eyes swung from the furious PA to the dazzling EA whose legs were tucked elegantly beneath the table.

Kim stepped between her colleagues before Jo could swat him. 'That's enough you two. Let's be professional for 10 minutes. You can thump him later Jo.' Kim tugged Wither's shirt sleeve. 'And there's no need to be a dickhead.' Kim turned to the reception desk where Zara watched the *Spotlight* domestic with a wry smile.

'Hi Kim.' Zara stood and walked around the desk. 'Do you need the conference room – or a boxing ring?'

Jo felt her face burn and vowed to hurt Withers when the interview was over. Physically she wouldn't touch him; she couldn't reach anything vulnerable without a step ladder. And Jo knew there were laws against justifiable homicide in the workplace. Pity. But she could punish her ex-boyfriend in more painful ways. Jo knew the shittiest jobs that every cameraman avoided like a steaming pile of vomit. Withers would find himself stuck with them forever. Plus, there wouldn't be any tickets to the footy, movie premieres, restaurant openings or any media conferences offering food and booze. Revenge would be sweet – and long.

Jo fumed beside Withers as Kim brushed cheeks with the executive gatekeeper and traded social pleasantries. The executive suite was Mac's tactic to outwit the cops. The aim was to make Kim part of the interview to squeeze more information from the detectives. Jo chewed at a fingernail while she waited. Withers leaned on his tripod, eager to record his shots and return to the dungeon.

Dugal was supposed to be there instead of Jo's former lover. However, he punctured a tyre during the lunchtime hamburger run. Jo pondered whether Dugal merited equal torture, then Withers whispered something; or did he cough?

'What was that?' Jo demanded. 'Are you being rude again?'

'No.' Withers mumbled. At the desk Kim and Zara laughed at a private joke. 'I said I was *sorry* – for being crude.'

Jo's face burned again. She and Withers had *dated* since the Christmas party, much longer than either expected. It had been fun, not overly serious – a mutual meeting of appetites when the urge arose. Usually after a night at the pub, the Big Bash cricket or the footy. They found spontaneity worked best – until Jo saw Withers escorting Jemma from the news library to their favourite coffee shop.

To be caught with a news department woman was bad enough, to share a sacred coffee site with her was unforgivable. Their natural spark was snuffed permanently when Jo bumped into Julian the following week. The gnawed nail was spared further punishment.

'Ok. I accept your apology. We have to work together, but don't be so precious again, right?'

Withers nodded as Kim waved them over.

'You can set up the camera beside Zara's desk. You'll get a shot of the cops coming out of the lift and can track them through the foyer to the corridor.'

That arrangement made Withers smile, while Jo nibbled at her nails again and shuffled nervously. She was way out of her comfort zone – the chariot was on the ground floor. It had been weeks since Jo spent half a day on her feet; they ached. Zara interrupted them as she replaced a phone.

'You had better hurry with that camera. Reception said two detectives are on their way up.'

Withers had the tripod set and swiftly clicked the camera into its lock. 'I'm good to go. Camera mic sound okay Kim?'

'Yep. Better if I'm not wearing a lapel mic. We'll greet them, explain you're getting set up shots for my story, then I'll take them to the conference room. You follow and get interiors as we sit. I'll tell you when to stop; hopefully by that stage they'll have accepted me as part of the deal.'

Withers pressed record, a few seconds later the lift doors opened to reveal two policemen in suits. Jo's stomach squirmed until the tall, good-looking detective spoke first.

'Kim!' Detective Sergeant Nathan Potter smiled.

'Nathan!' responded Kim.

Kim? Nathan? Jo looked sideways at the reporter who glowed. She glanced at Withers who discreetly smirked behind the lens. Jo was excited and annoyed. Kim had the hots for a cop – and she didn't know? Withers knew before her. Perhaps his apology wouldn't be enough to rescind his punishment.

Jo switched back to the main agenda as introductions were made. Detective Inspector Graham Dowell was a few centimetres shorter than Kim's new friend, stockier and older by about 15 years. He wasn't fat; broad shoulders and muscular arms filled his grey suit. Jo noticed that Dowell also picked up the vibe between the reporter and his colleague.

He raised an eyebrow. Jo couldn't avoid a smile. Maybe the interview wouldn't be as bad as expected?

Withers followed the foursome down the corridor. Zara had played her part by arranging two sets of chairs at one end of the six-metre oak table. Kim and Jo claimed a strategic advantage with the windows; the imposing Melbourne business district was behind their shoulders. Withers recorded another six shots on the shoulder and bid them farewell.

The senior detective looked at Kim.

'I thought we were supposed to be talking to Ms Trescowthick about her association with Julian Oliver?'

'You are inspector. Jo's happy to tell you everything about her brief meeting with Julian.' Kim remained in place.

'Well then, why are you here, Ms Prescott.'

'Please, call me Kim.'

Jo was impressed. Kim was 24 and here she was staring down a homicide detective who must have spent that many years chasing criminals. Who was going to blink first?

'Jo doesn't have much experience in dealing with police matters. She's our senior production assistant on *Spotlight*, but all her work is done from the office, via the phone. It can be intimidating to suddenly be swept into a murder inquiry. My first encounter with you frontline guys in Geelong last November was terrifying. Jo asked if I could support her during your chat.'

Jo noticed the young detective smiled discreetly as the older cop nodded. Then Kim played her ace.

'Besides, you know Jo would tell me everything as soon as you leave.' Kim smiled. 'We all want the same result inspector – Conor O'Leary's killer needs to be caught. You know the media can help in that quest. Shall we proceed?'

Dowell sighed. 'Okay. But if I decide something *must* not to be reported, you will obey that directive. We can't jeopardise a prosecution for the sake of an exclusive for *Spotlight*. Agreed?'

Kim nodded. 'Certainly inspector. I'll sit here, listen and take notes until you have all the information you need.'

Dowell sighed once more and laughed. 'The other news channels are going to scream. First you find the body.' He stopped, looked at

Kim and then DS Potter. 'Your second in six months – from what I hear. And now your workmate has intimate knowledge of our main suspect. With that sort of luck, your program will be a ratings winner for years. Okay, let's get some info on Mr Oliver.'

For the next hour Jo was drained of every scrap of knowledge about the man she met in a pub and later slept with. It was exhausting; mentally and physically. Several times Jo wanted to take her chair for a whirl around the room. She needed the freedom of movement, to hear the cries of pain as Mac's toes were mashed under the casters. That was her everyday existence and this – under the spotlight with two homicide cops in the corporate eyrie – was excruciating.

The policemen weren't rude or judgemental. They were meticulous, taking her through conversations with Julian several times to glean more information. It appeared to Jo they couldn't decide if the pub meeting was random. Did Julian seek her out; a ploy to get the current affairs program involved in his campaign?

The most embarrassing part of the interview for Jo was her recollection of Julian's body. They had pictures of their suspect, but he could change appearance in minutes. The Julian Oliver the police were trying to trace wore dark clothing: jeans and op shop gear. He favoured hoodies and wore his dark hair shoulder length. Smart casual clothes, a bottle of dye and a session with a barber who favours number two cuts could change that image remarkably.

'We know Julian is a New Zealander. Did he share that with you Jo?'

'Yes. He spoke about his time with the Red Cross. He's a sweet and caring guy; loves people and animals. That's why I'm shocked you believe he could be responsible.' Jo reached for a glass of water that Kim had topped up three times already. Anymore and she would need a loo break.

'He got burned out by his rescue work. I think there was one Pacific cyclone which really crushed his soul. The village he was assigned to help was obliterated. I remember his eyes were misty as he talked about it. There was nothing left standing – no homes, no trees, no shelter from the rain.

'The same families had lost everything a decade before. They got back on their feet only to be smashed again. They were so far away from the main island they were the last consideration for medical and food supplies. It destroyed him – he left to save his sanity. I can't see that man doing anything vicious.'

Dowell did most of the questioning, Potter took notes, just like Kim. Jo occasionally caught the two of them exchange looks across the table. A raised eyebrow, a smirk that was irrelevant to the information she provided. Jo looked forward to her own interrogation with Kim after the meeting. If not then, over a glass of sauvignon blanc. She desperately needed a drink after work.

'Now, is there anything physically *unique* about Julian that might help us with our inquiries. He can easily change his appearance to avoid surveillance at airports. Did he have any facial or neck tattoos that would be hard to disguise. Was there anything remarkable on his body? Any missing fingers or anything that might help us?'

Jo looked at her glass and smiled. Then she blushed. Again. She hadn't done that so many times in one day since the school ball when she was busted with a hip flask of Scotch and cigarettes.

Dowell saw the signs. 'There is something you can tell us?'

Jo didn't raise her face. 'He didn't have any tattoos or broken fingers, or anything obvious. But – well, he was – blessed you might say. Down below. He could stand at the urinals and make the other guys jealous.'

Dowell snorted; Potter laughed. Kim smiled. Jo gave her the look – *Don't ever share that tidbit with Kenny!* That was more information than the cops needed; Potter closed his note pad and tucked away his pen. Jo was relieved the ordeal was over and prepared to leap from her chair. Kim curtailed the escape.

'Just a couple of quick questions while you're here, guys. We know that Conor O'Leary arranged a meeting with a prospective owner on Saturday afternoon. Obviously, it was the ploy to get him alone at the property while Dwayne Milligan and Rene Harding took the dogs to the track. Have you traced that number and the phone?'

Dowell blew out a breath, Potter stayed silent. It was up to the senior man to answer, or not.

'Did Milligan or Harding give you that number?'

'Yes. They said it was in O'Leary's diary.'

'Have you tried to call it?' Dowell's tone was sharper.

'No. That's your job to investigate. Mine is to ask questions about what has been found. You can share, or you can withhold – but as a journalist I have a right to ask.'

Dowell nodded; satisfied Kim hadn't overstepped any boundaries.

'We've checked that number and – so far – we can't trace it. It was a pre-pay sim card. Most likely discarded either before or after O'Leary was attacked. We have other areas to investigate but I can't share that with you.'

Kim doodled with her pad and pen as she circled around her next question. 'Does that strengthen or weaken the case against Julian Oliver? It seems likely that he was setting up O'Leary to be exposed as a live baiter. Falsely as we now know. That's bad enough – but not as brutal as chopping up a man. Do you think he would seriously invite the media to witness a murder?'

Dowell pushed his chair back from the table and stood. The information flow to the media had ended.

'On the record, I'll say that Julian Oliver remains a person of interest until we can talk to him about the death at Steiglitz. Off the record, and I stress this is way off the record, he is still very much in the frame. We don't know enough about his psychological state of mind.

'He could be a psychopath who gets his kicks from the risk of exposure. Was the media meant to witness his handiwork – or publicise it? We've learned a few things about Julian Oliver from our New Zealand contacts this morning, but there is still much we don't know about him.' Dowell turned to Jo again. 'If he should contact you Ms Trescowthick, you must call us – immediately.'

The detective's tone made Jo shiver.

Twenty minutes later Jo was back in her comfort zone – the current affairs dungeon. Mac had nimbly escaped her chariot by millimetres as she sought a caffeine fix. Kim avoided an interrogation about the cute copper by escorting the detectives to reception. Jo would clip one journo and corner the other before the end of the day. Life was good again now that coffee flowed through her system. The polite and persistent approach of Inspector Dowell was an interesting technique. Jo wouldn't copy it with the reporter: she didn't need to be fair or impartial when grilling Kim about her love life.

The ambience of the *Spotlight* office had intensified during her absence; the program deadline approached. Jo sorted through half a dozen yellow post it notes stuck to the computer screen. They could be ignored until later. The email bin was littered with junk story ideas from PR companies. They could be deleted. She checked the station phone for messages. More chaff.

Jo breathed deeply and braced for the program frenzy ahead. Then she exhaled and sagged, reluctant to start. It had been such a strange day. She picked up her mobile as a distraction and saw there was a missed call. Unknown number, but there was a message. Jo had an uneasy feeling as she tapped the icon. The voice stunned her.

'Jo. I need help.'

Chapter 15

'Nice camera work guys.' Mac's office chair was tilted to breaking point, his legs on the desk, a beer in hand.

Spotlight had broadcast the pictures of the murder scene – before the cops arrived. That gave them the full package – the victim stuffed inside a starting box and where he was chopped to pieces. The other news services would have killed for that footage. They couldn't pinch it from Channel 5's on-air feed either. Mac ordered the editors to liberally watermark the vision with the *Spotlight* logo and name.

Fortunately, the night vision cameras minimised the gruesome aspects of the scene. It was light and shade. The blood patches were dark – not red; the small chunks of flesh and bone chewed up by the chainsaw were the same. Careful scripting from Kim and Curly portrayed the drama of a death scene without churning stomachs.

'I'm glad you didn't waste all the good shots on the weekend news.'

Dugal Cameron and Ken Withers flanked Mac at the command post. They were similarly inclined in office chairs as they watched the program.

'We have priorities Mac.' Withers held up his Crown Lager. 'You serve better grog than News.' He clinked bottles with Mac without taking his eyes from the program.

'I don't mind VB,' said Dugal.

Withers and Mac shook their heads. On the screen, *Spotlight* host Richard Templeton had thrown to the final commercial break. It had been a busy few, days they expected the pay-off to be a surge in the ratings. *Spotlight* hadn't creamed their news and current affairs competitors with just pictures – the content would have Melbourne news directors weeping.

Kim Prescott, with Mac and Curly's guidance, crafted a comprehensive package that *suggested* how the attack happened. Her friendly cop, DS Potter, discreetly confirmed that O'Leary had a head wound, a fact other media didn't know until 20 minutes previously. Kim said that injury indicated O'Leary was struck from behind when he approached the kennels. It wasn't enough to kill him; the dismemberment started while O'Leary was still alive. The trainer's own chainsaw was believed to be the weapon. Police couldn't confirm that because it was missing.

If opposition television, radio, newspaper and web reporters weren't cringing by that point, they would have been in tears when Kim revealed details about the phone number used to set up O'Leary. It was a pre-pay sim card, no longer in service. There was no speculation from *Spotlight* about the motive, apart from Julian Oliver's connection and that he was missing. Mac told his crew the cops had to do some work.

Templeton appeared on screen after the commercial break to wrap the show with a sit-rep. The studio director cut to a series of pictures on Julian Oliver. Many were obtained from former members of the Hound Liberation Party who were happy to push their volatile colleague in front of the media firing squad. They were mobile phone snaps: an agitated Julian during protests. Another three photos were lifted from media websites; they showed the humanitarian side of his personality, working for the Red Cross after a natural disaster. Templeton twisted the knife in the ratings battle with other networks.

'A reminder this is the man police want to speak to about the death of Conor O'Leary. He's 29-year-old Julian Oliver, a former Red Cross worker from New Zealand. We believe Oliver tried to get *Spotlight* to investigate the dead trainer, allegedly for using live animals to train greyhounds.

'The evidence was faked.

'We don't know why O'Leary's kennel was targeted. What we do know is that Oliver missed a scheduled protest with the Hound Liberation Party at Broadmeadows on Saturday – the night Conor O'Leary was brutally chopped to pieces. The last contact party members and friends had with Oliver was on Friday.

'If anyone has seen Oliver, you can contact police on the phone number on the screen now.'

Templeton closed the program a few seconds later and the titles played. Mac dropped his bottle into a rubbish bin without looking. He swivelled towards Kim Prescott's desk at the back of the office. 'Another bloody great yarn…Kim? Where's she gone? And Jo?'

Dugal and Withers emptied their beers and stood.

'They were huddled at Kim's desk last time I looked,' Dugal shrugged and dumped his empty as well. 'They've vanished.'

There was nothing magical about Kim and Jo's disappearance from the office, although the exit was deliberately quiet. They waited until the final commercial break when the cameramen wallowed in praise from their program producer. No jackets rustled, or keys rattled as they silently departed for Jo's apartment. It was 600 metres from the studio – away from *Spotlight's* regular post work watering hole at the Rising Sun Hotel in South Melbourne.

The apartment was a recent purchase thanks to an inheritance from Jo's maternal grandfather. The mortgage repayments were exorbitant, even with record low interest rates. Jo took a long-term view – keep her head above water financially for 40 years and superannuation might pay off the balance. Then she would sell and hop on a plane to Bali for a long and happy retirement. That was the plan, unless she found a billionaire. Monaco or San Sebastian would be more acceptable.

Not a word was spoken before they reached the second-floor abode. Jo swiftly produced a chilled bottle of sauvignon blanc and placed two glasses on the granite bench. Kim poured generously from a bar stool opposite while Jo emptied cashews into a bowl. The essentials were ready; it was time to drink and talk.

'Okay Jo. What have you done?' Kim sipped and held the glass ready for a follow up. She suspected it might be necessary.

Jo gulped her wine and avoided Kim's gaze. 'What makes you think I've done anything?'

'We sneak out of the office – never done that before – we come to your new sanctuary and you're more antsy than Mac before a Collingwood Grand Final. Come on – fess up. You've heard from Julian, haven't you?'

Jo's eyes widened. 'How did you know?'

Kim reached for a handful of nuts and munched. Jo waited.

'You were fine after the police interview. It was exhausting, but Nathan and the inspector weren't utter bastards. Then you suddenly went hypo. It looked like you were trying to cripple Mac. How many times did you run over his toes?'

'Only twice.' Jo slumped against the bench, the glass still in hand, Melbourne's city lights twinkled through the large window to her right. 'I got a message – it must have come in during the interview. Julian's desperate.'

Kim put her wine on the bench. 'Tell me you haven't done anything for him!'

'No! Not yet.' Jo shrugged and took another deep slug; it virtually emptied her glass.

'Regardless of what you feel about him Jo, he's a murder suspect. And, as you now know, there's a much darker side to his character.'

Jo glumly nodded. An emotional roller coaster day continued when Kim returned from escorting the investigators to reception. The younger detective had dallied, keen to chat privately with Kim. In the absence of his senior colleague, Potter revealed why they couldn't discount Julian Oliver as a suspect.

The New Zealand police revealed more about his exit from the Red Cross. Julian burned out – violently.

It was another fresh ingredient for Kim's story that made opposition journalists green with envy. Potter said the evidence was available on the internet – if you searched. Julian was arrested two years previously for wilful damage and threatening behaviour.

The Pacific cyclone and lack of resources for victims was the final straw for the fatigued aid worker. After six weeks of 20-hour days in oppressive humidity, Julian was sent back to Auckland suffering from stress. Instead of going home, Julian went straight to the devastated nation's High Commission in Auckland. Julian later told the police he wanted to make a special plea for supplies on behalf of the most damaged villages. But, upon entering the pristine air-conditioned office over-looking the Waitemata Harbour, Julian went troppo.

There was a lot of glass in reception: windows, tables, vases. Most of it was smashed by the time the first police officers arrived on the scene five minutes later. The only casualties were the flowers; birds of paradise mangled on the stone tiles. The receptionist was hiding in the High Commissioner's office and Julian was trying to smash the door down. He only came to his senses when the officers threatened to taser him.

The other Melbourne networks knew about Julian's physical outbursts with the trainer, but not the blow-up at the High Commission in Auckland. Kim was miles ahead on points and her contract renewal was due in a month.

'He was lucky to avoid a conviction, Jo. Julian has wealthy parents. They brought in one of New Zealand's best barristers to save his butt. Plus, the Red Cross gave him a glowing reference. They said he was a *victim* as well; he cared too much about the people he was sent to help. It did the trick: Julian avoided a conviction and agreed to undertake an anger management course.'

Kim paused and sipped more wine. 'He must have skipped a few classes.'

Jo didn't respond. She drained the dregs and reached for the bottle. The refill almost overflowed. Kim wasn't distracted.

'How did he contact you – phone or email?'

'My mobile.'

'How did he get your number?'

'I don't know.'

'Did he leave you contact details?'

'No.'

'What did he say?'

'He didn't do it and needs help.'

'What sort of help? A place to stay? Money?'

'He didn't say.'

'What about his rich parents?'

'It was a short message. I'm guessing he doesn't want to involve them with a murder allegation.'

The questions stalled; Jo seized the chance to turn around the inquisition.

'Anyway, I didn't drag you here to get the third degree. Are you getting Gestapo tips off your new boyfriend? Oh, and thanks for telling me about him.'

The distraction worked. 'He's not my boyfriend!' Kim reddened. She took a deeper draft than normal, causing a coughing fit. It was another minute before she could croak. 'We haven't been out for dinner yet.'

Jo beamed. 'So, we finally have a contender for your sex life – at last!'

'We won't even make the first date if Nathan finds out you're in contact with his main suspect!'

Chapter 16

A cold south westerly wind swirled a discarded newspaper outside the South Melbourne apartment. That was the only movement, although Wells Street wasn't empty. A male huddled against the southern boundary fence of Victoria Barracks in a woollen navy-blue jacket. His LA baseball cap, trim blonde hair and glasses wouldn't have attracted glances from post-dinner walkers. He was obviously a typical 20-something: absorbed with Twitter, Tinder or other social media on his mini life-support system.

That was the image Julian Oliver hoped to portray as he observed Jo and her colleague through the apartment window. Another breeze slapped the paper against the wire, Julian tugged his collar tighter. The jacket was a bigger size than normal; the chill found gaps to penetrate. But then beggars couldn't be choosers. Thieves couldn't be fussy either.

Julian spotted the garment at an outdoor café in Brunswick that morning. It rested over the back of a chair in the sunshine, the owner inside ordering a coffee. Julian tucked it under his arm and casually turned the corner, away from busy Sydney Road. Five minutes later his tatty overcoat was in a bin. The black jeans had been replaced by sandy chinos, taken from a backyard clothesline. He knew the owner – a member of the HLP he hated – and guessed they would be a good fit. The new garments helped transform the city's most wanted murder suspect into an anonymous citizen.

That opportunist snatch was preceded by a visit to a Vietnamese barber in Preston. The hair cut cost $30. The blonde dye job, administered by the barber's wife in their family bathroom, was $60. That was the last of Julian's cash.

Fortunately, neither husband nor wife were conversationalists. Julian chose the shop because it had no customers and the television was tuned to an Asian shopping channel. Reports about murdered Australian greyhound trainers weren't likely to feature. Julian didn't opt for the number two buzz cut as he needed to fit a certain image. He wondered if Jo would recognise him.

Julian was curious about the animated exchanges between the *Spotlight* colleagues. One minute they were laughing, the next they were glaring across the kitchen bench. No doubt sharp words were being exchanged. Were they talking about him?

He knew Jo was a tiny bundle of energy. She was also cute and sexy, attributes which had attracted him in the pub. Jo sounded confident and assertive as she drank with four friends. She laughed at risqué jokes but drew the line at sexist comments. Julian had hovered near her group for half an hour. He decided that, if you removed Jo's public armour, you would find a tender and caring soul. He was surprised when Jo approached him with an empty wine glass.

'You've been perving at me all night. I think that warrants a drink and at least a chat-up.'

Julian didn't go straight for his best pick-up line, preferring to engage Jo's heart with his humanitarian work and efforts to end greyhound racing. She was impressed. And so was Julian when he learned about her production job with one of Melbourne's top current affairs shows. The drinks and conversation flowed easily; it didn't take much encouragement for Jo to join him in a taxi to his rented room. They were two consenting adults who found an attraction.

Julian didn't feel guilty about that part of the evening, before Jo fell sleep. He had a few qualms about what happened next. His thoughts turned to capitalising on Jo's position at *Spotlight*. They had a fun night but there were no guarantees of a repeat encounter. Quietly, Julian had slipped out of bed and found Jo's mobile phone. He copied her number. For the next hour, as Jo slumbered, Julian pondered how to use that media access to embarrass the dog racing industry – and to inflict more pain on Conor O'Leary.

Julian was serious about saving greyhounds from the gambling world. He sincerely believed that live-baiting continued in greyhound racing. Not all trainers were involved, but he was certain that everyone in the industry was aware and turned a blind eye. To Julian, that made them as culpable as the guilty.

By the time a bleary-eyed Jo departed Saturday morning, Julian had a plan. He didn't want to directly involve Jo in case that personal connection made the journalists leery. He decided an anonymous tip addressed to the *Spotlight* office would appeal to her conscience. Jo sounded genuinely interested in the plight of racing dogs. She might *suspect* the tip-off was from Julian, but he didn't believe Jo would confess to her workmates it *could* be from a guy she shagged.

Julian was impatient to get traction in the HLP crusade. Digital campaigns, newsletters, protest banners and chanting outside racetracks weren't enough for him. The initial public outrage over the vision of butchered piglets, rabbits and possums had waned. The New South Wales government had even reneged on their ban because their power base was threatened. Julian knew the anti-racing movement needed a new spark – a fresh exposé to remind voters about the sport's cruelty. If it meant being underhanded in saving the dogs, so be it.

Details about Conor O'Leary's training base were easy to provide for *Spotlight*. Julian had driven to the property twice, both times at night. The first was to burn the utility shed. It was separate from the kennels. It was bad luck the wind changed and started a small grass fire.

Julian knew his arson attack was petty, but it felt good to get revenge against the older man who had shamed him. The dogs were hurting, so should the trainers. The blaze generated the same feelings he experienced after the carnage at the High Commissioner's office in Auckland. In his opinion, it was justified to cause suffering to uncaring bastards.

In both cases Julian regarded the damage as minor. It could have been much worse if he totally lost control. In Auckland, he surrendered before getting zapped by a 50,000-volt police taser. At Steiglitz, Julian knew everyone was at the track when he sneaked onto the property with a bottle of turpentine and a lighter.

Julian had taken similar care when baiting the hook for *Spotlight*. Television stations are full of cameras, inside and out. No way was he going to walk into reception and hand over the information. He waited until late Sunday evening when the channel was at its quietest. The lone security guard drifted in and out of the foyer with a coffee cup. Julian wrapped his face in a scarf, walked steadily to the entrance and slid an envelope under the door. He was out of sight before the guard returned. It was then up to the curiosity of the journalists. Instinct told Julian that the hype and Australia-wide exposure that the Four Corners program enjoyed after their story was enough to lure a ratings-conscious producer.

Julian didn't dare call or text Jo after the tip-off lest she became suspicious. It was a leap of faith that *Spotlight* would want to film the live-baiting the following weekend – the third Sunday of the month – before involving racing officials or police. That could jeopardise an exclusive story. *Spotlight* couldn't guarantee that a police raid wouldn't leak to other media. No, Julian believed *Spotlight* would gather the *evidence* – then alert the authorities. They could milk the story for days and stay ahead of the competition.

Julian's plan faced two challenges. The television crew had to find proof of live-baiting. There had to be animals – dead or alive – on the training track. Julian saw dozens of rabbits on the property during his previous visit. It wouldn't take long to snare a few; a chance to refresh the skills taught by his Uncle Garth in the North Island. One fluffy tail would be strapped on the lure to verify the trainer was live-baiting. The other bunnies could spend a cosy night in the spare utility shed; the one he didn't burn on his previous visit. Or would a possum be better? They're protected in Australia but a pest in New Zealand. Julian would have no problem sacrificing a possum for the cause.

Challenge one was easy enough to solve. The second – transport – was more difficult. Julian had to get to Steiglitz on Saturday night. In the past he had borrowed Kristin's car for personal matters. That wasn't possible because she always drove to the Broadmeadows track. The rail line passed The Meadows, yet most HLP members drove cars because it was a long walk from the station.

Julian had few friends in the HLP apart from Kristin; none who was likely to lend him a vehicle. A rental was out of the question as Julian's New Zealand driver's licence had expired in April; he never bothered to acquire an Australian one. Who needed a car in Melbourne with its network of trains, trams and buses? He couldn't approach a rental company with a sob story about getting to his Granny's funeral. No licence? No insurance? No car.

Julian briefly contemplated including Kristin in his plan. For about 30 seconds. He knew Kristin was besotted with him but didn't want to end up with a broken heart. She would flip out if he revealed his intentions. The publicity would re-ignite the animal cruelty debate. But Julian knew Kristin would never involve herself in such deceit. He needed another ally for the night; it came from a most surprising quarter. A first tentative chat with the HLP member on Tuesday was greeted with enthusiasm. The co-conspirator agreed a shock tactic would be good for their campaign. The planning flowed smoothly – until everything went tits up at Steiglitz.

Julian's musings stalled as Jo's colleague finished her drink and pulled on a jacket. That was good; he was worried his extended stay in the street would look suspicious. Victoria Barracks behind him wasn't the military hub that it used to be during the 20th century, but it wasn't a bluestone ghost town either. Julian couldn't see surveillance cameras, although he didn't know what security the military employed. A man lurking in the dark for too long might make even a half-awake guard nervous.

Julian's original plan was to follow Jo after she left the TV station: he would discreetly approach as she reached her car, or waited for a bus, tram or train. The exit accompanied by the colleague was a setback. Julian prayed they wouldn't get in the co-worker's car as he had no way to follow. He breathed a sigh of relief as they walked along Wells Street and entered the apartment block. He was even happier when they didn't draw the curtains; it became apparent that Jo lived there.

The call to Jo during the day was risky. She might have felt used by Julian and alerted the police immediately. He later sent a message from an anonymous email account which allowed for ongoing communications, if Jo wanted to reply. So far there had been no contact, which wasn't necessarily a negative response. Her media day was frantic and personal emails might have to wait until she was off duty. There was no message from the cops either, urging him to surrender. That was a positive as it did not appear that Jo had passed that information to detectives.

The next conundrum was to get inside Jo's apartment. There was a camera over the entrance which could be a problem. Would Jo call the cops if she saw him in her security screen upstairs? Another possibility occurred as he watched the friends. Could he slip inside the door as the colleague departed? It would require some acting skills, but he felt confident he could carry off the charade. The colleague was on the move: time to put the plan into action.

Julian dashed across the road and waited with his back to the front door. Twenty seconds later he tucked the mobile under his chin and started an imaginary conversation with a 'grumpy' girlfriend.

'I'm telling you Victoria – I can't find them.' Julian went through the pantomime of searching his pockets for a lost key as the colleague emerged from the lift. He glanced at the opening door and saw she was also distracted by her phone.

'I'm outside now Nathan. How far away are you?'

The colleague paused briefly as Julian played the flustered tenant.

'I know I picked the keys up this morning. I must have left them on the desk at work.' He reached out for the door as Jo's colleague passed through. He held it and smiled. 'I'm in luck Victoria. A kind lady is just coming out. I'll pop next door to Mrs Brambles and pick up our spare key.'

Julian thanked the good Samaritan and scooted across the foyer for the stairs as a vehicle stopped on the road. The first part of the plan worked, now he hoped his next assumption would. Within half a minute he was outside Jo's apartment. He rapped twice, hoping Jo would think it was her friend and not check the spy hole. A few seconds later the door opened. Jo had refilled her wine glass.

'Forget something Kim? Oh!'

'Hello Jo.'

Kim slipped her phone into a handbag and looked at the blue Ford Ranger parked in front of the apartment: DS Potter was behind the wheel. The suit was gone, replaced by a brown leather jacket, white shirt, no tie. Kim liked the casual style.

'Hey Nathan. Sorry to delay dinner.' Kim then appraised the truck. 'Are you an outdoor man when you're not solving homicides?'

Potter laughed. 'I need something big to carry the bodies after I shoot them.'

Kim paused with the passenger door half open. 'Um, I presume you're talking about kangaroos or deer – or something that's legal to hunt? I'm not being conned by a serial killer with the best job in the world.'

The off duty detective leered. 'I couldn't possibly tell you that.'

'I'm too hungry to worry – I'll take my chances.' Kim stepped up to the passenger seat and slammed the door.

Potter slipped the gear into first and cruised away from the kerb. 'What was the emergency conflab about?' He looked at the rear vision mirror. 'Anything a curious detective should know? I'm guessing that was Jo's place?'

Kim stared straight ahead, not willing to engage any eye contact. Were they watching the apartment for Julian? Maybe she should have looked closer at the man who lost his keys. *Was that an act?* Kim shook her head. Her quick glance at the resident revealed he was blonde, not dark-haired like Julian.

She suspected her friend wasn't totally honest about the latest contact with the suspect. Did Jo have a communication channel with Julian, despite her denials? The *Spotlight* colleagues reached a compromise – Jo would reveal the phone message on Tuesday morning. Her justification for the delay would be the frantic Monday; there was no time to clear her private mobile until back in the apartment. Jo could say she was exhausted and needed to sleep before getting involved with the police again. She would even surrender the phone for investigation if required. Both women were happy with that arrangement.

Now Kim was sitting in a car with a detective at the heart of the murder inquiry. He was also a handsome man whom she wanted to know better on a personal level. That was her dilemma – should she break a confidence with Jo to help a new relationship?

Kim turned to Potter who patiently divided his eyes between the road and his dinner companion.

'Nothing that can't wait until after an entrée, main course and a massive chocolate dessert. I told you I was starving. Anyway, you're supposed to be off duty.'

'Yeah, right.'

They laughed as Potter navigated the streets and light traffic towards the restaurant in Prahran.

Day 135

The prisoner was overdue for a beating on Monday evening. By almost a week. The wall chart below the bed marked the dates when the jailer had gone ballistic. It wasn't quite monthly, but it was regular enough to be prepared. She stayed on the far side of the cell during the two meal deliveries. Lunch always came with breakfast: a sandwich, two pieces of fruit, if she was lucky. If the bastard entered the cell with empty hands, that's when she pulled the blankets and pillow over her body. It didn't stop the blows, but it limited the damage and pain.

That evening her jailer was relaxed, no signs of the barely suppressed rage as he placed a bowl of thick Irish stew on the floor near the door. Communication was rare because her pleas for freedom were ignored. Requests for toiletries were usually filled within a day or two. He even granted a regular supply of books and magazines. That was surprising; she assumed he wanted to crush her spirit. Yet, the reading material kept her mind fresh.

The jailer's mood emboldened her. 'When is this going to end? You're achieving nothing but petty revenge. Not that I did anything to deserve this.'

The savage frown returned. A fist was raised. But he didn't advance on her.

'You're a whore. This is all you deserve.'

He turned on his heel, spilling her dinner. The door was slammed and locked. The first words in weeks – nothing had changed in his twisted mind. She ignored the allegation as she bent over the ruined dinner. Carefully she scraped the stew back into the bowl. Food was important to survival and she would do whatever was necessary. She held up one of the longer bones with stringy lamb. That might come in handy, with a bit of work. Gently she hummed Gloria Gaynor's 1978 anthem, *I Will Survive*.

Chapter 17

Mac entered the *Spotlight* conference room with a frown and dropped his pad and pen onto the table. He was more careful with his Collingwood Football Club coffee mug. Two had mysteriously cracked this year and been replaced. The Magpies bottle opener had gone missing – again. Curly Rogers looked up from his notes and raised an eyebrow as Mac stood at the head of the table.

'Still no sign of Jo?'

Mac sighed. 'Nope.' His legs felt weird, there was none of the instinctive twitching ahead of Jo's arrival at the meeting. 'She's never been late in her life.'

'Any response on her mobile.'

'Nada. Phone goes to voice mail.'

'Does she have a landline?'

That question made Dugal, Withers and Kim scoff.

'Come on Curly,' Kim said. 'Jo's still under 30. Working here was probably her first contact with a communication device that didn't require thumbs to operate.'

The ripple of laughter eased some of the tension in the room.

'I had a drink with her last night. It was a rough day; she was gulping it down. I'm sure she's looking for some paracetamol and will be here soon.'

Mac was sceptical. 'I've seen her guzzle more than you lot combined, and still be the first into the office. Did you talk about anything special last night? Anything that we should know about?'

Kim dropped her eyes to the notebook. 'No, no – nothing to…help us. But I did learn something interesting about the body. Or rather, what the killer did to Conor O'Leary.'

The distraction worked on Mac. 'What happened to him – apart from getting dismembered with a chainsaw?'

'I have a…ah – a new source. They told me O'Leary had his genitals mutilated.'

'What? His nuts chopped off? Stuffed in his mouth – like some Mafia contract killing?'

'No. No symbolic retribution. The autopsy revealed it was a frenzied attack – his penis and testes were ground to mince.'

Kim's description was received with a mixture of winces and one gasp from the men in the room. They tried to flush that imagery as Stephanie Grant suggested a motive.

'Have the cops received allegations that O'Leary was a sexual predator?' Stephanie paused a moment, then lobbed in the most damning possibility. 'Was he a paedophile?'

Kim went defensive. 'I didn't say this came from the police. I'm just delivering a fact from the autopsy.'

Dugal and Withers exchanged smirks, Kim noticed and blushed. Several other members of the production crew smiled. Curly and Mac were puzzled.

'Am I missing something here?' Mac asked.

Kim was saved by the rattle of casters bumping over the loose carpet tile at the door. Mac glanced over his shoulder but wasn't quick enough. His howl of pain announced Jo's arrival. He slumped into his seat and rubbed a bruised ankle.

'Sorry folks. I had one wine too many last night and didn't set the alarm. What have I missed?'

No blood had been drawn but Mac still glared at his perky production assistant. Curly diverted another rant and brought them back to the story of the day.

'Kim's learned that the killer was a sadist. Revenge was obviously the motive, but there was a sexual element to the killing as well. He mashed the trainer's manhood with the chainsaw.'

'Ewwwww.' Jo grimaced. 'That doesn't bear thinking about. And it's even less reason to focus on Julian as the suspect. He's not that kind of guy.'

Mac shunted his chair away from Jo. 'Well, until the cops identify another culprit, he's still a priority for us. Kim, good job with that inside information. You were about to tell us more about O'Leary's reputation – until the kamikaze arrived.' Mac ignored Jo's raised middle finger.

'The workers loved O'Leary as a boss. Rene Harding has worked at Steiglitz for 10 years and helped with the sheep and canola crops. Dwayne Milligan's considered a bit of a dog whisperer. He spent most of his time looking after them. They said O'Leary was a flirt and was always surrounded by women at the track bars. The only bad incident they can recall was the break-up of the marriage.'

Kim succinctly outlined the story of Siobhan hiding in the van to catch her husband with the female attendant. It prompted laughter and ribald comments amongst the crew until Curly stated the obvious.

'Does this new information about the wife make her a suspect?' Curly paused as that possibility was digested.

'She was an experienced farmer and could probably handle a chainsaw. She'd know where the tools were kept. It might explain why O'Leary turned his back on a killer.'

'Didn't she go back to Ireland?' asked Stephanie Grant. 'And why wait six years to take her revenge? If she wanted to give him a chainsaw vasectomy, wouldn't she have done it when they separated?'

Mac winced again. His own sterilisation was a smaller cut, but no less painful. 'Good points Stephanie. O'Leary's philandering certainly provides a motive. But time and distance would seem to rule her out. Does anyone know whether she is flying out for the funeral?'

'Dwayne and Rene said the earliest they would expect her was tomorrow.' Kim said. 'Siobhan would have to pack and arrange flights. They're going to let me know when she arrives, so I can get the first interview.'

'Jo tell the news guys we might need the chopper for an urgent flight to Steiglitz on Wednesday.' He turned back to the staff around the conference table. 'Right, we smashed the opposition yesterday with our program. What else have we got to give them another bloody nose tonight?'

Jo cast a quick glance at Withers who was conferring quietly with Dugal. She took a deep breath. 'I might be able to add something more.'

Withers' conversation stopped mid-sentence and all eyes turned to the diminutive PA.

'Julian made contact again.'

Chapter 18

Kristin Webb sighed as the phone at the HLP headquarters rang again: the 20th call since she finished breakfast. Was it the media wanting another quote for a radio deadline? The police inquiring if Julian had come in from the cold? Or another party member wanting to quit? Given it was the landline, Kristin assumed it would be the third option as it was cheaper than a mobile. Some had even parted company with the HLP via email – that cost nothing.

The voice mail would respond after 15 rings: much longer than most households or businesses. Kristin had set the delay because it was a large terrace and there were no extensions on the second floor. Normally she could dash down the stairs and beat the machine. If she wanted. As Kristin was already in the office there was no need for the digital support. She could pick up the handset and answer. If she wanted. Kristin knew she should respond; she was communications manager after all. She would gladly have relinquished that title after spending most of Monday with the phone against her ear. It was still red and sore from that weary experience, even with the help of Ryan Mathison.

Was the word *help* overstating Mathison's assistance? He spent three hours in the office, after he finally emerged from *unpacking* from his weekend trip. And most of that time Mathison was talking on the phone. It just wasn't the HLP hotline. They agreed to take alternate calls on the landline to allow each other time to get some proper work done. That arrangement lasted about six calls as Mathison was always on his mobile when the main line rang.

The phone bleated for the 13th time. She hadn't seen Mathison this morning and she most likely would have to listen to the playback. Why delay the inevitable? She snatched the handset.

'Good morning. This is the Hound Liberation Party and you're speaking to Kristin Webb. Can I help you?' It was such a practiced routine that Kristen was surprised she could inject any sincerity into the greeting.

'G'day Krissy. It's Marcus Denham from the Horsham branch. How are ya?'

Kristin cringed. She had lost count of the number of times Denham had been told she hated being called *Krissy*. Normally she could palm the bogan to Mathison. That gave her some pleasure: Ryan Mathison didn't lend itself to an easy Australian abbreviation.

'Not great Marcus. I don't have a lot of time to talk because of the current issue we're dealing with. I have to keep the line free.'

'Yeah. I guess it must be a cluster-fuck down in the big smoke. Did that dropkick really chop up the trainer with a chainsaw? Jeezus. We don't need that kind of shit publicity.'

Kristin sighed and didn't hide her exasperation from the party member.

'Yes, we are trying to deal with it, Marcus. So, if there isn't anything urgent, I had better get back to the job of saving the party.'

'Oh, sure, sure. I don't want to hold you up Krissy. I just wanted the bank account details.'

'Why do you need them?'

'For the money from the fundraiser on Saturday.' Denham laughed. 'It's burning a hole in my pocket and we don't want temptation to get in my way, do we?'

Kristen was so puzzled she ignored the latest *Krissy*. 'But why do you have the money? I thought Ryan brought it back?'

'Nah, nah. He didn't make it in time. Didn't he tell you? He had a breakdown in Ballarat on the way up on Saturday afternoon. By the time the RACV turned up and got him going again it was too late for the function. He told me to collect the money and he would send the bank account details. I've been texting him and sent an email. Nothing. I've got $437.50. They're a kind-hearted mob in Horsham and I'm sure you need the money, especially with the crap happening now.'

Kristin wasn't as thrilled as her regional enthusiast, but every dollar helped the cause. More concerning was Mathison's omission. What had her colleague said about the weekend fund-raiser? He didn't *confirm* he went to Horsham. All he said was it went well, and the money would be banked today. Would Mathison argue semantics if she challenged him about the cash? Or not declaring he missed the event? That discussion was best held in private, not shared with the country member who still babbled on the phone. It was time to get rid of him.

'Look Marcus, things have been frantic here the last two days. Ryan and I haven't been able to have a proper chat. I'll email you the bank account details; you can deposit the money today. Well done with the fund raiser.' Kristin replaced the phone before Denham had a chance to respond.

The 15-year-old office chair groaned as Kristin leaned back and stared at the mouldy plaster rose feature in the ceiling. The office needed more than $437.50 to restore its Victorian era grandeur. Mathison's bedroom was directly above. There hadn't been any noise: was he still asleep, or did he slip away early? That wasn't important – Mathison rarely kept her appraised of his movements.

The fact that he missed the Horsham function was annoying. It was important to maintain contact with the regions as it kept a regular flow of contributions for the party. If Horsham felt ignored the money would dry up. The HLP couldn't afford to lose more people. To stay registered as a political party they required 500 members. The current crisis had reduced that number to 521.

Kristin dragged fingers through tangled curls as she thought more about Mathison and his weekend. Did he have a new girlfriend somewhere between Melbourne and Horsham? Was the lure of a romp more important than HLP business? Mathison was vain and often flirted with women at their information booths and rallies. She regularly saw him write his private number on party literature for pretty ladies. Kristin wasn't jealous; their fling was over. She preferred Mathison spent more time getting the HLP a foot in the door at parliament rather than getting a leg over.

The ringing phone brought Kristin back to the mission for the day: saving their political dreams. She would get answers from Mathison about his mystery weekend later. She picked up the handset and summoned some cheeriness.

'Good morning. This is the Hound Liberation Party and you're speaking to Kristin Webb. Can I help you?'

Chapter 19

Dwayne Milligan was playing with the final two greyhounds in the wire enclosure of the kennels when he noticed a white sedan on the gravel driveway. The morning regime of training, health checks and feeding took a fraction of the normal time: two dogs required less work than when 40 were in residence. It was obvious to Milligan that Bitzer and Mandy were lonely; a few minutes of playing with a raggedy piece of rope lifted their spirits. And his. Now it was Milligan's curiosity that was being raised.

The car stopped in the same spot where Chauncey Quayle parked his Jaguar the day before. Milligan didn't think it was the old bookie in his wife's shopping cart, although he couldn't see the driver. The horn beeped. That was unusual for a visitor. Even more surprising was watching Rene Harding hurry down the front stairs 10 seconds later and open the driver door. A stout, grey-haired woman in her late 50s emerged.

She ignored Harding's outstretched hand of greeting and stared at the homestead instead. For almost a minute few words were exchanged as the woman slowly pivoted, appraising everything in sight: the house, sheds, paddocks and finally the kennels. Her gaze didn't linger, although Milligan was sure she spotted him through the wire fence. She walked up the stairs and entered the house.

It could only be one person – Siobhan O'Leary. But how did she get to Australia so quickly from Ireland? It's Tuesday; she couldn't have known about the murder until late Sunday. Milligan had never been overseas; a couple of weekends for Group 1 races in Sydney and Brisbane were the extent of his flying experience. Those flights involved delays, waiting and lots of shuffling around – and that was in Australia. He couldn't fathom how anyone could travel around the world in less than two days. It must have been a hell of a trip and, judging by Siobhan's demeanour, she was tired and grumpy.

Milligan wasn't eager to meet the new owner. He tidied the enclosure and poured the dogs more water as he watched Harding remove two suitcases from the car and carry them inside. Half a minute later his mate returned to the veranda and waved frantically. Time to meet the boss.

Milligan's Geelong footy club sweatshirt was stained with crap from the yard and torn from his latest rough-housing with the dogs. His jeans weren't in much better condition. It wasn't a great first impression, but could you expect much better from a kennel attendant at work?

If tea and biscuits were on offer, Milligan could cover the distance to the house in about 45 seconds. Milligan made his shuffle last almost three minutes. By the time he reached the house Siobhan had returned to the veranda. Harding quietly closed the door and leaned against a post; out of the new owner's direct eyeline.

Milligan's first impression wasn't encouraging. There was no smile or warm greeting. Siobhan had close-cropped hair with a straight fringe. Plain would be the word to describe her features; nothing was out of proportion, but then not much would leave an impression. Siobhan could pass through any security screening and officials would struggle to note anything memorable. Milligan was surprised to see she had a reasonable tan, much better than you would expect for anyone arriving from the Northern Hemisphere in May. Surely it was bitterly cold in Ireland? Wasn't Spring constantly wet? Summer wasn't much better, according to Conor. Milligan felt he might have been harsh to consider her stout. Up close, he realised Siobhan was wearing a red hooded rain jacket, the denims beneath revealed the strong and toned legs of a hiker. Siobhan broke the ice.

'And who might you be young man?'

'Dwayne Milligan, Mrs O'Leary.'

'And how long have you been working here?'

'About six years. I mostly work with the dogs. I help with the canola crops during harvesting, but not the sheep. Rene and Conor – Mr O'Leary – looked after them.'

Siobhan grunted. Milligan wasn't sure if the response was a reaction to her late husband's name, or Milligan's limited role at Tara. Harding shook his head and turned towards the distant grazing paddocks. Milligan realised he should have talked up his involvement.

'And how many dogs are there in the kennels?'

'Two Mrs O'Leary.'

'Two? And just you to look after them? How do you cope?' The sarcasm was as subtle as the sneer.

Milligan was annoyed but kept his cool. 'We used to have more than 40, sometimes up to 50, until just before Christmas. But there's been some bad luck in recent months and the owners have been fickle. Mr O'Leary's murder was the final straw, I guess. We lost more than a dozen since the weekend.'

'And how long are the last two mongrels going to pay their way?'

'Their owner is in Bali on holiday. He's back Thursday, so yeah, the kennels could be empty by the end of the week.'

Siobhan put her hands in her jacket pockets. 'Well, without dogs to train or race, and no likelihood of anymore as I hate the bloody things, what use are you to me?' Siobhan glanced briefly at Harding whose eyes stayed on the horizon. 'I know Rene has experience with the sheep and crops, but you're next to useless for farm work. I don't have the money to carry two workers. God knows why Conor ever saw fit to hire you after I left. He had such a soft spot for those skinny mongrels.' Siobhan shook her head, looked at the kennels and then back to Milligan. 'You can stay until Friday. If those last two dogs are still here Rene can look after them until their owner picks them up. We're out of the racing business.'

Siobhan turned her back on Milligan and clasped the front door handle. 'Don't count your blessings, Rene. I'm going to reassess the farm's direction before the next harvest.' She walked inside and shut the door firmly.

Milligan was shocked. He knew that losing his job was possible, but he never expected Siobhan's brutal dismissal. Nothing Conor or Harding ever said about her indicated she could be so ruthless. Maybe returning to Tara revived bad memories for the widow? Milligan didn't notice Harding descend the steps until he spoke quietly.

'C'mon mate. Let's go put a brew on at the kennels and have a chat.'

They covered half the distance when they heard Siobhan's voice. They turned to see the new boss standing on the veranda; more annoyed than before, if that was possible. She waved the ceramic teapot decorated with images of Ireland.

'And you two stay out of my home and kitchen.' The sacked and the reprieved nodded and turned back towards their sanctuary.

'I can't believe she's being so bitchy,' said Harding. 'She was never that mean, even when she suspected Conor was playing around. I don't know what's happened to her in the past six years. She's developed a cruel streak.'

They were soon inside their domain and out of Siobhan's sight. Milligan slumped onto the battered two-seater couch while Harding flicked on the electric kettle.

'I guess she's right,' Milligan said 'She doesn't need two of us with no dogs to look after. You've been here the longest and know more about the farming business. To be honest, if she's going to be such a cow, it would be better working somewhere else.'

Harding pulled down two mugs, the box of teabags and a packet of Arnott's Scotch Finger biscuits. The Tim Tams were gone, but they needed something sweet to cheer them up.

'I'm wondering if I should follow you.'

'What? Quit?'

'Yeah. It's not going to be any fun working here anymore. Conor's dead, you're being sacked, the dogs are almost gone. No bloody joy working for Cruella.'

The kettle boiled and Harding filled the cups. Milligan nibbled on a biscuit as he considered the latest blow in a stressful week. This had been his dream job. It was all he ever wanted to do since leaving school – work with greyhounds.

'I think you need to hang in here for a while mate. It's a pay packet. I'll need your help to cover the rent on the flat until I get something else. I can make some cash at the Geelong and Broadmeadows tracks catching after the races. The other tracks will cost too much petrol money to get there.' Milligan accepted his Earl Grey tea with milk and two sugars. 'And there's no way I'm ever going to sell the ute. I'll rob a bank before that happens.'

Harding laughed.

'Don't worry, Dwayne. We'll figure something out. Perhaps you should ring a few trainers to see if anyone has a vacancy? Maybe you could try Henry Wright near Ballan? He's got 20 dogs and there's just him and the missus, although I haven't seen her at the track for a while. He might give you a couple of days a week. That and the $10 per race catch will keep you going.'

'Yeah, I might do that. I'll line up a few trainers for the Geelong races on Friday and sound him out. His kennels aren't much further than Steiglitz from the flat.' Milligan sipped, then dunked half a biscuit. The skill was in getting the soggy bit to your mouth before it fell into the tea. 'Did you tell Siobhan that Chauncey Quayle's been sniffing about the property?'

'Briefly. I'm wondering if that soured her mood even more. She wasn't friendly on arrival. Then I mentioned that Chauncey might pop in to pay his respects. I hinted he was interested in buying the property. Man, did she turn crotchety in a heartbeat. She hissed – honestly, she hissed like a snake. Said that sneaky old bastard would never get his hands on her precious land.'

'Jeezus. It sounds like she's been nurturing that bitterness back in Ireland for years.'

Harding gulped his tea and placed the cup beside the kettle. 'Yes and no mate.'

'What does that mean.'

'She's been feeding her anger about Conor and the farm. But she hasn't been in Ireland all the time.'

'Eh? Where's she been? I noticed she wasn't as pale as you might expect most Irish folk to be at this time of year. Did she get an apartment in Spain or Portugal? I've seen that on those lifestyle programs. They call them snowbirds because they go south for the winter.'

'She flew south mate – all the way back to Australia.'

That caused Milligan to pause mid-dunk with his Scotch Finger. He waited too long; it fell into the mug with a plop. 'Bugger. She's been here? How long? Where?'

'Ballarat, apparently. I asked her how she got to Steiglitz so quickly after learning about Conor's death. Siobhan said she's been here for six months.'

'Doing what?'

'I didn't have time to find out.'

'Shit. That means she was nearby when Conor died.'

'Yep.'

The attendants looked at each other for 20 seconds, waiting for the other to ask the obvious. Milligan couldn't resist.

'Do you think Siobhan could have killed Conor?'

Chapter 20

For the second time in less than 24 hours Kim Prescott and Jo Trescowthick made a surreptitious exit from the Chanel 5 studios. Instead of turning right on Wells Street – the PA's home was a few minutes away – they went left. The reporter set a fierce pace; Jo had to jog to keep up. Not that she would say anything. She knew her colleague was cranky. It would be wiser to delay the verbal stoush until both had intravenous coffee lines attached.

Kim hooked left at Dorcas Street and marched up to Middleton Lane. Jo suspected their destination was a few metres down that road. It wasn't a preferred caffeine fix location. Kim used the café to practice her language skills with staff from the nearby French Consulate.

Again, it was better for Jo to hold her tongue a few more minutes. Neither wanted a shouting match on the streets of South Melbourne. A news camera crew might drive past and gleefully record the confrontation for the Christmas reel. She knew a couple of camera ops who would suggest the ladies put on bikinis and settle their differences in a plastic pool filled with jelly. *That* suggestion would be grounds for justifiable homicide. The current affairs crews were better trained. They might think about it; but feared for their lives if they ever mentioned it.

The café was quiet; only three of the 15 tables occupied.

Kim gave the coffee orders. 'Two flat whites please Gabby.'

Jo wasn't going to easily surrender control. 'No thank you. Make mine an espresso.' She wanted a good jolt. 'You can pay, seeing you dragged me here.'

'Fine. Anything to eat? A chocolate chip cookie? Banana muffin?'

'No. I'm sweet thanks.'

Kim didn't respond as she snatched the order number and looked for the most isolated corner. Jo beat her there and claimed the seat with the window at her back. Point One to Jo.

Kim squinted into the morning glare. 'Okay, what have you and Julian been up to?'

'What do you mean? I told everyone at the morning conference.'

'An email?' Kim glared. 'You expect me to believe that's all? You were late to work for the first time – ever – and yet there's no hangover from two bottles of wine. There are bags under your eyes from a lack of sleep, but you're positively glowing. Did you have a late visitor?'

The PA was spared that answer by the arrival of her espresso. The flat white was still being crafted by the barista who was experimenting with a new frothy design. It allowed Jo a few moments to consider how much to reveal.

The morning conference was easy to deal with. She told them about the voice message on the mobile *discovered* when she arrived home. That was the plan agreed with Kim during their Monday evening discussion. It covered her for not telling Mac or Curly before leaving the office. Then Jo opened her laptop and showed an email sent to her work address at 10.13pm. It was from Julian Oliver: another declaration of innocence and a second chance for Jo to contact him.

Hi Jo

First of all, let me apologise for getting you involved in this mess. Please believe that I had nothing to do with the death of Conor O'Leary. That was awful – you know what I'm like. I could NEVER do anything like that. I admit I was at his property, but I knew nothing about him being chopped up in the starting box. I was being petty and wanted to pay him back for embarrassing me at the track. I wanted him to be humiliated and to put more pressure on the greyhound industry. I understand that what I did was wrong and cowardly. I'm also sorry if you think I used you to get the TV crew out to Steiglitz. I like you Jo and really enjoyed our time together. Perhaps in other circumstances we might have been able to fan that spark we created. I know you are likely to

pass this message to the cops. So, to you and them, all I can say
is that I must go away until they find the real killer. It wasn't me.
Everyone – and I include the media – needs to look at other sus-
pects and I hope they do it quickly.
Regards
Julian

Mac, Curly, Kim, Stephanie and the other reporters weren't swayed by the declaration. They swiftly moved to Jo's terse response which was sent 10 minutes later. Its tone indicated her mood.

Julian
You put me in a very difficult position with my employers, col-
leagues and the police. I am angry that you abused my trust and
threatened my career to further your personal campaign. If you
are innocent of this heinous crime, I urge you to contact the po-
lice immediately. Call them and sort it out before it is too late. I
spent part of today with the senior detectives and they struck me
as fair and reasonable people. You shouldn't have anything to
fear if you did nothing wrong. I will be sending these messages
to the police in the morning as I'm too tired for another session
with the investigators tonight. Give yourself up and please stay
away from me.
Jo

The production crew were excited to find themselves with another edge over the opposition; they were part of the developing story – again. The suspect was communicating with *Spotlight* staff – unbidden – and they all believed it would continue. Plans were made for coverage and how to deal with the police. Mac took that responsibility to allow his reporters and producers the freedom to get on with the job of making television stories. They weren't convinced by Julian's denials but that didn't matter; it was their job to broadcast each development in the story.

Jo had zoomed back to her computer at the command post. She printed copies of the emails and the anonymous Gmail address Julian provided and gave them to Mac. Hopefully, the program producer could satisfy the cops to spare her another session under the bright lights. It wasn't that bad, but still not an experience she wanted to repeat. Joe had picked up the phone to check for messages left during the conference when Kim hissed in her ear, 'Coffee. Now!'

That was 15 minutes ago. Jo had her favourite life force at her lips but no easy answers to the conundrum of what to tell her workmate, an annoyed and extremely inquisitive current affairs reporter. She remained silent.

'I have a suspicion that Julian was at your place last night,' Kim said.

Jo clattered her cup onto the saucer. 'What makes you say that?' The defiance was meant to distract; Jo wasn't sure if Kim was certain, or fishing.

'These emails after 10 o'clock are too *convenient*. You didn't respond to his mobile message and suddenly he's sending an email to your work address. You replied immediately when you should have been almost comatose, judging by the way you were guzzling the wine.'

Kim's coffee and a heated muffin finally arrived, which gave Jo another brief respite. Jo vowed never to return to that café if she needed a quick caffeine fix. Kim resumed the attack.

'I also suspect that I might have given Julian access to your apartment building.'

Jo blushed, which encouraged her accuser.

'I think he was the man fluffing around at the front door, looking for his keys, as I left. He was convincing – talking to a wife or girlfriend on the phone, patting all his pockets, looking flustered. He conveniently didn't allow me to see his face.'

Kim paused a moment. It wasn't gloating, more to let Jo know it was futile to deny.

'The baseball cap couldn't hide his hair; it was short and blonde – not long and dark like Julian's. An hour and a few dollars at a discreet hairdresser could have produced that look. The glasses were probably a $10 pair from Kmart.'

The prosecutor rested her case by cutting a chunk off the muffin and sipping her coffee.

Jo knew she was guilty as charged. Her face was pink, a dead giveaway for a woman who normally had total control of her emotions. She had been consorting – amongst other things – with a murder suspect. Not that she believed Julian was the killer. She gave him food, a bed, cash and the sort of comfort that Kim didn't need to know about. But Kim wasn't her main problem – it was the cops. She could be charged even if Julian was cleared of the crime. Where was the bloody justice in that?

Kim allowed the silence to drag, an experienced interviewer's favourite tactic. Jo felt herself being pressured into filling the vacuum. Her espresso was finished, she had rejected a treat, there were no other props to help her delay. Apart from pinching some of Kim's muffin. She grabbed a chunk with mushy banana oozing onto the plate.

'It won't work Jo. Have as much muffin as you like. We have a problem – and you need to tell me how deep in the shit you are.'

Jo grabbed a napkin. 'Okay, okay, Torquemada.' She briefly dabbed at her lips and fingers. 'Jeez, Kim, you could have given the Spanish Inquisition lessons in how to grill suspects.'

'No distractions, Jo. We're running out of time.'

Jo slumped in her chair and sighed. 'Yes, that was Julian. I almost didn't recognise him. It's a radical change from his previous look – op shop grunge.'

Kim nodded, not wanting to halt the flow of information.

'Julian was desperate Kim. He doesn't have any cash and he can't risk using his credit card or an ATM. Everyone knows they have cameras and Julian didn't want to reveal his new look. He had nowhere to stay. He slept rough in Yarra Bend Park on Sunday night and he hadn't eaten all Monday. I had to give him at least food and shelter.'

'You should have told him to go to the cops. Nathan and his boss aren't fools. They're not going to convict the wrong person just to clear a case from their files.'

'He panicked. Julian had been at the property. The trainer was found chopped to pieces there. They'd had two confrontations – you can understand why he'd be nervous the cops would go for the easiest suspect.'

'Running hasn't helped his cause. What are the police expected to think? The innocent don't often hide.'

Jo felt her ire rising. 'Just because you're bonking a copper now doesn't mean *you* have to become one!'

Kim didn't flinch. 'That was uncalled for Jo. You've got a problem and I'm trying to help.'

Jo hung her head. 'Sorry. It's such unfamiliar territory for me. This sort of crap happens to other people. I met a guy in the pub a couple of weeks ago…now I find myself caught up in a murder investigation.' She lifted her head and laughed. 'It's always the stray pick-ups that cause problems. At least with Kenny I could make his life miserable if he pissed me off.'

The colleagues laughed; the tension drained away. Kim was amazed how the pint-sized Jo could bully the much bigger camera operator.

'How bad is it? You gave Julian food, a bed for the night – in the spare room we can say – and money? How much?'

'I only had $85 in cash. We didn't want to go to an ATM in case it was recorded by the cops. Probably a smart move by us in the end; too many digital checks to track our moves.'

'And where was Julian going? That amount wouldn't get him to New Zealand.'

'He wouldn't say – just out of Melbourne. Part of the reason was to protect me if the cops came back to heavy me. Little did I know it would be you hauling me over the coals by morning tea.'

It wasn't a spiteful comment, Kim let it slide. 'The emails were a set up to declare his innocence?'

'Yeah. He used my mobile and the anonymous email account to send it.'

'You know what gave you away?'

Jo waved her arms in frustration. 'I do now – answering a work email after 10 at night. Especially after we – well, mostly me – emptied two bottles of white wine.'

'If I picked up that point about the email timing, the cops won't miss it either. Or maybe they think us media types are slaves to the news – 24/7. Did you set up a system for future contact?'

'No. But I expect he'll try the work email if he wants to reach me again. He'll provide a clue that it's him.'

The coffees were finished, only muffin crumbs remained. Jo had no more information about the most wanted murder suspect in Melbourne; the one who left her warm bed four hours ago. She shared most of the details with Kim, but not all.

Julian revealed he was going to Sydney. He had Kiwi friends there who could be trusted to provide a haven until police arrested the real suspect, or the manhunt was scaled down. It wasn't her job to help the police catch an innocent man.

'You know we're going to have to tell Mac, Curly and Richard about this?'

'Oh shit. Then the whole bloody station will know within half an hour. I can hear the comments every time I go to the caff: *'Oooh – shagged any killers lately Jo?'* Her spirits tumbled again. What a shitty week!

'No. We'll keep it tight.' Kim smiled. 'You've been dumb, but we are a family – we'll protect you as best we can.'

Chapter 21

As Kim and Jo left the South Melbourne café the subject of their tete-a-tete was arriving at the V/Line station at Shepparton, in northern Victoria. It cost Julian Oliver $26.20 to get that far via Seymour. It was a significant chunk of the money Jo gave him, but he was safely out of central Melbourne. An online ticket would have been preferable. However, that would have left a digital trail back to Jo.

Southern Cross Station was all hustle and bustle; thousands of commuters pouring into the city at the start of another workday. It was Tuesday, the Monday blues overcome, the pace was business-like, bodies darted in all directions. Cops with pistols patrolled the building, yet none showed interest in him. Julian was anonymous as a bespectacled, blonde-haired traveller preoccupied with his phone. Two officers chatted with arms folded less than 10 metres from where Victoria's biggest suspect bought a ticket for the 7.11 train for Seymour, and then to Shepparton.

He hugged the wall on the way to the platform as worker ants surged towards offices and shops. He chose a carriage behind the engine and a seat at the front. Not for any quick escape at the end of the journey; Julian believed not many restless passengers would venture that far during the trip. Fewer people would see his face and wonder if they recognised him. The buffet car was towards the rear of the train and should hold greater interest.

It took almost three hours to reach the city at the heart of the Goulburn Valley: canned fruit processing country. He spoke to no other passengers or when passing through the station. Julian didn't believe his New Zealand accent was strong, thanks to a private secondary school education, Auckland University and international travel with his family and the Red Cross. There were occasional jibes from new HLP members in Melbourne about 'fush n chups,' not that Julian ever uttered the words. Trans-Tasman taunts were a fact of life. It didn't bother him, although he never obliged the teaser with a smile. He suspected any accent differences beyond northern Victoria would be attributed to him living in the city. They were all considered toffs down there.

Julian emerged from the station to a clear, blue sky autumn day that was cool, the temperature in the high teens. Jo would be surprised to learn that Shepparton was on his itinerary. It was closer to New South Wales, but not the most direct route to Sydney. That would have taken him through Albury, further to the east. Julian was deliberately deceptive with his short-term lover in case Jo was pressured by her producers and the cops to reveal his plans.

Julian had no intention of going to Australia's largest city. It would be a suitable hiding place with more than five million residents. A lot of Kiwis lived there; two he knew well enough to provide a bolt hole. But it was still a risk as he didn't have money. Julian reasoned those friendships wouldn't extend beyond providing a couch or sleeping bag on the floor. The cost of food and drink might test those bonds.

Julian checked the map printed from Jo's home computer. He was going much further north – Queensland. The Murray River wasn't far away at Tocumwal and that's where he would join the Newell Highway. It was the main north-south inland route between Victoria and the Sunshine State. Julian's plan was to hitch his way out of trouble. It was free transportation which left him cash for road tucker: pies, burgers, hot dogs, sandwiches, cans of coke. He hoped there would be enough truckies looking for a travel companion. There were plenty of major hubs along the Newell: Dubbo, Parkes, Forbes. If Julian was lucky, he might get a ride going all the way to Goondiwindi on the border. From there he would take a right turn to the coast.

It would be risky spending hours with one person. Julian used the train trip to prepare a back-story: his destination, reasons for hitching and the lack of funds to pay for a coach or train. There would be no chatter about humanitarian or animal rights causes.

The other concern would be a truckie recognising him. What would Julian do to protect his freedom? Julian hoped that point would be moot, reasoning that professional drivers spent most of their lives on the road. Would they have time to watch the television news? No doubt they had phones with mobile data, or even iPads. But would a truckie ever compare a digital screen image of a long-haired Julian to the blonde dude in their passenger seat? Hopefully not. Julian put out his left thumb as a big two trailer rig approached.

Chapter 22

Journalists always joked that the designer who turned their South Melbourne building into television studios was high on dope, opium, acid – or one of their 1950s equivalents – when he put ink to paper. The building had all that production crews required to broadcast news, sport, current affairs, drama and light entertainment programs for decades. There were studios, control rooms, offices and suites stacked with expensive digital equipment. They were all linked by corridors and, to that extent, there was a *flow* to the building. But put unfamiliar humans into that warren and there was a chance of losing them for hours. Possibly days. Rabbits would never be foolish enough to enter that maze. It took weeks for employees to feel confident enough to navigate the hallways without leaving pen marks at key intersections. Novices were even advised, only half-jokingly, to carry breadcrumbs for the first few days.

Consequently, Kim wasn't surprised that she *lost* Jo between reception and the *Spotlight* dungeon. Their office without windows was buried under 10 layers of shiny suits. *Spotlight* was the late arrival and had to accept whatever space could be found. Jo might have slipped into a bathroom en route. More likely, she had taken the alternative path around studios one and two to the news department. Either possibility was a delaying tactic; a chance to avoid telling Mac that she had screwed up. Literally. Jo had slept with a murder suspect.

It wasn't going to help. The program deadline crept closer with every movement of the former railway clock that hung over the edit suites. Mac put it there; a massive reminder to everyone that time was always in your face in the media business. Kim didn't mind breaking the news about Jo's latest dalliance with Julian. It didn't have anything to do with her new interest in one of the police investigators, DS Nathan Potter. The story was developing; *Spotlight* had to work out what to do with the new information.

Curly was pounding his keyboard across from Kim's desk as she dumped her handbag on the floor.

'Hey Curly.' She looked around the room. Stephanie Grant was on the phone, a smile on her face and scribbling furiously. The newsroom replacement was an ambitious reporter and a handful of years older than Kim. She dressed immaculately, looked and sounded great on camera and arrived via a newspaper cadetship rather than university. The hungry track. Steph wrote a good yarn and knew how to mine her sources for information. She would need watching while Pete Benson was in Europe. This was Steph's big chance to break into a current affairs team and Kim wanted to make sure she wasn't shuffled out the door to make room. Paranoia is critical for survival in the television business.

There was no sign of the scaredy-cat PA as Kim's gaze moved to Richard Templeton's office. Mac sat across the desk from their presenter and executive producer. Neither man looked happy. 'What's up with Mac and the boss?'

Curly rolled back from the keyboard, stretched and laced his hands behind his head.

'They've just heard the worst possible news, I'm afraid.'

'Oh? A death in the family?'

'Not quite. The CEO's being forced to take medical leave. He's had a heart attack.'

Kim looked back at Templeton's office. She understood why that would be a blow for him: Reg Bradley was his father-in-law. Clarissa, an only child and Templeton's wife, would be incredibly upset as she was devoted to her dad. But why was Mac so down in the dumps?

'That's tough for Richard and the Bradleys. But why does Mac look like Collingwood's lost a grand final replay?'

Curly allowed a wry smile. 'Because they've just been told Bradley's stand-in will be The Hatchet.'

'Oh shit. I thought we'd seen the last of him. Dad hinted the board would quietly announce his replacement by June or July.'

'Nope. Sod's Law bites us in the butt again. He's apparently been working from home since the start of March. It was convenient for everyone until they found a suitable replacement. But now Bradley's chair is vacant Andrew Hacket's done a Lazarus. No executive is going to pass up the chance to run a television station.'

Kim's seat squealed as she slumped into it. 'How bad is the prognosis for Bradley?'

'I don't think he's at death's door. He went to his doctor for an annual check-up. His blood pressure was up so the doctor ordered an extra test. That was yesterday morning. It seemed so routine that Bradley didn't even tell his wife. He felt fine and went back to work. Then four hours later the doctor called and ordered Bradley straight into hospital. The emergency department was 'expecting him.' By two-thirty they were doing an ECG and giving him handfuls of blood-thinners to swallow. Mrs B arrived at the emergency department an hour later and panicked when she couldn't find him – he was getting an ultrasound. The tests showed that he suffered a heart attack, a mild one. He probably shrugged it off as heartburn. Sounds like Bradley is being blasé about it, but not Mrs B. They said he needs an angiogram and might require a stent – or half a dozen.'

Kim was an educated young journalist, but most of the terms Curly mentioned had never featured in her conversations with friends. 'What's an angiogram involve? Do they have to slice his chest open?'

At 44, Curly was old enough to understand medical procedures that might afflict his future if he nudged the port bottle too frequently. 'Not these days. My Uncle Jake had two stents put in last year.' He pointed to his right wrist. 'They make a tiny nick here, send lines up to your heart, inject some dye in and check which arteries are full of pies and chocolate cakes. In Jake's case it was fried chicken. Once they identify the problem areas, they shove enough stents in to reopen the arteries and keep the blood flowing. It's all over in about 40 minutes and they don't even knock you out. Jake said he watched the surgeons work inside his heart on television, although he never felt them squeezing a mini camera through his veins.'

Kim and Curly laughed at that image. Even a 24-year-old understood the capabilities of modern fibres. 'If Bradley's not too bad, that might mean a quick recovery and a short stay in the hot seat for The Hatchet?'

Curly shrugged. 'You might think that. Most people who get stents walk out of hospital a few hours later and go back to work almost immediately. But the whole process has shaken Mrs B. She doesn't want him keeling over at his desk.' Curly looked over to Templeton's office as the door opened. 'The last I heard was that Mrs B has booked them on a long ocean cruise to relax. The Hatchet could be in charge for at least six months.'

Kim groaned and slumped over her desk; memories of The Hatchet's penny-pinching habits flooded back. The first cut would probably be the booze fridge. That wasn't such an issue for her, it would be more painful for the males in the office. And maybe Jo. And she knew how much Dugal Cameron, Ken Withers and the rest of the camera crews would moan about it. Road trips would be a never-ending whine about The Hatchet and better ways to kill him.

Mac ambled over and looked down at his grumbling reporter. 'I like to see my crew flat out at work but, given the latest health news, I have to wonder if I need to call a medic in case Kim is having a fit.' Mac scratched his ginger beard and looked at Curly. 'Can you enlighten me, my loyal scribe?'

'Yep. I told her The Hatchet's sharpening his scythe and eager to get back to the top floor.'

Kim moaned louder and thumped her head against the desk. 'Agh!'

'Well, I'm glad there's no new medical emergency to deal with. Cheer up my little ray of sunshine – six months will pass in the blink of an eye.'

Kim thumped her head again, not realising she was too close to the keyboard. 'Ow! That bastard is causing us pain already.' Kim lifted her head and checked for damage.

'Maybe you. We wise men have survived tyrants before – and will again. That was him on the phone with me and Richard. He wants a budget meeting with all the department heads when he gets back.'

Mac stopped his follicle scratching and rubbed his hands together. 'But that's tomorrow. We have a cracker program to dazzle him with tonight. Where are we at with our stories?' Mac looked expectantly at his senior producer and reporter.

Kim saw that Jo had slipped back into her seat; the delaying tactics hadn't worked.

'Jo, steer your chariot over here so we can update Mac and Curly.'

Mac's eyes widened. He stared at Jo, then back to Kim. 'There's more to tell about her time with the killer Kiwi?'

'Hush Mac. Don't wind her up.'

Mac perched his bottom on a nearby desk, hoping to avoid another flesh wound from his PA. It wasn't necessary; Jo took almost 30 seconds to tiptoe her temporarily non-lethal chair the 15 metres to the meeting point.

'Shit,' Mac muttered. 'This can't be good.'

Stephanie Grant was still occupied on the phone. Several editors roamed between the suites holding mugs of coffee. Their work started after lunch when the reporters returned. Kim saw no need for everyone to know the latest developments; she kept her voice low.

'Julian contacted Jo again.'

Mac's eyes lit up. 'Brilliant. Have we got him on tape, or was it via email? What's he saying now? Will he give himself up? What about an interview?'

'It wasn't today,' Kim said. 'It was last night – and in person.'

Mac often plunged one hand into his beard when ruminating. Two hands were a sign of stress. They both went to work furiously under his chin.

'Ah shit Jo. Did he spend the night with you?'

Jo didn't raise her head, her toes twirled on the floor ready to make an escape. Finally, she sighed. 'Yes. He stayed.' Then she looked up, a touch of the regular feistiness evident in her eyes. 'He was desperate Mac. He hadn't eaten for a day; he's sleeping rough and he doesn't have any money.'

'Shit, shit, shit.' Mac released the threatened beard and rubbed a hand over his mouth. 'So – you let him stay? Fed him? And gave him money?'

'Yes.' Jo maintained eye contact with the group.

'How much?'

'$85 – not enough to flee the country. Enough to keep him alive until the police arrest the real killer.'

'What about his appearance? Has he changed his hair and clothing?'

'Yes. It's short and he's dyed it blonde.' She didn't mention the cheap spectacles.

Mac grimaced. 'You're still convinced he's innocent?'

'Absolutely Mac. He's not that kind of person, I can tell that. He's worried the cops want to go with an easy suspect because he's a foreigner. He admits he was at the property on Saturday night to plant evidence. But says he knew nothing about the dead trainer in the starting box.'

Curly raised a finger to intervene. 'Something about faking the evidence has been bugging me. Did Julian say what he expected to happen on Sunday? There was never going to be any live-baiting. The trainer was innocent. We might have had evidence of animals being set up for the kill, but there wouldn't have been any follow up. We would have been suspicious if there hadn't been any racing the next morning. Plus, the trainer or his workers would have seen the possum on the lure. What would have happened then? When you think about it – his whole scheme should have fallen apart before we did a story.'

Jo clutched her chair and looked at her feet. 'The same thought occurred to me, Curly.' She raised her eyes. 'Julian was trusting our integrity – that we are good and decent people. He believed that once we found the possum and live rabbits, we would call the cops. He didn't think we would continue with the mini camera set up. We could have destroyed our own reputation if people knew that we had found the live animals; yet allowed the trials to proceed just to get our exclusive story. He believed we would be ethical and save the animals.'

Mac, Curly and Kim nodded at that conundrum; it was never tested because the crew found an innocent trainer chopped to pieces. The activist didn't question his own moral compass – just the media's.

'That's a fair point,' Mac muttered. 'But it's irrelevant now. The question is what do we do about your overnight guest? I've already sent the cops your email exchanges last night. They were content with Jo's advice for Julian to surrender. They have the IP addresses to trace if he uses that email account again. They'll be mightily pissed off if they find out the messages were bullshit.'

Silence descended on the group. They had valuable information on the murder suspect, but how could they use it without compromising a key member of their team. Jo finally asked the question which weighed heaviest on her.

'Will I go to prison?'

Mac shrugged. 'You could be charged – if we tell the cops.'

'If?' Kim asked. 'Do we have a choice?'

'We do – at this stage.' Mac looked around the room. 'Who else knows about Julian's visit?'

'Us four,' Kim said. 'And Julian. I don't think he'll share that information.'

'Exactly. We keep this to ourselves if we're going to protect our loose cannon. If, as Jo believes, Julian is innocent, the police might be willing to forget about your *kindness*. That's if they ever found out.' Mac looked pointedly at Kim who squirmed.

Curly picked up the theme. 'Time to reinforce the Chinese wall with your new boyfriend. It's one of the difficulties of the job when relationships get involved. You must control what information flows back and forth. In this case – nothing for Nathan from inside *Spotlight*. Including Julian's change of appearance.'

Kim glared at Jo, then sighed. 'I understand. We're both so busy that we're not likely to see each other for a few days. That means I won't have to lie – directly – or by omission. Hopefully they'll find another suspect. But the new look for Julian is important information. They could be wasting a lot of resources looking for a long-haired op shop refugee.'

Mac nodded. 'I'm sure the cops would have considered that Julian would dramatically alter his appearance. For now, it stays with us. We need to protect Jo.'

Another silence descended, broken only by Stephanie releasing a whoop as she replaced her phone. Then Kim's mobile rang; the number displayed was Dwayne Milligan from Steiglitz. She considered letting it go to voice mail, curious why her colleague was beckoning Mac and Curly to her desk as she scribbled notes. Jo used the distraction to escape to her computer, so Kim answered the iPhone.

'Hi Dwayne. What's happening at Tara? Any word on when Siobhan is going to arrive?'

'She's here now. And very grumpy.'

'Wow. That was a quick flight. No wonder she's tired, I guess.'

'She didn't come from Ireland, Kim. She was up the road in Ballarat. Apparently, she's been living there for about six months.'

'That's interesting. What's she been doing?'

'We don't know. But she's in a foul mood, that's for sure. She sacked me straight away. Said she's out of the dog business and told me to get out by Friday. Rene's okay because he can help with the canola crops and the sheep. Not me – I'm gone once the last two dogs are transferred to a new trainer.'

'I'm sorry to hear that Dwayne. I wonder why she's so stroppy? She can't be jet-lagged.'

'She's not rational. We told her that one of the old bookies – Chauncey Quayle – might be keen on buying the property. He came over yesterday without ringing. He wandered about the place, sizing everything up as if he would soon own it. But he didn't seem keen on the dogs or the kennels. When we told Mrs O'Leary about his inspection she flew into a rage. Told Rene to never let him set foot on Tara again.'

Kim weighed Dwayne's revelations as she watched Mac, Curly and Steph. They were excited about the results of Steph's research, although both producers were casting furtive glances towards Jo. Kim refocussed on her call. 'Is she certain that Conor left her Tara in his will? They've been separated for years.'

'They never divorced. Mrs O'Leary wouldn't surrender her rights to the property. I guess Conor didn't mind as long as she was on the other side of the world.'

That was a new part of the puzzle for Kim. 'What's so special about the land there? It's okay for sheep, crops and a few greyhounds. But I wouldn't expect it to make anyone rich.'

There was a pause.

'Rene reckons Mrs O'Leary has gold fever.'

'Gold? At Steiglitz? Didn't that run out at the end of the 19th century?' Kim enjoyed her history studies at secondary school and did several projects on Victoria's gold rush days. The Brisbane Ranges had been through several booms since the first discovery in the 1850s. Apart from a few weekend prospectors, everyone believed the last ounces from Steiglitz had long been turned into earrings and necklaces.

'Mrs O'Leary used to roam the farm, hills and old mines when they were still married. Rene says there's a legend that one of the original settlers discovered a rich gold vein when digging a well. Charles von Stieglitz didn't want diggers swarming over his land and the river, so he filled it up again. He made enough money from wool to retire in Ireland a few years later. We wondered if that's where she heard the story.'

Kim was momentarily lost for words. Gold fever could make people do strange things – including commit murder. She needed to talk to

Siobhan O'Leary urgently. Mac sat at his command post beside a dejected Jo. Kim swung her gaze to Stephanie who was talking animatedly with Curly. Kim feared she was being scooped. Not if she could get to the widow and learn more about the gold mine. Was it fact or fable? The news chopper was on standby and Kim knew she could be at Steiglitz early afternoon. The longest part of the journey would be navigating city traffic to the heliport.

'Dwayne, I need to interview Siobhan. I can get a chopper to Steiglitz. Is there somewhere I can land?'

'The dog zone is empty and there'd be room to land a chopper. But I don't know what Mrs O'Leary would say – or do. Maybe you should call her.'

Kim knew that wasn't a good idea. It's too easy to say no over the phone. She needed to take a chance to get face to face with Siobhan.

'How about I get in the air and we'll see what happens? Don't tell her you've spoken to me until we're a few minutes away. I'll say I needed aerial pictures of the property to portray the murder scene for our viewers. Once I'm on the ground Siobhan might be a bit friendlier with a camera around.'

The reporter had flown to Meredith three weeks ago and knew it was close to the former gold field: it would be Plan B for a landing. Kim was confident Jo could call someone at the pub and arrange a drive out to Tara if necessary. This story was taking another twist – gold was in the mix now. And what about Siobhan? Was an untapped gold mine on the farm a motive for dispatching an ex-husband?

'Listen for the Channel 5 chopper in about 90 minutes Dwayne, then tell Siobhan we want to land.'

Kim ended the call and hauled her handbag onto the desk. 'Mac, Jo,' she called over her shoulder as she swept a note pad, pens, phone and hair ties into the bag. 'I need the chopper ASAP. The widow's arrived in Steiglitz.'

There was no response. Kim turned to see the PA fleeing the office in tears.

'What's happened? Why's Jo upset?'

Mac stood, looked at the huddle around Stephanie's desk and beckoned Kim closer. 'Steph's got a source inside the police. Someone in forensics.'

Kim felt herself flush. Was it concern for her troubled colleague, or envy the new reporter was making an impression? Her voice remained neutral.

'What have they found?'

'The cops identified Julian's fingerprints on the starting boxes.'

Chapter 23

'No Mr Berry, for the tenth time the HLP has no comment to make about the police investigation. Nothing, nada, zip, zilch.' Kristin Webb doodled with a black pen on the blotter in front of her keyboard. The swirls became darker with every sweep of her hand. She was surprised Mike Berry from Channel 5 News bothered to call after his weekend hatchet job.

The reporter had been pushing for five minutes and wouldn't take the hints. Finally, Kristin's patience snapped. 'Look, you arrogant prick. You're not going to get anything from us ever again. Not after Sunday. Goodbye.'

Kristin slammed the phone into the cradle. That was one thing about old technology that mobiles couldn't match; an offensive caller knew they had been insulted by an abrupt hang-up. It made her smile, briefly, until she looked at the artistic creations inspired by Berry's call. What would a psychologist say about her dark mood? She stood; a herbal tea might improve her outlook before the next tinkle from the wretched device.

A clatter of paws on parquet flooring drew Kristin's attention. Molly, Mathison's pet greyhound, peeked around the door with doleful eyes. Could she sense Kristin's emotions? At least Molly was more aware than her owner. Kristin dropped to her knees and held her arms wide. The dog trotted into the embrace.

'Hello my darling. I'm glad you're here to brighten my day.' Molly showed her love with enough licks to bowl Kristin over in a fit of giggles. 'Okay, soppy girl. I love you too. But I can do without the slobber. If only your master was as sweet as you.'

'I think the days – or nights – of us sharing bodily fluids like that are long past.' Mathison smiled as he leaned against the door frame.

'Nice of you to finally show up to work,' Kristin rose, patted Molly and turned on the kettle. Tea would have to be the calming influence again. 'What have you been doing all day?'

'Stuff.' Mathison didn't move.

'Like what exactly?'

'Just stuff. Who decided I must account for every minute?' Mathison entered the room and perched on his desk.

Kristin was reaching boiling point faster than the billy. Too often she retreated from a confrontation with her co-founder and cohabitant. Not anymore. A frontal attack – verbally – wouldn't achieve much. Mathison had been evasive about his weekend. Kristin needed to trap him in a lie.

'This *stuff*, that has taken you until mid-afternoon to complete, did it involve your car?'

Mathison frowned. 'No, what makes you say that?'

'Your car is okay then?'

'The FIAT is fine. She runs like a dream.'

Kristin knew how vain Mathison was about his metallic grey 124 Spider. It was a highly inappropriate car for an animal rights activist and aspiring politician. They argued about it many times. Mathison claimed it was a freebie; a hand-me-down from his rich brother who drove a company-supplied BMW X7. The Spider was too flashy for Kristin. Plus, it was foreign. The carbon footprint it created was at odds with the values of the HLP. Kristin gave Mathison more line.

'Nothing wrong with the car then.' The kettle whistled. Kristin pulled one mug from the shelf above the sink and a single chamomile sachet from the box. She poured, then turned back to Mathison. 'Were you at the bank?'

Mathison's right eye twitched. 'No, I haven't been able to get to the bank yet.' He moved behind his desk and foraged through the loose papers. 'I'll do it in the morning,'.

Kristin dangled the tea bag in hot water. 'Tell me, Ryan. How much money did they raise at Horsham on Saturday?'

'I'm not sure.' He didn't look up. 'Marcus counted it and put it into an envelope. I'll double check at the bank.'

Kristin nodded as the chamomile aroma grew stronger. 'So, it could be hundreds of dollars in that envelope. Maybe thousands?' She was enjoying herself for the first time in days.

Papers continued to be shuffled between piles – and back again. 'Not that much. There weren't that many people. They're good folks in the Wimmera but a few hundred bucks is all we can expect.' Mathison looked up, a dash of defiance in his eyes. 'That amount isn't going to miss a day or two of bank interest.'

'No, $437.50 won't last long in the HLP coffers.'

Mathison blinked, then straightened and folded his arms. 'Okay, I'll bite. Where did you get that amount from?'

'It went into our bank account an hour ago.' Kristin's gaze was neutral as she dumped the tea bag in the bin.

Mathison clicked his middle finger and thumb. 'Damn. Did I leave the envelope with Marcus? I thought I had it in my overnight bag. I just hadn't checked properly.' The smugness returned. 'Well, that's one problem sorted. Are you going to get off my back now?'

Kristin blew on the tea. It wasn't that hot; it was more fun to keep the lying bastard simmering. 'Not quite, Ryan. Tell me, how many people did you see at the RSL club on Saturday night?'

'I've no idea,' Mathison raised his arms in frustration. 'There were dozens there, but not everyone in the RSL was part of the greyhound fundraiser.'

It was a safe answer. Bars would attract farmers and revellers from all around the Horsham district on Saturday night, especially if there was a top-of-the-table AFL game being broadcast. Her colleague was fudging. It was time to haul on the hook. 'I'm sure you made a speech. You always do, otherwise why would you go so far to forget to pick up an envelope full of cash? What did you tell them Ryan? How did you win hearts and minds and convince those folks to donate to our cause?' She sipped as droplets of sweat appeared an Mathison's brow. That was a first: he rarely allowed himself to be flustered. Would he come clean about missing the event – or lie again?

'I…I gave one of my usual speeches. You know, the greyhounds are a noble animal and shouldn't suffer because of greedy punters and callous owners. I was passionate, as always – they loved it.'

Kristin nodded, drank more tea and then placed the mug on her desk. Game over. 'That's bullshit Ryan.'

His mouth opened but no denial emerged.

'You didn't go to Horsham. I know.' Her voice rose. 'Marcus Denham rang me today asking where he could deposit the money.'

'I told you I must have forgotten it.'

'Denham said you weren't even there. He said you had car problems in Ballarat and couldn't get it fixed in time. Did you break down – or were you somewhere else? And think carefully before you lie again. I know your form when on party business. You raid the kitty for petrol money and always present invoices or receipts for accommodation, meals and even bloody chocolate bars as soon as you get back. Yet, this trip, there's been no requests for payment.'

Mathison wouldn't look at his colleague.

'You weren't in Horsham and you weren't home. Where were you Ryan…and what were you doing?'

Chapter 24

'Titles rolling. Twenty seconds to you Richard.'

The director's voice came through *Spotlight* presenter Richard Templeton's earpiece as the vision rolled on the monitor beside camera one. Two more cameras and televisions were spread around the studio. There was no sound. Templeton sat with his shoulders squared in a dark single-breasted jacket, white shirt and a blue tie. It was a typical uniform for a male TV current affairs presenter. A photo of the Melbourne business district filled the screen behind him.

'Five, four, three, two…cue.'

'Good evening. Thanks for joining us on Melbourne Spotlight for more exclusive developments in the Conor O'Leary murder investigation.'

The words on the autocue rolled in sync with Templeton's tempo. His delivery was authoritative and compelling; the exclusive pitch enough to prevent viewers changing channels.

'The main police suspect, Julian Oliver, reached out to Spotlight today to declare his innocence. The expat Kiwi sent an email to our editorial team, insisting he had nothing to do with the death of the greyhound trainer.

'We know that message was authentic – but new developments raise questions about the veracity of his denial. We have learned that Julian Oliver's fingerprints were found on the starting boxes where O'Leary's body was found.'

Templeton glanced at the script on his desk. It wasn't necessary, everything he needed was on the screens in front of every camera. But it gave viewers a few moments to understand the significance of what he said. Had the suspect been snookered? Did *Spotlight's* new evidence make a mockery of his innocence claims?

> 'Stephanie Grant will take us through those developments shortly. First, there was more drama at Steiglitz this afternoon. A gun was pointed at reporter Kim Prescott and cameraman Dugal Cameron when the Channel 5 helicopter tried to land at Tara – the farm where Conor O'Leary was butchered.

The presenter expertly transitioned to camera two which revealed an inset picture of Kim under lights beside the helicopter.

> 'Kim joins us live from our base at Tullamarine. Kim – we're glad to see you and Dugal are safe. Can you tell us who pointed the gun at you? And why?'

The reporter wore a dark green jacket with the Channel 5 logo and program name. A few strands of hair flicked across her face in the strong breeze despite her ponytail. She was poised and confident, no signs of being rattled by the gun confrontation.

> 'I can answer the first question Richard, but we're still unsure why we were threatened by a double-barrelled shotgun.'
>
> 'That must have been a terrifying experience?'
>
> 'It was Richard. We're grateful Frank Wilson – our RAAF-trained pilot – reacted so swiftly to get us out of range.'

The vision cut to the helicopter point-of-view of a smooth descent as Kim continued her commentary.

> 'We were told it was safe to land near the kennels as most of the dogs have been transferred to other trainers. The chopper was about 15-metres from the ground when Dugal Cameron spotted a woman running from the main house armed with the shotgun. We presumed it was loaded.'

Dugal was on the side of the craft facing the angry woman. It was a testament to his professionalism that the framing barely moved as the danger approached. His voice, recorded on the camera microphone, betrayed his fear.

'Gun! Gun! Gun! Get the fuck out of here Frank.'

Kim resumed the dialogue as the vision swirled for 15 seconds before stabilising on a long shot of the woman. She was stationary near the kennels, still pointing the gun. Again, Dugal's voice added a dash of drama.

'Are you sure we're out of range here?'

'The woman holding the weapon is Siobhan O'Leary, the widow of the victim. They separated more than six years ago when Mrs O'Leary returned to live in Ireland. We were told she arrived at Tara earlier today – a hurried trip around the world, or so we thought. We wanted to talk about her husband and if she knew of threats to kill him. According to our sources, the couple never divorced. We don't know why she was so agitated about talking to the media, but it wasn't safe to stay.'

The director returned to a single shot of Kim at the helicopter base as images of a dry paddock and buildings were boring. The chopper had been crabbing away in case the woman made another dash towards them.

'We landed in nearby Meredith and alerted police. We made further inquiries and found that Siobhan O'Leary didn't fly back from Ireland for the funeral of her husband. She returned about six months ago and has been living not far away in Ballarat. She arrived today to take over management of the farm. Her first decision was to sack one of the two workers – the man mainly responsible for the greyhounds.'

It was the perfect time to inject Templeton back into the report. The director cut to two inset boxes.

'Kim, have you been able to find out what Mrs O'Leary has been doing for the past few months?'

'Residents haven't seen her around Tara, Steiglitz or Meredith.

However, Mrs O'Leary is reported to be obsessed by the region's gold history. Our informants say she spent many years searching the creeks and old mines. Steiglitz has seen several gold booms since the 1850s, the last mine didn't close until 1941. Many believe there is still gold to be found.'

'I believe there is a legend about a lost mine with huge amounts of gold?'

'Yes Richard. The story goes that one of the first settlers discovered a gold reef while digging a well. He didn't want hordes of miners on his grazing land – so he filled it in again. He retired to Ireland a few years later.'

'And what does folklore say about the mine's location?'

'It's believed to be on Tara – the O'Leary's property.'

The director didn't need the producer to tell him it was the perfect point to wrap up the live cross. Everyone watching the program understood the police had a new suspect to investigate. Gold was responsible for too many murders to count.

'That's Kim Prescott at Tullamarine. Police are investigating the threat to our crew and we will update you tomorrow. But now – the latest on the first suspect in the death of Conor O'Leary. Here's Stephanie Grant.'

One switch plunged the ad hoc TV set at Tullamarine into darkness. Dugal and the live truck technician set about coiling power leads and packing equipment away as swiftly as possible. A few spots of rain fell as Kim finished her cross; that was enough incentive to hurry. Not only was all the camera and lighting gear expensive, it's an awful job when wet. The senior camera operator paused momentarily to check his phone for a text from Withers.

Good job mate. You can change your undies now! You owe a slab of beer for swearing on air. Haha.

Dugal chuckled and looped another length of cord as Kim approached. She held up her fingernails. 'Can you believe I just got a text from my manicurist?'

Dugal frowned. 'What did she say? Shoot back at the crazy woman next time? We don't have a gunship – it's a news chopper for goodness sake.' He looped more cable.

'She saw my nails holding the microphone and scolded me for missing last weekend's appointment. She says they weren't presentable enough for live television.'

Dugal looked at the offending digits. 'Who looks at bloody fingernails when you're talking about getting shot out of the sky?'

Kim laughed. 'Oh, you don't know Madelaine. She can spot a chipped nail from 20 metres. I've been going every week since I left university; one of my little indulgences. Now that I'm appearing on camera, I've been bumped up to *celebrity* status at the salon. I get all the gushing attention of being a *TV star* – but no discount.'

Dugal shrugged and walked over to dismantle a light stand. Kim's mobile vibrated again. This time it was Nathan Potter. It made her hesitate – was he Nathan the potential boyfriend, or Nathan the homicide detective?

The last bars of the *Spotlight* theme had barely finished when Curly Rogers and Stephanie Grant walked into the office, deep in conversation. He was the supervising producer in the control room; the fill-in reporter was using every opportunity to learn more about the program production. Richard Templeton followed them 15 seconds later with a warm cloth in hand to remove studio make-up.

Mac clapped his hands as he stood at his command post. 'Another great show guys. I love it when we scoop Seven and Nine. I bet some hard questions are being asked over in Docklands right now.'

His three team members modestly nodded their heads. They perched against computer desks as Mac continued.

'Nice ad lib Boss about Julian being the 'first' suspect. From what we're learning about the nutty widow, the cops must take a closer look at her.' Mac listed the reasons on his fingers. 'She was secretly in the area, she hated her ex and a lost gold mine is a powerful incentive to claim sole ownership of the land.'

'Well done Kim for that nugget,' Curly said. 'She couldn't land at Steglitz, so who told her about the widow's gold obsession?'

'One of the farm boys,' Mac responded. 'It was revenge because Siobhan sacked him.'

'What are the cops doing about her threatening behaviour?' Stephanie asked. 'Was the gun loaded?'

'The workers say yes, the widow says no. By the time the cops arrived the shells were back in the box. Hard to prove they were ever in the chamber. Siobhan O'Leary claims she was defending her property from trespassers. The cops will caution her but won't prosecute unless we want to press the point.'

Mac looked at Templeton. 'We can chat about that tomorrow. I don't want it to become acceptable practice to point weapons at news crews. However, I don't think a court case will produce any winners.'

'Fair point Mac. I want our people to feel safe on the job. But that woman might already be heading for a world of trouble with the cops.' Templeton walked the half dozen steps to his office and dumped the cloth in a container left by the make-up woman. He poked his head back around the door and grinned. 'Andrew Hackett might appreciate us if we save some legal fees.'

Curly and Stephanie groaned at mention of the financial nemesis.

'When is The Hatchet back on deck?' Steph asked.

'Tomorrow morning. I've got a budget meeting with him at 10 o'clock.'

'Wonderful,' Mac turned for the kitchenette. 'Is there any beer and wine in the fridge – or do we have to make that last until Christmas?'

Chapter 25

Jo Trescowthick tugged a black beanie over her ears as she emerged from her apartment building. She tightened the belt on her thigh length woollen jacket to keep out the evening chill. The denims were the after-work favourites: faded, raggedy, totally comfortable. Jo wasn't trying for the Cold War spy look. She wanted warmth and a degree of anonymity.

She looked both ways along the street. No movement from any person or vehicles. Every parallel park was filled. She checked for silhouettes, or signs of movement in them. Reporters weren't the only media people with healthy appetites for paranoia. Jo had more reason than her office crew to be worried about covert police surveillance. None of them had slept with a murder suspect.

Jo turned left and walked towards Grant Street. It would take her up to St Kilda Road. Another left onto the main thoroughfare, 10 minutes brisk walking, a third left turn at the Flinders Street Railway Station before a right at the traffic lights into Elizabeth Street. It would take her about 25 minutes, depending on the pedestrian crossings. Plenty of time to ponder her new predicament.

The afternoon in the *Spotlight* office was another frantic blur. Stephanie's coup on the fingerprints was trumped by Kim's mid-air drama. The forensic evidence advanced the police case, but in television visuals it couldn't beat the near *shootout* at Steiglitz.

That wasn't her interpretation of the crazy woman with the shotgun. That was Mac and Curly talking up the dramatic components for the story promos. Jo couldn't eat lunch as her stomach would have rebelled instantly: too much acid. She wanted to pour a large white wine when she reached her apartment. One glass would have become two, before she knew it the bottle would be empty. Jo wouldn't have been in a fit state to complete her mission.

The pedestrian traffic multiplied as she approached the Arts Centre. Southbank would have been a preferable destination – a night of music and culture followed by a late supper at one of the many restaurants and bars along the Yarra River. Jo sighed; that was for ordinary folks, not women who consort with killers. *Alleged* killer. Well, not even that. The detectives *urgently* wanted to talk to Julian regarding their homicide inquiry.

Julian had vehemently denied on Monday night that he murdered the trainer. Jo believed him, mostly. Until that afternoon when Stephanie's police informant revealed Julian's fingerprints were found on the starting boxes – the murder scene. It was one thing for Julian to say he was at the property but wasn't involved in the killing. Now evidence contradicted that denial. What was she to believe?

The famous Young and Jackson Hotel beckoned Jo from across Flinders Street as she reached the station. A quick tipple to steady the nerves? Fortunately, the pedestrian crossing turned red. It would be a few minutes before she could yield to temptation. She continued the pathway to the left until Elizabeth Street.

Her destination was vague. She knew it was somewhere up that bustling road towards the Bourke Street mall. She spotted the café when shopping for new boots a fortnight ago. In fact, the Sunday after she met Julian. It was a chance observation really; Jo was bumped by a nerdy teenager as she admired a window display. The kid mumbled an apology and staggered away shielding his eyes from the daylight glare. Jo had turned to look at the pit the teen emerged from. It was filled with rows of computers and game players. Jo shuddered, grateful that it was a cafe she would *never* enter. Two weeks later she was outside, summoning the courage to cross the threshold. It was necessary, so she stepped inside.

The interior wasn't as grotty – or smelly – as she assumed. There were 30 terminals with headsets and controllers. Most seats were occupied, the screens a mixture of graphic violence. Dozens of bodies were being shot or mutilated with weapons that Jo had never seen before.

All eyes were glued to the visuals, not the petite woman trying to blend into the gloom. Jo scanned the five rows of players carefully. Two of the *Spotlight* editors were computer marvels; they spent hours gaming with friends around the world. Thankfully they chose another cybercafé; or preferred to waste aliens or win World War 3 from the comfort of their homes.

All Jo wanted was an anonymous computer to send a message. She could have used her iPad at home, or mobile phone. But were the cops monitoring them? Modern surveillance techniques were beyond her comprehension. Would Jo even merit scrutiny from the cops? Possibly, possibly not. She didn't want to risk further police inquiries into her contact with their murder suspect.

There were dozens more convenient terminals she could have used closer to home. They were in public areas, with security cameras and were well lit. If the police ever intercepted the message to Julian, they could perhaps trace it back to the source. She had seen that in the movies. The innocent sender was identified by cameras they never considered. Again, it might be paranoia fuelling her suspicions, but it was wiser not to take chances. That's what had brought her to the gamer den. There were probably cameras around the café, but Jo was hoping the murkiness might shield her.

The other advantage was indifference from the players. They were so focussed on their screens Donald Trump could have sat beside them and they wouldn't have noticed. Or cared.

Jo paid for an hour and located a terminal at the end of a row of five. No heads raised as she quietly sat and opened a web page. Within a few minutes she had created a new email address that carried no information which could identify the writer. Jo had a fresh digital persona as Spiro Chronis, a 46-year-old bus driver from Dandenong. The name was inspired by a Google search.

With the preliminaries out of the way, Jo was ready to communicate. That was the hard part – what to say to Julian? They arranged to stay in touch daily, when possible, via his own anonymous email. Jo had a code to include in the subject line. It would confirm her identity and ensure the message wasn't dumped in the spam bin.

Jo clicked compose and entered the subject line – All Blacks Forever! It baffled her; Jo was purely an Aussie Rules fan and had only a vague idea about the All Blacks. Were they a Kiwi rugby team, or the cricket side? Whatever, the code was the easy part. She sat for a minute, then her fingers attacked the keyboard with none of the emotion of a middle-aged male bus driver.

I don't know what to believe tonight. Here I am in a dingy cybercafé communicating with a man who insists he's not a killer. I can't write this from home because I don't know if my computer is being monitored – or hacked? – by the cops. I have to sneak out under the cover of darkness and find a place where nobody will remember me. No doubt there are cameras here, but I've had to skulk around and hide my face. That's not me. I've never done anything worse than get a few parking tickets. I'm not a criminal but I feel like I'm being forced to act like one.

You put me in this situation! I'm in danger of going to prison because I helped you. I believed your denials of involvement in murder. You were so passionate that I was convinced about your innocence. You admitted you were at the farm for a noble cause but denied knowledge of the dead trainer.

Why my change of heart? Did you watch Spotlight tonight – our story about your fingerprints being found on the starting traps at Steiglitz? The box that held the butchered remains of O'Leary had your prints all over it. How do you explain that? How could you touch those boxes and NOT know – or smell – there was a body inside? Or did you put it there? Were all your denials another con to get my help? Spin gullible Jo another smooth line of chat to get cash and back into my bed. Are you that low?
Have I misjudged you so badly?

I'm risking my freedom again by writing this message. I don't know why I'm even doing it. The police evidence against you is mounting. You must talk to them. If there is a valid reason for your prints being on the box convince them. And get me out of this mess. My nerves are frazzled, my colleagues are losing trust in me. I've lied to them and I don't want to continue doing that. They are putting their own careers in peril by trying to protect me. A lot of people are in danger because of what you have done. It's time to man up and do the decent thing.

Jo read through the message one more time. She should have told Julian to cease all communications. *No reply, please,* it would only drag her further into the crime that horrified Victorians. Murders were common enough not to shock many people. But not the case of the dead dog trainer. How often did men get their genitals turned to mince? Yet, Jo yearned to hear Julian's response. He wasn't a sexual sadist. Was there a valid reason for his prints being where they shouldn't be? She wanted answers as much as the police and the public.

Jo pressed send. Would Julian have to sneak into a similar café to read her message? It could be a day or more before she received a reply. If Julian answered. The latest revelation might cause him to vanish forever.

With the night's mission completed Jo closed her new email service, logged off and discreetly looked around the room. Wouldn't that have been freaky if Julian was a few rows away? Was he sitting at a terminal, waiting for her promised communication? Would he be embarrassed by the fingerprint revelation?

No heads lifted, no one paid Jo any attention; the other patrons were consumed by their cyber battles. Nevertheless, Jo tugged her beanie over her forehead and silently exited.

Day 136

The screw did its duty, another day in confinement scraped on the stone ledger. Just like the previous weeks and months. Her spirits had struggled in the 24 hours since the tormentor spoke. He called her a whore. This was her punishment. She was at the mercy of a madman. Listlessly she scratched at the wall. Sixteen days into May. Her birthday was another four months away. Could she find a way to escape before then? He was never going to let her go. She had to outsmart him.

The first two escape bids coincided with her monthly beatings. She tried the oldest trick – the fake body in the bed. It was doomed to failure as two thin blankets were never enough to imitate her body. The next attempt was an attack in the bathroom. He would have to investigate when he didn't find her in the cell. She stood on the vanity to lash out at his head as he entered. Unfortunately, he twigged that plan. She kicked at the first sign of movement – it was an arm. He latched onto a leg and tipped her onto the floor. That beating left her unconscious for at least an hour.

She needed a weapon next time. The sheep bone could be turned into a prison shiv. The stone floor under the bed could hide that diligent work. But what would happen once she left him lying in a pool of blood on the cellar floor? He still had the main line of defence. The guardians were still out there. He obviously didn't want to kill her. They would – instinctively.

Chapter 26

Dawyne Milligan's ute burbled in second gear as he cruised up the driveway to Henry Wright's property on the Geelong to Ballan road Wednesday afternoon. There was no need to make a dramatic entrance. That's what Rene would have urged if he was in the passenger seat. The offsider would have encouraged Milligan to hoon into the roundabout 50 metres away at full noise, then haul on the hand brake to stop them outside the main house.

The gravel drive was perfect for that larrikinism. And Wright was a good bloke; he loved a party and appreciated red-neck humour. The evidence was parked in front of the double garage attached to the house: a 2013 model Ford 150 with a Confederate flag on the rear window. The American Civil War standard wasn't politically correct, not that Wright cared. He enjoyed provoking people.

Despite Wright's reputation for a lark, Milligan decided it wasn't the day to be a clown in his driveway. The unemployed greyhound attendant urgently needed a job; he didn't want to piss off a potential boss. In fact, he was an hour early.

The departure from Tara had been expedited to Tuesday; the final exit, without pay, was a few minutes after Siobhan O'Leary threatened to shoot down the helicopter. There was no sign of Harding during the confrontation: he'd run as soon as Siobhan emerged from the house with the shotgun. Milligan was terrified but didn't bolt.

He felt responsible that Kim Prescott was flying into an unexpected shitstorm. Why would Tara's new owner object to a television interview? Surely, Siobhan wanted to generate publicity to help find Conor's killer?

Unfortunately, Milligan hadn't revealed the current affairs chopper was on its way until they could be seen approaching from the east. To be fair, it was mostly Siobhan's fault. He knocked on the front door to inform her of the imminent arrival, she yelled at him to go away. The chopper had swooped in and the fiasco unfolded.

Guns were a part of life on the farm. Conor had the shotgun for rabbits and pesky sulphur-crested cockatoos that raided his crops. The birds were protected in Victoria, not that Conor ever worried about being dobbed in. The nearest farmhouse was two kilometres away and their owners used the same deterrent for feathered raiders. There was a .22 rifle for injured sheep that needed to be euthanised. The air rifle was for fun when the lads wanted target practice with empty tins.

The television camera had flown to safer pastures by the time a livid Siobhan confronted Milligan with the shotgun still in hand.

'Who was in that helicopter?' Siobhan bellowed. 'What do they want on my farm? They'll not get anything from me. It's all mine. I can do what I want with it. It's there in Conor's will. It's mine, you hear, mine.'

Siobhan's eyes were wild, there was froth at the edges of her mouth. The shotgun was still loaded.

Milligan's throat was dry. 'I tried to tell you Mrs O'Leary. It was a reporter from Channel 5 in Melbourne. They wanted to talk about Conor and what happened on the weekend.'

It wasn't wise to tell the agitated owner the reporter also wanted to ask about Siobhan's activities since the return from Ireland. And, most importantly, where Siobhan was on Saturday? Ballarat was 40 minutes away by car. Conor had known and trusted his killer. He had his back to them when he was bludgeoned.

'I don't have to talk to the media. I don't have to tell them anything. You've been doing enough prattling for all of us. I saw you on Sunday night.' Siobhan finally opened the breech and removed the shells.

Some of the tension seeped from Milligan until Siobhan spoke again.

'You're a nuisance. Pack your stuff and get out – now. I don't need you and I'm not going to pay you. You were Conor's dead weight with those damn dogs. Be gone and never show your face around here again.' Siobhan didn't move or pocket the cartridges.

That was enough incentive for the sacked worker to walk as steadily as jelly legs could carry him to the green ute. He was down the road towards Meredith and the pub before the shotgun was returned to the rack inside Conor's study. Now Mrs O'Leary's domain.

Harding joined him at the bar an hour later. Milligan's two-beers-only rule when driving was ignored; five full strength Carlton Draughts had been consumed. He only paid for the first pot. The rest were supplied by curious patrons who heard about the showdown between the chopper and the new boss at Tara. Harding was peeved when he saw the state of his mate; he would have to drive home to Geelong.

A more loquacious than normal Milligan used that journey to call Henry Wright and inquire about casual work. The timing was perfect as the whole district had seen the confrontation on television. The trainer wanted to hear all the gossip about Siobhan and her shotgun solutions. Wright chortled throughout the call and then told Milligan he could help with the dogs for the Ballarat meeting the next day. There might be regular work as the trainer admitted he was short-handed. His wife was *visiting* her parents in Brisbane and there was no return date.

The phone call cheered both occupants of the ute. There were prospects of employment for Milligan and Harding could still have a ride to work – the Wright kennels were only 10 kilometres from Tara.

'You can drop me off and pick me up – as long as Siobhan doesn't see you. She might use the rifle next time.'

Milligan's head wasn't as sore as it should have been on Wednesday afternoon, given the alcohol consumed at his farewell party. He attributed it to good vibes created by the chance of a job. Pink Floyd's *Dark Side of the Moon* was on the radio as he parked on bare ground across from the main house. It was one of his father's favourite bands; it would have been disrespectful to cut it short.

The song had just started; that left Milligan with two and half minutes to check out Wright's property. The rectangular sandstone house, with obligatory wrap-around veranda, almost blended into the flat, sun-bleached landscape. Neither Mr or Mrs Wright were gardeners, the only greenery within cooee was on the gum trees 100 metres away. The house was saved from obscurity by three rows of solar panels on the tin roof. Australia has baked in the sun for aeons; technology has finally given inhabitants a way to harness its power to stay cool. Air conditioning units were outside every window that Milligan could see.

The kennels were 150 metres to his left. Wright usually had 20 dogs in training, their accommodation was three quarters the size of the O'Leary set up. A timber wall with a single door faced the family home; Milligan presumed that was to reduce noise. The dogs could bark and howl into the boundary trees and the neighbours. The race day transport – a white Ford Transit with custom built cages – was parked outside. It faced the kennels; the rear doors were closed. A trailer with six cages was beside it. All was quiet: no sign of Wright, or that preparations for departure were underway.

The first race at Ballarat was a few minutes past six. There was plenty of time to load the dogs and drive the 50 minutes to the track for kennelling. That process would be the busiest part of the day; each greyhound had to be identified, weighed and checked by a vet before given a kennel to await their race. It had to be efficient as almost 100 dogs were processed in 45 minutes. The pressure stayed on throughout the event: the dogs were retrieved 20 minutes before their race, identified again, dressed in the rug corresponding to their box draw and prepared for a chance at glory. An extra pair of hands, like Milligan, could be a necessity for a trainer with a big team.

Pink Floyd segued into Creedance Clearwater Revival's *Proud Mary*; time to find the new boss. Milligan stepped out and walked to the right of the garage. Perhaps the trainer was working a pup elsewhere on the property? It was sunny, but cool enough to give them a romp as the young ones wouldn't be going to the track.

Spread out in a line behind the garage were eight paddocks with the greyhound training run in between.

Two rusty starting boxes made that obvious. The fields were about an acre each, all fenced and as dry and flat as the rest of the property. They looked more like a housing subdivision awaiting construction crews. Was that Wright's retirement fund? In the distance was a forest that was growing closer to being brought back to earth. There were thousands of trees, but Milligan couldn't identify them. They might be pines, but Milligan didn't care. Farming was not in his DNA.

No dogs were on the run and there was no sign of Wright, although a wheelbarrow stood close to the practice boxes. Maybe Wright had been doing repair work? Milligan continued his exploration around the family home.

Behind the garage were three water tanks, each holding 30,000 litres; Wright was an optimist. He tapped one, the hollow boom confirmed the dry summer. Next was a blue perspex wall that ran for about 20 metres. It was weathered by the sun; in several places the plastic had fractured which allowed Milligan a view inside. There was a pool and a covered outdoor entertainment area, complete with six burner gas barbecue and an equal number of loungers.

Wright was regarded as a generous host. Milligan heard a rumour about pool parties where swimming togs weren't required. The attendant was at least a generation younger than the trainer and had never been invited to verify those stories. It wasn't a party day; no steaks or sausages were sizzling and there were no naked bodies in the pool.

Milligan walked all the way around to the front door and knocked. Several windows were open, but no sounds emerged, not even a radio or television. The Wright children had left home in the last two years. One boy was studying law at Melbourne University, the other was backpacking through Asia. Wright had regularly shared his disappointment in the lads over post-race beers; neither showed interest in the farm or greyhounds. Milligan knocked again and waited, too polite to test if the front door was unlocked. It probably was, but his mother raised him to never enter a home uninvited. A third, louder knock produced the same response – nothing.

The vehicles indicated that Wright was on the property. It was unlikely he had gone to visit a neighbour; no one was close enough to walk. He could only be in the kennels. Perhaps the dogs were making such a racket that Wright never heard the V6 enter his drive? Dust clouds swirled above Milligan's boots as he ambled towards the timber building. It was in excellent condition; a fresh stain recently applied, the dogs shielded from winter south-westerlies off Bass Strait.

He heard the dogs from 45 metres. It made him stop and cock an ear. Greyhounds had been Milligan's life for the past six years; he knew their moods, the highs and lows, and the sounds of joy and pain from injury. The tone coming from the kennel sent a shiver down his spine. An inexperienced person might call it howling from several dogs. Milligan knew it wasn't the whole pack and it wasn't excitement at the approach of a stranger. It was a pitiful cry, mournful – harrowing.

Chapter 27

A wad of $20 notes was placed on the counter in front of Benedict Beacham at The Meadows track. Race four had been kind: $200 on the dog in box two at $3.20 for a place paid a handsome return. It followed a similar collect in race three. The punting gods were on his side. He slipped the money into a bulging wallet; grateful the TAB bookies didn't do their homework.

'Thanks Sheryl. I'll give the next one a miss but keep your terminal hot for me.'

Sheryl Kearney had seen thousands of winners and losers at The Meadows in her decade behind the counter. She knew the Dapper Pom was cannier than most.

'You keep up that winning streak Benedict and my boss might take *me* out of service.'

They laughed before Beacham gave a one finger salute and turned to scan the other punters, owners, trainers, handlers and unclassified attendees at the midweek meeting. Generous portions of comfort food at cheap prices attracted a few non-racing people.

Of the 90 people in the ground floor lounge, Beacham estimated that half would gamble on the tote. The mood was cheerful; the greyhounds provided a pleasant break from mundane routines for a few hours. Beacham smiled, it was a win for the club as they still made money either way.

Beacham limped to a tall table near the entrance to browse the form guide. His knee and thigh were sore from the old injury. Not much he could do about that. It was quieter in that corner, fewer distractions. Most activity was between the bar, cafe and the TAB counter. Race five was a Maiden and held no interest; seven and eight had a couple of possibilities.

He didn't need to confine his race selections to Broadmeadows. Televisions on every wall offered odds on meetings throughout Australia and New Zealand. Beacham loved to punt, and he had talent: he diligently studied breeding and form for every bet. The trainers were equally important in his selections; high rankings in the premiership indicated consistency and success. Not many good dogs went to average trainers. Or if they did, they never stayed long.

Dogs had been circled in black pen on his guide. Several had question-marks. A last-minute appraisal as they paraded past the grandstand to the starting boxes might tip Beacham in their favour. Often that gut instinct paid off for the canny Pom. That was another moniker he occasionally heard while collecting winnings. Beacham didn't mind; or being called the Dapper Pom. It was the name Benny, especially uttered in *Strine,* which irritated. Beacham didn't have an English Public School education, but standards had to be maintained. His mother christened him Benedict and he insisted on being called that since he started school.

Beacham looked up from his selections to see Chauncey Quayle shuffle into the lounge in an agitated state. The bookie's face was flushed, the tie askew and his shirt wasn't tucked in.

'Hello Chauncey. You're looking flustered there, old boy. Everything okay?'

Chauncey dropped his fedora on the table and retrieved a large handkerchief to wipe a sweaty brow. He waved half-heartedly, neither confirming nor denying there might be a problem, but didn't reply.

'Can I buy you a drink Chauncey? Something to settle you?' Beacham looked to the bar, hoping to catch the eye of Cliff. No luck, the manager had his back turned. Beacham pulled out a stool. 'Sit yourself down Chauncey and I'll fetch you a Bundy and Coke.' Everyone knew it was the bookie's favourite.

Chauncey nodded and finally found his voice. 'Thanks Benedict. Tell Cliffy to make it a single. I've got more driving to do today.'

A few strides took Beacham to the bar where he gave the drinks order – the Queensland golden rum for Chauncey and a mineral water for himself. He looked over his shoulder as the drinks were prepared. The older man shook his head and mopped his brow.

Within two minutes Beacham returned to the table where Chauncey was muttering.

'What a crazy bitch.' Chauncey looked up as Beacham approached. He accepted the drink, took a deep swallow. 'An absolutely crazy bitch.'

Beacham looked out the lounge windows that framed the track and smiled.

'I'm sure there's a few of them out there in this race, Chauncey. But somehow I suspect you're not talking about a greyhound.'

'You're right there, Benedict. The dogs are predictable – but not that mad woman at Tara.'

'Ah!' Beacham nodded. Everyone at the track had seen Siobhan's shotgun performance on television. But why would that rattle Chauncey so badly. Unless…

'You went to Tara today? Even after she pointed a double barrel shot gun at the TV crew.' Beacham struggled to hide a smirk. 'Maybe we should question your sanity as well?'

Chauncey dragged the hanky across his forehead one more time and tucked it into his coat pocket. The rum helped restore some of his traditional crustiness.

'The cops gave her a bollocking after the media changed their undies. I thought they'd take all the guns away for a cooling off period. She's obviously deranged. Why would they leave her with an arsenal to shoot innocent businessmen?'

Beacham shook his head and raised his mineral water to hide the broadening smile.

'You're a braver man than I Chauncey Quayle. You wouldn't have caught me within 10 miles of Steiglitz. I don't like guns – they're too dangerous. What happened? I'm sure you didn't arrive in a helicopter; did you ring ahead to announce your arrival? That would have been courteous for a recent widow.'

'I told Conor's young lads I would be out to pay my respects. They were supposed to tell Siobhan.'

Beacham placed his glass on the table and folded his arms. 'Slight problem there Chauncey. The word around the kennels today is that Siobhan gave Dwayne Milligan his marching orders, straight after chasing away the TV chopper. She blamed him for the intrusion. I don't know whether Rene stopped running after seeing the gun. He probably didn't go to work.'

'Christ. I walked into a minefield.' Chauncey finished the drink and waved the glass at the bar. This time Cliff was looking. He held up two fingers to indicate a double. The latest survivor of widow O'Leary gave a thumbs up.

'Neither of us were Conor's greatest fan, but I didn't even get a chance to offer condolences. She was on the front deck with the shotgun in hand by the time I got out of the Jag. Said I had 10 seconds to get back in and drive away before she started shooting. I opened my mouth – you know, just to tell her to point the gun away from me. The bloody bitch fired.'

'Shit!' Beacham looked the dishevelled bookie over once again. No blood. 'I presume it was a warning shot. What about the car?'

'No damage from what I could see. God knows where the shot went. I didn't hang around to let Siobhan improve her aim.' The barman delivered Chauncey's second drink.

'What was the important matter that required such a risk?'

Chauncey dropped his eyes to where both hands had a strangle hold on the glass. 'Oh. It was just a business proposition. I can't really talk about it.'

'Did you call the police? Have they arrested her?'

Chauncey's face turned sheepish. 'No. I…ah…um, I had an urgent meeting to go to.'

'More important than telling the police about getting shot at?'

'Aye, it was something that had to be done this morning. It couldn't wait. By the time I sorted it I'd had a change of heart about the shooting. It was bloody scary. But now I think it might help Siobhan and me come to an – arrangement.'

Beacham was incredulous. He doubted the widow and bookie could ever form a partnership to run Tara. Not after she shot at the courting entrepreneur before the sales pitch. And what would the joint venture be? Tara was out of the greyhound game. Canola and sheep were the money spinners, but Siobhan knew that business. What could a pensioned bookmaker offer her – apart from capital?

Beacham considered the unlikely duo as the dogs in race five burst from their boxes. The only sound in the lounge was the commentator. No eyes were on the track – the television provided a close-up view of their winners. Half a minute later Beacham had an answer as the lead dog crossed the line.

The reporter at *Spotlight* was on the money.

'The gold!' Beacham's smile returned. 'You believe that legend about the lost gold mine! You want to be part of the search.'

'Keep your voice down Benedict!' Chauncey looked around the room. It wasn't necessary; punters had more tangible riches at their fingertips – the form guide for race six. 'Why shouldn't I get rich? The mine in the well at Tara isn't a myth – it's true. Been there billions of years. Steiglitz used to be one of Australia's richest quartz mining operations. Miners said there were more veins to explore, but landowners ran them off at gunpoint.

'I've had experts doing geological research for years; they're convinced the Brisbane Ranges is filled with gold. They reckon the veins stretch for miles – out towards Ballan and other areas that were never considered likely in the 19th century.

'Sinking shafts and developing mines cost money – and Siobhan doesn't have any.' Chauncey sat up straighter with a smug smile. 'The bitch shooting at me actually gives me more leverage now. I can dob her into the cops at any stage. Unless she sells me a slice of Tara.'

Beacham shook his head. It was the first time he had witnessed gold fever.

'Good luck with that quest Chauncey.' He retrieved his wallet and picked up the form guide. 'I'll try mining Sheryl's TAB terminal over there.'

Chauncey grunted. 'How much have you won?'

'Enough to keep the wolf away for another day.'

The bookie appraised the golden punter's newest bespoke suit.

'I'm sure no wolf – or debt collector – would have the temerity to knock on your door. You always have been a jammy beggar. C'mon. I've shared the gold story – how about a tip for the day.'

Beacham weighed the request, then nodded. 'There's not much more to plunder here at The Meadows. But I've heard that Henry Wright has a chaser that's been flying below the TAB's radar. It could pay a nice dividend in the first race at Ballarat tonight.'

Chapter 28

The forlorn howls turned to excited yelps when Dwayne Milligan opened the kennel door. The dogs were agitated, their routine was out of kilter. There were rows of ten cages against the front and back walls. All were full and the dogs were eager for Milligan's attention. He reached out to nuzzle a fawn bitch whose tongue sought him through the wire. The touch calmed her.

Wright had a reputation for treating his dogs well. A sweep in both directions confirmed that: every cage appeared to meet industry standards for size, construction and security. It was the same for the sleeping areas; they were all enclosed on three sides with plywood. There was ample water as well. Apart from being ruffled, the dogs were in excellent health. Milligan slowly walked the line of cages, holding fingers out for the dogs to sniff and be reassured. Where was their trainer? It was spooky.

There were sliding doors at either end of the caged dogs. Milligan chose to inspect the western side first. It led to a large room which was the heart of Wright's domain: stocks of kibble lined the wall along with all the accoutrements a racing kennel requires. A dual treadmill was in one corner. Two dogs could be safely exercised while Wright concentrated on other duties. A long bench against another wall served as an examination and treatment area. Racing dogs need regular assessments for soreness or muscle injuries. Milligan was impressed with the operation: Wright was a responsible and dedicated trainer, like Conor. He was keen to work for the man – if he could find him.

The door at the eastern end of the complex most likely led to an exercise and play enclosure. He couldn't imagine Wright being out there by himself while the dogs whimpered inside. Maybe the trainer was having a post-lunch nap? He was in his 50s and Milligan remembered his Dad loved an afternoon snooze on the weekends. Another glance towards the kettle, fridge and sink didn't reveal any plates or crumbs from a midday meal. He could have eaten at the house. Did the dogs sense something tasty on his breath and that set them off? Their meal-time was hours away, but it never stopped them trying to cadge an early treat.

The dogs were quieter, just the occasional bark for attention as he walked to the far end. Milligan hoped Wright was dozing in a lounger outside the door. The next option was a 600-metre walk to the forest at the end of the paddocks. That would be a long trudge with no guarantee of solving the mystery.

Milligan opened the door and stepped into the sunlight. He didn't find Wright, but he almost stepped into a grisly clue: a massive blood stain in the dirt. It was too much to have come from a dog. And there was no gutted carcass either.

Oddly, Milligan wasn't shocked. No bile surged into his throat, threatening to spill onto what was probably a crime scene. He was more curious; was that human tissue and gristle mixed with the gore? Has Henry Wright met the same fate as Conor O'Leary – chopped to pieces by a deranged animal rights activist?

Milligan wasn't worried that a chainsaw wielding lunatic might suddenly appear. The blood was spilled a few hours ago. He stayed close to the doorway and rubbed a hand over his mouth as he surveyed the rest of the enclosure. No arms, legs, torso or head were scattered about. To his right was a gate in the three-metre-high wire fence. It was open. Milligan noticed a deep groove in the gravel. He looked beyond the exit and saw the practice traps in the distance. And the wheelbarrow.

'Oh god.' There was no one to hear his despair.

Chapter 29

The aroma of onions and heart attacks wafted throughout the *Spotlight* office and edit suites as Mac, Curly, Jo, the camera crew and editors demolished their burgers with all the trimmings. Conversations were sparse, the main sounds were chomping and murmurs of pleasure. A lone greasy paper bag sat on the conference table. The two largest members of the dining party – Mac and Withers – alternated bites with yearning looks at Richard Templeton's lunch.

Kim knew the burger from *Spotlight's* favourite taxi depot café would be safe for a few more minutes. Templeton had shouted the working lunch so he could update the team on the budget meeting with The Hatchet. That thought, or the balsamic dressing, almost curdled Kim's stomach as she nibbled at her tuna salad. She hoped her arteries were grateful. They bloody should be – the burgers smelled *divine*.

Kim piously looked at Stephanie Grant who had become Curly's shadow in recent days. She was parked beside him at the table, eating a bagel with salmon and cream cheese. At least one member of the production might survive to claim their superannuation.

Mac finished his burger, licked his lips and reached for a stack of handy towels that Jo dumped on the table. He wiped his mouth and hands, scrunched the mucky paper into a ball and tried an over-the-shoulder shot for the bin near the door. It missed. Jo sighed but didn't shift her chariot.

The program producer checked a text message on his phone.

'Right, the boss is on his way down with termination notices for everyone who has been coveting his hamburger.'

A chorus of grunts greeted the predictable joke. More hands reached for paper towels and practiced their basketball three-pointers. None would attract interest from NBA scouts.

Jo was exasperated.

'Come on guys! Who's going to clean that? Some of us had a proper upbringing.' Jo rolled her chair over to the bin, slam dunked her paper ball and raised her arms in triumph.

All male heads turned towards Dugal Cameron who was still eating. Foolishly he had taken the seat closest to the waste pile. He looked around the table and then at the missed points. He shook his head and dutifully cleaned the mess.

'Good lad, Dugal. You'll make a fine wife for a pretty wee lass one day.'

The senior camera op playfully took a swipe at Mac's head before reclaiming his seat.

'Richard is really on his way down. Before he decides that my hunger is greater than his, where are we at with our stories? Kim?'

The reporter should have joined the males in a cardiac binge as that would have been the highlight. She was running out of exclusives after three days of leading the media pack. That made her nervous; Stephanie had been working the phone hard all morning. Her contacts were full of information while Kim's was giving her the cold shoulder. Especially after the Tuesday night report about Julian Oliver's fingerprints being found on the starting boxes at Steiglitz. Detective Sergeant Nathan Potter wasn't happy.

'My source hasn't been able to provide anything new.' She glanced at Stephanie again. 'The police were miffed that we ran the fingerprints story. They're shutting me down. I have some other calls to make, but I don't have any fresh angles – at this stage.'

The phone conversation with Nathan after *Spotlight* the previous evening wasn't pleasant. He was wearing his police hat, demanding to know how *Spotlight* obtained the prints information. Kim knew that wasn't going to happen. Journalists never revealed their sources to police, or anyone else, including potential boyfriends. She didn't even offer Stephanie's name as the recipient of the police leak. Was it only Monday night that they were exchanging a goodnight kiss, or two, in his car outside her Richmond apartment?

Then Nathan had berated her about almost getting shot out of the sky. That's when Kim's temper peaked. He had no right to stop her from doing her job. How was Kim to know the dead trainer's wife was a nutter? Grieving widows are not renowned for pointing shotguns at helicopters. Kim then turned her anger on Nathan; she was amazed the country cops hadn't emptied the farmhouse of every gun or potential weapon.

The feisty exchange eventually reached a stalemate. Kim believed that Nathan was genuinely concerned about her safety. That was a positive. There was another – neither had cancelled their dinner date for Thursday. Perhaps they might be more civil then. That was tomorrow – right now Kim and *Spotlight* needed to advance the story. Her heart sank as Mac turned his attention to Stephanie.

'Steph. You've been chewing on the phone all morning. Anything new from your tame cop?'

Kim noticed the reporter smirk.

'I think we might have something. My guy says the lead detectives, Dowell and Potter, were very excited about an hour ago. He hopes to ferret out the information and let me know by three o'clock.'

Kim's face burned. Her police confidant had a new lead – and hadn't shared. Or was Steph trying to wind her up? Kim glared across the conference table but missed her target; Steph's eyes were on the arrival of Templeton.

'Hi guys. Sorry to keep you waiting – The Hatchet avoided me for hours.' Templeton scooped up the greasy paper bag, smelled it and sighed. 'Don't anyone tell my wife!'

'Has The Hatchet returned in typical fashion? Wants to slash all the news and current affairs budgets? Dump half the staff?' Mac asked.

Templeton put aside his burger. 'Basically – yes. He jumped back on his old hobby horse: our departments waste money, television is a business to keep shareholders happy – Yadayada.'

Withers groaned. 'Do we kiss goodbye to Friday drinks?'

'No. And no need to worry about retrenchments either. I saw the CEO last night. Reg is in good shape and the stents will make him stronger. The cardiologists agree it was a minor heart attack. If he takes his medications, lays off the booze and fatty food they estimate he's got another decade in the top job. That world cruise won't last long – Reg is itching to get back to work.'

Withers and Dugal exchanged smiles and high fives.

'Reg told me to give Hackett both barrels. So I did. I said *Spotlight* is Channel 5's flagship program; if he fucks it about, Reg will make sure the next crossbow bolt from a deranged daughter doesn't miss.'

That brought a round of applause.

Templeton held up a hand as he retrieved the lukewarm burger. 'I did have to make a concession. The chopper.'

All the road crew were horrified. Were they going back to Melbourne's incessant traffic delays?

'I said concession – not surrender.' Templeton looked at Kim and Dugal, then grinned. 'Hackett panicked after the gun woman. Not that he was worried about you two. It was the cost of losing the chopper. He checked our insurance policy this morning – hence my long delay. Our pay out wouldn't have covered the cost of a new bird. He wants to copy the other news networks – consolidating operations through a single supplier. If a chopper gets shot down the rental firm carries the cost.'

Most heads nodded at the economic justification.

'I said we don't care who provides or pays for the chopper – just make damn sure there's one available when we want it.' Templeton couldn't resist any longer, he bit into the greasy delight as the crew chattered about the merits of the new arrangement.

Kim's mobile vibrated on the table. It was from Dwayne, the sacked greyhound attendant at Steiglitz. She picked it up and left the noisy room.

'Hi Dwayne. How did you go with that new trainer?'

'He's dead.'

Kim steadied herself against a seat. 'Who's dead? Another trainer?'

'It's Henry Wright. I just found him at his farm – chopped and boxed like Conor.'

Chapter 30

Jo Trescowthick navigated her chair to the entrance of *Spotlight's* kitchenette and looked at the track back to her computer. Everyone was filming, reporting, editing, producing – apart from Mac. He was standing in the clearway, obstructing her, as he watched three news channels simultaneously. He was fair game; 10 toes could be crushed in one pass and no referee would call a foul. At times like this Jo wished she had decals made – like the old Spitfire pilots. The back of Jo's chair would be full of row-upon-row of toes.

Jo held her arms to the side for balance and advanced on the command post. Mac was oblivious to the danger as the news services wrapped their bulletins with updates from the scene of the latest murder.

'Excuse me, Mac.'

Mac jumped. He looked down at his co-pilot and accepted a chilled beer. He stepped forward and Jo glided smoothly around him and set her white wine on the desk. Mac pulled out his own seat and flopped into it.

'Cheers mate. Good to see you back in the game and smiling.'

They touched glass and bottle, waiting for their turn to dazzle the television audience. Mac took a generous slug, Jo sipped. The tension was seeping away. It was show time, nothing more she could do except watch – and wonder if Julian knew about the second victim. She couldn't imagine her runaway lover was responsible. Not that she believed he committed the first murder. The crimes were similar, but the circumstances were different.

The previous four hours had been frantic, everyone flying on the adrenalin buzz of a major story unfolding. It's even better when you're ahead of the opposition media. Two words had galvanised the production crew – 'who's dead?' Producers, presenter, reporters and camera ops swiftly surrounded the reporter. Kim had turned her mobile phone to speaker. The important information had been gleaned within seconds: a second trainer had been murdered near Ballan. Jo had grabbed a phone in one hand to alert the chopper pilot, the other clutched a pen to record the instructions that spewed out of Mac. Curly ran down the corridor to alert the news department; Dugal and Withers raced to their camera cars.

Experience taught Jo to follow several conversations at once. Mac was giving directions to the Live Truck; Kim deftly drained her source of information. It was one of Conor O'Leary's workers who stumbled upon the body. The death scene was almost the same: the victim chopped up – most likely with a chainsaw – and dumped in a greyhound starting box. This time there was no attempt to disguise the crime scene as live-baiting. That gave Jo a spark of hope: Julian wouldn't be responsible. She didn't fan that flame as there was too much work to do.

Once Kim ended the call, Jo's priority was to secure them a landing spot close to the trainer's property. Dwayne Milligan gave them an amazing head start on the story; he called Kim before the cops. A no-fly cordon would be established, but if the pilot was fast – and lucky – they might get pictures of the practice traps and kennels before the police were organised.

In that respect, Jo felt she had done her best work of the day. They were given permission to land on the property to the south of the dead trainer. The neighbour was a mate of Henry Wright. Jo assured Bazz Davidson that publicity would help catch the killer, so the friend was prepared to help.

Wright's farm had a belt of gum trees around the boundary, apart from a 20-metre section where the neighbours installed a gate 15 years ago. Bazz told the crew to land nearby; it provided the best view between the paddocks and there were no crops or sheep to worry about. Bazz didn't even grumble when Jo said a *small* live truck would follow the air crew. His reward for being a good bloke would arrive in a few days: Jo would dispatch a courier with a bottle of Laphroaig as Bazz admitted he was partial to a smoky, single malt Scotch. Jo took another contented sip of her wine and sat back to watch the weather segment.

In Ballan, news reporter Mike Berry handed Kim Prescott the microphone and accepted the headphones in return. They were trading roles from reporter to floor manager. Berry had completed his two live crosses and packaged report from the scene. They went well, no other news service had the forensic scene as their backdrop for the live shots. The camera crew remained the same: Dugal and Withers adjusted their framing as the newsman was 10 cm taller than Kim and 20 kilograms heavier.

The lights didn't need to be moved, although Farmer Bazz was on standby to shift anything required. He was enjoying the media presence. It was fascinating to see what happened behind the scenes in television and it was rewarding. When the other news services called, seeking landing rights, the Channel 5 reporters offered him $500 for exclusive use of the paddock. Bazz was sorry to lose a neighbour and mate, but he wasn't going to turn down easy money the taxman would never know about.

'Three minutes, Kim,' Berry called. He was beside Dugal.

Studio directions still came to Kim via her earpiece; the impromptu floor manager was a back-up in case the live shot turned to custard. Sod's Law made frequent live television appearances. Kim took a deep breath to the count of four, held it and then released it to the same tempo. It always settled last-minute butterflies. The whole production crew's efforts for that afternoon were about to be visualised for an expectant television audience: Kim's job was to ensure it was informative, fluent and seamless.

Milligan's tip off literally gave *Spotlight* a flying start, but it also posed a complication. The police might check the body finder's phone log if the media arrived soon after the first responders. Kim told him to wait 10 minutes before calling the cops. He was to sound *panicked,* then to hang up immediately after providing the crime and location details. Kim knew from her own experiences with two bodies that the police controller would want to keep Milligan on the line: he was a potential suspect. By breaking the connection, Milligan could call Channel 5 again and *then* provide the news tip. They agreed the first call could be explained to police as an apology from Milligan for the mid-air drama at Tara the day before.

The off-air monitor on the ground in front of Dugal's camera showed the graphics for tomorrow's temperatures.

'Two minutes,' Berry called out, a fraction later than Curly Rogers in her earpiece. There was no sound from the monitor; the pictures would chart the countdown: final forecasts, Channel 5 news wrap, *Spotlight* titles, Templeton's introduction. It was always a challenge for a current affairs program to follow a news service: any major story was devoured like vultures by their colleagues. Mac was forced to compromise with his news colleagues to keep their exclusive element.

Channel 5 News used the chopper aerials taken on the approach to Ballan. The pictures showed the farm, house, kennels, forest and two police cars flanking the boxes at the top of a long run. The pilot managed one circuit before a uniformed officer on the ground waved him away. The next media choppers were an hour behind; they never got that close.

Spotlight needed to progress the story to keep viewers. Fortunately, Kim had the essential ingredient that would stall the remote-control twitch – an interview with the man who found the victim. Dwayne Milligan stood out of camera frame, waiting his cue from Mike Berry to move onto the farm paddock set. Kim gave him a thumbs up. He didn't look as nervous as his TV debut on Sunday. Was that only three nights ago?

Good people skills are crucial for a reporter. They need to encourage shy, nervous, or terrified witnesses to share their stories. Kim was chuffed her handling of Dwayne since the brutal murder of his boss was paying dividends. He had called *Spotlight* before the cops about Wright's murder! When she asked him to walk to Bazz Davidson's property when the police cleared him, he was happy to comply. Milligan preferred to talk live with Kim than get mobbed by the media pack at the front gate. It was a win-win situation for reporter and body finder.

'One minute,' Berry called. The news was finished, *Spotlight's* titles were running. Next would be Richard Templeton's introduction. The 30 second cue was followed by another at 15, and then a countdown from 10. Everything was on track – and then Farmer Bazz moved.

The 65-year-old wasn't as nimble as he used to be: gout in his right foot caused him to hobble. He moved to his right to get a wider perspective of the upcoming interview and his lame leg almost ruined *Spotlight's* program. Bazz accidentally hooked a cable to one of two light stands and toppled it.

'Shit, bugger, damn, sorry,' Farmer Bazz wrestled with the blazing beast that had plunged half the set into darkness five seconds before the studio director cut to Ballan. There was an alternative. Ken Withers' camera was framed on a long shot of the forensic team working under their own stable lights in the next paddock. The audio was fine, so director and producer urged Kim to talk about the crime scene.

Withers was the closest to the novice staging hand. In two quick strides he clamped a hand over Bazz's mouth, then grabbed the light with the other. He wrenched it free from the chastened helper and rapidly turned the paddock back into a studio set. The cameraman shuffled the farmer to a position where he couldn't do any more damage.

To her credit Kim, although startled, quickly adjusted to the new sequence of coverage. There was only a momentary pause before she acknowledged the handover and change of pictures on the monitor at her feet.

'Thanks Richard. You're watching live pictures from a farm near Ballan. That is the homicide scene – a set of practice boxes used in training greyhounds for the track. Crime scene officers have been working since mid-afternoon following the discovery of a body inside one of the two boxes. It's a grim task, one that will continue throughout what is now a chilly night. We can tell you it's a homicide scene these officers are familiar with – they performed the same tasks four nights ago at Steiglitz. The murder scene for greyhound trainer Conor O'Leary.

'We know the identity of the victim but, out of respect, will withhold that information until all the family has been notified. What we can say is that he was a greyhound trainer.'

That was the point when full lighting returned. Kim waved Dwayne Milligan into his pre-arranged spot beside her right shoulder. Sod's Law had been thwarted – unless Farmer Bazz moved again. Kim continued as the director switched Dugal's camera to air.

'The reason we can be so certain about the identity is that we have the man who discovered the crime. Dwayne Milligan, who formerly worked for Conor O'Leary, was supposed to be starting a new job at the property. Instead, he stumbled into an horrific murder scene like my crew and I encountered on Saturday night.'

Withers had swung his camera during the transition to frame it on Milligan. It revealed a gaunt man whose orderly world of dogs and racing had gone through a massive upheaval.

'Thanks for joining us, Dwayne. Can you take us through what happened here today?'

Milligan raised his hangdog expression and shuffled his feet.

'It's unbelievable Kim, first Conor was butchered – now it's Hen…I mean, this other trainer. And the same thing was done to him. It was horrible…just horrible. Neither of them deserved that. They were good blokes.'

'How did you come to find the victim, Dwayne? The practice boxes are in the middle of a paddock – away from the house and kennels.'

The director cut to a single shot of Dwayne who was nodding, his eyes staring at the ground.

'It was spooky when I first arrived at about one. There was no one around, no sign of…um, the trainer. I got sacked yesterday and desperately need work. I knew the trainer and he said I could help with his dogs at Ballarat tonight. Like a trial to see if we all got on well. His truck was near the house and the transporter was over by the kennels – but there was no sign of him. I looked around the house and then walked over to the kennels.'

Milligan shuffled again; Kim nodded for him to continue.

'I could hear the dogs howling when I approached. It was pitiful, they were all in their cages, but they must have known what had happened. It was like they were crying. I patted a few of the skittish ones and – after finding no sign of the trainer – went out into the wired enclosure.'

The director stayed on a single shot of Milligan as Kim prompted him.

'What did you find out there Dwayne?'

'Blood. Lots of blood…and gristle. Too much blood for it to be a greyhound. And the flesh…and bone. It wasn't a dog – or two dogs – that were mutilated there. It had to be human.'

Millgan swallowed; obviously reliving a mental image of carnage that was being served up for dinner in Victorian homes.

'It looked like a crime scene Dwayne. But there was no body. What made you go to the practice traps? Was it the thought of what happened to your boss on the weekend? That this could have been the work of the same killer?'

'Yes. Exactly. I could see the boxes from the enclosure, a few hundred metres away. There was a gate in the fence. And that's when I saw the grooves in the dirt.'

'Grooves?'

'Tyre marks. Two or three of them overlapping. I could see a wheelbarrow by the boxes.'

'You guessed that was how the killer transported his victim?'

The director was back on a two shot of reporter and interviewee, catching each nod or reaction.

'You suspected that the victim was placed in a box, just like your boss. Yet, you bravely went to confirm that was the case.'

'I didn't want to seem like a panic merchant. It looked dodgy – I was sure something or someone had been killed – but in case Hen…I mean the trainer…just in case he'd slaughtered a deer or whatever and was dumping the carcass in his forest…I wanted to make sure. I didn't want to embarrass my new boss. You know.'

'So, you followed the trail?'

'Yes. Whatever was in the barrow must have been heavy. The grooves ran deep where the dirt was soft. Occasionally they went crooked. I saw blood as well. A few spots here and there.'

'And what did you find at the boxes? Were the starting lids or loading doors open?'

'No. Both were closed.'

'Was there more blood on the ground?'

'Yes. Not as much as at the kennels.'

'Which door did you open?'

'The rear door. It slides up.'

'What did you find?'

Milligan closed his eyes and grimaced.

'It was…the trainer. He was chopped to pieces. He's a big guy, like Conor was. There were body bits crammed in everywhere. It filled the box.'

Kim allowed a moment for that imagery to settle on her audience before asking the next question.

'How could you be sure it was the trainer?'

'I saw his face. The bastard cut his head off and put it in front of the body parts.'

In South Melbourne, Jo Trescowthick was disgusted.

'What a sick man. Sick, sick, sick.' She turned to Mac who glanced at his watch. Kim's interview had another 30 seconds to run; next was Stephanie's background story. That was a difficult task without the victim's name. The parallels with the murder at Tara made the job slightly easier: two dead trainers within 10 kilometres gave the reporter enough content to work with.

There was the animal activist theme to pursue as well. No connection had been made to the live-baiting foray on the weekend. However, *Spotlight* had a duty to at least raise the questions.

'Surely no one can believe Julian, or any activist, is behind these killings,' Jo said.

Mac laughed and tilted his head to swallow more beer. He was surprised to find the bottle empty.

'I don't know if there are any Hound Liberation Party members left to claim the credit.' Mac dumped the empty in the bin. 'The news boys rang their communications guru this afternoon for a comment. Kristin

Webb gave them a verbal spray. She claimed the media had destroyed her party and any hope to bring down the greyhound racing industry. Dogs would be injured and killed by the thousands. If they weren't motivated to kill trainers before – they certainly are now. And maybe a few journos.'

Mac paused as Richard Templeton segued from the live shot to the feature on death stalking the dog business. He previewed the story in an edit suite and didn't need to watch again. He turned to his PA pal who hadn't crushed a toe all afternoon.

'As for what this means for your AWOL lover. Well, we might think he's innocent, but the police could still have a different opinion.'

Jo was mortified. The brutal second killing had secretly fanned her hopes detectives would turn their attention to someone else.

'But there's no animal rights connection here. It's a crazed killer who happens to be targeting greyhound trainers. I know that's not Julian.'

Mac held his arms up. 'I have to play devil's advocate here Jo – and look at it from the cop's perspective. They have a suspect on the run. There's a second murder – another greyhound trainer. They were both killed in the same fashion. There's still no sign of the first suspect.'

Mac paused to allow Jo to comprehend the official view. 'We know Julian was at the first crime scene, which doesn't help his case.'

Jo's mood was plummeting. Toes were being endangered.

'However, if your lover boy has an alibi for today – well, then he might be able to divert attention from himself.'

The PA's spirits spiked a few degrees. 'That's the key – Julian needs to prove he was nowhere near Ballan.'

'Yep. Julian must come in from the cold. Now, I know you're not a journalist young Josephine Trescowthick.'

That made her cringe. No one dared use her full name at home – let alone work. Mac continued, unaware how close to being crippled he might come in the following days.

'As you're surrounded by scribes every day, I'm sure you've picked up some of our more dubious habits.'

'As in being obnoxious?'

'Not quite. I meant our sneakiness. It's ingrained from the day we pick up a notebook, microphone or camera. We're born to get what we want, by any means. At times, for ethical, moral, legal or safety reasons, we're ordered to sever all connections with suspicious people. Yet we disregard that advice because *we* know better.'

Jo remained mute.

Mac lowered his voice, although not another soul was in the main office. The editors watched the program from their booths.

'I'm sure you have a backdoor way to contact Julian. Perhaps a mobile number?'

Jo shook her head.

'An email?'

Jo nodded.

'Bingo!' Mac beamed and rolled his chair to her computer. 'Ignore the need for discretion. We're trying to solve a crime – and help ourselves. Open your private email account and let's make a heart-rending plea to get Julian to surrender. His alibi should get the cops chasing more evil villains.'

Jo was back on Cloud 9. Julian could save himself. Her fingers flew over the keyboard as she opened an email server.

'Oh, one other suggestion – get him to come to us first. We can record his alibi – and then drive him to police headquarters.'

Day 137

Hunger pangs were her only companions as she lay on the bed Wednesday evening. Breakfast and lunch never arrived. That happened a couple of times before, in the early days when she was punished for belligerence. The portions served were never large, which was probably for the best. The exercise options were limited in the former wine cellar; seven steps from end to end if she shortened her stride. Touch the wall, turn and start again. She instigated a training regime in the first week. It was to burn calories, keep her muscles toned and the mind active. Three times a day she would do the wall-walk for about 15 minutes. On the return, she would raise her knees to waist level to vary the routine. Those sessions would be followed by callisthenics, improvising to work as much of her body as possible. The weight continued to slide, but her mind and body stayed agile.

The jailer's absence was concerning. Had he been involved in an accident? Was he unconscious in a hospital bed, unable to tell anyone about his prisoner? Or worse, was he dead? His body mashed to pulp. It was a pleasing thought that a captive former nurse couldn't feel guilty about. It might also be her only chance of escape. He would be identified by his driver's licence. Would that bring investigators who could become rescuers? That's if they got past the dangers outside. She shivered at that ever-present threat.

Her stomach grumbled when the aroma of food drifted through the lower floor. It smelled like Pad Thai. More takeaways? Twice in less than a week. What had he been doing?

Chapter 31

Sexy Rexy patiently panted in the bedroom doorway as Kim Prescott slithered into black jeans. Was it her imagination, or did they feel a teensy bit tighter than normal? She looked at her most faithful companion.

'Does my butt look bigger this morning?'

Rex's ears twitched; saliva drooled from his tongue. But he would never stumble into that mine field.

'Oh Rexy, you're such a gentleman,' Kim gave him a pat as she searched the lounge for her keys and phone. 'I should have made that a small seafood pizza last night instead of a medium.' She zipped a yellow rain jacket over an old tee-shirt. The greyhound had taken his usual position at heel.

'And maybe I didn't need that second wine. You'll have to make me run it off before we go to work. Well, *I* go to work my darling. You would be most welcome – but no one would get anything done. They'd spend all day cuddling you.'

Kim clipped on a lead and let him guide her into a damp, cold Melbourne Thursday. She blamed the takeaway dinner on another late arrival home. The fridge was severely depleted after a week without time to shop: out-of-date eggs, wilting lettuce, manky mushrooms, soggy tomatoes and chilled wine were the only nutritional offerings. Maybe an omelette could be whipped up? If she could summon the energy after the drive back to Channel 5 and then a taxi home. There was no chopper to chauffeur the reporter back to the city; it had been seconded to cover a car-versus-truck crash on the Hume Highway. Fresh bodies took precedence in the news business.

The six-year-old former racer had been denied attention and exercise since the weekend murder. Kim could only spare him a half hour canter. The gardens were off the circuit: it would be down to the Yarra River, along Alexandra Parade, across the Church Street Bridge and back home to Richmond. Kim softly told him the foxes were tucked up for the day. Rex understood.

Kim didn't feel the same contentment as her four-legged running mate, even if they were compensating for dietary sins. Nathan texted before seven to cancel their date that evening. He blamed work pressure – two murders didn't leave time for a social life. The rain-check wasn't unexpected, especially after a brief and terse phone call from Nathan in DS Potter mode on Wednesday.

'How did you get to the crime scene so quickly?'

'Dwayne Milligan called me. Right after he reported the crime.'

'You flew over the scene soon after the first patrol cars arrived at the farm.'

'We were on our way to the helicopter base when Dwayne called.'

'And Mike Berry from news – he just happened to be in the crew car with you?'

'He was coming back from a story in the chopper.'

It was all true; Kim didn't need to admit the witness who found the body had spoken to her twice. It hadn't mollified the grumpy investigator.

'It doesn't look good Kim; you are miles ahead of your competitors I'm getting grief from Inspector Dowell. He accused me of being a snitch for Spotlight.'

'Well, we know that's not the case, don't we DS Potter.'

Frosty was the politest way to explain the conclusion to the call. Both had important jobs to focus on; personal relationships would have to wait. The early morning text indicated there would be no rapprochement for another day, at least. Perhaps they were doomed to never get beyond drinks, dinner and a few snogs? Kim increased the pace along Church Street. She would be a few minutes late to work, not that it would be a problem for Mac or Curly. She had already clocked more than a normal working week – and there were still two programs to fill. Kim would feed and water Rex, shower and call an Uber; still plenty of time to beat Stephanie Grant to another exclusive story.

Jo rolled to the command post with two coffees as Curly Rogers entered the office.

'Perfect!' Curly snaffled a mug. 'I missed my caffeine hit because the kids slept in. Threw the whole routine out.' He continued to his desk against the back wall.

Jo glared, but the lasers failed to fire; no holes burned through the cheeky sod. Mac was preoccupied with an online news service and snatched the second cup, unaware the coffee-addict was empty-handed. A volcanic eruption was approaching until Curly chuckled. He walked back with the fragrant coffee extended.

'Sorry Jo, it was too good a wind-up to miss.' The steaming elixir was returned, no blood was spilled.

'You guys live dangerously,' Jo breathed in the aroma and settled the mug out of reach of other reckless arrivals.

Mac was still absorbed in his computer as Curly looked around the room; Stephanie was already on the phone, but there was no sign of Kim.

Jo's radar was working. 'Kim texted – she's about 10 minutes away. Sexy Rexy needed a gallop this morning. The poor soul must be lonely with the hours she's working. Steph's pumping her police contact for a fresh update.' She watched the reporter scribble furiously. 'I think Steph is peeved that Kim keeps trumping her for the top story.'

Curly smirked. 'Competition is healthy in a newsroom. The tricky part is making sure it's productive rather than destructive. I think Kim and Steph are smart enough to keep their focus on the stories, rather than going for the jugular.'

Curly lowered his voice. 'They're both doing a brilliant job and Mac and I want to keep Steph after Pete Benson returns. You can never have enough hard-working reporters. Plus, Steph is keen to learn more production skills. That's a bonus as most want to stay solely on camera.'

Jo grinned mischievously. 'I wondered why she's been your shadow all week. And here I was about to start a rumour that she fancied you.'

Curly rubbed a hand over his smooth pate. 'I know we solar-powered sex machines are irresistible, but Mrs Rogers doesn't share.' That prompted the giggles, which distracted Mac from his reading.

'I hope that jollity is because you have uncovered our next exclusive.'

'Not yet Mac,' Curly said. 'Give us another hour and we'll have it gift-wrapped. What were you researching – who's going to smash the Magpies this week?'

Jo turned back to her computer as the producers exchanged barbs and fanciful predictions about their favourite AFL teams. It was irrelevant – it was going to be Richmond's year! She scrolled through another half dozen emails that arrived in between making the coffee and considering an assassin for the faux thief.

The messages contained nothing important: more PR companies pitching story ideas. She laughed at one *exclusive*. It was addressed to the chief of staff at a rival network. Rule 1: if you copy and paste media handouts, make sure to get the name of the recipient correct.

The coffee was ready for consumption. Jo took one sip, then two. She sighed and felt the energy course through her veins. It was empowering, encouraging her to check once again for the most important email – a reply from Julian. One hand typed, while the warm mug nuzzled her cheek. She almost spilled the precious contents when the inbox registered a new arrival.

'Mac! Julian's responded.' The subject line made her heart flutter. 'He's got the perfect alibi for yesterday's murder – he's in New Zealand!'

Chapter 32

It was a few minutes past nine at the Hound Liberation Party headquarters and the answering machine was full. The phone rang again, the beeps climbing towards 15 when messages should have been recorded. Dozens had been collected. The influx started during the television news the previous evening. There was no space left to record the membership cancellations, or the bitter rants.

Kristin Webb could have answered most calls. She sat at her desk, drinking herbal tea and twirling strands of hair that were getting more knotted by the minute. She could have picked up the handset, tried to persuade the faithless to ride out the storm. It was a media beat-up – the HLP was being unfairly maligned without evidence. It was all guilt by association.

Julian Oliver was the main police suspect. He was still on the run; therefore, he must be responsible for the latest crime. The calls were from *important* people; they couldn't be associated with an organisation that spawned brutal killers. It was the antithesis of their values and reasons for joining the campaign to save greyhounds.

Kristin knew it would be futile to argue with the callers. No words she could summon from a decade and a half as a communications whiz would save her dream. The membership had plummeted beneath the 500 threshold – the party was doomed.

More chamomile tea was consumed as the connection was severed by a frustrated caller. A few seconds later the phone beeped to continue the pattern. Kristin hadn't bothered to switch on her computer. It would only deliver more bad news – emails severing ties to the HLP. A few would probably demand refunds for the remaining months of their subscriptions.

The only silver lining, that Kristin could see, was that her grandmother's legacy was safe from creditors. The building belonged to her. She had resisted half a dozen attempts by Ryan Mathison to use the terrace as collateral for a loan. He wanted to increase campaign funds, showing no concerns for risks it posed to Kristin's inheritance and home. To Mathison it was there to feed parliamentary ambitions.

It would be her sanctuary. The front door was locked, as was the door from the back lane. Kristin had done a stocktake before tottering into the office; there was enough tea, milk, eggs, vegetables and wine to last a few days. She could ignore the incessant phone calls and doorbell until at least Saturday; maybe even Sunday. Hopefully the police and media would assume she had left town, just like Julian.

It pained Kristin to think of him. Julian had caused this catastrophe and he wasn't man enough to front up and take the consequences. How could she give her heart, or body, to a person like that? He was cunning and manipulative. She never wanted to see or hear from Julian again.

Kristin gave an ironic laugh as her thoughts shifted to Ryan Mathison. Another part-time lover who had betrayed her. And their cause. Male vanity and stupidity were the seeds of the HLP's destruction. At least he was no longer around to physically remind the party co-founder of foolish mistakes. His bedroom upstairs was empty. The fancy sports car was banished. Mathison was told to find his stupid partner in crime – and to rot in hell.

Chapter 33

Kim entered the *Spotlight* office to find Mac, Curly and Stephanie hovering around Jo and her computer. *Damn!* Would her tardiness cost her the lead story?

'Hey guys, sorry I'm a bit late. Sexy Rexy needed some love and attention.' Kim dumped her bag and noted Stephanie raise an eyebrow. 'My dog, Steph. What's happening?'

Mac beckoned the recent arrival. 'Read this.'

The men parted to allow their reporter to read the new scoop – an email from the suspect in a double homicide. Kim scanned Jo's computer screen.

Hi Jo

It shouldn't be good news to hear about a death, but in this case, I can't help but feel ecstatic. It proves I didn't do the murders. I'm in New Zealand!!!!!

If the crimes are the same – trainers chopped up with chainsaws and squeezed into the training boxes – it means it must be the same killer. And I'm 2000 kilometres away across the Tasman. I flew in from Brisbane last night, just before midnight. The police will have to take me off their suspect list and focus on the real killer – or killers.

Sorry I couldn't tell you that NZ was going to be my destination on Tuesday. I know you were incredibly kind and generous. But, as your email about my fingerprints indicated, your moods have swung wildly this week. I couldn't take the risk you might tell the cops I had flown back to Auckland.

I'm still a bit groggy from hitching to Brisbane and the late flight. I'll think about your suggestion to talk to the cops, but I'm not sure about getting the local police involved. They won't understand all the details and how this latest murder clears my name. They're more likely to lock me up until they talk to their Australian counterparts. I think I might lay low for a while longer. Does anyone at your work know about our backdoor link?

Julian

'Wow,' Kim straightened. 'When did it arrive?'

'Ten minutes ago,' Jo replied. 'Mac and I crafted a message after the program. We told Julian about the second murder and urged him to come in with an alibi.' Jo spread her arms wide. 'And there it is – he went home.'

It was just the three of them at the command post as Curly and Stephanie were at her desktop computer.

Mac scratched his beard. 'Apparently Julian slipped past border security and found enough money for a flight to the Shaky Isles.'

Jo was stunned. 'Apparently? You don't believe he's on the other side of the Tasman?'

Mac folded his arms.

'We have to be cautious Jo. It's an anonymous email account – it could have come from anywhere.'

Jo's shoulders slumped; her cheeks reddened. 'But ...'

'We want to believe him Jo, but we need evidence he's actually across the Ditch. Not sitting in a cybercafé in the city with a bunch of sweaty nerds.'

'He's right Jo,' Curly said. 'We need to question his claims until we get verification.' He pointed at Stephanie's computer. 'We've just checked the departures from Tullamarine yesterday. Air New Zealand had a direct flight at 6.35 which arrived in Auckland at 10 minutes past midnight. Qantas had a four o'clock flight via Sydney which arrived at 11.55. Even if he is in Auckland, either flight would have given Julian time to get to the airport from Ballan. We know it's not far.' Curly shrugged.

Kim saw the PA's eyes moisten and placed a hand on her shoulder. Then inspiration struck.

'The plane ticket!' Kim looked around all her colleagues. 'He must have a paper record from the flight. It would have the seat number, date and times. If we get him to show the ticket, that would help prove he caught the flight from Brisbane.'

That brought mixed reactions: approval to scepticism from Mac.

'How easy are they to forge?' Mac didn't wait for an answer. 'Whatever – we need Julian on camera today. He claims he was in New Zealand at the time of the second murder and that's the story. It's up to the police to confirm or disprove that.'

'It's too urgent for us to fly over,' Kim said. 'Should we get one of the local news crews to interview him? I can send them the questions.'

Curly vigorously shook his head. 'That's too risky. There are two main networks – TVNZ and TV 3. They could easily record an interview – if Julian agrees to front – and send it to us. However, they've been following the story closely. They would expect a quid pro quo – some juicy sound bites for their news programs. Even if we say no, the temptation would be too great to sit on the material until after we run it. Their bulletins are two hours ahead of us – there's too much risk that clips of Julian could be pirated and sent to 7, 9, 10, the ABC, SBS and anyone else who wants to spike our exclusive. Even the bloody radio stations could upload clips of Victoria's most wanted man on their websites before we went to air.'

Kim offered another option. 'What about a freelance camera crew? They could record it and send a file via the internet. No need to take it to a television station for a satellite transfer.'

Mac and Curly shook their heads. 'Even riskier. We don't know any crews over there. They could do the interview and flog it to everyone else for more than what we pay. They would burn any association with Channel 5, but it's probably the only time we would ever need them. I'd like to think most media crews are professional – but the temptation could be too much.'

Mac spun Jo's chair back to face her computer.

'Come on Tonto, we worked some magic last night. Let's create another email that will have Julian begging us to record his life story on Skype.' Mac turned to Kim as Jo opened the email server. 'Kimbo, get yourself set up at a terminal with a camera crew. Talk to Lachlan in editing about recording the New Zealand end of the conversation.'

Kim saw Stephanie pout. The temporary fill-in obviously hoped to get the story: she was first into the office. Mac continued to fire instructions.

'Curly, sit down with Kim and work out the questions. You're on standby if Julian gives us the thumbs up. Stephanie, I need you to call around the cops and get updates on both murders. What about your inside source? Has he got anything new on what happened to the body?'

'Sure thing Mac. The autopsy was scheduled for nine, my contact might have something by lunchtime.' She stalked back to her desk.

An hour later everything was in place for a chat with the murder accused. Stephanie had verified with Inspector Dowell that Julian Oliver was still their only suspect. Kim's texts to Nathan hadn't been answered. She toyed with an empty espresso cup and studied the questions prepared in collaboration with Curly.

They agreed to take a sceptical tone from the outset. They had to be objective; it was up to the accused to provide evidence of his innocence in their media court. They knew the passport wouldn't provide any verification. Both countries used electronic gates at airports: there wouldn't be a stamp as proof of arrival. All the data – and Julian's proof or ruination – would be on a server at New Zealand Immigration. The police could access it, but *Spotlight* didn't want to tip them off before recording an interview.

Kim's mobile distracted her. It was the greyhound handler who had lost two employers in less than a week.

'Hi Dwayne. Are you having any luck chasing some new work?'

'Not really Kim. I've got a few people who want me to catch their dogs at The Meadows on Saturday. It's $10 each race. But I need a guaranteed six to cover petrol money to the track and home. Eight and I might eat next week.'

'That's a bummer. Is there anything I can do to help? Maybe a story on the career of an attendant? Our viewer interest in the murders will wane by the weekend – unless there's an arrest. We'll want to keep the story simmering for a while longer; a backgrounder on track life might generate interest. Have a think about a trainer who is photogenic. He might offer you a job as a reward for good PR.'

The feature would assuage some of Kim's guilt about the live-bait escapade.

'That might be cool. I'm getting used to the camera now. Not that I want to keep appearing on your program talking about dead trainers.' That caused an embarrassed pause. 'I remembered something that might help your coverage. A photo.'

'One of those you sent on Monday?'

'Yeah. Do you remember the group shot – Conor beside Paddy? He was our champion chaser until a snake bit him.'

'Hang on a second. I've got it on my computer.' Kim clicked through her photo document folders and identified the image. 'Yep. It's the one with several people standing around the dog.'

Kim looked at the group shot with renewed interest. They had cropped the smiling face of Conor and discarded the rest. There was an attractive, tanned, happy dark-haired woman in her late 40s beside Conor – definitely not Siobhan – and a second man snuggled in tight beside her. She stopped on that face.

'Is that Henry Wright beside Conor and the woman?'

'Yep. Weird eh? Two dead trainers and a dead dog in the same picture.'

'That is a bit creepy. Who is the smiling woman? Mrs Wright?'

'No. That's Carolyn Beacham. She was married to the other guy on the far right of the picture.'

Kim's eyes took in the disgruntled gent. 'He doesn't look happy.'

Milligan laughed. 'No, he doesn't. I didn't take the picture. It must have been Rene playing around one night. It was taken at The Meadows, but I don't know anything more about it. The sad thing is that Conor, Paddy and Henry are all dead – and the woman has gone.'

'What do you mean by that?'

Another laugh. 'I don't think she's dead. She's a Pom who got sick of the Australia summer. Her husband – Benedict – he says it was the unrelenting heat. Reckons she was moaning about the nights where the temperature never dips below 35 degrees. She packed up and went home to England.'

'I can understand that. Sometimes I would rather be in chilly London in mid-January.'

'But there's something that doesn't add up for me. Take another look at the photo.'

Kim noted it might have been taken on a warm evening. Carolyn Beacham wore a sleeveless top. Her face, neck and arms were tanned.

'Mrs Beacham doesn't appear to have been hiding from the sun.'

'No, and I remember her and Conor once joke about how lucky they were to escape the brutal northern hemisphere winters.'

'Hmmmm. Maybe the marriage soured and that was her only option?'

'Could be. I don't think they divorced, although Benedict has another girlfriend. It's been such a shocking week; I guess the photo spooked me when I found it on my phone.'

Kim looked at the image again and noted the grim visage of the husband. He didn't look impressed as he stared at the cuddly threesome and the greyhound. But who was Benedict unhappy with – his wife, the trainers or all three? That uneasy feeling that Milligan talked about seeped through her bones as well.

A sudden movement at the command post caught her attention. Mac had leapt to his feet and was peering intently at Jo's screen. Did they have a reply from Julian?

'Dwayne, I have to go as I have an interview to record. I think you'll be very interested in the subject tonight.' Kim stood up and waved at Dugal who gave a thumbs up. 'Do me one more favour and talk to Rene about the photo – ask him when it was taken and where? What were the circumstances and anything else he might be able to add? It's made me curious, but it will have to go on the backburner for the moment.'

Kim checked the battery charge as she dumped the mobile on her desk. Mac's face was flushed.

'We're on. Julian Oliver is ready to talk to us and wants to prove his innocence.'

'How soon Mac?'

'Now. Julian says he's sitting in front of a computer in New Zealand and he's ready to go.'

Chapter 34

Victoria's most wanted suspect stood on the balcony of a fifth-floor apartment building in Auckland and enjoyed its most famous landmark – Rangitoto Island. The volcano sits majestically in the Hauraki Gulf, looming large over a steady stream of marine traffic and much of the city: an ever-present reminder of a violent geological past. Scientific consensus for the most recent eruption is about 600 years. Auckland's million citizens – scattered across 50 volcanoes on the isthmus – pray the next lava flow is well beyond that time frame.

Inside the sliding glass doors was a desktop computer, the screen opened to the Skype greeting: Welcome Miriam. The terminal, account and the luxury three-bedroom apartment were not his. Julian was once again reliant on the generosity of others. He was blessed with friends – old and new – and family who were prepared to help him evade arrest.

In this case help came from the paternal side – his father's sister. Julian had always been her favourite nephew. Miriam would never hear a bad word against Julian, even from her brother whom she regarded as a career-driven bully.

Julian glanced at the screen. No request yet for a conversation. He considered Jo's email for a Skype interview for about an hour, weighing the pros and cons. In the end he accepted a public appearance – from the safety of another country – might secure his freedom. Julian's only proviso was that the interview had to be within the next half hour. He implied that he would be on the move in case the New Zealand police were on his trail.

Once *Spotlight* agreed to that condition, Julian sent the details for Miriam's account. He knew all the passwords because he set up the email and internet for his aunt six years before. Julian was the only person to appear regularly on her Skype chats, until the wealthy widow stumbled upon an international dating site. Miriam was besieged by brazen lotharios and conmen: that called for another tutorial for the vivacious 60-year-old. Her latest dalliance had taken Miriam to the Gold Coast.

Julian had his own key and the security codes for Miriam's Tamaki Drive apartment. It was prime real estate without any of the ubiquitous Pohutakawa trees to block the world-class views. Beneath his sanctuary, a road and walkway snaked more than 10 kilometres along the waterfront. No strings of cafes, restaurants or bars were permitted to blight the seascape.

Multi-coloured yachts, former America's Cup boats, ferries and container ships churned through the waterway between the shore and Rangitoto. Windsurfers and paddle boarders hugged the coast. They were all familiar sights and Julian felt himself relaxing after the tension of the past six days. He leaned against the door frame; Miriam's apartment felt more homely than the family abode five kilometres away.

The sprawling Oliver mansion on the Remuera ridge had more generous views of the Gulf and 10 times the space. With Miriam, Julian was away from the disappointed looks and barbed comments of parents. He was the only son, yet he failed in his duty to follow in his father's entrepreneurial footsteps. The parental despair was a barrier that solidified with every new mishap. Consequently, Julian hadn't contacted them since his life in Melbourne imploded. They would be aware, but neither parents nor son had reached out.

The bubbling audio of an incoming Skype call broke Julian's nostalgic memories of sea kayak trips to the lava caves on Rangitoto. It was barely an hour away from the beach at Kohimarama – if you picked the right tides. Julian sat down at the desk. He saw Jo's colleague on the screen. He was amused as the reporter checked his dramatically altered appearance. Or did she remember him from the Wells Street apartment on Monday?

'Hi. I'm Kim Prescott from *Melbourne Spotlight*. Thanks for agreeing to record this interview. Before we get underway, can you confirm that you're Julian Oliver, currently wanted for questioning by Victorian police in connection with the deaths of two greyhound trainers?'

'Yes. I'm Julian Oliver – and let me say that I had nothing to do with any serious crimes in Melbourne. I admit I was at the O'Leary farm on Saturday night to cause mischief, but I had nothing to do with his murder. And I couldn't have killed that second trainer because I'm in New Zealand.'

'Where exactly?'

'Auckland. It's the private residence of…friends. They're overseas.'

'When did you arrive?'

'Last night, about midnight.'

'Given that we know you were in Melbourne on Tuesday morning, you obviously caught a plane. Where did you board it?'

'Brisbane.'

'Do you have any evidence of that?'

'I do, but I can't show you.'

'You're being pursued by police for two violent deaths – and yet you won't verify proof of your flight. Why not?'

'I…had to borrow the identity of…another friend. I can't jeopardise them by showing a passport or boarding pass with their name. I'm sorry, but that was the condition I agreed to. I'm always loyal.'

'Did you change your appearance to use a borrowed passport?'

Julian was peeved; but couldn't afford to show it on camera. The interview was more confrontational than he expected. Okay, he had committed passport fraud and maybe a few other minor crimes. They were necessary because he couldn't trust the Australian cops to be objective. They wanted a scalp and a Kiwi was an easy target. No matter what was said, Julian had to protect Rawdon.

They had been best mates since primary school. In those days, teachers dubbed them the terrible twins because of their similar appearance and naughty natures. Rawdon had readily agreed to help when contacted on Sunday, although Julian required an urgent dye job to match his friend's new Aussie look. The long pause saw Kim fill the gap.

'You say you're in Auckland, yet – looking at your camera feed – it could be any suburban living room. You could be in Fitzroy or Sandringham. You won't present proof of your flight – no boarding pass, no passport. So, why should Victorians believe your alibi for the second murder?'

'Proof? You want proof? Ok – look at this.'

Julian stood up and grasped the camera mounted on top of Miriam's computer. It was an eight-year-old model and didn't have an inbuilt lens. It had been velcroed to the top of the screen. He didn't care that the framing was chaotic. He stepped through the doorway and let the camera reveal the seafront.

'That's Rangitoto Island – you won't find that in Port Phillip Bay or Sydney Harbour.' The camera panned sharply to the right. 'That promontory is Achilles Point, named after one of the Kiwi boats that fought the *Graf Spee* at the start of World War Two.'

There were no warships, just a sandy beach, clay cliffs and multi-million-dollar houses with views to justify the prices. Julian continued the commentary as the camera drifted left. 'That grass-covered volcanic crater is Browns Island – which proves we Kiwis have a sense of humour.'

Julian's bitter tone didn't indicate any jocularity. 'You want more?' The camera did a whiz-pan across Rangitoto to a white, crab-like structure in the water. 'That is Bean Rock Light House. It's made of timber and has been keeping ships off the reef since 1871.' The camera shifted left again. 'That grassy dome is North head – again, no resemblance to anything in Sydney as it's much nicer. The city and bridge are further around the harbour. Unfortunately, the camera cable doesn't extend that far.'

It took another 10 seconds for the framing to stabilise and reveal a disgruntled Julian.

'Satisfied Ms Prescott? I think that confirms I'm in the middle of bloody Auckland.'

Julian was annoyed that his tourist tirade hadn't ruffled the reporter. She looked composed on her screen in Melbourne.

'We accept that you are in New Zealand. However – your arrival time wouldn't clear you of police suspicion in the case of the latest homicide.'

'What do you mean?' Julian was confused by the reporter's tone. She was supposed to be a friend of Jo's!

'We believe the police would be interested in two departures from Tullamarine yesterday afternoon – a Qantas flight via Sydney at four o'clock and a direct Air New Zealand flight at 6.35. Both landed about the same time as the Brisbane plane. It's suspected the trainer was killed in the morning. Ballan is roughly an hour from Melbourne Airport.' Kim allowed a dramatic pause. 'You must understand that, without proof of which flight you caught, the police would still be interested in you.'

Julian's shoulders sagged and his head slumped. To save himself would mean throwing his best mate to the wolves. Rawdon would be arrested, charged and quite possibly jailed. Border security since the Twin Towers on 9/11 was taken far more seriously. Rawdon was already on the Australian police radar after a bust for cocaine possession outside a night club. Another black mark could get him deported.

Kim interrupted thoughts of betrayal. 'Let's change tack for a moment Julian.'

He raised his eyes, fearful of where the reporter would take the interview. 'What do you mean?'

'Your fingerprints. Can you explain how police located them on the starting box where we found Conor O'Leary?'

Julian grimaced. That revelation had been a shock. He guessed how they got there – and when. To explain that would create more cause for Victorian cops to get their mates in Auckland to track him down. Aunt Miriam's refuge wouldn't be safe for much longer.

Kim prompted him. 'We understand that you denied being near the boxes on the weekend. That you didn't know the body…parts…had been crammed into the box'

'That's true. I had no idea he was inside. I didn't go near the boxes… on Saturday night.'

'I'll come back to my original question. How do you explain the prints getting there?'

Julian sighed and rubbed a hand across his sweaty neck. 'I'd been to the property before.'

'Before? Did you scout the track and homestead to plan your fake live-bait venture?'

'No.'

'When was your first visit – and what did you do?'

Julian believed Kim was wasted in the media. She should be leaning over a prosecutor's lectern at the Old Bailey in a horsehair wig and black silks. He didn't agree to record this interview to get grilled.

'I can't say. It has nothing to do with the death of that man and I don't have to tell you anything about it.'

Kim wasn't perturbed. 'Did your previous visit have anything to do with the spate of greyhound deaths at the O'Leary property from snake bites?'

'No! I wouldn't hurt any animal – or person.'

To scare greyhound people was another matter, and that's how Julian knew his fingerprints were left on the crime scene. The fire he started in the utility shed flushed out two snakes. The smallest reptile was slow; Julian scooped him into a hessian bag. The excitement and success of the arson attack provided fresh inspiration – he would dump the singed serpent in a starting box. He wanted to give the trainer a massive fright the next time he used the contraption. The handlers opened the sliding door at the back, so the dogs wouldn't be in danger. He never heard if that sneaky trick led to a hurried change of underwear at Tara. Kim brought Julian back to the present.

'Did you start the fire that burnt a shed to the ground and threatened the kennels and homestead?'

'No...comment.' That was stretching the truth, there was no danger of the fire getting out of control. That's why he held the hessian bag, until he heard a car on the gravel driveway. She was really winding him up.

'Well, then what logical explanation is there for forensics experts finding your prints on the crime scene?'

'I...think...I touched the boxes when I was looking around the property for evidence of live-baiting. I have no idea how long fingerprints can last.'

That left another flank exposed and Kim stabbed again.

'We both know the live-bait issue was a con, Julian. There has never been any live-baiting at Conor O'Leary's farm. You were setting up an innocent man – and our program. You either took live animals to the property – or caught the rabbits and possum there – with the intention of ruining the career of a respected and hard-working team. Why?'

Julian was flustered. His hand hovered over the icon to disconnect; the temptation was overpowering. Downward pressure and she was gone. She was in Australia; he was in New Zealand. Good luck trying to find him again after that kangaroo court. But still, there was the primal urge to defend himself now that *Spotlight* had drawn him out. If the cops tracked him down, he might never get another opportunity to tell his story properly. Julian turned to the Donald Trump media defence: attack and divert.

'We know the greyhound industry is rife with animal cruelty. They've been getting away with murdering dogs for years. Too slow or crippled to run anymore and they get a bullet in the head. Or it might be a hammer. Then they're chucked in a pit or left to rot for the scavengers. Greyhound racing must be banned. The governments won't do anything, so we had to take action. We couldn't let it go on. We had to take positive action to save those poor...'

Kim interrupted the harangue with a single word. 'We?'

Julian was confused. 'What do you mean?' Perspiration trickled from his brow.

'You keep saying *"We."* Was there someone else with you at the O'Leary property?'

Chapter 35

Across from the Edinburgh Gardens in North Fitzroy, Kristin Webb dipped her spoon into a bowl of hot courgette soup but didn't raise it. Instead, she pushed the contents around for a minute or more, wondering why she bothered to heat the remains of Wednesday's dinner. *Waste not, want not* sprang to mind when her eyes spotted a wall-mounted photo of Bessy. It was the proverb her depression-era raised grandmother often preached when Kristin visited as a child. She obediently sipped and continued, welcoming the extra pinch of nutmeg. Granny Bessy would have smiled.

The only co-founder of the Hound Liberation Party in residence methodically emptied the bowl. The phone had forced her out of the office into the kitchen down the hallway. Two closed doors helped block Alexander Graham Bell's contribution to communication. However, the terrace's design couldn't isolate Kristin from another intrusive instrument.

Dogged inquirers were able to defeat timber doors, brick walls and long halls with a finger and the doorbell. Granny Bessy was so deaf by her final years that Kristin's parents installed a booming ring tone and flashing light for the kitchen. It was occasionally still convenient for Kristin, until now. The latest visitor hadn't removed their digit from the button for more than three minutes.

Another 30 seconds passed as Kristin carried the empty bowl and spoon to the sink and rinsed them. The light flashed and the doorbell howled; it was connected to the mains and wouldn't run out of juice. The saucepan and a ladle went under the tap next. The visitor alert continued. Was five minutes of that unrelenting cacophony enough for justifiable homicide? Kristin slammed the pot into the sink, turned on her heels, wrenched the handle and marched to the front door, ready to deliver a tongue lashing.

If Granny Bessy had opted for a different portal, it might have saved Kristin from a final bout of public humiliation. Many terrace homes had glass panels in the front door, or beside it. They provided clues about the visitors. Encyclopaedia salesmen and debt collectors could be ignored in the 1960s while owners tiptoed back to the safety of the kitchen. But Bessy never saw the need to change the solid wooden rectangle that provided shelter and security to her family for more than a century. Consequently, Kristin's hissy fit fizzled as she opened the door to a blazing sun-gun, camera and microphone. That was when Stephanie released the doorbell.

'Ms Webb. Stephanie Grant from *Melbourne Spotlight*. We've learned that a second member of the Hound Liberation Party was on the property of greyhound trainer Conor O'Leary on Saturday – the night he was brutally murdered.'

Kristin groaned and threw up a hand to cover her face from the harsh light. Had the camera operator deliberately cranked up the luminance to blind her? Or was it a ploy to make the HLP spokeswoman look suspicious? Her anger ratcheted another notch; she was a veteran communications manager who had allowed herself to be ambushed – again!

That adrenalin burst gave Kristin the impetus to fight back. 'I don't know what you're talking about. You're slandering the HLP and its hard-working and loyal members. This is gutter journalism and I won't make any more comments.' Kristin backed into the hallway and tried to close the door. The reporter and her large cameraman eagerly filled the surrendered ground. The onslaught continued.

'You deny knowing that two members of your party went to Steiglitz to deliberately frame Mr O'Leary for live-baiting?'

Kristin pushed back against the door, but it wouldn't budge; someone had a foot against it.

'No! No! Get out, please!' Kristin should have left it at that plea. The television audience might have felt sympathetic; she was being bullied by the media. Foolishly, Kristin gave Stephanie another opportunity to hammer the HLP.

'I don't know where you get these wild ideas from.'

'One of your party members Ms Webb. One of the two men who planned the raid at Tara spoke to us today on camera. He told us what they planned – and what they did.'

The battle over the door subsided as Kristin's dismay disarmed her. Julian's gone underground; would the media find him before the police? Not likely. That left only her ex-house mate. Without thinking Kristin blurted his name.

'Ryan? What has Ryan been saying?'

Kristin's horror grew as she watched the *Spotlight* reporter's eyes widen. Stephanie Grant had been bluffing! The program set a trap for Kristin with their aggressive doorstop tactic – and she fell into it.

'I know that Ryan Mathison lives here at party headquarters. Is he inside now? Can he come out and explain his actions at Steiglitz?'

'No. No. He's…not here.'

'Does he know anything about what happened to Conor O'Leary?'

The questions continued, but Kristin couldn't process them anymore as tears welled. Her head sagged against the door, releasing thin waterfalls down her cheeks. That's when she felt the pressure against her safety barrier ease. Slowly she pushed, shutting out the people who sealed the fate of the Hound Liberation Party.

Ken Withers buttoned off and stepped back onto the footpath. Stephanie Grant grinned and handed him the wireless microphone. It was wiser to go in without cables on a doorstep ambush. There was less chance of camera operator and reporter getting tangled if the browbeating prompted a violent response.

'I feel a bit guilty about that,' Withers said. 'I've done a couple of freelance promos for Kristin before. She's a nice lady.' He placed the camera on the ground and stretched his arms and back. The camera was recording on his shoulder the whole time Stephanie had her finger on the bell. The plan was to drive the communications manager to the front door, or bonkers. The footage would show that Stephanie had done a superb job. The reporter's skin had been toughened by dozens of similar encounters.

'We had to get that second name. Julian cut the Skype connection to Kim without revealing his collaborator. Kristin Webb wasn't answering the phone. Emails were ignored. The same with texts. We had another potential breakthrough in the case and the ends justified the means.'

Stephanie pulled out her mobile and pressed the speed dial for *Spotlight*. 'Even if Kristin agreed to talk, there was no guarantee she would sacrifice the party by confirming there were two mavericks involved. We had to play hardball.'

A tram rumbled past as Mac's eager voice burst from the phone's speaker.

'Steph! How did it go? Did she give you the other name?'

'Yep. It's Ryan Mathison – her HLP co-founder and parliamentary candidate.'

Chapter 36

Julian's abrupt exit from the online interview had frustrated the *Spotlight* team. They stumbled on another tantalising thread of the O'Leary case, only to be isolated by geography. The suspect was across the Tasman Sea and – after Kim's inquisition – wouldn't respond to further Skype calls. Two emails from a grumpy Jo also failed to produce a response. They presumed Julian had already fled the bolthole. Then Stephanie suggested engineering a confrontation at the HLP.

Kim grabbed her notebook and jacket ready for a new skirmish; after all, it was her story. She could drive across the city and back to South Melbourne in time to package another blockbuster exclusive. Mac didn't agree.

'Hold your horses, Kim.' He turned to the other eager reporter. 'Steph – grab Kenny and scoot across to Brunswick Street. Get that second name.'

Kim was horrified to watch her colleague snatch her bag and disappear out the door in 10 seconds. She rounded on the program producer, eyes ablaze.

'It's my story Mac! How could you give it to her?'

Mac held up both arms to prevent a meltdown. 'It's still your lead Kim. But I need you here working on the bigger picture – not standing outside the HLP for half the afternoon trying to get a comment. The party is in lockdown; there's no guarantee we'll get anything.'

Mac turned towards the empty doorway that Stephanie had bustled through moments before. 'But Steph is hungry to make her mark with

Spotlight. It's better to set her loose on those dog huggers as she won't play nice. Plus – we can afford to leave her knocking on the door for a few hours if necessary. You – I can't spare. Go find Curly and get to work.'

Kim reluctantly conceded. She wanted to be in control of the whole story, certain the crucial information could be squeezed from the HLP in half the time. But it made sense to take pressure off everyone later in the day.

The producer and reporter huddled at their desks, bouncing ideas back and forth. Curly decided they would approach the story chronologically. The intro would be compelling – the main suspect had skipped the country and a second HLP member was implicated in the live-baiting fraud at Steiglitz. And possibly murder.

The start of Kim's package would deal with the new information on Julian Oliver. The original suspect 'reached out' to *Spotlight* to clear his name after learning about the latest homicide. He confirmed he was home in New Zealand, although wouldn't verify how he evaded border security in two countries. In *Spotlight's* opinion, it wouldn't end police scrutiny of Julian for Henry Wright's murder. The edited Skype interview would allow viewers to make their own decisions about Julian.

There was a debate about how to portray the abrupt end to the interview. The black screen could have been a technical failure; a power break in Auckland, or problems with the local ISP. Curly decided to report it as a deliberate move by the suspect. Most viewers would treat it the same way; Kim had trapped him in a damning admission about a previously unknown conspirator.

That raised fresh questions about the HLP's involvement. How many people at the HLP were aware of Julian's plan? Did the party leadership know about the scheme despite their repeated denials? That would segue into whatever Stephanie Grant could film. It might be a closed door, or they might get lucky. Thanks to the ambitious news reporter, it was the latter.

By four o'clock Kim was at her desk with a flat white. The script was written, the voice over recorded and the editor conjuring magic with Kim occasionally stepping into the booth to look over his shoulder. They were in a happy place; their lead story should be ready by 5.30 – even before the Channel 5 News went to air – a rare feat in daily current affairs. Kim had known too many nerve-wracking nights where the last shot was edited seconds before the studio director gave the play command. Television production was not healthy for people with cardiac problems.

Kim had to be magnanimous, Stephanie's footage was priceless. It was dramatic and revelatory: Kristin Webb had blundered into the trap and revealed the second man. Her new rival had saved the day. Kim despaired when Julian shut her down on camera. She had deliberately gone hard in the interview – *Spotlight* couldn't be perceived as too soft on the fugitive. All the journos understood that, but not Jo; she was giving everyone the cold shoulder. A second coffee collected from the café sat untouched beside the PA. Kim guessed the thaw wouldn't start before a bottle of white wine was opened. Or would it take some expensive French bubbly?

The HLP was in disarray, a recipe of the activists own making. Julian was on the run, now the party co-founder was implicated. He wasn't responding to phone calls. Were they killers? Kim had significant doubts. But there were too many questions and neither man was around to provide answers. The cops were eager to find Julian. Soon Ryan Mathison's name would be added to their workload.

The timing of their program and the information *Spotlight* had uncovered was causing consternation. The brains trust – Mac, Curly and Templeton – were behind a closed conference room door with Channel 5's lawyer, Stewart Easton. The issue was whether *Spotlight* should immediately alert police that their main suspect had left Australia and there was a second man to find. Or should *Spotlight* cite media independence and let the cops watch it on television like everyone else?

Jo was supposed to have surrendered all email contacts and phone numbers for Julian. How did they explain being able to Skype him? Their own video evidence would show *Spotlight* initiated the call. The PA, Mac, Curly, Kim and Templeton could be in deep shit if the cops wanted to punish the bolshie current affairs team. They had been poking around in homicide investigations, matters where police claimed exclusive rights.

Currently *Spotlight* had vital information in two murder inquiries – the police needed to reallocate their resources. But telling detectives in the afternoon could threaten their exclusive coverage. Someone was bound to leak that information to other media. A payback for *Spotlight* getting above their station. Cops solved murders, not TV journalists. That's what prompted Mac to call in Easton to untangle their legal dilemma. Did withholding information until *Spotlight's* normal broadcast slot amount to obstruction, or a dozen other charges that could land them in court?

Kim watched the animated debate behind glass. Mac was on his feet, both hands worrying his beard as he spoke. For a moment, Kim envied Mac's facial fuzz. His hairy ruminations usually provided answers to problems. The closed door prevented Kim from sharing another complication with the senior muse. It was connected to their discussion in the conference room. But revealing personal details to a lawyer who also did business with her father – a member of the Channel 5 board – made her hesitate. Dad didn't know about the fluctuating circumstances of her love life.

A phone slammed into its cradle at the command post. Few production crew members had ventured into the Siberian zone since the Skype call. There was a serious risk of frost bite if Kim shared her conundrum with Jo. She looked at the text message from Nathan that was causing the anxiety.

> *Sorry for being a grump. Would still like to meet. Can be free 8ish. Any more surprises – or do I need to watch your show????*

It arrived at 3.49. That's rush hour in the media business and gave the reporter breathing space. Kim would normally be at Warp 9.9 to get her story of the day ready. The mobile never strayed far from a reporter's hand – at any time – but personal messages were often ignored until the show started. Did Nathan understand that, or would he think he was being ignored? Kim's thumbs hovered over the miniature keyboard, mentally composing a neutral response. The snick of the conference room door stalled the reply.

Mac emerged first but avoided Kim.

'Lachlan!'

The 25-year-old backed his chair out of Edit 3 where he worked on Kim's feature. A black hoodie shrouded his head and contrasted the paleness of his skin and spiky blonde hair. Lachlan avoided direct sunlight whenever possible; his world consisted of the dimly lit booth at

Channel 5 and a gaming console at home. Eccentricities were forgiven for creative brilliance. In that respect, Lachlan was a star at *Spotlight*.

'Mate. Convert that Skype interview to a media file that I can send to the cops. It doesn't have to be high resolution – something they can view on a computer or mobile. Dub it quickly. I need it ASAP.'

The editor nodded and rolled back into the shadows. Kim approached the three wise men. 'Will giving a copy to the police keep us out of prison? What about the risk of the cops leaking the story? We've embarrassed them a few times this week – even the inspector might be miffed enough to spike our exclusive.'

Mac glanced at the lawyer who was on the phone in the meeting room. 'Stewart says it's a chance we will have to take. The cops are wasting resources looking for Julian Oliver in Victoria. We know he's left the country. Telling them now might avoid some of the anger and retribution if they don't find out until we go to air. Besides – the other media don't have the footage of Julian. It would be a shame if we lose the edge about the HLP collaborator, but I think we're still miles ahead of everyone.'

Kim held up her mobile. 'You might need to get me off the hook with Nathan. He wanted to know if we have any more *surprises* on the show tonight?'

Curly chuckled as he joined them. 'Two bombshells might have spoiled any tête-à-tête you were planning. I'm glad I'll be at home in Middle Park tonight with a bottle of port instead of some hairy git in a remand cell.'

Mac stopped his beard scratching and glared at his colleague. 'You would have been in the top bunk.'

'Should I text Nathan – or let you deal with his boss, Inspector Dowell?'

'Give me Dowell's mobile and I'll take the flak.'

Kim thumbed through her contacts and sent the number. She looked across to Jo who was on the phone again, her back to the colleagues that had crucified her runaway lover.

'What about Jo's involvement? How do we explain her latest contact?'

'Our standard protection – confidential sources.' Mac folded his arms. 'It's a sacred trust – we never reveal their identities. I can't see the cops – or a judge – wanting to lock us up. Especially when we're giving the cops a breakthrough in a double murder. In fact, two new strands to investigate.'

Curly cracked a sly grin. 'What if we get a beak who wants to intimidate the media? You know most of the judiciary want us under their thumb. Who would we sacrifice for a few days behind bars?'

Mac turned to Richard Templeton's office where the presenter was also on the phone. He raised a questioning hand and eyebrow at the broad smiles of his two senior producers.

'That's why the boss earns the big bucks.'

Kim joined their laughter, but it hadn't solved her problem with DS Potter.

'What about Nathan? Do I tell him – or wait for his inspector to break the news?' There was more than drinks or dinner at stake for Kim.

'Lachlan!' Mac yelled, although the edit booth was three metres away.

Lachlan didn't bother rolling to the doorway. 'File's ready. Check your inbox.'

Mac picked up his landline. 'Give Nathan the gist of what I'm about to tell Inspector Dowell. That might keep your dinner date on track.'

Chapter 37

Dwayne Milligan's two-bedroom unit in Corio felt bleaker than usual on Thursday afternoon. The rent was $210 a week; for that, you get what you paid for – not much. The aluminium sliding windows were jammed because of frequent burglary attempts. The only ventilation on hot days came from the lockable front wire screen door. It had enough gaps for a mozzie battalion to infiltrate.

The place was always clean, life at the kennels taught the boys the virtues of tidiness. Their home could never be described as cheerful, but it was only two good torpedo punts away from the Geelong greyhound track. That was one advantage.

Normally Milligan would be at Tara, or maybe on the way to a night meeting at Sandown. That was when they had a full kennel and strong chasers in the pack. If there was good money on offer, and a couple of dogs or bitches were in form, then Conor would travel across Melbourne. But those days were gone for Milligan. Was it only last week they considered going to Cranbourne for their feature? Milligan shook his head; so much had changed in seven days.

Two trainers were dead – and for what reason? The handler didn't share the current affairs reporter's scepticism that activists were involved. They were as nutty as the tree huggers: all extremists. There was a madness Milligan could see in their eyes whenever they chanted their slogans at the track. They were so obsessive. Who knew what they were capable of? That guy Conor tangled with was the weirdest of the lot. Kim Prescott might have dismissed Julian Oliver as more noise than action, but not him.

Milligan looked at his mobile on the charger. The battery had flatlined while he was talking to Harding at the farm. The home's sole paid worker was whinging about extra duties Siobhan had thrust upon him. And he was still responsible for the last two greyhounds. They had to be fed and exercised. The owner arrived back from Bali that morning but wasn't in a hurry to collect his investments; or arrange a new trainer. Milligan had listened to Harding gripe for half an hour. Fortunately, there was sufficient battery life to question his mate about the photo with Conor, Wright, Paddy and the Beachams.

'Yeah, yeah. I remember that now. That was in October, I think. At the Beckley Centre. Paddy picked up a good win in Race 7.'

'Paddy was in great form last Spring, I remember that. But I don't know why Henry Wright and the Beachams were part of the photo. They don't own any dogs. Did the dapper Pom have a big flutter on Paddy?'

'Not that I recall. They had just come back from a holiday in Queensland. Noosa Heads. Yeah. Carolyn was raving how wonderful the weather had been. Lots of sun. She went over to the nude beach at Alexandria Bay to get an all over tan.' Harding laughed. 'That made Conor and Henry all frisky. I think his dog finished third in that race. When Wright saw the boss getting a winner's cuddle, he wanted to join in. Carolyn didn't mind and they told me to get a photo.'

'I suppose that explains it. Mind you, Benedict didn't look impressed.'

'I never noticed, mate. The boys were getting a bit playful. I think they had a grope of her arse. Not that Carolyn objected. She just giggled her way through it.'

'I didn't know her that well. Was she – a bit loose?'

'Well, I heard a couple of rumours. She was a party girl – loved a few drinks, a dance…and maybe more. Apparently, she went to a few of Henry's more risqué barbecues. Conor did too.'

'I never knew if that was gossip, or true.'

'You're a straight arrow mate.' Harding laughed. 'Everyone thinks you're a nice guy. They knew you'd be horrified to hear about some of the shenanigans that go on behind the scenes. I remember your eyes almost popped out when I told you about Conor getting busted in Eastern Gardens with the blonde.'

Milligan didn't know whether to be embarrassed or offended by his prudish reputation. He wasn't a wowser; he hadn't encountered much permissive behaviour as a 23-year-old. His life experience was limited to greyhounds, the ute and watching sport on TV.

He disconnected the phone from its charger and dialled Kim Prescott. That made him smile. He would never have dreamed a week ago that a television reporter would be on his speed dial.

Five members of the *Spotlight* production crew struggled to restrain their mirth as Milligan's call found Kim. She turned her back on them and retreated to her desk. Curly, Dugal, Withers and two editors were absorbed by another phone chat, although they could hear only one side of the conversation. It was Mac on the landline, his chair under pressure at full tilt and size 12 boots on the desk.

'I keep telling you superintendent – journalists cannot reveal their sources. No. Never. You know that and the courts know that. If Moses was here, he'd set our solemn vow in stone: we never talk about confidential sources.'

More chuckles from the chorus. Mac went silent while the senior cop pressed his futile case.

'You have everything on Julian Oliver that we have. We were given a Skype contact but no physical address. We called him and recorded the conversation. He used a camera to prove he was in Auckland. It was on the waterfront. That's all we know. You also saw he refused to verify his boarding pass or passport details.

'We have no idea who helped him escape or who is sheltering him. He cut the line when our reporter tripped him up about a collaborator. We haven't been able to reach him again. We've given your investigators two valuable lines of inquiry. Why would you want to persecute us – pardon, I mean prosecute. There's nothing to gain by that. We've saved you valuable time by sharing the information promptly.'

The lead story was ready and most of the program was in the can. That's why the crew had congregated early and caught Mac's performance. It was only one half of the impromptu show. Kim had been getting text updates from Nathan Potter.

The detective sergeant and his inspector were realists: *Spotlight* had saved the investigation many fruitless hours and a lot of money. With detectives allocated new duties, Nathan sat back to provide text coverage of his apoplectic superintendent at police headquarters. A week of being humbled by amateurs stoked a monumental rage. Kim shared the histrionic details with her colleagues until the phone call from Dwayne Milligan. The crew just had Mac to make them laugh, although the smirks faded with his parting shot to the superintendent.

'How many in the *Spotlight* production crew, you ask? There's about 15 of us on duty today. Have you got enough handcuffs for everyone?'

Chapter 38

'Is that you on the telly?'

Ryan Mathison raised his head from a pot of beer and looked above the bar in the Rathdowne Street hotel. Even Molly peered at the screen then back to her master. It was the aspiring politician and HLP co-founder: a still taken from the party website. Had the media connected him to Julian Oliver and what happened at the farm? Who told them? Has Julian been caught – or was he talking? There was a watermark at the base of the frame to identity the program. Even without the audio, Mathison guessed that *Melbourne Spotlight* was about to turn him into a lame duck.

The 20-year-old barmaid, dressed in matching black tee shirt, jeans, lipstick and eyeshadow wanted to be helpful. 'Shall I turn it up?' She reached for the remote control.

Mathison quickly scanned the blue-collar pub; no other eyes were on the idiot box. Their interest in Thursday television ended after the sports news. If the volume was increased that might change and Mathison's humiliation would go public.

'No, that's all right. I'm a…human rights campaigner. It's just a background feature I helped with today. I know what's in it. No need to disturb your customers.' Mathison gulped the rest of his beer. It was time to depart in case the lass assumed he was too modest. Curiosity was winning until a thirsty patron decided the matter.

'C'mon Chantal. Do ya want to be the first pub in Carlton where a man died of thirst?'

The barmaid replaced the remote and reached for a glass.

Mathison waved farewell and left with Molly on her lead. It was dark, no pedestrians were in sight. He didn't want to be recognised, but then Mathison didn't know exactly what he was running from. He stepped back to the door and discreetly peered at the source of his hasty exit. He was shocked a second time. Julian was on the screen, obviously being interviewed by a reporter. Mathison looked at the baseline graphic: Auckland! The scheming weasel had run home. How did he get there? And what the hell was he saying about Saturday?

Agitation overcame caution; Mathison pushed his way inside with Molly silently at his heels. They stayed by the door as Chantal had turned up the volume. She watched the screen, her back to the unexpected TV celebrity. It was hard for Mathison not to cringe as he listened to the reporter put Julian through the mill. Mathison's next facial tic was a grimace as the besieged fugitive on TV turned to belligerence, only to be skewered a final time. The reporter worked out Julian had help at Steiglitz.

Molly whimpered as the pictures changed to the HLP headquarters and a distressed Kristin Webb. Guilt seeped through Mathison. An idiotic plan had boomeranged. Instead of wounding the greyhound racing industry, they might have destroyed his political ambition. By the time the story was finished Mathison understood his problems were more serious – the police would be looking at him as a murder suspect. He tugged on Molly's lead and made a second exit as Chantal pulled a mobile phone from her back pocket.

Outside, Mathison looked up and down the street, fearful a police car with flashing lights would halt in front of him. He needed a bolthole, a place to think. There were friends – not all in the HLP – sprinkled throughout Carlton, Brunswick and Fitzroy. Would they provide a bed for the night and a receptive ear to consider his prospects? Or would they slam the door in his face, too scared to get involved? Mathison flicked through his contacts wondering whom he could take a punt on.

Chapter 39

Mac's voice boomed from the studio corridor. 'Jo!' Three seconds later he entered the *Spotlight* office. 'Have you got a phone number in England for...?'

There was no sign of the PA at her post. The program producer looked around the room until he found Kim at her desk. 'Is she still sulking because you crucified her boyfriend – or have the boys taken her to the pub?'

'Both. She asked Dugal to drive her. Kenny tagged along – no invite for the bitch at the back of the room.' Kim shrugged; it had saved her a makeup bottle of vino blanco that evening.

'I presume that Templeton gave us the thumbs up to hijack Pete Benson's holidays?'

'Yep. I slipped in for a chat during the last commercial break. He didn't even want to run it past The Hatchet for approval. But how do we reach Benson? I was hoping Jo would have a number, or at least his email.'

Kim held up a piece of A4 paper. 'Don't worry. Our ever-reliable colleague emailed us his itinerary and hotels before he left – in case a major story broke.' She looked at the list. 'According to his schedule – he's in London for the next few days. I've checked on Google – Bath is about two to three hours away by car on the M4. The train is half the time, but I'm sure Pete would rather have his own wheels.'

Mac looked at the clock over the edit suites. 'What's the time difference – nine or ten hours?'

'Nine, I think. Which means Pete should be awake and enjoying a traditional English breakfast.'

'Ahhhh! Lucky boy. No one does breakfast like the Poms.' Mac reached out for the email and led the way into the conference room.

A few minutes remained in the broadcast, but another angle on the murders took priority. If they could find *Spotlight's* senior reporter. Mac tapped in the international codes while Kim assembled her notes.

The latest call from Dwayne Milligan had aroused more curiosity about Carolyn Beacham. The early preparation of the lead story allowed time to share thoughts with the senior producers. She showed them the picture of the happy trio – plus dog – with a grumpy husband on the outer. The dog and two males were dead, the woman was gone.

Did that October photo cause a marriage breakdown, rather than the public excuse of an escape from the Australian heat? Milligan's mate said Carolyn had a reputation for flirting. Was it merely track gossip? Carolyn was an attractive woman; did she push Mr Beacham's buttons once too often? Was a wayward wife enough to prompt Benedict Beacham into brutal acts of revenge?

It was circumstantial. The cops would laugh at *Spotlight* if they suggested the investigation focus on a punter, all because of gut feelings about a photo. *Spotlight* needed more information about the couple. Kim could research the husband, but they felt that Carolyn Beacham should be included. There were many questions to pose: was the separation acrimonious, did her ex-husband make a fuss about that photograph with the dead trainers, was he a violent man?

Answers could be provided over the telephone; a face-to-face might produce more interesting results. It was easier to think of follow up questions depending on visual reactions. Kim wouldn't be able to see a grimace, or fearful expression, from 20,000 kilometres away.

Julian Oliver demonstrated the limitations of Skype calls when interviewers touched on sensitive topics. Pete Benson being in the neighbourhood was a bonus for the team. That's if he hadn't booked a day at the races or Buckingham Palace. The ring tone ended as a handset was picked up in London.

'Hello?'

'Pete! Mac and Kim here. Howzit going in old London town?'

'Mac! Jeezus. This is a surprise. I was dreading it might be bad news from home when the hotel phone rang. My grandfather has been a bit crook with pneumonia – I was worried it was my mum calling to say he was slipping away.' Benson's tone brightened. 'But you're a different story. Does it mean you need my help?'

'Yep. Have you caught up with our dead dog trainers?'

'Too right. You guys have owned that story from the start. Well done Kimbo. Two dead bodies at your feet in six months – that's awesome!'

Kim gave Mac a wry smile; trust Benson to view the murders in purely journalistic terms.

'It's too freaky for my liking Pete. And I'd like to make sure no more trainers get caught by the chainsaw maniac.'

'Oops. Forgive my enthusiasm – but it's still a great yarn. I've been catching up with the clips on *Spotlight's* website. There's free wifi everywhere. What's happened now that you're calling me?'

'Are you free today?' Mac asked.

'I was going to visit the Tower of London. It's been there almost a thousand years, so I reckon it will still be standing on the weekend. What do you want me to do?'

'You might get another history lesson instead. Have you been to Bath yet?'

'No. Didn't the Romans build it. Lot of hot spas I gather.'

'You might find time for a soak later. Templeton's given you approval for a rental car and a night in a nice hotel.'

'Sweet. What do you want me to do?'

Chapter 40

Drinks at *Spotlight* 's favourite South Melbourne pub had been infrequent in recent months. The need for alcohol hadn't evaporated, it was more a matter of economics. Especially for the eternally frugal Dugal Cameron. Why pay for your beer if the company was giving it away? Jo Trescowthick knew he would have raided the office fridge if she hadn't insisted on an escort to The Rising Sun Hotel. The demand for company didn't extend to Ken Withers, but he volunteered to be the other prop for their bar scrum.

The first wine didn't touch the sides. The second was ordered before the camera crew were halfway through their first pots. They exchanged nervous glances.

'Don't you dare say anything!' Jo took the second glass and emptied a third of it. 'I've had a shitty day and no way was I going to drink with that back-stabbing bitch.'

The props nodded, not game to contradict their stroppy colleague.

'How could she be so brutal to Julian? He must think I'm an absolute cow. I arrange for him to talk to a *friendly* reporter. He believes he's going to get a fair hearing – a chance to present his case. After all, he was out of the country – or at least Victoria – for the second murder. Despite that evidence, Kim as good as paints him as a double murderer!'

Dugal and Withers nodded and emptied their glasses. They waved for two refills. Jo continued with her rant while they watched the closing segment of *Spotlight* on the bar TV.

'He's probably running from the New Zealand cops now. He found a safe house – but we've exposed that. I don't know why I bothered helping when…'

Jo was interrupted by the pop of a champagne cork: the text alert on her mobile. The sender was unknown.

Julian trusted you. Can I? We're innocent. Will you talk to me?

'Oh Christ.' Jo reached for her glass.

'What's wrong?' Dugal asked. 'Does Kim want a make-up drink? I think it would be a good idea.'

'No, it's not her. She's got more sense than to grovel this early.' Jo waved at the phone on the counter. 'I'm not even a bloody journalist, but everyone wants to drag me into this story.'

'Who is the text from?'

'I think it's Ryan Mathison.'

'How did he get your number?'

'I've no bloody idea.'

Dugal returned to his beer, leaving the floor open to his mate.

'Does he want to be roasted on camera by Kim as well?' Withers laughed briefly, until Jo dug an elbow into his ribs.

'Ooof! Okay, okay. You need to lighten up Jo.' Withers rubbed the fractured bones. 'What does Mathison want?'

'He wants to talk to me.'

'Damn. He's now a suspect as well. We're already in the shit with the cops. Mac stopped a posse coming over with handcuffs for all of us. Should you talk to Mathison – or call Mac first?'

Jo was confused. She was angry with her colleagues, yet she felt the urge to help – again. Every time she assisted someone in this case, she took another step closer to a prison cell. How far could her loyalty to *Spotlight* stretch?

With a prolonged sigh Jo snatched the phone and looked at the door. 'Better you guys aren't party to this.' She thumbed the phone icon to call the phantom text messenger. 'We need someone free to keep the program going until idiots like me get paroled.'

The cold wind whipping down Eastern Road made Jo regret leaving her jacket inside. A male voice answered before she could retreat. Jo took control immediately to minimise her liability.

'Don't say anything for a moment. Just listen.'

'Okay.'

'I think I know who this is, but I'm not going to risk saying your name as I'm not sure if police are monitoring my calls.'

'Christ! Are they? I never thought of that.'

'You and…your mate…didn't think this escapade through very well. And I'm angry it's risking my liberty.'

'Okay, I can understand that.'

'However, I don't believe either of you are guilty of the worst crimes. You were Dumb and Dumber, but I don't think you are killers. I tried to help him, but my over-zealous workmates might have made things worse. I wanted to give him a chance to clear his name. I guess you want to do the same?'

'I do. Yes, we were silly to have tried to implicate the trainer. But we're not psychos.'

'You saw what happened to him tonight?'

'Yes.'

'How can you trust us? Once you're on camera, the reporter takes control. You risk the same shit that…he…copped today.'

'Not quite. I have a plan – if you can get your program producer to do it my way.'

Chapter 41

The English Spring was warmer and sunnier than Benson expected. His puffa jacket hadn't emerged from the suitcase after five days of sightseeing around London. It was his first visit and the bachelor had ticked off many of the traditional tourist venues. A Jack the Ripper walking tour was on the agenda for Saturday night. He was having a brilliant time and didn't mind a detour to the West Country – especially when the company paid for the transport and accommodation.

The Ford Focus wasn't exciting, but Benson decided not to test the largesse of Channel 5's accounts team. He heard The Hatchet was back at the helm. However, he would splash out with a boutique hotel and hope his receipts were paid in full.

Traffic on the M4 moved steadily – even the truck drivers were courteous – and he expected to reach Bath by three o'clock. Benson's perusal of the map before departure revealed that Stonehenge was 50 kilometres from the spa town. He could squeeze in a trip to the prehistoric monument on his way back.

Benson's mind switched back to work mode as he approached the UNESCO World Heritage site. There were no fears about getting lost with a GPS in the rental. It directed him off the M4 near Chippenham; a good choice as quaint villages were more appealing than the motorway. His destination was a town house in Northampton Street. Benson was chuffed because it was close to the famous Royal Crescent; maybe another chance to be a tourist after his main duty?

Kim had spent 20 minutes on the phone, providing details and her instincts about Benedict Beacham. She discovered Carolyn had returned to Bath and was believed to be living with her brother, a professor at the university. There had been little communication with her Australian friends: a couple of cards at Christmas. Benson respected Kim's tactic to treat the visit as a cold call. Carolyn never worked in Melbourne and it was hoped she would be home by mid to late afternoon. If she had interesting information, Benson had the number for a freelance camera operator to record an interview. The Hatchet would pop a fufu valve for those charges.

The Ford found the property easily enough – a beautifully preserved four-level Georgian town house – the difficulty was parking. It took ten minutes to find a space near the professor's home. That was the price for having famous neighbours: Royal Crescent attracted tourists every day of the year.

Benson stood at the front door and realised his first estimate of the property was wrong – there was another level below ground. He presumed the professor had a large family, or was it split into several apartments? He looked at the entrance and saw one bell. Benson pressed it and stepped back. It was opened almost immediately by a man in his late 40s dressed in grey jacket and slacks with a floral open-necked shirt. Natty was the word that sprang to mind for Benson; the trim, dark-haired man on the doorstep didn't look anything like a mathematics professor. A chic leather holdall indicated he might be off to the university.

'Oh! You surprised me. Can I help you?'

'Professor Smedley?'

'Yes. Are you one of my students?'

'No, I'm a journalist from Australia and I was hoping to talk to your sister, Carolyn.'

The professor released the door handle and smiled.

'I think you would have more luck in your homeland. Carolyn moved to Melbourne about five years ago. She and her husband bought a lifestyle property.'

Benson's instincts twanged. 'You sound like you don't have a lot of contact with her?'

The professor shrugged. 'She was four years older and didn't get home much when she joined the army as a nurse. We weren't the greatest communicators as a family, mainly gossip or news via our parents. Sadly, they were killed in a car accident two years ago.' The professor gestured to the limestone town house. 'We inherited this but haven't decided what to do with it. She sent a text at Christmas to say she was happy to keep the status quo.'

'Okay, as far as you know, Carolyn is still in Australia?'

Professor Smedley frowned. 'Yes. Why wouldn't she be?'

'Was she still with her husband, Benedict, when she sent the most recent message. Late December?'

'I presume so.' The professor placed his bag at his feet. 'I'm getting the feeling that something is wrong.'

Benson nodded. 'I'm getting the same inkling. I'm on holiday from my job as a television current affairs reporter. My senior producer asked me to contact Carolyn and talk about the deaths of two greyhound trainers in the past week.'

The professor paled. 'Deaths? At the track?'

'They were murdered. Butchered, in fact, with a chainsaw.'

'My God.' The professor steadied himself against the brick frame. 'But what does that have to do with Carolyn?'

'My colleagues told me that Carolyn knew both men – very well. However, her husband said she left Australia because she couldn't stand the heat.'

'When was that?'

'In December – well before the homicides. She's supposed to have been living with you – here in Bath.'

'If Carolyn isn't with me…and she's not been seen in Australia for months. Where the hell is she?'

Day 138

The prisoner counted the steps as she paced. Like an Olympic swimmer she prepared to pivot perfectly and push back the other direction for a similar count. This was an additional walk to her regular regime. It was thinking time; a chance to work out what was happening with her captor.

She stopped on that thought. For so long she had deliberately dehumanised him. She had simplified her own life as well. She considered herself the prisoner, trapped by a monster. Carolyn Beacham's life was on the outside. She wanted to reclaim it. To do that she had to outwit the bastard.

Carolyn ran fingers through long dark hair and held them up to view – more grey strands. It hadn't been cut, dyed or styled in months. The proud spiky bob was down to her shoulders. Scissors were never allowed as they could become a weapon. A brush became a necessity after a fortnight to tame the wild growth. Cheap shampoo was supplied, but no conditioner. Her nails had forgotten the feel of polish.

Carolyn laughed at the unexpected vanity. It had been suppressed as she focussed on the necessary skills to survive. She had done that, but was no closer to attaining her goal – escape. Strangely, the jailer's frame of mind that week had renewed her hopes for freedom. His meal routine was out of kilter. Yet his mood was relaxed. In fact, she thought there was a smile as he entered through the cellar door that morning.

Chapter 42

Ryan Mathison stood outside the crumbling façade of the Court House Hotel in Sydney Road, Brunswick. Molly was handed over to the care of Kristin Webb in the Brunswick HQ for the morning. It was 10.45 and his lawyer was late, deliberately. He looked towards the Supa IGA across the road; Angelo Russo emerged with a brief case in one hand while shoving food into his mouth with the other.

Most likely it was a cherry ripe; his legal mate was addicted to the chocolate treat long before they met at Melbourne University. His dark pin-striped suit strained to contain that passion. Russo waited for a city-bound tram to pass and shuffled across the road.

'Is this fashionably late enough for you Ryan?'

'Yep. It's lucky I told you to meet at 10.30. You're always 15 minutes behind on every appointment.'

The youngest grandson of Italian immigrants shrugged and finished his snack. The foil wrapper was discarded to the wind. Mathison didn't notice as he looked north towards Coburg and the *Spotlight* camera car. He gave a discreet thumbs up. Stephanie Grant emerged from the passenger door with notebook in hand. Dugal Cameron went to the rear of the station wagon to retrieve his camera; it was loaded and ready to record.

'Okay Angelo, send the email now.'

The lawyer opened an account on his iPhone, selected the draft that had waited two hours for electronic release and showed it to Mathison.

May 19 – Media Release

Hound Liberation Party co-founder Ryan Mathison will be talking to detectives at the Brunswick Police Station, 630 Sydney Road at 11 o'clock Friday. He is prepared to make a brief statement before that interview. Mr Mathison is being represented by Angelo Russo LLB, DIP CRIM

Mathison looked at his watch – 10.49 – and nodded. The message departed for every major media company in Melbourne. It would be a miracle if any news crew, apart from *Spotlight*, could make it in time. Not many TV channels, radio stations or newspapers were likely to be in the area. It was a risk to give one channel exclusive access. But experience had taught the veteran campaigner it was the only way to control the message. A frenzied media pack was a greater peril.

Mathison had lived up to his part of the agreement. Now he had to make sure the reporter and cameraman played their roles. The new murder suspect and his lawyer waited for a tram to trundle north, then crossed to the police station entrance.

Stephanie waited. The camera was recording before she spoke.

'Mr Mathison. Mr Russo. By chance we were in the area when our office received your email a few minutes ago. I believe you want to make an announcement before you talk to police?'

Stephanie held out the microphone. It rankled that she couldn't pressure Mathison about Saturday night. He was being given a free run to declare his innocence. But that was the price for sole access. It was the fifth exclusive in a row – and this time it would have Stephanie Grant's name on the baseline, not Kim Prescott.

Russo spoke first.

'My client has volunteered to meet detectives this morning. He wants to clear himself of malicious allegations that have surfaced in the gutter press. He also wants to protect the party that he established for the welfare of greyhounds. Mr Mathison felt it was important to speak to the media first.'

Russo looked around. 'I apologise for the late notification. I had to deal with another crucial legal matter.' The lawyer smiled theatrically. 'And you know how judges frown upon mobile phones in their courts.' He stepped back and ushered his client forward.

Mathison engaged Stephanie rather than the camera directly. He looked smart in a dark sports jacket, linen shirt and beige chinos. Confident and believable was the image he wanted to project. Deep in Mathison's heart there was a flicker of hope that he might save his political career. The HLP was stuffed. But the main political parties loved a cool and professional operator under pressure. Allegiances could change with a signature on a membership card. He had one chance to sway the public.

'The police are about to question me about my visit to a farm at Steiglitz on Saturday where the body of a greyhound trainer was found. Let me say very clearly – I had nothing to do with his death. Neither did Julian Oliver. I admit we were both there. My involvement was purely as a driver. I stayed with the car the whole time and never entered the property.

'Mr Oliver said he had credible evidence that live-baits were being used to train racing dogs. I drove Mr Oliver to Steigltiz to obtain that evidence. I waited for about an hour. Mr Oliver eventually returned and said he was unable to find the animals. We drove to a bar in Ballarat and discussed whether the tip was false, or we had the wrong training establishment.

'I did not – and I emphasise that – I did not know until after the event that Mr Oliver had fabricated the evidence. If I had known, I would have released the animals and immediately banished Mr Oliver from the HLP. He made a silly mistake which has had terrible consequences for me and the party.

'I don't believe he had anything to do with Mr O'Leary's death. We are pacifists who treasure life and the welfare of all living creatures. I hope to clear the issue with police today and return to the HLP to continue the campaign against greyhound racing in Victoria. Thank you.'

Mathison nodded to Stephanie, walked up the short ramp to the station entrance followed by Russo and stepped inside. That was as much of the truth he was going to share with anybody. Mathison's fingerprints weren't at the property and there was no video evidence that he ever left the car. Even Kristin didn't know the extent of his involvement with Julian's hare-brained scheme.

Mathison had used guerrilla tactics with other welfare campaigns. If done well, they could generate massive publicity for the cause. The current mess was the other side of that coin. Experience taught him to minimise his exposure to the fallout. Good luck finding Julian to contradict the spiel he was going to give detectives.

The lawyer's smile was shielded from the television camera by tinted glass.

'Jeezus mate. I never realised how ruthless you are. You chucked Julian Oliver under the bus – and drove over him again.'

Mathison snorted and looked around the empty foyer. 'Stupid prick. I gave him a lifeline – I said he wasn't guilty of murder. That's the best he can hope for. I've got to save my own butt.'

'You know the HLP is fucked? No matter what happens with the cops, you can't save that dead dog.'

'Yeah. But there are other options.'

Russo smiled again. 'That's my boy. You know I've got contacts on both sides of parliament. After that performance – who do you want me to approach first?'

Dugal finished packing his camera gear as Stephanie leaned against the side of the vehicle.

'What a lying bastard he turned out to be. It grates that I wasn't allowed to question him. He's so full of shit. He's going in there to dump on Julian Oliver to save his own career.'

Dugal closed the hatch. 'He's a politician Steph, can you expect anything better?'

'No, I guess not. He's cunning, that's a pre-requisite for anyone wanting a career at the top of Bourke Street. He knows we'll run the whole statement. There might be enough gullible voters who believe him. You notice he was careful to avoid the second murder altogether? He was Lee Harvey Oswald – a patsy.'

A squeal of tyres caught their attention. A Channel 9 News car was in the no parking zone outside the cop shop. A dark-haired reporter was soon on the footpath, anxiously scanning for a media conference. A fist slammed into the roof of the SUV when he spotted Stephanie and Dugal. It was 11.02 and they had been scooped again.

The Spotlight crew could have driven away with their victory. But reporter and camera operator felt like gloating. They walked down the road to *console* their competitors.

'Hey Simon,' Stephanie said. 'You just missed Mathison and his lawyer. Tough break – the cops whisked him away as soon as he walked into the foyer.'

'Shit. We ran every red light to get here. How did you make the deadline? A job in the area was it?'

'Funny you should say that.' Stephanie laughed and her beaten opponent couldn't avoid a grin.

'I suppose we're going to have to wait. Any chance the cops will release him before the bulletin starts?'

'Two murders to question him about – what do you think?'

Chapter 43

Mac's fifth sidestep in the valley of crushed toes would have earned him high praise from Collingwood's coach. Self-preservation was making the senior producer nimbler by the day. It was lunch time and he had avoided every kamikaze run to the kitchenette from a hung-over Jo. Kim saw the danger and begged to escape the office. Mac knew it was sensible to provide the death chariot with two targets. Wisely, Kim didn't stray far from her desk. Curly had been enlisted as her chai wallah.

Perhaps it was these adrenalin bursts that were making Mac fleet-of-foot. He hoped it would last the day because Jo's wrath was going to linger. For a long time. Nobody would dare raid the coffee kitty for the horses at Flemington that weekend. To be fair, *Spotlight* played the right game with the first suspect. News organisations could turn into doormats for politicians and news setters offering exclusives. Mac was comfortable with their handling of Julian Oliver, even if his co-pilot wasn't.

The production crew were flabbergasted when Jo rolled into the morning conference and declared that Ryan Mathison wanted to talk. Her loyalty to the program rated higher than her fury. Mac was also impressed that Jo's deviousness was at journalist levels. She arrived with a plan to secure the scoop and not make the police suspicious. Self-preservation wasn't confined to the current affairs hierarchy.

Mac was surprisingly bright-eyed despite little sleep after a late-night phone call from an excited Pete Benson in Bath. The Carolyn Beacham inquiry provided more substance than expected. The reporter had hired a freelance camera operator to record the professor's information. It was ready to view in a media file on Mac's computer by the time he arrived. The main question was what to do with it? To broadcast it on Friday night would leave the door open for other media – especially newspapers – to dig deeper while Spotlight enjoyed their two-day break. *Spotlight* could lose the advantage it earned in the past six days. There was also a chance that Carolyn Beacham didn't travel to Bath. There might be an undeclared sibling rivalry, or she found a new lover. In Mac's opinion, there was more to explore before they alerted viewers, or the cops, about a fresh angle in the story.

It had been a boisterous morning conference; opinions flew back and forth across the table. Mac parked the Carolyn Beacham story to focus on the HLP leader surrendering to the cops. That sparked an equally spirited dialogue. The program producer was happy to listen, but he made the tough decisions – Mathison would be the lead story. Stephanie would do that job and Kim would dig deeper into the lives of Mr and Mrs Beacham.

That was the perfect allocation of resources and Mac was grateful he didn't have to pacify an agitated Kim. She was delighted with the treasure trove Benson had gleaned from the professor. It was circumstantial, but all journalistic instincts were tingling. Channel 5's lawyer warned the current affairs team it was on thin ice with the cops. They wanted to make an example of any media organisation that interfered with the investigation. Stewart Easton directed *Spotlight* to share all relevant information with detectives.

Mac was prepared to gamble and wait until Monday – the police had Ryan Mathison to interrogate. Perhaps *Spotlight* was wrong? The HLP activists might be responsible for one murder, or both. All the journalists had was suspicion, which might be laughable to the cops. But Mac felt *Spotlight* was on the right track. Benson discovered the source of Beacham's wealth – a £10 million lottery win. His previous occupations were also intriguing.

Chapter 44

The clink of glasses was lost in the hubbub of Friday festivities at the Rising Sun. The *Spotlight* fridge – with help from newsroom staff – emptied in record time. The camera crews, with Ken Withers a pace ahead, led the charge to the next watering hole. By nine o'clock the males – and Stephanie Grant – were gathered around the sports bar television and the live AFL game.

That left Kim and Jo mending fences at a table on the far side of the room. Reconciliation came easier than they expected, thanks to Jo's wine consumption. Kim was on her third glass; Jo had lost count.

'I must have called you a bitch 20 times last night.' Jo used her glass to point at the bar, spilling a few drops. 'Just over there. Between Dugal and Kenny. You were public enemy number one – not my Julian.'

'I know.'

'You weren't here.'

'Your drinking buddies told me I needed to make amends. Quickly. They had sore heads – and Kenny reckons you broke half his ribs.'

That brought a chuckle. 'He's such a wuss. I only tapped him a few times for stupid comments. Just like this.' Jo swung her right elbow and almost pivoted out of her chair.

'Steady there, Jo. No wonder the boys are staying out of reach.'

They looked at the media scrum around the television. It was Geelong playing one of the interstate teams, no need for them to take an interest. Jo had forgiven her colleague, but revenge could be taken in small doses.

'I see Stephanie is making herself part of the team.'

Kim's smile tightened. 'Yes. She's been like a limpet with Curly all week. Now that he's escaped, she's found a new host. Look out Dugal.'

'Oooo. You're being really bitchy now!' Jo laughed and tried to drink at the same time. More wine was spilled. She swiped it off her denims. 'Steph wasn't impressed when you volunteered to *research* at the track tomorrow night.'

Kim shrugged. 'Tough. She's got her angle and I've got mine. Let Steph focus on the worried greyhound people. I'll go after the killer.' Another half shoulder lift. 'Maybe.'

Ryan Mathison's police station performance ended a perfect week of exclusives for *Spotlight*. The missing Carolyn Beacham and her husband was held back for further investigation. Steph's delight at securing the lead story was intensified when Mac asked her to work Saturday. He wanted a feature at The Meadows. The greyhound racing industry was in turmoil: two trainers were murdered in less than a week and animal activists tried to ruin the industry. Did other trainers fear for their lives and careers? Did owners, attendants and punters know why greyhound racing was being targeted?

It was an easy story; there wouldn't be a shortage of people ready to offer Steph their opinions. A lot of fear and emotion would be caught on camera, maybe even some tears. It also guaranteed a strong story for Monday. Viewer interest in the murders wouldn't wane over the weekend; Mac was covering his bases in case the Beacham story didn't go anywhere.

Steph's jubilation was swiftly dampened. Kim suggested she should visit the Broadmeadows track as well. She wanted to discreetly observe Benedict Beacham. Could he be a real suspect? Kim clinched her ride in the camera car when she declared that Dwayne Milligan would help. Mac gave her the thumbs up.

Jo giggled. 'I've never seen a greyhound race. Are you going to take Sexy Rexy?'

'No. Imagine if he jumped the fence and joined the pack. What would they do if Rex won the race – or caught the lure?'

That brought more laughter – and inspiration. 'Actually Jo – why don't you come with me? You would be brilliant cover – Steph's doing the colour story and we could be on a girl's night out. We could mingle and chat – without a camera around us. Nobody would be suspicious.'

Jo finished her wine and almost tipped the glass over trying to place it on the table.

'That might be fun. My love life has gone to the dogs – why not watch them race? But first – more wine!' Jo swayed as she stood. She reached out with both hands for the table. Only one connected, the other slid beneath the timber causing her to stumble. 'Ooops.'

Kim took Jo's arm. 'Come on. I'm about to call an Uber, how about I drop you home as well?'

Day 139

Carolyn licked blood from the knuckles of her index and middle fingers. It was the third time she had scraped them in the past hour. It was worth it. She held up the handiwork that caused the injuries: a lamb bone sharpened to a point. As weapons go it wouldn't do serious damage. It was five centimetres long and brittle. She read enough crime stories to know prisoners called them a shiv: a makeshift knife to kill, wound or terrorise inmates and guards. Carolyn's weapon had another purpose – surprise.

Her captor was only slighter taller, but stronger. It would have been impossible to overpower him with her hands and escape. But if Carolyn could draw blood, that might be the distraction that could work.

The question was where to stab him? An eye would be the ideal target. It might partially blind him, giving her precious seconds to flee the cell. It would be a risky move; Carolyn was not a violent person; any hesitation would alert him to the danger. She had one chance and couldn't afford to have him deflect the weapon. A body jab wouldn't cause the necessary harm and confusion; his clothing could absorb much of the impact.

Carolyn pondered for another half hour. It had to be the throat. The carotid artery would be perfect. But her makeshift knife wasn't strong enough to sever that lifeline. And she couldn't guarantee hitting the right spot. However, a blow to the throat and a spray of blood would be a great shock tactic. The challenge would be luring him close enough to make the crucial thrust.

There were still the other dangers beyond her cell door. She called them the guardians, another attempt to depersonalise the threat. How many were out at any time was a guess: at least one, possibly two or three. They had contained her for too long.

She would find a way to deal with all threats. Instinct told her this weekend would be her best – maybe her last – chance to escape. Her captor's mood had changed. Why? Carolyn couldn't tell, she just knew it was time to shape her own destiny.

Carolyn hid the bone shiv inside a tear in the mattress and recovered the screw that recorded every day of her imprisonment. Methodically she scraped at the stone, pausing every few strokes to blow away the dust and lick her bloodied knuckles. Day 139 – she was determined there wouldn't be many more to etch into that wall.

Chapter 45

'Come on red. Come on,' Jo yelled through the window at The Meadows track. Her bet in race two had led from the start. But 525 metres was proving to be a challenge for the young black dog and the field was closing as they turned for home.

'Go Magic,' Kim shouted. 'Catch her.' Magic wasn't the fawn brindle's full name, but she didn't care. Kim was caught up in the excitement of the race. Her dog had exited the squeeze box in the yellow rug at the back of the field. With less than a hundred metres to go she swept around the pack and threatened Jo's lead.

The finish was a blur of flying greyhounds, colours and hooting. The *Spotlight* intruders' adrenalin was inflamed by the track commentary and the 200-plus patrons in the lounge with race fever.

'Who won – you or me?' Jo asked. 'I hope red held on.'

'I couldn't tell. They're so fast.' Kim looked up at the television screen above their heads and groaned as the director swiftly cut to a replay of the finish. 'Damn. Mine was second!'

To the amateurs it was a photo finish, the slo-mo footage revealed a wider margin: Jo's dog won by a head.

'Yay!' Jo twirled, waving her ticket. The Meadows veterans smiled at the newbie and several raised their beers in a toast. 'A third in the first race and now a win. How much will that pay?' She looked at the monitor for dividends. '$1.70 – that's $17. Add the $13 from the first race makes it $30. Yay! I could make a profit on the night. How many races are there?'

'Another seven.' Kim hid her envy with a sip of wine. She bet $20 for a win at $2.70. An each way bet would have returned some compensation for her novice judgment. But where was the thrill in that?

On the track the three place-getters returned to the dais for photos. The losers had already been cleared from the catching pen. A few pats, hugs, water and a ride home were their reward for another fun chase. In about 20 minutes it would all be repeated for race three.

Kim looked at the form guide and wondered if her luck might improve. The first selections were based on the dogs' ages, class and recent performances over the race distance. Her purse was $30 lighter. Was that an indication of her betting experience, or luck?

Jo's tips weren't as analytical – her punts were chosen by the dog's rug colours. She went for a place on the pink rug in the first race. Bravely Jo jumped to the other side of the starting boxes for a win on the red in the second. Both choices paid off. Go figure that formula for success.

Laughter from the next table interrupted Kim's musing. Jo was surrounded by four middle-aged men impressed by her new-found racing knowledge. The new punting club reached a consensus within a minute – blue rug. The happy group then queued at a TAB terminal: Jo to collect her winnings and reinvest them.

A television camera light bathed the bettors. A few metres away Stephanie Grant was recording another interview. Kim admitted her newsroom colleague was industrious: that was the sixth male to air their opinions about the turbulent week. Steph was attractive and engaging; Kim guessed that most married men in the room would line up to chat – if their wives weren't there.

Many race patrons identified Kim as a TV reporter but were surprised the *Spotlight* star wasn't in front of the camera. Kim worked hard to demonstrate it was a social evening: drinks, laughs, races and bets. She wanted to blend in and listen to gossip about the deaths of Conor O'Leary and Henry Wright.

There wasn't a shortage of opinions, especially after the afternoon radio news update on the second murder. The autopsy report on Wright revealed that his genitals were also mutilated by the chainsaw attacker. That information was too gory not to leak to a media source. Each new sharing of that story was greeted by grimaces or wry laughter. Kim also heard several comments about the victims being 'too randy for their own good.'

Technically it was Kim's first day off after 12 in a row. An evening at the racetrack for research wouldn't earn over-time pay. Not even expenses to cover her betting losses. It had been an expensive day so far. Guilt about Sexy Rexy's lonely week saw Kim splash out on a grooming session. The lady who ran the service parked a Mercedes van outside Kim's apartment and ushered Rex aboard for five-star luxury treatment: bath, blow dry, brush and nail trim.

Kim's weekend pampering didn't extend beyond the overdue manicure. First, she had to endure a ticking off from Madelaine; how could her famous client broadcast to the world with tatty digits? They didn't look *that* bad to Kim. But her manicurist compensated for the public flogging; Madelaine urged her other clients to watch *Spotlight* next week to see the remedial work. New polish and a boost in ratings wasn't a bad deal.

It was compensation for a love life that was once again stalled. Thursday dinner with Nathan didn't happen because of the homicide inquiries. Friday was never an option – drinks with the work crew took precedence over fledgling romances, especially when the potential beau was busy. Kim left him a voice message about her visit to the dogs on Saturday. She emphasised it would be a social evening. It was up to DS Potter to make the next move.

A cold breeze swept from the southerly corner of the lounge as a door opened; it was Dwayne Milligan and Rene Harding. They were on catching duties in the first two races. Neither were required for races three and four, which gave them time to meet Kim in the lounge. Harding greeted the reporter and headed for two women at the back of the lounge. Milligan laughed.

'Friends of Rene – or something more?'

'In his dreams. They're sisters, their father is an owner/trainer. They visit the track occasionally and Rene always gets suckered in to buying them drinks. He's never got beyond being Facebook friends.'

Kim sipped a white wine. 'Is this a good crowd – or did the murders scare a few away?'

'The reverse. I reckon there are more punters tonight than normal. And everyone is talking about Conor and Henry. Must be morbid curiosity as they're not the ones in danger.' Milligan pointed a thumb over his shoulder. 'Some of the trainers are edgy. If those animal activists didn't kill anyone, then who is it – and why? Yeah, there're a few shaky guys, especially those who were mates with the boss and Henry.'

Kim looked at the kennels beyond the finish line. The semi-circular tin roofs hid all the pre and post-race activities. Should she tell Steph to talk to some of the nervous nellies. Maybe. Perhaps Steph had already sniffed the fear?

'Are any trainers making suggestions on who is responsible? Could it be business related? Did Conor and Wright clash with someone over dogs or money?'

'Nah. They would never do anything to tarnish the sport. I wouldn't know about Henry's business dealings, but Conor was a fair man.'

'I guess a motive will be the key to finding the killer.'

Kim surveyed the room. The punters were a mixed bag of ages and ethnicities, reflecting Melbourne's multi-cultural diversity. The gender split was about 60:40 in favour of the males. The mood was buoyant: alcohol and a Saturday night at the track overriding most concerns about a crazed killer. At least for punters.

'Any sign of Benedict Beacham?'

Milligan's eyes turned to a table on the far side of the room.

'That's him over there, in front of the window.' He nodded discreetly. 'See the cute blonde? The one who sat down with a glass of wine. That's Abigail – his girlfriend. The Dapper Pom is the guy in the suit beside her. The other guy is the bookie, Chauncey Quayle.'

Kim drank more wine as she turned to observe her quarry; he lived up to the nickname. Beacham was the most elegantly dressed male in the lounge in a tailored grey suit, light blue shirt and a contrasting blue tie. He looked more appropriate for Flemington on Melbourne Cup Day than a night at the dishlickers. He was in his early 50s, trim and had a full head of hair with splashes of silver over his ears. The bookie was the only other patron wearing a suit, but it couldn't match the Dapper Pom.

'The old guy's suit looks like it hasn't been pressed in the last decade.'

Milligan laughed. 'Everyone says Chauncey was born in that.'

'He's the one that wanted to buy Tara – the guy with gold fever like Siobhan?'

'Yeah. Rene and I had our doubts about him earlier in the week. He turned up on Monday and inspected Tara like a buyer. Chauncey carried a bag in the days when bookies had to be tough. They had a lot of money to protect. The old-timers say Chauncey had some muscle on call if needed. We wondered if he might get someone to top Conor. But then Henry getting killed knocked that theory. If he was after the missing gold mine, why would he bump off Henry? The same goes for Siobhan. They wanted Conor's land – why create trouble with the cops by killing two trainers?'

Kim shrugged. 'A distraction? Get the cops thinking there's a lunatic with a chainsaw – rather than an old bookie and an angry wife.'

'I still don't think they're guilty. Anyway, you can make your own assessment. Look – Chauncey is waving us over.'

Kim saw the bookie offering spare seats. No need to worry about Jo, she was the centre of attention for her new gambling buddies. 'Okay, time to earn my keep.'

The eight dogs and their handlers for race three paraded past the lounge windows in step with Kim and Milligan. The next start for the chasers was from the 600 metre boxes. Kim's targets were a few metres away.

Milligan didn't have to make the introductions as Chauncey assumed the role of genial host.

'Ms Prescott – nice to see the media taking an interest in our humble sport. That other lass is doing all the camera work so, is it business or pleasure for you tonight?'

'I don't know if giving the TAB $40 could be described as fun but, in theory, this is a night off.'

Chauncey winked and picked up a large rum and coke. 'I see the cops released that HLP guy, the one who tried to plant false evidence against our good mate Conor. If the animal loonies aren't guilty, who is?'

Good mate? Kim waited a moment until the bookie had the drink to his mouth. 'Have the detectives spoken to you – or Siobhan?'

The barb produced the anticipated response. Chauncey spluttered, the drink sprayed sideways and forwards.

'Oh Chauncey,' Abigail pushed her chair away from the table. 'That's disgusting.'

Kim had one eye on Benedict as he passed a napkin. He laughed as a flustered Chauncey mopped his face and suit.

'Why would the cops talk to me? I can understand them chasing that crazy woman, but why me?'

'We know Siobhan believes the long-lost von Stieglitz gold mine is on the farm. That's a powerful motive to get rid of her husband.' Kim looked at Beacham and Abigail, then went for the jugular. 'But aren't you keen to buy Mr O'Leary's farm? Do you have some gold prospecting in mind as well? You know how police always like to follow a money trail.'

'But, but…' Chauncey wiped his face one more time then swallowed more rum without spilling any.

'Sorry to upset you like that Mr Quayle,' Kim said. 'I was putting myself in their shoes. The animal activists are out of the murder picture. They're guilty of trying to frame Conor and being stupid, but not much else. The cops need to focus elsewhere, you might get called in for a chat at headquarters.' Kim didn't think it was likely, but she wanted to keep the focus away from her real quarry.

'But I'm a businessman. I don't kill people to make deals.'

Kim went back to the inside information provided by Milligan. 'How would you describe your relationship with Conor O'Leary?'

Chauncey reeled. 'We weren't best mates – but we were okay. We talked at the track.'

'Didn't you once have a fight? Public fisticuffs?'

'Who told you that? That was years ago.' The bookie's eyes swept the table. Benedict and Abigail as recent arrivals to The Meadows were oblivious to that history. Milligan twirled his water glass and didn't return Chauncey's gaze.

Beacham's curiosity was piqued. 'I never heard anything about that Chauncey.' He smiled to lessen the blow. 'I knew you and Conor had a frosty relationship, but I can't imagine you two going toe to toe.'

'There was nothing in that.' Chauncey waved his hanky. 'He was drunk and let his hands get too familiar with Mrs Quayle. I dragged him outside and taught him some manners.'

Kim assessed the bookie. He must be in his 70s. He was tall, close to two- metres. She guessed in his prime he would have been able to handle himself. But now?

'When was that?' Beacham continued his interrogation.

'Must have been 20 years ago – at Geelong. He always was a randy bugger. None of the wives were safe around him after a couple of drinks. He was like an octopus – arms and hands all over them. You've seen what he's like? It's a wonder Siobhan stayed so long.'

Beacham nodded and let the matter rest. From what Kim had learned, neither man landed a punch during the affray. The sparring had been vocal ever since. She doubted he could wield a chainsaw these days. Time to tack.

'How well did you know the trainers Mr Beacham?'

'Call me Benedict, please.'

Kim nodded, waited.

'I met Conor and Henry soon after I arrived, about five years ago. I enjoyed the racing scene in the UK and I now have more time to indulge that passion. A flutter on the horses or dogs is good for the heart.'

Most people at the table laughed, except Chauncey.

'Your luck wasn't good for my old ticker. I had to retire before you put me in the poor house.'

'Come on Chauncey,' Benedict said. 'I won a mere trifle off you. It was the online invasion that made you punch the clock.'

Kim shut down that tangent. 'You follow all the racing codes Benedict? Which is your favourite?'

'I have to admit to a fondness for the greyhounds. They are such beautiful, fast and regal creatures. I love watching them race. My father owned dogs and I guess the interest runs in the family.'

'Do you own any?'

The question wasn't answered as the boxes opened for race three; the commentary demanded all the attention. Within seconds the field raced past their window, the black rug dog in the lead. The blue was mid-pack. Kim looked across to Jo who was cheering loudly. The excitement she generated was contagious, dozens joined the chorus for their own dogs as the field raced down the back straight and swept into the home turn. In a few more seconds it was over. The dog in the white rug was the winner in a tad over 34 seconds. Kim watched the screen for the placings; blue missed out. That didn't seem to worry Jo's betting buddies. Their tickets were discarded, all heads were soon buried in the form guide for the next race.

Kim's table suddenly emptied. Abigail headed for the bar. Milligan was being summoned by Rene Harding. Was persistence with the trainer's daughters getting him somewhere? And Chauncey was also on his feet with empty glass in hand. He didn't offer to shout anyone, perhaps eager to escape Kim's scrutiny.

'I've got to chat to Raymond about a couple of dogs. Ah…nice to meet you Ms Prescott. Are you going to Healesville tomorrow Benedict?'

'I think so. I've been given a couple of good tips for races seven and eight. It would be nice to watch them win – and make some money.'

Chauncey grunted and waved goodbye. Kim was alone; how hard should she push the Dapper Pom?

'You seem to have a lot of time for racing, Benedict. Do you still work?'

'Not these days. I made a good profit selling the business in London. Our pound buys a lot more here, so we bought a nice lifestyle block at Mount Macedon. I always wanted land but could never afford it in England.'

'Well done. What was your former career?'

'I was an electrical engineer. Had a few guys working for me in North London. Sold at the right time and life is good in the land downunder.' Beacham smiled, all charm and – Kim hoped – no suspicions. Time to rattle him.

'Abigail doesn't sound English.' Kim looked to the bar where the girlfriend chatted to two women.

'She's not. We met recently.'

'Oh, sorry. You said *we bought* so I assumed it was your lovely lady. She's very pretty.'

Beacham shifted in his seat. 'Yes, she is.'

'Did you have another partner? Are you separated – or divorced?'

He shifted again. 'Yes, well – no. My wife came to Australia with me. She didn't like the heat and went home last year. We haven't divorced, or anything yet.' Beacham reached for his beer and drained the dregs. He waved it at Abigail, she turned and ordered a fresh pot.

'Oh, that's a pity. I love the climate, can't get me away from the beach on a hot summer day. Where did your wife go? Back to chilly London?' Kim smiled, hoping she didn't sound disingenuous.

'Somerset, actually. She has family there. We don't communicate much anymore.'

Bingo! Two lies. Kim wondered if she should go for strike three?

'What else keeps you busy – apart from following horses and dogs? Do you have stock at Mount Macedon, or are you into formal gardens? Those mansions have the most amazing autumn shows. My mother drags me out there every April to traipse through lush wonderlands. Do you like gardening – or do you have other hobbies?'

Benedict looked at Kim for a long moment, she held the *friendly* smile. 'Ah no. Nothing really. The property is more woodland, not much for me to do there apart from mow a bit of grass. I dabble in the stock markets online. I've had a busy professional life; it's time to relax.'

That curve ball missed the edge of the plate. Kim prepared for another pitch when Abigail stalled play with Benedict's refill.

'There you go love. Remember you're driving tonight.'

Beacham nodded, but still swallowed deeply and then stood.

'Excuse me a moment. I have to use the bathroom.'

Kim watched him limp through the crowd and turned to the girlfriend.

'It's not far to Mount Macedon from here, but I wouldn't fancy being behind the wheel on Saturday night.'

'Oh, we're not going back there. I live in Albert park. I've only been to Benedict's place once. That was enough.' Abigail shivered.

'Oh – what's wrong with his home.'

'The house is beautiful, so are the grounds. Quiet and secluded.' Abigail lowered her voice. 'Benedict won't let me talk about it. Never.' She checked that no patrons were close 'I don't visit because of the guardians. Benedict's snakes creep me out.'

Strike three!

Day 140

Saturday was disappointing for Carolyn, more so than the previous 139 days. She woke early, a plan in place to use the carefully crafted weapon. It was simple but workable. She pretended to be sick, lying on the bed, facing the wall. Her jailer would investigate when there was no response to his breakfast delivery. She hunched in a foetal position, the bone shiv in her right hand. One strike at his throat. Her only chance. Push it deep and twist – hope to shock and draw blood. She would spring for the door and keep running. Speed might beat the most dangerous guardian – the cobra. Carolyn didn't know about its habits, or striking capability. King Charles was deadly, if bitten there was little hope of survival. Did Australia have any cobra antivenom? A magazine article revealed death usually occurred within an hour. Could she get help within that time? Not likely. But they wouldn't be a deterrent any longer.

Not that she had a chance to outsprint the serpents. Her ploy to draw the jailer close failed. He dumped the breakfast and lunch tray inside the door and left. No curiosity, no compassion. Her stomach grumbled as she repeated the ploy Saturday night. She maintained the bed pose for most of the day, leaving the food untouched. Surely, he would investigate if nothing had changed from the morning. She was a pitiful, helpless wretch – no danger to him.

There was more disappointment. No dinner. No sounds from above, just the occasional hiss and slither from beyond her prison door. Carolyn picked up the screw and scratched at the wall. Tomorrow. Freedom – or death – would come tomorrow.

Chapter 46

Stephanie Grant's gym bag bumped along the walls of the narrow corridor to the *Spotlight* office on Sunday morning. A vigorous cardio and weights session energised the new current affairs reporter eager to make an impression with her new bosses. Daily news programs rarely allowed the luxury of extra time on story production. There was always a deadline looming. If the best story of the day broke at 5.30 television audiences still expected coverage on the six o'clock news.

Steph knew she had great interviews from The Meadows. She was prepared to sacrifice a few hours on a rostered day-off to view the footage and write a script. The story could be edited Monday morning, leaving her free to chase new breaks on the trainer murders. Kim Prescott couldn't cover every angle by herself.

The office lights were on as she approached, which was unexpected. Who else was prepared to sacrifice their weekends? Steph entered and wasn't totally surprised to find Kim at Mac's command post. But she didn't anticipate Jo would be at the computer as well.

'Oh. Hello. What are you up to? I thought I was the only zealot.'

'Hey Steph,' Jo replied. 'Kim's got another wacky idea and she wants some company – as usual.'

'What have you found? Something new on the English guy?'

'Possibly.'

Steph offered an olive branch. 'I got Dugal to record pictures of you chatting to him at the table. In case you need footage.'

Kim hesitated, then accepted the professional peace offering. 'Thanks Steph. It might come in handy. I think our Dapper Pom is whiffy, even if he dresses like a shop window mannequin.'

Steph dropped her gym bag and rolled a chair to Jo's computer. It displayed a Google satellite map. 'Where's that?'

'Mount Macedon.' Jo said. 'It's Benedict Beacham's property.'

'Why are you looking at that?'

Jo turned to Kim and raised an eyebrow.

'We think it might be worth a sneaky inspection.' Kim pointed at the computer.

The aerial revealed a long, rectangular building from above with two extensions. Most likely for window views over the gardens. There was a 20-metre strip of lawn around the house and then trees all the way to the boundary.

'It's about three hectares and secluded.' Kim clicked on the mouse; the image changed to street view. There was a double gate and dry-stone wall which merged into high hedges. 'The Dapper Pom loves his privacy.'

Steph nodded but was unsure about the fascination with the manicured grounds and mini forest 60 kilometres north west of Melbourne. Kim didn't say much in the crew car on the trip home from The Meadows. The PA dominated the chatter; Jo was fizzing about her first punting experience. A night of fun, food and booze had produced a profit of $75 – thanks to lucky guesses and tips from her new admirers.

Steph folded her arms. 'What did you learn Kim?'

The younger reporter reached for keys on a shelf above the desk.

'Come on Kim. We're on the same team. We want to make the best stories possible for *Spotlight*. Sometimes you need to share. If you have information that relates to my story, I should know.'

'There's no connection to your feature. That's about an industry and people in fear. This is a guy who might be of interest.' She stood up. 'I'm going to the crew room to get the Sony camcorder.'

Steph watched Kim leave and shook her head. 'I don't know why she won't share information with me. We're bloody colleagues.'

Jo sighed. 'I'll never understand you journalists. You can't tell the difference between single-minded and paranoia.'

'Can *you* tell me why she is being so secretive?'

The crew room was at least 100-metres away through the station rabbit warren. Steph knew it should take Kim at least five minutes to find the camera and return.

'Come on Jo. I'm not going to steal her story. But there might be a crossover to what I'm doing – or what I might find out.'

The PA looked at the empty doorway. 'Beacham lied about his wife. He said she is in Somerset. The brother says she isn't. Beacham said he owned an electrical engineering business. We know he was in the British army and his money came from a lottery win. And then there was the big secret – Beacham's hobby.'

'Okay – you've got me hooked. What is it?'

'He's obsessed with snakes – there's a private collection in the cellar. Most of them are lethal – local species and imported. The deadlier the better according to his girlfriend. She's too scared to visit. None of the greyhound people know about his love affair with serpents.'

Steph joined the dots that Kim connected the previous evening. 'Three of the O'Leary dogs were killed by snakes, weren't they?'

'Yep.'

'And the former wife hasn't been seen for months?'

'Nope.'

'Kim thinks she might have met the same fate?'

'Yep.'

'You're going to look for a grave on his property?'

'Yep.'

'How can you do that?'

'Kim heard him say he's going to the races at Healesville today. It's an hour and half each way from Mount Macedon. We know he's going to be there until at least race seven or eight.'

'That gives you a few hours to…dig around?'

Jo nodded. Two minutes later Kim returned to the office with the camcorder.

'We need to get going Jo. The races start at 11.' Her mobile beeped. 'Damn.'

'What's the problem?'

'It's Nathan. He's been given the day off and wants to meet for lunch.'

Jo grinned. 'You can always invite him along.'

'No thanks. He can wait.' The reporter pocketed the phone and picked up her keys.

'You're going to ignore him?'

'For the moment.'

Chapter 47

The hook gently slid beneath the slow-moving guardian. Its duty was over for another session. The diamond python was three years old and, at full stretch, measured more than two metres. The steel shaft lifted the head of the dark olive and yellow snake from the brick floor. It didn't mind; bred in captivity it was docile if handled properly. It wasn't venomous but a bite would be painful and bloody.

Benedict Beacham had a deft touch; he'd never felt the fangs of an angry serpent. He knew snakes would rather back away from a confrontation than strike. Even his most fearsome pets – for all their dramatic hissing and posturing – preferred the security of their private domains than attacking.

Reptiles had fascinated him all his life. His first encounter was at St Materiana, in Tintagel, during a family holiday to Cornwall. The 10-year-old spent every spare minute hunting vipers between the grass-clad gravestones. They were venomous, but generally not lethal if a bite was treated swiftly. Not that Beacham's family knew about his dalliance with the snakes. They thought he was walking the rugged coast and coves like every other holidaymaker. Boarding school and the army restricted opportunities to nurture that interest for many years.

Beacham held the python by the tail as he hobbled to DJ's lair in the corner. Five years in Australia saw Beacham finally succumb to a local habit; consequently, Diamond Jack had been abbreviated. DJ's tank was 2.2 metres long and 700 mm in width and height. It couldn't replicate the forests of New South Wales where an entrepreneur bagged him for the black market, but a mixture of soil, rocks and foliage made it homely. A thermostat kept the tanks – and the whole lower floor – at the right temperature. DJ wouldn't have enjoyed the May climate around Melbourne without central heating.

DJ slid off the hook inside the glass panel and coiled himself beneath a branch in the corner. It was the carpet python's classic ambush position. Beacham wondered if DJ knew his reward for another guard shift would be a nimble rat. The panel slid back into place.

'Patience DJ,' Beacham said. 'I'll get your meal in a few minutes. I have to organise the live stream first.'

There would be a few seconds for the predator and prey to assess their face-off. Did the rodent believe it had a chance to escape, or was being the main course inevitable? How quickly would the python strike? Did it enjoy the panic of its quarry? That was beyond Beacham's knowledge. But he did know humans enjoyed Darwinism in action – and they were prepared to pay for the thrill. DJ's natural instincts drew a regular audience of about 300 people on the dark web, each prepared to pay for the privilege. Who would have guessed that feeding pets could be so lucrative?

DJ wasn't the only internet star in the cellar. Beacham inserted the hook into its slot beside the tongs on the brick wall. The pistol grip was used to secure the lethal members of the troupe. He surveyed them in their tanks: 10 in a variety of sizes, most flush against the 19th century cellar walls. Each habitat created for maximum comfort. The massive cellar was a major reason for buying the property, along with the thick bush with a regular food supply for his pets. There were another 10 empty tanks scattered among the collection: awaiting new arrivals.

The media favourite was King Charles. The King Cobra reigned in a four-metre tank which stood at centre stage. Charles was young, measuring 2.5 metres. He could reach up to four metres as an adult and that posed future problems for Beacham. He couldn't handle such a large and dangerous reptile alone. That would be the time to cash in on the underground celebrity and sell him to another owner. Most likely in America or South Africa. Maybe even Russia. That's where many of his viewers were based. It wouldn't be a problem to transport King Charles to a new home, or continent; the reptile black market had flourished for many years.

Beacham would be sorry to lose the King. He was a great earner – double the price of DJ per view. Hundreds switched on their computers when an alert went out for a new show. The fans loved to watch King Charles hunt lizards, rats or mice in the cellar. Sometimes it was another snake. Nothing venomous; Beacham didn't want to risk his star having an off day.

There were five remote cameras in the cellar and the paying public would never miss the climax. Before the catch and kill sessions, Beacham displayed the defensive nature of cobras. They loved to feint at threats with mock bites. The flared hood was the most attractive feature and Beacham liked to keep his viewers entertained. Not that they ever saw the snake charmer. Only his heavily gloved hands. The killer pets were exciting to own and show, but he wasn't silly about revealing his identity. You never knew who was watching.

The rest of the cast were native Australians: an inland taipan, a coastal taipan, a tiger snake, a copperhead, a red-bellied black snake, a death adder, an eastern brown and a mulga – otherwise known as the king brown. Until King Charles was sold there would be only one resident king.

Beacham wanted more snakes, especially international species. A rattlesnake, bushmaster and a black mamba were on his wish list. In time he would acquire them and other exotic pets. It would require more space than the cellar of this Victorian era homestead to house his dream team. Reptile collections were not illegal, but Beacham preferred to avoid regulations and bureaucracy by keeping his domain secret. Few people within Australia knew about his hobby; only two were in Victoria.

Milking the local species could provide another revenue stream. But selling venom to the laboratories which produced antidotes would put him on the radar. And that would have thwarted Beacham's payback against Conor O'Leary. He wanted to torment the Irishman for his sins. To ruin a thriving greyhound training business was the start of his revenge. The chainsaw coup de grace was always planned as the final act.

It took incredible patience and skill to hide his anger and bitterness. Beacham had to be civil for months: friendly, chatty and full of bonhomie until he could complete his plan. There was no problem finding poison for the dogs, it was merely a matter of choice. Should it be from the tiger snake or eastern brown? Both were found in the Steiglitz district. He knew he was stretching his luck by using the tactic three times. The original intention was to kill the best two dogs, the group winners and cash cows for the kennels.

The assassinations were so easy and exciting that Beacham was inspired to commit a third. By then the dogs were terrified of the black-clad intruder and didn't howl or bark when he entered the kennels. They whimpered at the doggy grim reaper; but it wasn't enough to disturb a sleeping Conor in the main house. If they didn't make a fuss, maybe he wouldn't visit them. It was almost human-like.

Death came quickly for the victims. Beacham entered their cages, clamped a hand around their jaws and injected the dogs twice with a thick syringe to make it look like a snake bite. The poison swept through the slight 25 kilo frames; the dogs soon collapsed in his arms. It would have been easier to kill two the same night. But that might have made Conor and the vet too suspicious. A predatory tiger snake in a greyhound kennel was already testing credulity.

Beacham watched with delight as the O'Leary racing team withered. Three deaths to snake bites were too much for owners of the best-performed dogs. The kennels were jinxed. Those that stayed with the embattled trainer did so out of loyalty, or apathy. Yet Beacham had to bide his time, delayed by the unexpected fire at Tara. It wasn't an accident. Who else had a grudge against the Irish expat? Beacham wondered if the animal activists were involved. The track confrontations were witnessed by too many to keep that story under wraps. Little did Beacham know that Julian Oliver's vendetta would aid his own plans.

Day 141

Carolyn seethed as a Dire Straits song played outside the cell. The anger wasn't about the music, it was the loss of her weapon. Her chance to escape.

She was starving by breakfast on Sunday. The previous meals were ignored on the floor to create a scene of illness. She stayed hunched in the foetal position around his expected appearances. Her nerves jangled when she heard him arrive and greet the guardians, each reptile receiving personal attention. Then it was the captive wife's turn.

Mentally she had rehearsed this moment a hundred times since Friday: once he was close, roll and thrust for the throat or face. Push, jump and run. Don't dally to lock the door. Swift movement was the key.

He didn't say anything. She heard the plastic food tray slide on the floor. More silence. Then movement – steps coming towards the bed. She sensed him over her shoulder, then smelled his after shave: Sauvage. How close was he? No touch yet. The light over her head dimmed – he must be within reach. Carolyn twirled, stabbed and tried to leap off the bed.

Her shiv was engulfed by a thick blanket. A gloved right fist smashed into the side of her face; once, twice. Her vision blurred. The hand then easily snatched her weapon. She was powerless again. How did that happen?

Beacham stepped backwards from his distraught wife with a knowing grin. That irritated Carolyn almost as much as her failure.

'You bastard!' she screamed. 'You can't do this forever! I've done nothing wrong – let me go!'

Her husband was through the doorway by that stage.

Tears poured from Carolyn's eyes for the first time in weeks. She was so close to freedom. But how did he know she was about to attack? There was nothing in her preparations to alert him. Unless…he was watching. Her eyes scanned the smooth limestone walls. There had to be a camera. He knew she had the makeshift knife; he'd watched her sharpen it and prepare for the escape. He knew the whole time – was he laughing at her now?

Slowly Carolyn stood and examined every centimetre of her prison that she could reach. Nothing. No sign of a lens or anything to indicate she might be Benedict's private Big Brother show. That didn't mean there wasn't a hidden camera. He was a technical whiz – he could have 20 tiny cameras and Carolyn wouldn't find them. She shivered. The beast was watching all the time. Who else could see her?

Chapter 48

Beacham hummed the Dire Straits tune *Money for Nothing* as he swept the floor of the reptile zoo with a soft bristle broom. There wasn't much dust, as usual. Half a lifetime in the military instilled habits on cleanliness. The entire 310 square metre home – above and below ground – was spotless. Rodents silly enough to investigate it as a winter retreat would become the menu.

For a moment, the army veteran was Mark Knopfler, strumming a broom guitar. He was in his happy place; memories swirled with the music. The leather-covered lead sap that laid out Conor O'Leary wasn't military issue. But it had been part of Beacham's kit during his 25 years in the military. The Royal Engineers served in many of the world's troubled nations; the sap was convenient for defence and offense when a gun wasn't appropriate. It had rarely been employed, but the ex-soldier knew that several swift blows to the back of the head would take down most men.

It was easy to get the desperate trainer to meet a new owner in secret. O'Leary and every trainer in Melbourne and Geelong had tried to get the Dapper Pom to buy a few chasers. They saw his smart suits and luck with the TAB. Why shouldn't he put money back into the sport? Beacham had to hide his loathing as O'Leary made his sales pitch over a Jameson's in the Tara homestead. Twenty years ago, the dishlickers left at the property that night might have been given a whack on the back of the head and a bonfire farewell. They were too slow to race, yet O'Leary embellished their records for the potential co-owner as they strode towards the kennels.

'Take no notice that these dogs and bitches aren't racing tonight, Benedict.' O'Leary stopped in the driveway. 'They're young dogs – all potential Group winners. One of them I reckon could make the Melbourne Cup field next year. Imagine getting a share of $600,000? I know a couple of owners are struggling financially and would be open to a deal.'

O'Leary laughed as he turned and opened the wire door to the kennel enclosure. That's when Beacham struck with all the skill and muscle of an ex-soldier – and a husband who had been cuckolded.

The sap struck twice; O'Leary was unconscious within seconds. The blows weren't overly energetic, but Beacham found himself breathing heavily.

'Bastard!' he shouted. 'That will teach you to molest my wife. No one…no one…touches Carolyn…except me. She's mine! Mine!'

Beacham kicked his victim in the side. It felt good; he did it again – two, three, four times. No grunts emerged.

'Noooooo!' he howled, froth at the edges of his lips. 'You can't be dead. That's too easy.' He felt for a pulse on the neck. It was faint. He ran to the Commodore parked near the front steps. From the boot he retrieved overalls.

It was one of the rare days that Beacham wore denims and a sweatshirt, an outfit that surprised O'Leary. The suit was on a coat hanger over a rear passenger door. The Meadows was also on the agenda for the Dapper Pom after their business deal. Beacham stripped naked and donned the navy-blue cotton drill coverall. It cost $90– but would only be worn once. Same with the boots. The pull-on size 10s were worth $120. The black balaclava cost much less. They would all go up in smoke.

The final item to emerge from the car was a 20-inch petrol powered chainsaw. Water was splashed on the victim's face as he lay in the dirt. It roused Conor to semi-consciousness. Beacham revved the chainsaw, watching bleary eyes widen in terror. Within 20 minutes the bastard was minced and boxed. That was a satisfying experience.

The soundtrack in Beacham's cellar segued to *Brothers in Arms*, another favourite from the band. A gun would have been too quick and easy for the trainer. Venomous snakes too risky. A brutal execution had been Beacham's fantasy since witnessing the infidelity. He wanted to emasculate and destroy. Dismemberment was his dream scenario, just like his own heart had been torn apart. Conor had to *feel* pain.

Beacham believed every farm had a chainsaw; but it was wiser to take a reliable second-hand one to be sure. Conor's implement was found in the garage beside the house. He took it to confuse investigators. Beacham placed it in the Commodore, separate from the plastic-wrapped blood-stained clothing. It would survive four days longer than the first murder kit.

Chapter 49

'I want to search for the body.' Jo folded her arms and stared through the windscreen. 'You're not going to have all the fun.'

Kim lifted one hand off the steering wheel in frustration. 'I need a lookout. In case Beacham comes home early.'

They were on the M79 to Mount Macedon. It was 11.20, race seven was at 12.57; Beacham should be on his way to the track. But you never knew when fate might intervene: a change of plans, a flat tyre, roadworks could turn her suspect around.

It wasn't an inspiring drive. Double lanes north and south surrounded by brown paddocks and scrubby trees. The next kilometre unlikely to be more memorable than the last.

Kim didn't want to concede. 'Anyway, you're not dressed for searching the bush. A jacket and jeans are okay, but proper boots would have helped.'

Jo hoisted a brown Windsor Smith with elastic gusset onto the seat. 'What's wrong with these? The shop sold them as boots, ergo they must be boots.'

'We're not searching the wilds of Chadstone Shopping Centre. There are dirt tracks, tree roots, creepy crawlies and who knows what else. I don't need you twisting an ankle.' She glanced at her own intruder gear: the same fleece, jeans and footwear worn the night she found Conor O'Leary's body. Was that a good or bad omen?

The boot slammed onto the floor of Kim's Mazda Roadster. 'Well, how good is this for an undercover vehicle?' She gestured to the gleaming red bonnet, polished on Saturday by Kim's father. 'A flash sports car *won't* stand out parked in the leafy lanes, will it?'

'How else were we going to get there? Ring Nathan and get a police escort?'

That silenced both women. Should they really be sneaking into the private grounds of a murder suspect? Beacham was only dubious to the media, although it didn't make him any less dangerous. Especially when snakes were his secret hobby.

'Maybe your new boyfriend should be there looking for chainsaws and bodies.'

'He's not my boyfriend. We're just *friends* – at this stage.'

Jo rolled her eyes. 'Whatever. This is risky. But I think we need to stay together. A snake can't bite two of us at once.'

'I hope the poisonous ones prefer smaller morsels – like you.'

They passed the exit for Sunbury: less than 30 kilometres to Mount Macedon, almost time for the GPS to take over.

'By the way,' Jo said. 'Do you know exactly where his snake pit is?'

Chapter 50

Henry Wright's fate was sealed the same night as Conor O'Leary's. His takedown was a work in progress at the time of his friend's death. There couldn't be a plague of poisonous snakes sneaking into kennels or homes to kill. That would be too coincidental for police. However, Wright merited an equally painful death.

He knew the Ballan Road property. It was the source of his bile. That's where it started – at one of Wright's drunken parties. The pre-Christmas evenings were too cold for naked shenanigans in the pool. Groups hovered around the barbecue and bar: drinking, laughing, chatting. The regulars danced on the concrete terrace to a medley of hits from Spotify. Beacham was sprawled in a low Cape Cod chair and watched as the usual pranksters flirted with the easily led.

Carolyn was always chattier than her husband, a social butterfly, flitting from group to group. Beacham preferred to find a comfortable perch and observe. He wasn't a party recluse, always ready to talk. But he preferred chatters to come to him. His party base allowed him to keep Carolyn within sight, or sound. Her laugh was distinguishable; high-pitched and infectious. Perhaps it was that missing sound that made Beacham curious that last night. Music and laughter filled the terrace, but there was no sign of Carolyn.

He had scanned the party area and noticed the host and his best mate were also absent. The fear of betrayal caused stomach acid to rise. It had taken all his strength not to react when the trainers groped his wife at the dais in November. He could have handled one, not two. That might have invited more humiliation.

Casually, and with a smile on his face, Beacham cruised the house. Smaller groups congregated in the kitchen and lounge. They nodded or said hello as he passed. The bedrooms fanned off a central hallway. Beacham used the party noise to shield his approach. There were four closed doors. Militarily he knew how to enter and search without being shot. On those occasions he had a flak jacket and helmet for protection. One of Wright's bedrooms had the potential to fatally wound him.

The first three rooms were empty, apart from double or single beds and dressers. He stood outside the fourth door and quelled the angst as muffled voices filtered through. The red mist rose. He clasped the handle, steeled himself for a horrifying scene and stepped inside.

A semi-naked woman screamed on the bed. A man lay on top. Beacham flushed like a beetroot – both participants were married, but not to each other. The lady caught *in flagrante* wasn't his Carolyn. It was still a betrayal; another whore who should be punished. Let her husband sort her out. Beacham had to find his own wife and prayed it would not be in a similar scenario.

His face felt like a blazing sun; he couldn't return through the house to the party. Instead, he exited via the front door and turned left past the double garage. A cold breeze from the south might settle his heart and return his pallor to normal.

The adrenalin was dissipating a minute later when moonlight revealed three figures returning from the paddocks. They were laughing, two men and a woman. Her voice was distinctive – Beacham had listened to it every day of his married life. A sensor triggered a spotlight on the house as they approached. The trio greeted it with more giggles; Beacham was mortified.

Wright was bare-chested, Carolyn was in his over-sized sweatshirt: a green silk blouse and dark bra was in her hand. How could she be so brazen? O'Leary was dishevelled and had an arm over Carolyn's shoulder.

Rage surged through Beacham. If he was back in Afghanistan, his SA80 assault rifle would have chopped them to pieces in seconds. He would have reloaded and shot them again. Two magazines, three. Maybe even a fourth. That was the depth of his shame. Carolyn had stripped him of his dignity. They had to be punished. Not now, not there. Revenge didn't have to mean spending the rest of his life in prison.

The threesome couldn't see Beacham in the shadows under the eaves of the house. He retreated to the safety of his car. Carolyn eventually found him there. It was too late for apologies. Her fate was settled, along with O'Leary and Wright. It would take planning. A quarter of a century in the army as a combat engineer made Beacham a master organiser; lethal when required.

The Wright death was designated for mid-winter – two months after Conor O'Leary. The trainer had to endure similar torment until Beacham believed the timing was right. It would be well after their party betrayal, long enough for Beacham to show no public rancour towards either man. He would provide no reason for police to suspect him.

Julian Oliver created a new opportunity to hasten the revenge plan. The cops already had a strong suspect. He was on the run. Why not use the same tactic to kill Wright? He wouldn't have the pleasure of destroying the trainer emotionally or financially. For that, Beacham planned to torch Wright's retirement fund – the 40-hectare forest.

A good soldier capitalised on confusion. Detectives were looking elsewhere for their killer. The animal activists made themselves guiltier by the day. Therefore, Beacham had turned himself into a *buyer* – again. Wright's death was as thrilling and satisfying as the first murder. It was better than dealing with the Taliban in Helmand Province. The terms of the Geneva Convention hindered battlefield revenge.

Beacham replaced the broom and dustpan in a cupboard. He checked the time. It was about 80 minutes to the Healesville track. If traffic was bad, he might miss the races he was targeting. He could always place his bets online and watch the races on television. But it wasn't the same as the live experience. The skitter of paws, the whirling of the electric lure, the cheers of the crowd. The magic of race days had captivated him from the first time his grandfather took him to the Belle Vue Stadium in Manchester. He loved all racing codes, although the dogs were his favourite because of Pappy. That first £1 bet in 1973 as a 10-year-old was a winner. He'd always been lucky, in racing at least.

The jailer looked at the steel door set into the limestone. No tears, screams or whimpers emerged. He was surprised at Carolyn's mental resilience. He thought his wife would be a basket case, although the detention was never meant to last so long. She was supposed to be the second execution, between her sexual playmates. Ironically, Carolyn was making too much money to kill.

All combat engineers had a secondary trade: Beacham was an electrician. A brilliant sparky and internet genius who thrived on complex challenges. The £10 million lottery win allowed Beacham to satisfy every whim in the Mount Macedon sanctuary. He turned to a bank of eight monitors that portrayed every movement of the below ground residents. He used a desk console to tweak camera three, zooming into DJ's tank and sharpening the focus.

One star was ready to perform, time for the prey. Beacham lifted the lid of a metre-square timber box and extracted a white rat by the tail. It was bred for scientific research. Breeders didn't mind selling a few on the side as *pets*. The extra expense was worth it; white rats were easier to see on internet screens. Viewers could watch DJ slowly crush them. It was twisted, but who was Beacham to argue with easy, untaxed cash?

He returned to the reptile room, slid open DJ's panel and released the doomed rat. The panel was closed. A few seconds later the video feed was broadcasting to the sickos who wanted another lesson in survival of the fittest – and fastest.

Day 141

Was Benedict the only person watching? Or were there others? Carolyn had always been impressed by her husband's electronics skills. The lottery money and move to Australia allowed him to indulge every passion. She thought they were reasonably happy – until November. Benedict had always been possessive about her around other men. She learned to live with that trait. But overnight he turned into a monster. Did that twist in his psyche extend to the internet? Had he turned her into a weird show for other fruitcakes? The thought made her shiver. But it also gave her renewed hope. If people were plugged into the prison feed, would someone help if they knew her location?

It was a long shot, but she had nothing to lose. But how to send an SOS via the camera feed? *If* there was one. She had no writing materials or paper. No lipstick or mascara to use on the limestone walls. There was soap, toothpaste and deodorant – all white. Could anything be mixed with them to stand out against the wall?

Carolyn looked around the spartan room. There was the single bed, a few clothes, books and not much else. How had she tolerated this for so long? The wall calendar marked the passing days. Could the tiny screw scrape a large plea for help? It had to include their address and that would take hours. Benedict might be watching even now. He could cut the television feed within seconds. If he didn't intervene, did that indicate she wasn't an internet star? This was all his own fantasy?

'You're making too many assumptions, girl. Think!'

One hope had been quashed that morning. Now another flickered. Why not take a chance? Carolyn's eyes roamed the room again. Her food tray lay by the door. Breakfast was scoffed after a day of hunger; a chicken and salad sandwich were lunch. She saw the beetroot. Two slices. It might be her salvation.

Chapter 51

Beacham's 6.2 litre Commodore gobbled up the kilometres on the Calder Freeway. It guzzled petrol, but he didn't care. He was still a multi-millionaire, despite paying more than $4 million for the Mount Macedon home. His pets and Carolyn earned money even as he drove to the track. Another good day at the races would boost the bank balance.

The key to punting was research. Study the breeding, long term form, box performances and success at the different tracks. Not many small-time gamblers put the effort that Beacham did into preparing his bets. He wouldn't have a flutter on every race. Rarely did he put a large sum on the nose. A consistent performer with excellent results from a certain box on a familiar track was more appealing. If the bookies left the place dividends too generous, that's when Beacham would strike. A dog virtually guaranteed to place at $1.70 was his ideal target. A thousand dollars would return $700 in less than a minute. Sometimes luck and fate played a hand; the mutt might get bowled or checked by a dippy dog on a turn. But Beacham's success indicated his formula worked.

Good returns from the TAB didn't surprise Beacham, the live streams popularity did. Especially the pictures of Carolyn. She was basically a woman in a box, why would weirdos want to pay for that? He charged by a 24-hour bloc to watch Carolyn sit, read, walk, eat, wait. There wasn't a camera in the bathroom, although they occasionally caught glimpses of her naked 48-year-old body when changing. The numbers had increased over the months, rising to a peak of 743 daily views in February when she often spent hot days in a bra and panties. Currently it fluctuated between 511 and 527. Easy money.

It was risky keeping Carolyn as a media star. There was always a fear that a neighbour or greyhound industry person might recognise her. You never knew which people enjoyed these fetishes. Beacham had degraded the live stream to obscure her identity. Maybe the viewers wouldn't care if they knew her. It was her plight that captivated them. Beacham admitted the whore was still attractive. Her wanton nature had cost the trainers their lives. It made her a condemned woman as well.

Abigail was another factor to consider. Fortunately, she was terrified by the snakes and never ventured beyond the kitchen or lounge on her only visit. That also helped extend Carolyn's life. Abigail wouldn't even use the loo on her only visit – worried that a snake might slide out of the S bend. That fear always made Beacham laugh, although it suited him. The relationship was casual, Carolyn would be gone before any Abigail-replacements entered the home. He had given his heart twice and been rejected. Never again. But a man still needed company.

Beacham barely noticed the scenery as he drove towards Healesville. The northern fringe of the city wasn't an inspiring drive, especially post summer. It was dry and brown, a contrast to the green fields of England. Their origins helped prepare the false story about Carolyn's departure. It was a stretch to say she hated the heat: they made regular trips to Queensland or Fiji. However, mixing the narrative with yearnings for village life, coastal walks and other trappings of English society made it believable.

The escape bid was anticipated, thanks to the hidden cameras. Carolyn never suspected she was under observation, by him or voyeurs around the world. Was that secret out? Probably. She wouldn't find the cameras. He was too clever for her. The blanket and glove could be explained as a soldier's instincts for an ambush. If Carolyn was truly sick, she should have been begging for help, not curled ready to strike – like his pets.

Carolyn's own fears helped keep her imprisoned. She rarely visited the cellar during the happier days of their marriage. The King Cobra terrified her: the flared hood and swaying symbolised instant death for Carolyn. The thought that King Charles slithered around the floor every night deterred any breakouts from her box. She never knew it was the python; harmless, cuddly DJ enjoying his freedom. His patrols didn't last the night. When sleep beckoned, DJ returned to his tank and curled up in the corner.

The Commodore was joining the M80 from the Calder Freeway when Beacham's mobile ruined his day.

Chapter 52

Kim passed the Mt Macedon Trading Post and a vine-covered Uniting church. It was quaint, like much of the region. The roads were quiet, the autumn garden festivals finished as the brilliant foliage had fallen. She checked her speed; it was easy to edge over the 60-km limit and get pinged by a sneaky camera. They continued past the turn off to the Mount. Their destination wasn't far down the road. The sky was overcast, although not threatening rain. The wind swept yellow and brown leaves across their path. The temperature was in the low teens, several degrees colder than Melbourne.

Jo's head was buried in her mobile phone. 'Did you know that Mount Macedon is covered in wet sclerophyll communities? Hope I pronounced that right. The native forest is made up of alpine ash, mountain ash and snow gums.' Jo looked out the window. 'They all look like gum trees to me. I never knew there was a difference.'

'You need to get out of the South Melbourne bars more often. Or spend more time on Google.'

'Ooooo – saucer of cream for kitty?'

The sarcasm was ignored. 'We're almost there – keep your eyes open for a park.'

A few seconds later Kim's mobile chirped with a text. It was charging through the USB port on the dash. 'Can you check that for me Jo?'

The PA tapped the screen and smiled. 'Lover boy is persistent.'

'What? It's Nathan again?'

'Yep.' Jo paused. 'I think he might be in cop mode.'

An embankment and hedges shielded lavish homes on the left. On the right, their parking options were limited by trees, shrubs and a culvert.

'He says: *"Unusual for a reporter not to answer. Makes a cop wonder if she has a new story?"'*

The road curved. Kim looked left and right for a space, ignoring Nathan's latest message. 'Damn. That's Beacham's property there.'

The sports car cruised past imposing double cedar gates, arched stone supports and a thick box hedge. It wasn't a fortress, but it wouldn't be an easy entry – unless the gates were unlocked. Everything was at least two metres high.

Jo looked at the humble, green-painted wooden entrance across the road. It was open.

'Why couldn't that be his lair?' She shrugged. 'That would have been too easy.'

The road twisted the other way. There wasn't anywhere to park either side of Beacham's entrance and view the gates. It settled one issue.

'I guess you join me as a grave robber.' Kim slowed the car and turned into a driveway. 'There was an antique shop a few hundred metres before Beacham's. There were two Mercedes parked outside; a sports car won't stand out. Did you see any cameras?'

'If you'd dropped back to second gear, I might have seen more than the hedge. Why would he need cameras out here?'

Kim glanced at the entrance as they passed for a second time. No obvious security and no latches on the gates. They stopped near the shop.

'Maybe we should have brought Sexy Rexy?' Jo said. 'We could pretend to be out for a country walk.'

'I considered that.' Kim turned into a bay near the shop and switched off. 'But then I thought of Beacham's snakes. I wouldn't want to put my baby in danger.'

Jo stopped with one foot out of the car. 'I forgot about them.' The boot returned to carpeted floor and the door shut. 'Do you think they might be loose when he's out?'

'Probably.' Kim stepped out and pulled on a rain jacket. Her colleague remained seated. 'But I'm sure they're all locked inside a warm room. We're not going inside the house – we're looking for a grave.'

There was no need to mention the deadly neighbours who lived permanently in the bush.

'Come on. I'm going to need your help to get through the gates.'

Beacham was agitated. There were five lanes on the Western Ring Road and nowhere to pull over. He couldn't even take a sneaky look at his mobile as a police patrol car kept pace in the compressed traffic. The alert was for the front gate – it had been breached.

The Airport Drive sign saved him. He indicated and powered the Commodore towards the elevated roundabout. It would hook him back to Mount Macedon, if necessary. There was space to pull over about 100 metres before that decision had to be made.

Dust from the emergency stop hadn't settled by the time Beacham logged into his server. All cameras were recording; the one at the entrance and the four around the house were well hidden. He retrieved the alert file and watched the video.

A small woman in a dark rain jacket, jeans and fashion boots scrambled over the arched stonework and into his property. She turned and opened the gate. A taller woman in a green jacket slipped inside. She looked familiar but the feed from the camera wasn't high resolution. A few seconds later they ran out of frame.

Beacham selected the next file from a camera mounted on a light post halfway down the gravel drive. It was lower and closer; he identified the taller intruder: the TV reporter from The Meadows!

The video lasted a few seconds. Beacham moved to the house cameras. The pair stopped at the manicured lawn that encircled his rectangular home. The original 19th century homestead had been extended by the previous owners. The roof now had three hips, thanks to the addition of a guest accommodation wing and a library. They were built of rendered brick and shingle that complemented the original style. The interior was equally imposing, not that the women could see inside. Beacham always drew the curtains when he left. He switched from camera one to four, watching the women circle his home. They showed no inclination to get inside, not even testing if a door was unlocked. That was strange.

He couldn't fathom why the journalists might be suspicious. There was nothing to connect him to the deaths of O'Leary and Wright. Kim Prescott had asked about Carolyn – where she was living in the UK.

Beacham lifted his eyes from the feed. Have they learned that Carolyn never arrived in Bath? He looked back at the video and was surprised again. The pair disappeared into the thick bush 20 metres from the house. *That's weird.*

Beacham tapped a few more keys on the iPhone and called up the camera in Carolyn's cell.

'Shit!'

Carolyn had smeared an SOS on the wall. It was a creamy red: perhaps blood mixed with something? He cut the cell feed from the internet, slammed the Commodore into gear and accelerated towards the roundabout. Five minutes later he'd left six irate motorists in his wake but was on the freeway to Mount Macedon. Home was 48 kilometres away – less than half an hour with his foot flat on the floor.

Chapter 53

The formal garden didn't extend far from the rear of the house. A pristine white stone border path and a rose-covered pergola were lost from sight as Kim and Jo stepped cautiously through the undergrowth. They chose the bushland away from the road as a more likely location to hide a body. Occasionally Kim recorded a 10 to 20 second clip of their search on the camcorder. They alternated camera op duties, to include both *Spotlight* members in the hunt. They never gave any thought to their search being illegal.

'I wonder what kind of ash these trees are – alpine or mountain?' Jo whispered. She followed in Kim's footsteps, hoping that any lurking snakes would go for the leader.

'No idea. You're supposed to be looking at the ground.' Kim's eyes scouted behind trees and shrubbery.

Jo sighed. 'How do we know what the grave will be like. It's not going to have a white cross on it: RIP Carolyn Beacham, bitten by her husband's snakes.'

'The soil should be different; scraped into a mound, the grass maybe not as long as the surrounding area. Don't you ever watch crime movies?'

'Until the wine bottle is empty. If it's Netflix, I fast forward to the end to find out whodunnit and go to bed.'

'What if it's a Channel 5 Sunday thriller?'

'I text Jeannie in scheduling. She watches everything.'

Kim shook her head and used a stick to poke behind a fallen gum. 'Anything?'

'Something has been digging around here, but I think it's too small and fresh. She's probably been in the ground for almost five months. There would be some regrowth, I think.'

'Ewww. We don't have to dig her up, do we?'

'No. That's when we hand it over to Nathan and the proper detectives. They can do the dirty work. It's another reason why I brought the camera – evidence. I'll mark the location on the phone GPS.'

Jo looked at the wild terrain. 'That's *if* we find her.' She guessed they were 60 metres from the house yet couldn't see its roof. It was a needle in a haystack search – or body in the bush – with little chance of success.

'What's the time?'

'12.25. Beacham should be at the track for at least another hour. Then it's a 90-minute drive home. If we're gone by two-thirty we should be sweet.'

Jo used a thin branch to prod a bare patch beside a lichen covered tree. 'Was Dwayne going to the races at Healesville?'

'I don't know.' Kim followed a narrow trail. 'Why?'

'It might have been a good idea to keep an eye on Beacham.'

'To text us when he left the track?'

'That – and to confirm he arrived.'

Kim stopped, looked at her fellow grave hunter and shrugged. 'How far do you think Beacham could carry a body?'

'He's got that heavy limp.' Jo looked in the direction of the house, then at the wilderness. 'Yeah, I don't think he would want to go far – or would need to. According to Abigail there aren't many guests. Who would ever venture this side of the house? Should we try closer to the tree line?' They moved down the slope. 'By the way. Do we get expenses for these escapades?'

'Why?'

'My boots – they're getting trashed.'

The double gates opened silently. Beacham resisted the urge to gun the Commodore along the gravel drive. The media intruders could be anywhere. No sense giving them a chance to escape while he was still in the car. He had to know if they were there because of Carolyn's SOS. He glided to a stop outside the garage at the south end of the building.

His left foot dragged annoyingly as he hastened to the front entrance. No sign of a forced entry. But he had to make sure. He pressed the four-digit code and entered. He hurried through the main hall to the utility room at the rear. Another stout timber door with a security panel was still secure. Beacham entered that code and limped to the cellar.

The video wall with split screens showed all cameras were functional. The pets were coiled in their tanks, but of the intruders there was no sign. *What are they looking for out there?* He checked Carolyn's monitor. It was recording, but isolated from her adoring audience on the dark web. He didn't imagine there would be any complaints procedure on the host TOR Network.

Beacham looked at the rescue message more carefully with the PTZ function. He could pan, tilt or zoom anywhere in her main cell and listen. Not that Carolyn showed signs of mental debilitation by talking to herself. It wasn't blood on the wall. Was it something from her lunch? Maybe the beetroot in the salad roll, mixed with – what? The message texture wasn't as crucial as what it contained: the universal appeal for help with an address for her imprisonment. Did the reporters see that? Or anyone else?

Beacham scanned the exterior cameras as he considered that possibility. It wasn't likely, he concluded. He was less than a third of the way to Healesville when the intruder alert pinged on his mobile. Carolyn had to wait for his departure to start the SOS. The reporters couldn't have been waiting nearby. No, it had to be something else.

Further speculation wasn't worth the time; he must find the *Spotlight* women. He glanced at his wife's camera; she was safely boxed, sitting on the bed beneath her futile message. Beacham stood at a grey metal cabinet near the entrance to the cellar. He drew a key from his trouser pocket to unlock the double doors. They swung open to reveal the armoury: a SA80, a M16, a double-barrel shotgun with boxes of ammunition for each weapon. On a separate shelf sat a Browning 9mm with a 13-round magazine. It had always been Beacham's preferred semi-automatic.

The nearest neighbours were 400 metres, further if the women were at the rear of the property. A shotgun blast wouldn't be unusual in the country on the weekend. But it could do too much damage at close quarters. He needed to question the women, or at least one of them. The distinctive sound of an assault weapon might draw attention. The handgun would be more suitable for a confrontation. He checked the Browning magazine and returned to the video feeds.

Stay Calm. Beacham repeated that mantra over the next 10 minutes as he searched for signs of Kim Prescott and her friend. The cameras were his best hope. He could blunder through the bush, yet still be a hectare from the women. Or, if he was close, his disability could warn the prey.

Beacham took two years to accept the abrupt change to his life and career caused by the IED in Afghanistan in 2007. His left leg was shredded and broken by nuts and bolts in a Taliban ambush in Helmand Province. It was the result of months of boredom during the construction of Camp Bastion. Snake hunts, disguised as village tours to win hearts and minds, were popular distractions for soldiers. The Oxus Cobra was their favourite quarry in the stony, desolate country. Beacham loved the hoods and mesmerising movements of the lethal reptile. They could never return to base with their prize. But several hours hunting, then admiring the majesty of the cobra was a welcome distraction. Until their Land Rover was blown off the road when approaching a friendly village.

The driver saw the bucket near a culvert too late. No reason it should be suspicious, apart from it being Afghanistan and instincts were tuned for that sort of trap. He swung the vehicle to miss the full blast, but not enough to save his life. There were two of them in the Land Rover that day, another followed 40 metres behind. The pair in that avoided the ambush and saved Beacham's life.

His leg suffered the most damage. Bits of scrap metal were also embedded in his torso and skull. It was the surgical skill of the team at Camp Bastion that avoided amputation and ensured he walked again. Carolyn was the nurse who played a crucial role in his recovery.

Beacham's patience at the video screens paid off after 15 minutes. The smaller woman emerged from the treeline near the pergola. She looked left and right then retreated. He had used the waiting time to prepare for the hunt; the race-day suit was discarded for camouflage jacket and trousers. The women would never see him coming.

Beacham picked up the Browning and climbed the stairs. He locked the door to the cellar then did the same with the door from the utility room. He moved steadily across the lawn and entered the bush 20 metres to the right of the pergola. He knew the terrain and how to compensate for his gammy leg.

Day 141

Carolyn felt uneasy. Her bold plea, applied with the toothbrush, was bound to earn the overdue beating – if it didn't prompt a rescue before her jailer returned. There was no watch to gauge how much time had passed since she mixed beetroot with toothpaste on the food tray. It was sloppy, but enough of the red mixture adhered to the stone to spell out the prison's location – her Mount Macedon home.

The waiting was the most agonising of her months in captivity. Was anyone watching? There was no sound from beyond the door. Was Benedict looking at her and laughing? Taking pleasure in her futile gesture. She sensed he was out there, although there was no sound from the guardian's room. He wasn't with his pets – but he was in the house. Her home. What was happening?

Chapter 54

Nathan Potter stared at his mobile screen. Two texts to Kim and neither had been answered. That was unusual for their relationship, even in its early stages. The phone was a life support system for Gen Y. What made it more surprising was his new lady friend being a journalist. They *always* had their phones nearby, even on a day off. Was he an ignored beau, or should he be a worried cop?

His Ranger was parked on the outskirts of Bacchus Marsh, close to the Western Freeway. Nathan stopped to send the second text to Kim after the unexpected leave pass. Sunday morning was spent at Henry Wright's property. Half a dozen uniforms and detectives made another sweep of the paddocks and home to see if anything had been missed. It wasn't likely, but their investigation had run out of suspects.

Julian Oliver was out of their jurisdiction and most likely had dropped down the order of suspects. The slimy Hound Liberation Party co-founder, Ryan Mathison, had virtually guaranteed the pair with his voluntary interview on Friday. Detectives were still making inquiries to test their alibis, but Nathan's instincts told him the animal activists weren't responsible for the murders.

The widow was briefly under suspicion, especially after threatening to shoot down the *Spotlight* helicopter. Siobhan was *intense* but wasn't anywhere near Tara on the previous Saturday. She was with a group of gold historians in Ballarat; poring over maps of the old diggings, debating which might still yield riches.

An anonymous tipster suggested police look at Chauncey Quayle, a bookie. He didn't stay under the microscope for long: Chauncey was downing rum and cokes at a Flemington pub when Conor O'Leary was boxed. The hotel's security cameras were his verification. The investigation was back to square one: two dead trainers and no strong suspects. Detective Inspector Dowell suggested an afternoon off might clear the cobwebs.

A two-trailer truck rocked the Ranger as it swept past. It was doing at least 130 kilometres an hour. Nathan wanted to chase it and issue a ticket, but there were no lights or siren under the bonnet. Maybe a speed camera would snap the truck down the freeway? He turned his attention back to the phone and wondered what could be occupying Kim Prescott?

Nathan knew she went to The Meadows with Jo Trescowthick. Stephanie Grant was there as well, recording a feature with a cameraman. Nathan's source was a plain-clothed constable sent to listen for gossip. He reported that the production assistant was in a party mood; drinking wine and winning a few bets. The reporter was circumspect: having the occasional flutter, but mainly focussed on the track's best dressed punter, Benedict Beacham. She spoke to him briefly. Beacham left her table and never went back within the reporter's orbit, although she constantly watched him.

Police computer checks didn't raise any red flags on Beacham. No arrests, convictions, complaints or fines. He was a model British immigrant living at Mount Macedon. Why would he make Kim curious? Beacham was a regular at the greyhound tracks, that was the only connection to his murder inquiry. Was there more?

Nathan checked his vehicle's GPS. Beacham's property was 40 kilometres away, less than half an hour on quiet country roads. It might be worth a detour on the way back to the city. The media program that had been ahead of the cops for much of the week was curious about Beacham. Should DS Potter be as well? Nathan flicked the indicator to re-join traffic.

Chapter 55

A heavy carpet of autumn detritus didn't make the grave search easy. To Jo it felt like they had been wandering for hours. Kim was 15 metres away, probably to avoid being asked what the time was every 10 minutes. No body, bones or tombstones had been discovered. On the positive, no snakes had poked their heads out to investigate the bush-bashing. That made Jo braver to probe around fallen logs.

She kicked aside a pile of mulch and paused; the ground beneath her ruined boot had recently been disturbed. Jo used her stick to sweep away more debris. It wasn't as big as a grave should be. But it looked – to her – like something was buried beside the dead tree.

'Kim! I've found something here.'

The reporter was filming towards the mount through a gap in the foliage. The trees had thinned in that area. She lowered the camera but didn't show great enthusiasm. The amateur sleuth had found three *somethings*, already. None proved productive.

Kim turned slowly and froze – there was a man dressed in camo gear a few metres behind Jo. He held a pistol.

'Run Jo! He's got a gun!' Kim bolted in the opposite direction.

The production assistant didn't get a chance to react. A hand grabbed her jacket by the collar as Kim weaved between gum trees.

'Don't move or I'll blow your head off.'

The gun poked over her right shoulder: it was pointed at Kim. It exploded once. Against her ear it was deafening. Kim kept running. *Go Kim!* She was almost 30 metres away. *Get help!* The pistol fired again. A tree splintered near Kim's head, she stumbled. There was a third blast – Kim face planted like a rag doll.

Jo wailed. There was no movement from the downed reporter. Tears burst forth. 'You've killed her!'

She was still trapped by the killer's hand. He was strong, but Jo was angry.

'You bastard!'

Jo lashed out; her right arm barely made an impact against his chest. The grip tightened. A moment later her head was numb; she was staring at leaves, bile filling her stomach, panic rising. Had he shot her?

'Damn!' Beacham was furious. Both women were down. That would make it difficult to move them. He stared at the feisty hobbit at his feet. Her blow didn't hurt, but he might have retaliated too heavily. Beacham wanted to subdue her, not knock her out. He needed information and this woman might be the only source.

Drool dribbled from her mouth, eyes flickered. That was good, not totally out to lunch. The Browning grip knocked the fight out of her; she couldn't get far without assistance. That gave him a minute to check the shot one – Kim Prescott. Beacham scampered through the underbrush, the acrid stench from his pistol a reminder of a previous life. It was energising.

The reporter had made it almost 40 metres. Another 10 steps and she might have escaped: too many trees to protect her and too fast for an army veteran with a dodgy leg. He looked down at Kim Prescott's head. There was a splinter several centimetres long sticking out above the right ear. The third bullet had struck the reporter high in the back. Did it deflect into the heart as there wasn't a lot of blood? If so, it was an incredibly lucky shot over the distance.

Beacham was bending to check for a pulse when he heard a thud. The accomplice was trying to run on jelly legs. She stumbled a metre and fell. He glanced back at the reporter: no movement, not likely to be any ever again. She could wait. Battle experience told him to put another bullet in her head. Would that be one shot too many for the neighbours? Jo's second freedom run made the decision for him. Get the bolshie one inside the cellar, then come back to finish this job – with a spade.

Jo was almost to the lawn when Beacham caught up. 'You're a plucky one.' He hoisted her over his shoulder and hustled towards the rear door. Hands feebly struck at his back but didn't halt the momentum. Within two minutes he was safely inside the house and easing down the cellar stairs. The Browning was placed carefully in front of the video console. The keys to Carolyn's cell hung on a hook beside the door to the reptile zoo. There was no danger to him in either quarter: his wife sat forlornly on the bed, his pets were coiled in their tanks.

Beacham unlocked the steel door and smiled at Carolyn's shock. Her first contact with a different human in months – but there wouldn't be any rescue. If anything, it heralded her own demise. He lowered Jo to her feet on the brick floor. She was unsteady. He was about to shove her towards the bed when a mobile rang. It was in the woman's back pocket.

Beacham snatched the phone and looked at the caller ID: Nathan Potter. 'Who is this?'

Jo swayed. No answer. Beacham grasped her by the jacket and shook violently. He hadn't thought about their link to the outside world. Who did the reporters tell about their adventure? He still didn't know what they were after.

'Who is it? Does he know you're here?'

Jo put her hands on her knees and vomited.

Beacham was annoyed; he hit her too hard, she was probably concussed. Carolyn moved to support the newcomer.

'Stay there.'

She stopped. Her arms opened as her husband pushed the stricken woman towards the bed.

Beacham shuffled out of the room and locked the door. In his haste the keys didn't return to their hook in the video room. The phone ceased ringing. Was this Nathan Potter part of the *Spotlight* crew, or was he a boyfriend? Would he be worried that Jo hadn't answered? There were too many unknowns and that was ratcheting the stress levels. Beacham went to a bench at the back of his utility room. There was a mallet on a shelf. He picked it up and smashed the phone to pieces.

It didn't solve the problem. It reminded him there was another complication lying out in the bush: Kim Prescott would have her own mobile. Was Nathan Potter trying to call her next? Two reporters not answering their mobiles might raise too many alarm bells. He had to act fast. Get rid of the second mobile – then dispose of the reporter.

Inside the cell Carolyn Beacham cradled a distressed Jo. Her injuries weren't as bad as she made the killer believe.

'He killed my friend! Shot her like an animal.'

Carolyn sighed. 'I'm so sorry. I didn't want my rescue to cause harm to anyone else.'

Jo wiped her eyes and pulled away. Her head spun for a few seconds, but she was coherent, if not confused by the woman providing comfort.

'Rescue?'

Carolyn pointed to the sign on the stone wall above the bed.

Jo stared at the reddish SOS and the location – the property they were searching for a grave. Her sore brain finally made the connection.

'You're Carolyn Beacham?'

'Yes. And who might you be, apart from a brave woman?'

'I'm Jo Trescowthick. I work for the *Spotlight* current affairs program – on telly. My friend and I came here to look for you. But we never expected to find you alive – we thought your husband killed you with the snakes.'

Chapter 56

Nathan Potter's ute stopped outside the antique shop – behind Kim's Roadster. He had only seen the car once on Monday, but the cop in him remembered the number plate. Beacham's home was a few hundred metres down the road. This could be potentially embarrassing. The relationship was new, still so much to learn about hobbies and interests. There might be a mutual interest in antiques with the British expat. Was Kim inside the building looking at 19th century gold era knick-knacks? Even a casual appearance in the shop would make Nathan look like a stalker. That would be wonderful for the relationship – and his police career.

On the drive through Gisborne Nathan debated whether a call to Kim – after two texts – would be too much. Patience won the day; he stayed in cop mode until he spotted Kim's car. That was a new can of worms. He parked beside Kim's Mazda and scrolled through his call list for Jo Trescowthick's number. She might know what the reporter was doing in Mount Macedon.

He was about to press the green symbol – but paused. He needed a valid reason to call. Julian Oliver was the obvious excuse, but it was weak. Everyone knew he was out of the country and out of the frame. Another minute of thought didn't provide a better reason. Perhaps Julian had sent another email? Victorian Police still wanted to get his version of events at Steilgitz. He could make another plea for Jo to persuade Julian to call. Pathetic, but the only option.

Nathan entered the number and waited. It rang, but Jo never

answered. He waited for voice mail, instead the line dropped out. That was strange. He tried again. No connection: a recorded message to say the number was out of service. There was no other choice: he had to call Kim's mobile.

At least it rang. He hoped she hadn't programmed it to divert to voice mail after two rings. It kept going. On the eighth beep he felt certain he was destined for the message service. But then it was answered. It wasn't a voice. It sounded like the phone was being dragged through dried leaves. Then a voice, ever so faint.

'Help…I'm shot.'

'Kim! It's Nathan. Where are you?'

Terror gripped the experienced police officer. He had to be professional. The line was open. Ten seconds – nothing. Nathan tried again.

'Kim!' he shouted. 'Can you hear me? I'm in Mount Macedon. Where are you?'

Another agonising 20 seconds passed on the open line. Then a name.

'Beacham's,' she rasped.

There was nothing else.

The nearest police station was in Macedon township – five kilometres away and it wasn't staffed 24 hours. He didn't have his police weapon with him. If Nathan called triple zero for back up and an ambulance he would be hamstrung. A senior communications officer would order him to wait until armed support arrived. Kim needed help urgently. He had one choice. He found the inspector's speed dial and prayed Dowell answered.

'Nathan. I thought we had the afternoon off.'

'Sorry boss. No time to talk. Kim Prescott has been shot at Mount Macedon. I believe she's on the property of Benedict Beacham.'

'Whoa – slow down. Nathan. What's this all about?'

'I think it's connected to our dead trainers. This Beacham's a successful punter. He knew O'Leary and Wright. Kim must have followed a lead and she's in trouble.'

'Boss I need you to call out the cavalry and the paramedics. I'm a few hundred metres away. I have to go in. More lives are in danger.'

'Have you got your Glock?'

'Yes.' He had to lie, otherwise the inspector would order him to wait. He gave the address clearly. 'It's one of those lifestyle places – a few hectares. Tell the patrol boys I'm wearing a dark San Francisco Giants hoodie and blue jeans. Gotta go boss.'

It took less than a minute to drive to Beacham's property. He revved the accelerator to smash open the cedar gates. But that could tip off the shooter. He backed up and ran his Ranger into the culvert. He turned the mobile to vibrate as he exited the cab, jamming it into his pocket. He leaned into the rear tray and opened the aluminium box for the tyre repair kit. The only potential weapon was an L shape wheel brace. Better than nothing.

There was no handle on the front gates. He was tall enough to reach the top, adrenalin gave Nathan the strength to scramble over. He landed on a gravel drive which curved away through evergreens. There was no obvious camera mounting and no bullets blasted his way. He clasped the makeshift weapon like a pistol. It might make a shooter hesitate – for a precious moment.

The magpies that warbled as Nathan climbed the gate went silent as he glided up the driveway. It was impossible to be quiet on the small stones, but he stepped as lightly as possible. A hundred metres and two sweeping bends later the home appeared. There was no time to be impressed. Nathan blended into three conifer trees on the drive to watch and listen. No gunfire, no cries for help. Kim needed him – he had to go forward.

Beacham puffed as he shuffled across the back lawn. He tried to stay fit after leaving the army, but the leg injury restricted his exercise. The upper body strength was powerful, the legs were weaker. Plus, it was a decade since the Taliban enforced retirement. He paused for breath as he entered the treeline. A sixth sense alerted him to danger. Some soldiers said it never left you. He crouched beside a shrub and looked at the house. A few seconds later a man carrying a pistol stalked around the corner from the guest wing. He was in a sweatshirt and denims. Both hands were wrapped around a pistol – was he police?

He was 20 years younger and fitter. It would be silly to engage with the Browning from this distance. He couldn't count on lucky shots twice in a day. Beacham chided himself for leaving the house without changing the magazine. He was down to 10 bullets. Goodness knows how many the intruder had.

The gunman couldn't see inside as the curtains were closed. He reached the back door and tried the handle. Open – another mistake. Beacham didn't move, his 9mm pointed at the ground. He waited. The intruder disappeared inside. That changed things. Beacham looked over his shoulder into the bush. There was no sign of the reporter, nor any sound. A cry of pain might have helped his cause. The gunman would have diverted to investigate. Beacham could shoot him within a dozen steps. Inside the house it was a different game. If he moved stealthily, he might catch all three in the cell.

Nathan had chased robbers, rapists, wife-bashers, burglars and more as a patrol officer. He'd never been required to use a gun to arrest a murder suspect. Many cases were domestic related. The evidence was built steadily, the accused often surrendered to the inevitable. In Mount Macedon he was hunting a possible killer armed with a *loaded* wheel brace. He would never go anywhere without the Glock again. If he survived the afternoon.

Was the second open door too much of a coincidence? It led down from the utility room. Several male jackets hung on pegs, a pair of gumboots and more outdoor shoes sat beneath them. There wasn't anything feminine about this domain. He breathed deeply and descended. Nathan forced himself to move steadily; the stairs were stone; no creaks would give away his presence. A lit doorway awaited after 12 steps. He peeked around the frame – nobody there. The glance alerted him to a bank of monitors.

Nathan took another deep breath and stepped inside, the faux gun still in the pistol grip. Empty. He walked the six paces to the television screens. The owner had serious security: cameras covered upstairs, downstairs and outside. Nathan's eyes were drawn first to two women huddled on a bed. It was Jo and another woman. No sign of Kim. Were they in a cell? Then he noticed the contents of the glass tanks. It was King Charles showing off that confirmed Nathan's fears – there was a snake pit a few metres away through the door. He shivered.

There was no sign of a gunman. A few more seconds in front of the screens showed that all the tanks were secure; no reptiles slithered around on the floor. Nathan braced himself and opened the door to the serpent world. He stared wide-eyed for a few moments, recognising a bevy of Australia's most lethal belly crawlers. How would a wheel brace fare against them?

A steel door was 10 metres across the room. To get there involved passing the cobra's tank in the centre of the room. It had to be done. Nathan moved quickly which prompted King Charles to make a feint. Even knowing there was glass in between couldn't prevent Nathan from over-reacting. He jumped sideways, his right arm swinging wildly, the metal brace shattering another glass tank. In horror, he watched as a large brown snake inside uncoiled.

'Shit!'

Instead of striking, it slowly curled around a branch, its tongue forking incessantly. Spooked, but not ready to attack.

Nathan reached the cell door and was relieved to see keys in the lock. He stepped inside and slammed it shut.

'Nathan!' Jo squealed. 'Have you caught him?'

'No. I haven't seen anyone. Is it Benedict Beacham you're talking about? Where's Kim? She said she'd been shot?'

Jo was shocked. 'Kim's alive? I thought the bastard killed her. Beacham gunned her down as she tried to escape. Then he belted me and dragged me down here. She's lying out there in the bush. He went to get her mobile phone – so we couldn't be traced.'

'When was that?'

'A couple of minutes ago.' Jo looked at Carolyn who was standing by the door, eager to flee. 'We need to get out – now!'

'There's a slight problem.' Nathan scratched his head. 'The cobra scared the crap out of me...I accidently smashed a glass panel. I don't know where that snake might be.'

'What snake was it?' Carolyn asked.

'A thick brown one.'

'That's Billy – a king brown. He was caught in the wild and can be unpredictable. But I can't stay here any longer. I'll take my chances.'

Nathan grabbed a blanket from the bed. 'Okay, we might be able to smother an attack.' He held up the wheel brace. 'This will have to be the second line of defence.'

Jo looked askance. 'One cop, a doona and a tyre changer. Brilliant.'

Carolyn opened the cell door for the first time, Nathan led the trio out. The smashed tank was empty: the king brown had done a slider.

'Billy's on the move. I can't see him – but let's go.'

They bunched and ran for the exit. Ten anxious metres: King Charles feinted again but was ignored, six eyes were scouting for Billy. Nathan breached the doorway and skidded to a stop – Beacham pointed the Browning at his face.

'Drop it. Now!'

Jo smacked into the back of her rescuer. Nathan dropped the wheel brace and blanket. Carolyn heard the clang and retreated into the snake pit.

The gun didn't waver.

'That won't do you any good Carolyn.' Beacham yelled. 'Billy is very upset. You'll be the first to die.'

He glanced quickly at the *weapon* on the ground and shook his head.

'You weren't even armed. I should have shot you as soon as I came inside.' The pistol flicked at Nathan. 'Back you go.'

There was nothing to fight with and Beacham was out of reach for a charge. The detective wrapped a protective arm around Jo and slowly edged back into Billy's domain. Words were his only option.

'It's too late Beacham. I'm a cop and I called for back-up before I entered. Patrols will be here within seconds. There's no need for anyone else to die.'

The gun nudged them backwards.

'The whore must be punished, just like O'Leary and Wright. No one betrays me.'

Nathan glanced to his right as they were forced into the danger zone. He stopped as the pistol reached the threshold. Only Beacham's hand was exposed. It was enough.

Carolyn lunged. She held the tongs – in its rubber grips was the agitated Billy. The captive of 141 days thrust the deadly king brown onto Beacham's bare hand. Billy reacted instinctively. The bite went deep; Beacham screamed and jerked, the gun exploded.

The bullet missed the captives and ricocheted from the floor and into King Charles' tank. Glass shattered. Billy wanted a second bite and Carolyn struggled to control him.

Nathan stepped forward and smashed a fist into the killer's nose. He crumpled; the gun fell from his hand. Billy tried another dart at his keeper but couldn't sink any more fangs before Carolyn twisted his writhing body away. Jo jumped over the fallen Beacham into the video room. She didn't stop – there was a cobra loose and her friend was lying wounded in the bush.

Nathan pointed towards the central tank. 'Throw the snake and tongs over there and run,' Carolyn obeyed and dashed to safety. Billy skittered across the floor and escaped his noose. King Charles slithered from his throne. Nathan dragged the unconscious killer away from the looming royal battle and closed the door.

The detective sergeant was torn between following Jo into the bush or doing his duty. Police patrols would be approaching the property: anxious colleagues with guns in hand and little information on the dangers they faced. Nathan had no idea how serious Kim's injuries were. Would a minute or two make a difference to the reporter's chances of survival? At least Jo knew where her friend fell, there was some comfort in that as professionalism won the battle for his attention. A few seconds later Detective Inspector Dowell was on Nathan's mobile.

'Boss. Tell the troops the suspect has been disarmed. We need a second ambulance – we have a woman with gunshot wound and a man with a snake bite. We'll need antivenom for a king brown. We also need a snake catcher.'

Nathan looked at the closed door. 'In fact, make that a cobra expert.'

Chapter 57

Mac sat in the hospital visitor chair gobbling grapes like they were Maltesers at a movie matinee.

'Do you want my jelly and ice cream?' Kim asked.

Her boss missed the sarcasm. 'Ta, Kim. I didn't get any morning tea – Jo's still claiming time off for concussion and stress.' Mac lifted the raspberry blob from his wounded reporter's tray. He combined the sugary treats, scooped a spoonful, then grimaced. 'Hospital meals haven't improved since my last visit.'

'When was that?'

'Fifteen years ago. The birth of my Collingwood football star.'

Kim let her head rest on the inclined bed. Mac's son was never going to be premiership material; let him have his dreams. She fingered the bandage above her right ear. Beneath was bare skin and a dozen stitches that joined flesh split by a chunk of Alpine Ash. The surgeon said scalp injuries bled heavily, but the wood didn't penetrate her skull. Kim's hair stylist would have to be creative for a few months.

The third 9mm round did the most damage. It lodged in her left shoulder blade. Kim felt like she was run down by a bus. Any closer to the shooter and the bullet might have been deadly. The twin blows knocked her out – and possibly saved her life. Beacham should have issued the *coup de grace* immediately. Kim never expected there could be pleasure in watching Mac scoff the remnants of her lunch.

Four days had passed since the surgery late Sunday night. Kim was sore and tired. The weariness came from the morning TV interview with Mike Berry. He was doing double duty for Channel 5 News and *Spotlight*. Kim's enforced absence had created an opening for another ambitious news hound. Stephanie Grant had hogged the lead story for the past three nights. That made Kim grumpier than the bullet hole in her scapula. Rehabilitation was going to take many weeks. How many stories could Steph and Mike do in that time?

Kim's eyes roamed the 23 bouquets that sat on the windowsill and floor. The largest was from Dugal and Withers: hidden inside was a bottle of wine. Her smile broadened at Jo's personal floral arrangement – complete with rubber snake.

'Will there still be a reporting job for me when my hair grows back? Or is it back to the research department?'

Mac's laughter almost stopped his assault on the dessert. Almost. He spooned more ice cream.

'Kim. You've got to control that paranoia. I love ambition among my reporters. We get great programs when the news gatherers are hungry for stories. But you've got to have faith in your own skills. Look at what you've done in the last six months. No television network in the world is going to dump a reporter who gets shot in the line of duty.'

Kim felt marginally better. It had been an incredible run since her elevation from the research desk in November. *Spotlight* helped stop two killers. Mac reached over and dumped the empty bowl on the tray.

'To be honest. My biggest worry is you being pinched by another network. Remember how Channel 9 almost snatched Curly after Tugga's Mob were laid to rest?'

Kim grinned. Mac didn't know the full story. Curly was tempted but had already rejected the offer before *Spotlight's* management learned about the poaching. Curly played it brilliantly and secured a pay rise. She remembered that lesson well.

'When's your contract up for renewal Kim?'

'Next month. *That's* why I was worried. Who wants to pay for a half bald reporter hobbling around like the hunchback of Notre Dame?'

Mac chuckled. 'I guarantee there won't be any problems. Any special requests you want to throw in?'

'A bulletproof vest?'

Mac slapped his knees and roared. 'Oh – I want to be on the 10th floor when that invoice lands on The Hatchet's desk!'

Kim dozed after Mac returned to the office to oversee another exclusive program – the gunshot survivor's personal story. It was the shoulder pain that woke her. She tried to be brave, reluctant to get dependent on medication. The throbbing made her reach for the button to summon relief.

A minute later a woman's pale face appeared around the curtains; it wasn't the nurse.

'Hello. Are you well enough for a visitor?'

The woman looked familiar. But there was something different – the nose was crooked, broken and not set properly? Kim trawled through her memory to find a connection. Her visitor came to the rescue.

'I'm Carolyn Beacham – I wanted to thank you for saving my life. And I'm so sorry my husband almost killed you.'

The nurse bustled in behind Carolyn as Kim waved her to a chair. The pain meds were a welcome relief, but curiosity about the captive's story ensured she didn't drift off into dreamland.

'What made him lock you up? I heard from my colleagues that Benedict said you betrayed him.'

'Pure fantasy.' Carolyn's eyes were sad, grey strands stood out in her dark mop. Her black jacket and slacks were a size too large. There hadn't been time for a hairdresser or shopping. Her prison pallor would take weeks of sunshine to remove.

'We've been married for 10 years. We were happy, until last year.'

They met in Afghanistan after Benedict's Land Rover was destroyed in a Taliban ambush. Carolyn was visiting Camp Bastion to share battlefield nursing skills. An army career was ruined, but a romance blossomed. They returned to the United Kingdom where – after extensive rehabilitation – Benedict secured a job with another former army veteran at a reptile park.

'It was supposed to be an electrical contract, looking after the buildings, displays, tanks and anywhere else his engineering skills could be applied. But Benedict has been fascinated with snakes since he was a child. He naturally gravitated towards the handlers to learn more.

'Then came the lottery windfall – £10 million was life changing. Mostly for the good. We both enjoyed sunnier climes. New Zealand always appealed to me. Benedict preferred Australia.' Carolyn paused. 'He wanted a private collection – and that swayed our decision.'

'If everything was going well, what caused his meltdown?'

'Jealousy. Benedict thought I betrayed him with Conor O'Leary and Henry Wright.'

Kim remembered the photo of the trainers and Carolyn. The unhappy look on the husband's face. 'I saw a photo of the three of you – with a winning greyhound. I'm not trying to be impolite – but everything looked *cosy*.'

Carolyn blushed. 'That was the start of it all. Not that I understood. Conor and Henry where being cheeky that night, pushing their luck. They both grabbed my bottom at different stages. I slapped their hands away. Twenty years as a nurse gives you a thick hide. You keep the wandering hands at bay and move on.

'Benedict fumed all the way home. I tried to laugh it off. I never understood the depths of his obsession.'

Carolyn rubbed a hand over her dress.

'I've had two counselling sessions with a psychologist since the rescue. We've talked a lot about Benedict's irrational behaviour. He can't do a diagnosis without talking to Benedict. But he believes my husband suffers from a delusional disorder known as morbid jealousy. They also call it Othello Syndrome – he's preoccupied with the fear his spouse is being unfaithful.'

'Was that enough to tip him over the edge?'

'No, it was a party at Henry's that made him snap. They could be raucous affairs, lots of drinking, dancing, flirting. Sometimes a bit more in summer – the pool was a skinny-dipping zone.' Carolyn grimaced. 'It was harmless fun.

'Benedict was in a sour mood because I made him drive. I let him stew on the terrace and circulated. We've met many lovely people in the racing industry and I'm a social butterfly. I just wanted a fun night out.'

'What happened?'

'I was talking to Conor and Henry about the starting boxes. There was a set of practice traps a few hundred metres away. We were joking about how easy it might be for a human to make the jump like a dog. Henry bragged that he could beat me. It was stupid.' Carolyn smiled wistfully. 'You do things that sound silly after the event. We took our wine and beer down; Conor was going to be the starter. We had a bet – first from the box to a gate 20 metres away.'

A shiver shook Carolyn.

'The box was horrible. It was narrow, cramped and pitch black. I'd never felt claustrophobic until I squeezed inside. I wanted to escape so badly. I was pushing at the front almost immediately. The trap sprang open and I burst out.

'Unfortunately, my blouse and bra caught on part of the trap. They were ruined – but I kept running. The boys thought it was hilarious. I calmed down and soon saw the funny side. Henry was a gentleman – he handed over the $20 and his sweatshirt. We returned to the party and everyone laughed about it.'

'Except your husband?'

'Yes. He saw us return – me wearing Henry's sweatshirt and holding my clothes. I found him in the car half an hour later. I tried to make it clear there was no hanky panky – it was just a silly stunt. Benedict wouldn't listen.

'I guess that explains why Conor and Henry were dumped in the starting boxes.'

The women sat quietly for almost a minute.

'When did he lock you up?'

'The next morning. I slept in a spare room. He bashed me from behind as I entered the kitchen. I was his prisoner for the next 141 days while he plotted his revenge on Conor and Henry.'

'An extreme reaction.'

'Benedict's always had issues with betrayal. His first girlfriend left him for another man when he joined the army. It took him years to trust me. I've been wondering if that pathological jealousy has always been there, hidden from everyone, or the bomb explosion in Afghanistan did more damage than we ever suspected.'

The room fell silent, neither woman knowing where to pick up the conversation. One man's unreasoned vengeance had tragic consequences for too many innocent people.

A man's appearance in the doorway was a welcome distraction. Nathan Potter was dressed in a dark suit, with a striped, blue tie.

'Detective Sergeant Nathan Potter,' Kim's face brightened. 'Is this business or personal?'

'A bit of both.'

Carolyn stood up. 'I should leave you two.'

'Actually, Mrs Beacham, you might want to hear my update.'

'Want to – or I need to?'

Nathan approached. 'More the latter, I'm afraid.'

The policeman looked at the spare visitor chair but remained standing.

'I've just come back from the intensive care unit. Your husband is still too sick to interview – or to learn that he has more problems when he recovers.'

'What's happened?' Carolyn asked.

'You know the story is big news in your homeland? It's perfect tabloid fodder.'

'Yes. I've had requests for interviews from every newspaper, radio and television station.' She looked at Kim. 'I can't talk about it – not yet. The pain is still too raw.'

Kim understood. She also guessed the media frenzy in Britain might have uncovered some damaging history.

'Has the story brought new information about Benedict?'

'Yes. A former detective in Oxford saw a report on the BBC. He remembered the name from an unsolved murder case that has niggled him for 33 years. Benedict was interviewed at the time because he knew one of the victims. Cynthia Milton was Benedict's girlfriend before he joined the army. He claimed their parting a year previously was amicable; he chose the military over domestic life.'

'One of the victims?' Kim asked.

'There were two – Cynthia and her fiancée, Bryan Edmonds. They were 23 and 21.'

'What makes an old cop dredge up a cold case?'

'Their deaths. They were tied, gagged and abandoned in a six by four packing crate in a disused warehouse.'

Tears welled in Carolyn's eyes. She reached for a tissue. 'That's horrible.'

Kim looked at Nathan. 'But there's more, isn't there?'

'Yes. Their killer left three vipers in the box. They're venomous, but not normally deadly if treated immediately. Cynthia and Bryan weren't found for 10 days.'

Chapter 58

The opening titles for Channel 5 News were a nervous sight and sound in Jo Trescowthick's South Melbourne apartment – it was wine o'clock. She used both hands to carefully pour a smidgin; enough to test if her taste buds had returned after the concussion. It had been a shock to find the Monday, Tuesday and Wednesday tipples were not totally palatable. She vowed to sneak a deadlier serpent into Benedict Beacham's prison cell if she couldn't appreciate a sauvignon blanc again.

Jo sipped – the wine was delicious; life was back to normal.

The news opened with an update on the killer: British police wanted to talk to Beacham about the death of an ex-girlfriend.

The mobile phone on the kitchen bench vibrated as she filled the wine glass. It was Curly Rogers. The television was silenced.

'Hey Curly, I just caught up with the latest on the psycho. We should have left him in the cellar with the cobra.'

Curly laughed. 'Good to hear you're back on form – I was worried about your noggin. How about the booze – found your taste buds yet?'

Jo slurped loudly. 'Yep, this Oyster Bay is divine. But don't tell Mac – I could do with another day of rehab.'

'The secret is safe. You know we've got an interview with Kim?'

'Yeah. If Kim can talk about what we experienced – I don't think it will traumatise me. My head was sore for a few days, but I'm not having nightmares.'

Jo's mobile buzzed.

'Have you got another call?'

'It's a text.' Jo replaced the glass to hold the phone steady. She was grateful Curly could not see her cheeks blush. It was Julian Oliver, the lover who sparked the drama that almost cost Jo and Kim their lives.

Early snowfall in New Zealand. Fancy some après-skiing?

The End

About the Author

Stephen is an Australian-born writer, TV producer, kayaker and traveller who now plots crime fiction from his garret overlooking the Tamaki River in Auckland.

His debut novel Tugga's Mob was inspired by three seasons working as a tour guide on double decker buses around Europe in the '80s. It was a finalist in the 2020 Ngaio Marsh Awards for Best First Novel.

Boxed is the second book to feature the Melbourne Spotlight television crew. The amateur sleuths encounter more bodies and drama in the third novel which follows their motorhome adventures in New Zealand.